THESE ARE NOT SEÑORITAS

THESE ARE NOT SEÑORITAS

BY

RUBY McDOW WENDT

LIBERTY BELL PUBLICATIONS

ISBN: 978-1-59364-060-6 Color Edition

ISBN: 978-1-59364-061-3 Black and White Edition

ISBN: 978-1-59364-059-0 Spanish Color Edition

ISBN: 978-1-59364-058-3 Spanish Black and White Edition

Liberty Bell Publications
655 Sandifer Road
York, SC 29745
1-704-560-4880 or dmartyo@protonmail.com

Printed in the United States of America

For Ruby

A Dream That Mattered

TABLE OF CONTENTS

EDITOR'S NOTE

This Edition includes a glossary for those with a vocabulary not as well enhanced as some others. I found myself quite periodically having to fetch my dictionary to clarify the meanings of words that I knew and had used many times but, in fact, I actually didn't know the true meaning. Only an idea of what was being said. I decided to provide the meanings (as used here) of many words that I was having difficulty with, in the hopes that others experiencing the same would not have to constantly look up their meanings and thereby lose the flow of this truly remarkable and interesting story.

Many of these words we all use but are we sure we understand them? At my sixty-nine years, I thought I did and was truly surprised at my inability to define them accurately as I was reading. After puzzling over how many there were, I realized that many people may just give up and not continue reading. I didn't want that. So to encourage others like me, I have provided this glossary for a good number of the words I was having some difficulty with. Some will say an excessive amount of words and I must agree. But being someone who was above average in school, I never realized that I couldn't actully give a proper definition when push came to shove. To those of you, both young and old, native or foreign, brilliant or not so brilliant, fluent in English or not, who may need a little refresher, it is for you. You may be surprised how helpful it is.

All who purchase the book will be provided a pdf version at no charge. Simply email the publisher with proof of purchase at:

dmartyo@protonmail.com for your copy.

Cast Of Characters
(In Order of Appearance)

Micaela – Servant in Luzare household.
Esmeralda Constant – First wife of Luzare. Daughter of Dr.
Moran.
Lorita – Pet parrot of Micaela.
Ricardo Constant – Son and first child of Esmeralda and
Luzare.
Dolores – Servant in Luzare household.
Rosa – Cook servant in Luzare household.
Eva – Servant helper in Luzare household.
Luzare Constant – 53 years. Head of family.
Diana – Wife of Ricardo.
Victor Constant – Youngest child of Luzare and Esmeralda.
7 years old.
Libia Constant – Second wife of Luzare.
Laura – Libia's faithful child servant.
Carmen – Painting on wall. An ancestor.
Arturo Constant – 18-year-old son of Luzare and Esmeralda.
Paulo Constant – Brother of Luzare. Owns large dairy.
Named Lecheria.
Felipe Quesada – Father of Libia. Dentist in Cartago.
Catalina Quesada – Mother of Libia.
Martita – Friend of Libia.
Enor – Head concho on Luzare's plantation.
Francisco – Servant in Ricardo Luzare household and
brother of Enor. 15-year-old.
Doctor Moran – Father-in-law of Luzare.
Marie – Sister of Libia.
Lucien Constant – Grandfather of Luzare.
Jerome – Son of Lucien. Died of malaria in 1850's.
Louis Constant – Son of Lucien. Husband of Amelia.
Grandfather of Luzare.

Amelia Constant – Mother of Luzare. Wife of Louis.
Elena – Eldest sister of Libia. In Asylum.
Helena – Sister of Libia. Had turned mad.
Albert – Brother of Libia. In penitentiary.
Luira – Teacher of Libia.
Anabella Constant – Eldest daughter of Libia and Luzare.
Margarita Cecilia Constant – Daughter of Libia and Luzare.
Sara – Became wife of Arturo.
Yolanda – Servant Victor liked.
Virginia – A friend of Margarita.
Roberto – Boyfriend of Anabella.
Edwin – Boyfriend of Margarita. (Eddy)
Olga – Became wife of Victor.
Renato – Son of Ricardo and Diana.
Juan Quitituy – Molester of Libia.
Rafael Valverde – Wanna be boyfriend of Anabella and
        becomes her husband.
Ester – Distant cousin of Margarita.
Lina – Sister of Esmeralda. Married name of Escalante.
Nena – Girl who lives across street from Margarita.
Dora – Student at school who had a crush on Margarita.
Flora – Oldest girl in school.
Nastalia Mora – Edwin's Mother.
Claudia – American friend of Margarita.
Jaime Aragon – Doctor who likes Margarita.
Olivia – Girlfriend of Roberto.
Amelia – Los Angeles. Distant cousin of Libia. Runs
        boardinghouse.
Sara Williams – Owner of boarding house in New Orleans.
Estrella – Friend of Margarita at school in New Orleans.
Roy – Boyfriend of Estrella's in Atlanta.
Maurice Du Clerc – Student at Georgia Tech. Likes Margarita.
Barton – Student at beauty school. He likes Margarita.
Barr Tully – Student at night school who likes Margarita. 19-
        year-old. Becomes her husband.

Lucy Tully – Barr's mother.
Jack – A friend of Barr.
May – Girlfriend of Jack.
Gabriela – Servant helping Margarita.
Charlene – Daughter of Margarita and Barr.

Cast Of Characters
(In Alphabetical Order)

Albert – Brother of Libia. In penitentiary.

Amelia – Los Angeles. Distant cousin of Libia. Runs boardinghouse.

Amelia Constant – Mother of Luzare. Wife of Louis.

Anabella Constant – Eldest daughter of Libia and Luzare.

Arturo Constant – 18-year-old son of Luzare and Esmeralda.

Barr Tully – Student at night school who likes Margarita. 19-years-old. Becomes her husband.

Barton – Student at beauty school. He likes Margarita.

Carmen – Painting on wall. An ancestor.

Catalina Quesada – Mother of Libia.

Charlene – Daughter of Margarita and Barr.

Claudia – American friend of Margarita.

Diana – Wife of Ricardo.

Doctor Moran – Father-in-law of Luzare.

Dolores – Servant in Luzare household.

Dora – Student at school who had a crush on Margarita.

Edwin – Boyfriend of Margarita. (Eddy)

Elena – Eldest sister of Libia. In Asylum.

Enor – Head concho on Luzare's plantation.

Esmeralda Constant – First wife of Luzare. Daughter of Dr. Moran.

Ester – Distant cousin of Margarita.

Estrella – Friend of Margarita at school in New Orleans.

Eva – Servant helper in Luzare household.

Felipe Quesada – Father of Libia. Dentist in Cartago.

Flora – Oldest girl in school.

Francisco – Servant in Ricardo Luzare household and brother of Enor. 15-years-old.

Gabriela – Servant helping Margarita.

Helena – Sister of Libia. Had turned mad.

Jack – A friend of Barr.

Jaime Aragon – Doctor who likes Margarita.

Jerome – Son of Lucien. Died of malaria in 1850's.

Juan Quitituy – Molester of Libia.

Laura – Libia's faithful child servant.

Libia Constant – Second wife of Luzare.

Lina – Sister of Esmeralda. Married name of Escalante.

Lorita – Parrot pet of Micaela.

Louis Constant – Son of Lucien. Husband of Amelia. Grandfather of Luzare.

Lucien Constant – Grandfather of Luzare.

Lucy Tully – Barr's mother.

Luira – Teacher of Libia.

Luzare Constant – 53 years. Head of family.

Margarita Cecilia Constant – Daughter of Libia and Luzare.

Marie – Sister of Libia.

Martita – Friend of Libia.

Maurice Du Clerc – Student at Georgia Tech. Likes Margarita.

May – Girlfriend of Jack.

Micaela – Servant in Luzare household.

Nastalia Mora – Edwin's Mother.

Nena – Girl who lives across street from Margarita.

Olga – Became wife of Victor.

Olivia – Girlfriend of Roberto.

Paulo Constant – Brother of Luzare. Owns large dairy. Named Lecheria.

Rafael Valverde – Wanna be boyfriend of Anabella and becomes her husband.

Renato – Son of Ricardo and Diana.

Ricardo Constant – Son and first child of Esmeralda and Luzare.

Roberto – Boyfriend of Anabella.

Rosa – Cook servant in Luzare household.

Roy – Boyfriend of Estrella's in Atlanta.

Sara – Became wife of Arturo.

Sara Williams – Owner of boarding house in New Orleans.

Victor Constant – Youngest child of Luzare and Esmeralda.
7 years old.

Virginia – A friend of Margarita.

Yolanda – Servant Victor liked.

Illustrations

Maps

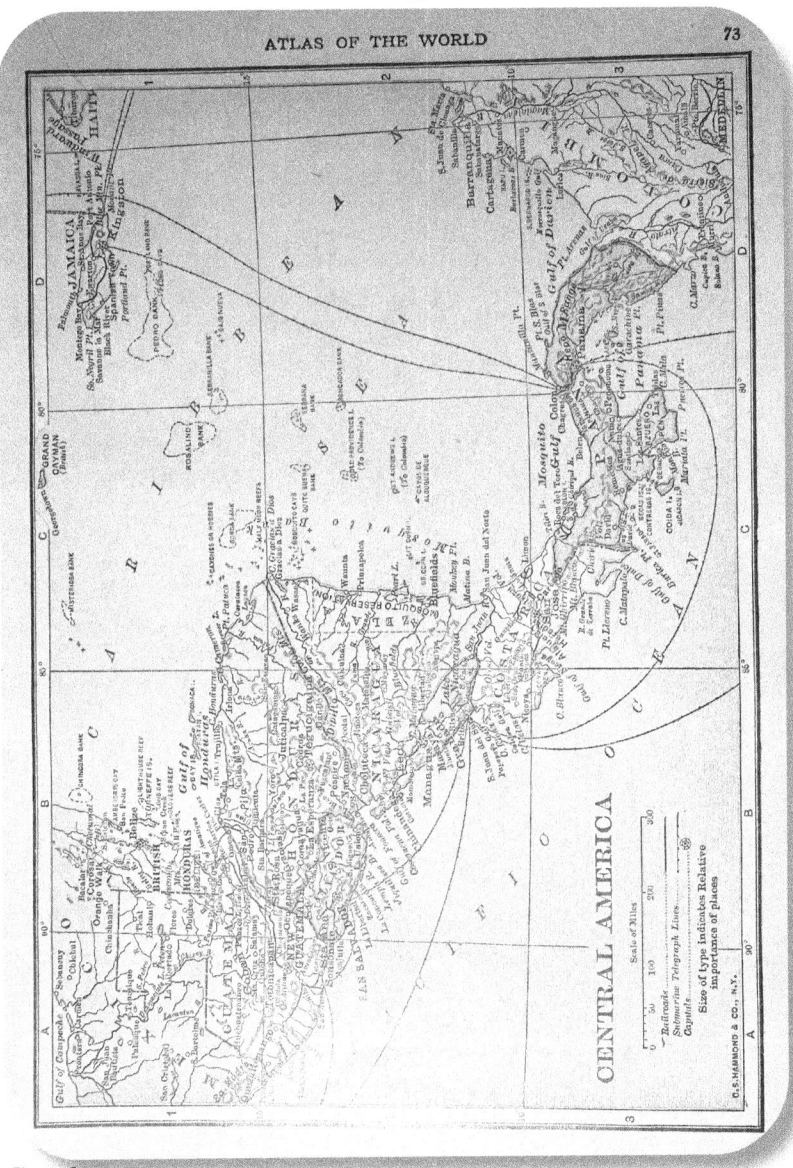

Figure 1

1910 Hammond Atlas of the World

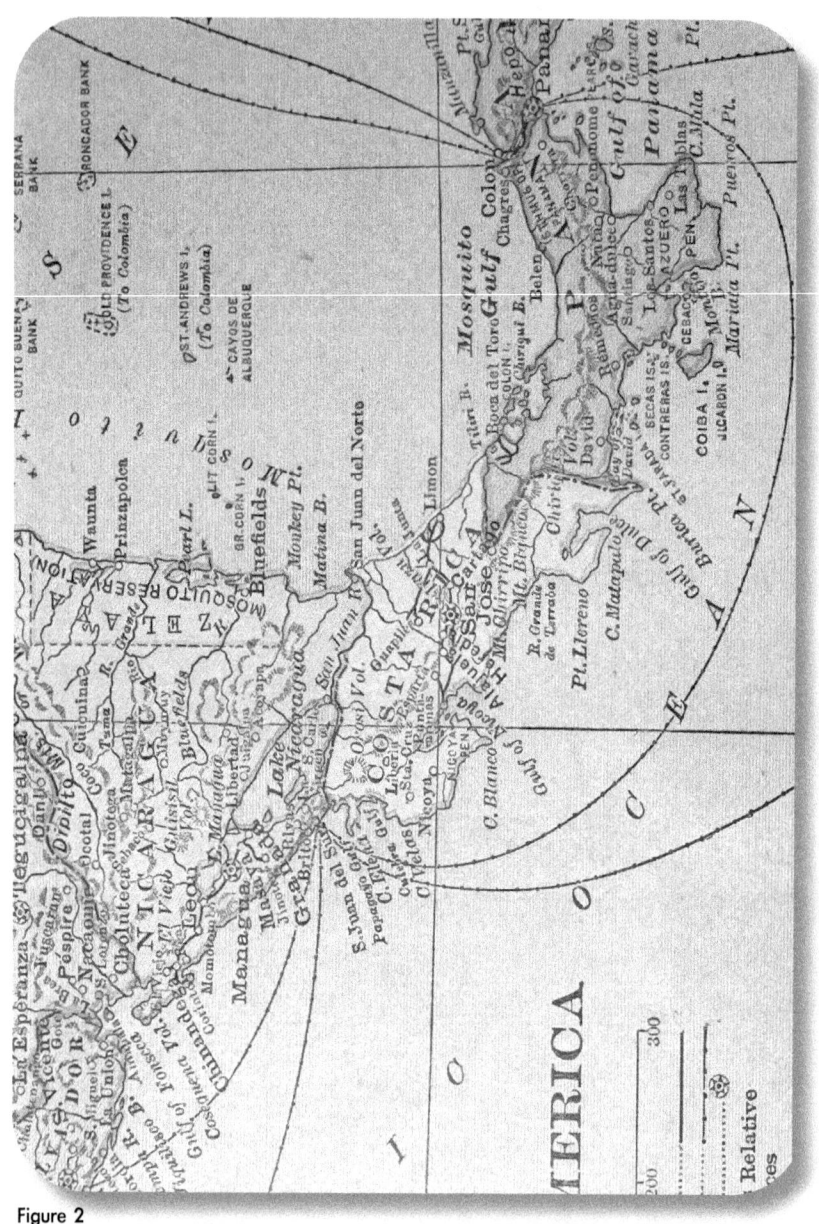

Figure 2

1910 Hammond Atlas of the World

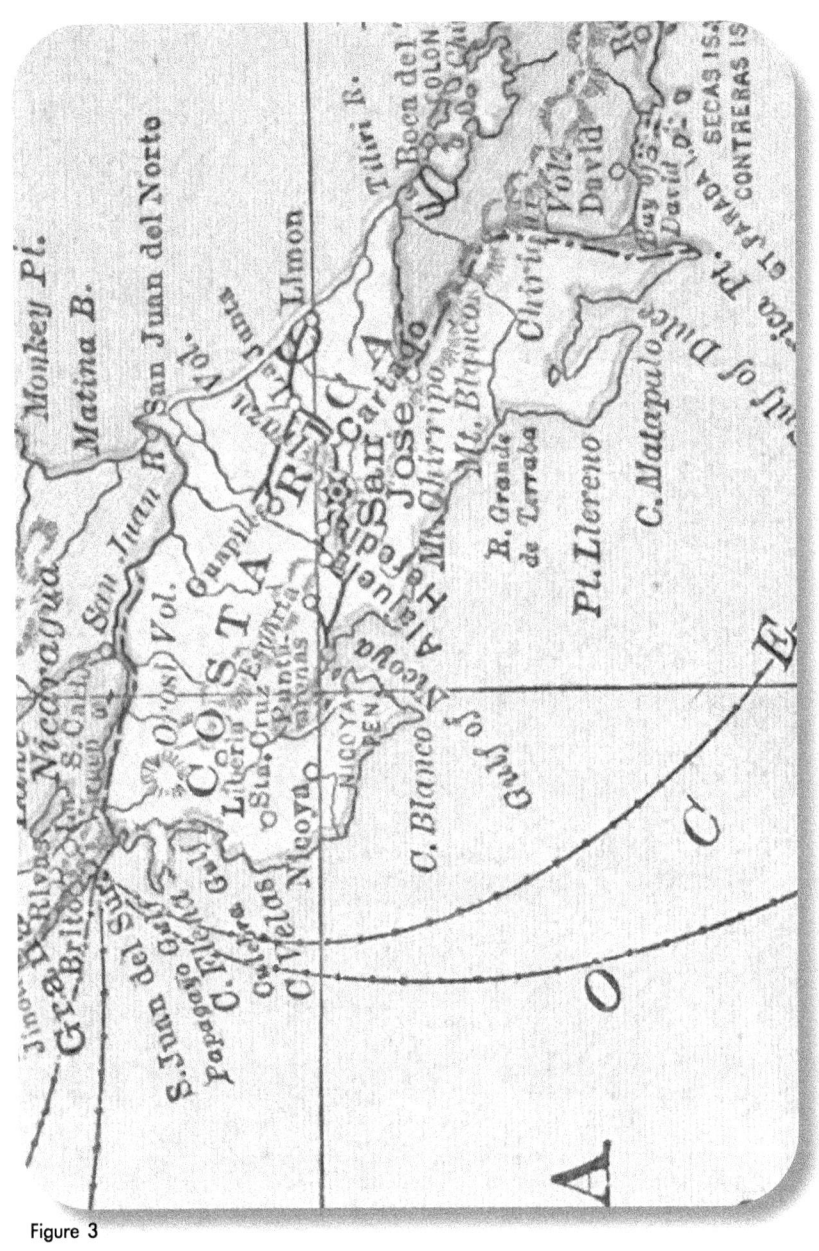

Figure 3

1910 Hammond Atlas of the World

Figure 4   Costa Rica Topographical Map
istockphoto.com/FrankRamspott
https://www.istockphoto.com/photo/costa-rica-3d-render-topograpic-map-
border-gm909754816-250566678?clarity=false

Figure 5

Costa Rica Provinces
istockphoto.com/-Panya-
https://www.istockphoto.com/vector/the-detailed-map-of-costa-
rica-with-regions-or-states-administrative-division-gm956739476-
261232375?clarity=false

Figure 6

Arenal Volcano National Park in Costa Rica with Arenal Lake.
istockphoto.com/OGphoto
https://www.istockphoto.com/photo/arenal-volcano-and-arenal-lake-costa-rica-gm1388560096-44616239?clarity=false

Figure 7

The Constant Home

Figure 8

Back Porch Of The Constant Home Viewed From A Balcony

Chapter I

CHAPTER ONE

The Constant Family

1924

THE BURNING COSTA RICAN SUN glared down on two grumbling servants who stood at the bleaching table of the back patio. The voice of old Micaela croaked above the flapping of wet garments. A crone-like, ageless creature she was, blacker than ebony. But wrinkles could not disguise her origin. Her small, sharp features, her glittering, beady eyes, and high cheekbones attested to her Jamaican birth. Her figure was hunched into a vulture-like stoop, her shrouded black skirt was gathered at her waist and hung to the ground, covering her bare feet. Her black blouse was caught high at the bony neck, leaving a crevice where she always tucked her crumpled handkerchiefs, and on her blouse against the concave breast, amulets, crosses, and medals of Saints warded away the clamoring evil spirits that beset her on every side. Her blouse sleeves hung full to the emaciated wrists. And whenever she opened her mouth, strong, square false teeth grimaced and clicked hideously. The shriveled heart of this creature knew but two fidelities. The first and supreme devotion was to the verdant memory of her dead mistress. Micaela felt that by talking of her kind, generous, Catholic Esmeralda, then doña Esmeralda lived

Figure 9

Micaela

again, if but for a moment. The other fidelity was to her Lorita, the gorgeous multi-plumaged green and red parrot, which, as a fledgling, had come with her when she, at the age of sixteen, left her Jamaican island to come to this small country of Costa Rica to enter the service of Esmeralda's family. At that moment, Lorita sat perched on the fence of the chicken yard nearby, cocking her green head interestedly at all Micaela's mumblings and pretending the mutterings were news she had not heard before.

Micaela wheezed and sniffed back an asthmatic cough, then continued her raucous lamenting. Her baleful, rasping voice crackled, "O Dios, she will wish she was dead before this is over." She bent over and grabbed a handful of thin, lawn garments, noticed they were a young woman's underpanties, spat and hissed, "Caramba, it is too bad, but thank God Ricardo is married. I can go there." She gazed at her hands, dry as potsherd, and continued, "These old hands won't serve an intrusa who lies in Esmeralda's bed. Ricardo loves this old woman. Ricardo, my Esmeralda's firstborn, my baby, loves this old woman."

Dolores, the other servant, comfortable on her full hips, shifted her position and hummed in a deep, croupy voice a song she always made up as she went along, "*Sing, sing little bird, because I want to cry.*" She shrugged her fat shoulders at Micaela and retorted, "It's none of your business, shut up! Let people marry, die—what is it to you? The señor has been married for seven months now, and you still grumbling. Can't you ever hush? Besides, how do you know what the new mistress will be like?" And Dolores paused a moment herself to consider the question. But she hastily took up her conversation again with, "And the noise they made last night coming in! I didn't trouble myself to get up and get a look at them. But I have heard that she is pretty, the new mistress."

Micaela shot a viperous glance at Dolores and began another dirgeful monologue: "You, you don't know my feelings if you can talk like that. You didn't spend forty years with doña Esmeralda. Since I was just a little kid, I worked for nobody else, almost my whole life. And now here is that skinny, long-legged intrusa, I had a look at her last night. I saw her. How do you expect me to act? I wish I could leave this place today."

Tolerantly, Dolores remarked a little less brusquely, "I'm ready to go too, but have patience; keep your mouth shut. We will be away soon; your Ricardo will see to that, I'm sure, and his wife will be like a second doña Esmeralda to you, I'll bet."

But Micaela didn't hear the intended consolation. She was too far back in the nebulous, shadowy gloom of her mind, where she often slipped. Yet her lips kept muttering, "No more intrusa in place of my poor, dead Esmeralda. Lorita, Esmeralda is dead, cold, dead, gone." Then she collapsed into another dry, racking cough so violent all her bones seemed to rattle and creak in their rusty sockets. Finally, catching her breath in short, exhausted puffs, she grabbed her handkerchief away from her throat with her small, black talon and wiped her wet eyes that always moistened at the mere mention of Esmeralda's name.

Across the patio in the wide, square kitchen, Rosa was moving efficiently, rapidly. Dinner was already late. She was new to this kitchen, and the young servant helper, Eva, was inexperienced. Brought over from the former home of her mistress, Rosa was eager that the first meal for her young mistress in this house should be perfection in preparation and service. She herself, tall and skinny, with her long, black braids dangling down each side across her breasts, was preparing every dish. She broke the eggs into a red-glazed clay bowl, folded in the chopped onions and tomatoes, poured a splash of sweet milk from a small jug, stirred the mixture with a powerful whirling motion, and stepped over to the old woodstove where a skillet of melted butter simmered. While the hot butter spattered with the cooking eggs, she eyed the broiling steaks and cautioned Eva to fluff up the rice and stir the black beans. Then, placing the scrambled eggs on a platter, Rosa turned to her pièce de résistance, which she always saved until the last possible moment, the ensalada. She examined every leaf of crisp lettuce, gave each a final fling to dry off water, dumped in the diced carrots, cucumbers, beets, avocados, and tomato pieces, then doused the concoction with vinegar, oil, salt, and pepper and pushed the bowl aside, confident of her absolute achievement.

Figure 10

The Constant Dining Room

Figure 11

Luzare Constant

Next door to the kitchen was the dining room, vast and beautiful. A long dining table was laid out in snowy linens and set with blue and gold china. Luzare Constant sat in his rightful place at the head of the table, drumming his strong, stubby fingers impatiently against it from time to time. Second only to beautiful women was his enormous and passionate desire for punctuality and correct, neatly written figures. At the age of fifty-three, Luzare Constant was healthy and vigorous, and he considered his fine, black mustache and hair to be a source of vanity. His round head sat neckless and solidly on his sturdy, thick shoulders. His gray eyes, quick, inquiring, always alert, studied first the new napkin ring at the other end of the table, then turned their attention to his eldest son,

Figure 12   Ricardo Constant

Ricardo, in whose presence he always felt vastly well-contented.

Ricardo sat at his father's left. Much taller and broader but not heavier than his father, he bore a striking resemblance to the older man. His head was large and strong-boned. His complexion, like his father's, was clear, thin, and ruddy over his cheekbones. His nose was longer and more aquiline than Luzare's, and his full nostrils were always a little distended. Even now, at twenty-three, his black hair was sparse, and his scalp shone through translucently as it caught the bright January sunlight from the windows. But it was always

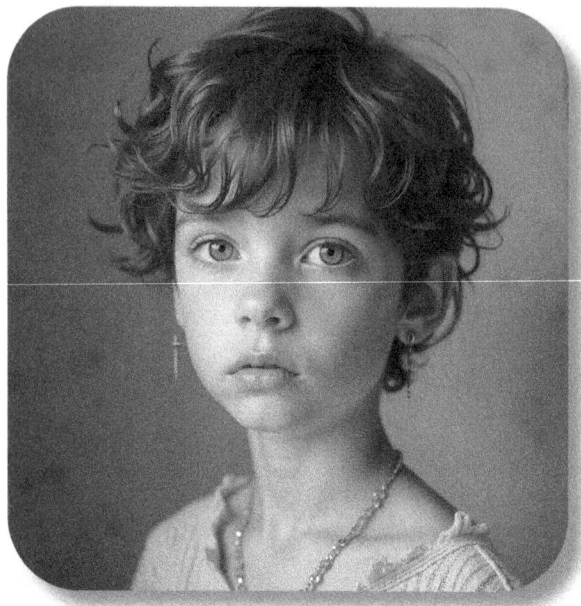

Figure 13

Victor Constant

Ricardo's eyes that held one's attention; wide and liquidly clear they were, as gray as moss behind water. Occasionally they were as inscrutable as a mystic's. Again, he could catch and capture other eyes with a blank stare that could mesmerize. Or they could snap with sudden interest. But usually they were seemingly guileless except for a peculiar glint. Ricardo, too, like his father, favored gray suits.

Luzare had not seen his eldest son for two months. They had parted company in Paris when, on their double honeymoon, Ricardo had decided to return home for the sake of checking on the business; though nearer the truth, he was in a hurry to get started on the construction of his home, incorporating all the advanced ideas he had accumulated on his travels. Luzare inquired, "And how is Diana? Is she feeling well? I'm sorry she couldn't be with us for our first meal back home."

Ricardo replied, "Diana is well, but she is beginning to pall, that's all. The hotel is fatiguing her, so she went with her mother to Puntarenas. She enjoys the beach there."

After closing the door to his mother's room, Victor, who is Luzare's youngest child, snail-paced down the hall. He could have easily been the *Gainsborough Blue Boy* that hung larger than life on the opposite wall. His slender, fragile body was as dainty as a little girl's. Back from the delicate face, his brown hair grew thatch-like,

Figure 14

Libia Constant

waving slightly at the forehead. His large, dark eyes were fringed with blue-black lashes that swept to his brows. His small lips were compressed into sullenness, and his whole expression was cloyed in unveiled contempt. With all his young soul, little Victor Constant despised his stepmother. He plodded on down and crossed over into the dining room.

Libia Constant sat upright, facing the reflection in her dressing room mirror. She thrust her brush vigorously at her tight, black curls that grew cap-like and short about her head. Her sad eyes scorned what she beheld. Sighing an inexpressibly worn-out, vanquished sigh, she sat idle, her hands still holding the brush handle. If she could only look the part she was supposed to fill, she could feel boosted, but her wide eyes in the young face and the lithe, slim body only abetted her feeling of total unfitness for her role. She glanced about the pink-papered room; Esmeralda Constant, from various positions in the room, met her gaze. Esmeralda's face was full of the solemn dignity plain-faced people always seemed to possess. Her lips were drawn into an unyielding tight line, and her eyes were calmly aware of her austere position.

Libia's eyes caught the reflection of the posters of a small bed, and again she released an involuntary sigh. She had welcomed the little boy's constant presence during their travels, even though she recognized that it stemmed solely from the child's selfish desire to separate his father from her. She had been grateful; he served a purpose. Luzare had shown more restraint in his passionate, hovering attendance toward her. The days had been spent thusly, with only the nights to dread. Here with the boy in the very room, the embarrassing fear of being heard was more than she could bear. Luzare's passion certainly could never be controlled by whispers. Her eyes shifted their stare to the heavy, black, iron safe in the other corner. The massive sides of the safe were wrapped around money and valuables as tightly as Luzare wished to crush her in his arms.

Another tinkle of the bell roused her from her quagmire trance of misery. She arose, patted away the wrinkles on her lap, and checked to ensure she had actually put on Luzare's wedding gift: the pearls that he liked to see her wear. Even the advanced 1926 dress she bought in Paris could not disfigure the purity and grace of her long body. The tight bodice enhanced her slenderness. The demurely rounded neck revealed her mellow, tawny skin, flawlessly smooth. Her small feet, in their pointed pumps, carried her out into the tile-paved hall. Upon the wall, the painting of Carmen, garish and bizarre, flinging and whirling her petticoats in wild abandon, spread a derisive smile as Libia passed. Libia felt her taunting eyes full of mockery, and she wondered if Carmen could hear her shackles. Down the hall and the sweeping stairs, she sashayed her way to her waiting family.

At the door of the dining room, she paused, lifted her chin, and put on a faint smile as she approached her husband. Luzare held her hands warmly, caressingly for a moment, then helped her into her chair. It was always an unutterable delight to have his young wife come near. As she sat down, Libia greeted her stepson Ricardo politely. Victor slid sideways into his chair. The sight of the little fellow sitting there so forlorn and lost-looking, dwarfed by the high-backed chair, his small hands crumpled in his lap, flooded Libia with enormous tenderness. Her hand stole over his small ones, and she patted them softly. But little Victor pushed her hand back and gave her a stony, scornful look from under his lashes.

Ricardo and Luzare immediately began eating, leaning their heads close to their plates like greedy, ravenous beasts. Even after seven months, Libia could not endure the horrible revulsion of their overgorging and cramming. It was like gazing at swine slopping. It always sickened her anew to watch. Luzare looked up from time to time as if to assure himself they were all still there, then went back to his food. Today he held determinedly on to his good humor even though waiting had irritated him. But Libia's loveliness always soothed him. Occasionally, he looked up and beamed benignly at his wife and young son. How indescribably magnificent they were sitting there together!

Ricardo was always affected with annoyance at the very sight of Libia. With his taste for superlatives and the impeccable, he realized that in the incandescent radiance of Libia's beauty, his wife's piquant prettiness was only a flickering candle. And when the two

Figure 15 A

The Stairway

were together, Diana's glow was completely in the umbra. After five months of being seen publicly with this woman, Ricardo realized she was just as breathtaking to others. Her brilliant black eyes shaded by heavy eyelids, her haughtiness, her majestic shoulders, her high breasts, and her rich coloring made her a veritable Madonna of Perugino. Moreover, she had always possessed a coldness and hauteur towards him that always rankled his very being. Even when they attended high school in the same classes, she always looked through and beyond him but rarely had ever spoken to him. He had, a few times in their teenage years, become emboldened enough to ask her for a dance at the fifteen-year-old parties. She danced with him, but her body had been as rigid as a corpse and her face just as expressionless whenever she was near him.

Looking toward Libia, Luzare became aware of her wristwatch and remarked, "Ricardo, Libia's watch we bought in Switzerland. Do you like it?"

Ricardo cast a smoldering glower, and his calculating eye estimated the cost to be very dear. Swiss mechanisms were expensive. Although it riled him and made it difficult to hide his disapproval, he still smiled appreciatively and responded, "Nice, very nice. Diana and I bought nothing of a personal nature. I felt everything should go into our business contracts. But then Diana has a fine collection of jewelry her mother provided." Libia felt the prick of his barb. And as if to assuage the wound he had just inflicted, he added, "But Libia needs no embellishments; she is a jewel herself." Ricardo's every remark to Libia for the past three months had been an innuendo, a subtle insinuation, or an allusion to her family's impecunious state. She brought nothing to her marriage but a lineage of high Castilian birth, a descendency from aristocratic old Spanish colonists, who for four hundred years had remained free from mixtures with native strains. She lifted her eyes from her plate in time to see Ricardo's triumphant smirk. Nature, in a capricious mood, had stuck three buckteeth in front of Ricardo's handsome godhead like a revolting deformity. Ricardo sucking in and out his lower lip only accentuated its unwholesomeness. He was a man of monumental self-composure. One would naturally expect pomposity from such a person, but instead his deprecatingly mild and half-apologetic tones did not seem a part of him. He stammered and stuttered as though only the dictates of a righteous conscience forced him. In such a manner he always uttered his double meanings, his inferences, and his noxious insults. Libia anticipated his next gesture, the hand rubbing. He always washed and wrung his hands in an invisible ablution whenever he felt pleased with himself.

Suddenly, Libia knew she was going to be sick. She gazed at the trees on the wallpaper and tried to control herself, but it was no use. She excused herself hastily and fled up the hall into her room, flung herself across the bed, grabbed the plato from within the cabinet of the bed table, and succumbed to the violent inundations of her stomach muscles until she could no longer heave. Her nose smarted and burned with the acidic liquids. She leaned farther over the china interior and fixed her eyes on the yellowish stain and sediment that smelled faintly sweet of old urine. Then she became so blindingly nauseous she held onto the bed with all her remaining strength and slid her head back on the pillow. Noon times had affected her like this since her miscarriage two months ago. And if she were not actually retching, she felt lightheaded, natant, and weak. Even the stepson, Arturo, ordinarily affable in his careless eighteen-year-old manner, had been irked by her eternal sickness.

Lifting her blurred eyes, she focused them on the silver crucifix hanging overhead. The suffering Prince was stretched on a cross, His head lowly bowed, a victim of his spoilers. *Esmeralda's crucifix!* Libia thought desperately, then groaned hopelessly and whispered, "O God, do You belong to Esmeralda too?" She crossed herself feebly to free herself from impious thoughts. Dizzy and dazed, she descended into the hell of her remembrances. She could see a quiet, studious girl, untouched and aglow with secret plans for her ambitions, strolling to her music lessons or practicing at the conservatory. Tranquil in spirit, she had delighted in tantalizing herself with the decision of where she would go when the scholarship, a certainty, was offered to her. She had visualized herself in the United States and then again in Europe.

Then one day she accepted an invitation to sing at a wedding, a fabulous affair. She remembered how much fun she'd had designing her costume for the masquerade to be held after the ceremony and the breathless thrill of viewing herself in the mirror before she left home. She had rarely been out socially, and she had never attended such a grand event of high society before. She bedecked herself as a cigarette girl in a black sateen skirt, white frilly apron and low-cut blouse, with cigarettes and cigars tied in red ribbons to her wide sashes. She sang behind the foliage embankment before the ceremony, and then when the festivals began, she drifted among the dancers. Balancing her tray, she made her way over near the refreshment table, where everyone seemed to be giving a particular greeting to a distinguished, older man. Gliding up, she accomplished a coquettish curtsy and bubbled, "Mr. Constant, your party is beautiful; the costumes are so wonderful! I do want to thank you for the wonderful time I'm having." She then presented him with a cigar.

The middle-aged man spoke in a concise, tight manner, which she soon deduced was just his way of speaking, for he was visibly pleased with her attention. He smiled and said, "My dear, your graciousness pleases me. But I'm afraid I'm taking the honor that belongs to my brother Paulo. This is his house." Libia remembered how she had flushed with confusion, losing her poise. But the older gentleman wanted to ease her acute discomfort and immediately begged, "Please, may I have the honor of the next dance?" Luzare Constant was completely taken by the girl's lovely face. He smiled often into her sparkling eyes, and as they danced, he inquired, "And what is your name, Miss Cigarette Girl?"

Libia looked up and answered, "Oh, I am Libia Quesada de la Esprilla."

The man questioned her, "Not Felipe Quesada's daughter? It is incredible! Incredible! And how is my good friend Felipe?"

Libia's face clouded. "Papa is not well, but it is so strange; I don't remember you."

Luzare chuckled, "Well, I remember you! Have no fear, little girl. I have known you since I used to hold you on my knee. You were just a little dirty-faced, apple-cheeked kid with long curls. I used to tease you by pulling them." Luzare danced again with Libia to make sure the understanding was clear that he would take her home after the party.

Figure 15 B

Butterfly-shaped Flag of Costa Rica
https://www.istockphoto.com/vector/flag-of-costa-rica-in-the-form-of-a-butterfly-gm485104814-71832883
iStock.com/Bolsunova

CHAPTER TWO

Libia

1925

L IBIA COULD STILL REMEMBER THE chill of the night air on the way home as she sat breathing deeply, Luzare beside her. He never drove his automobiles himself. Mechanical contrivances unnerved him, so he always employed a chauffeur. At her home he held her hand briefly and asked, "When am I going to see you again, apple-cheeked girl?"

And with shy charm, Libia replied, "You may look in on Papa any time. I am sure he will be glad to see you." Luzare showed his interest in Papa the very next evening and continued to visit three or four times a week, either playing cards or just talking, mostly with Catalina and Felipe.

Luzare's proposal came as such a surprise five months later that Libia, more confounded and baffled than flattered, took her problem immediately to Papa, upon whose unfailing understanding she always relied. With a childlike simplicity, she stated, "Papa, Luzare wants to marry me. What must I tell him?"

A different Felipe drew his daughter close, and looking down through her chaste, trusting eyes into the unblemished purity of her being, he gravely answered, "Search your heart, my baby. Let your heart tell your head what you must do. Do you love him?" But he himself knew that answer. She was just a little child, despite being nearly twenty-five years old, and there was a certain quality about Luzare—a rapaciousness he himself sometimes sensed. But maybe age had quieted that.

Libia shook her head in a quandary, answering, "I don't know; he's very nice, and his gifts are thoughtful; he's considerate, and if he's your friend, he's fine."

Felipe lacked the courage to reply as he wanted; however, he recognized this as fate, and fate had been the earthquake that leveled his business office in 1910 and rendered him humble. He still felt himself struggling with the despondency, the bitterness, and the debris of spiritless depression left by it. Fate was a harsh master with whom he could no longer contend. Felipe's chin sank to his breast as he admonished, "Go ask Mama; she always knows best."

Catalina took the news with no trace of surprise, only astonishment that Libia hadn't already given her answer to Luzare. In moments of vexation like this, she lifted one of the combs from her black hair, which was piled high away from her forehead, and combed it in agitated little strokes while walking back and forth across the floor. "Don't be stupid, Libia. You are pretty, true, but the boys don't flock here. You show them no interest; that is why. And you never will. You think you live only to sing. Well, you can sing after you're married. Use your head. Here is a man of property, rich, responsible, and able to give you everything. What more could you ask? Love? That will come in time. Think of your father! He could go at any time, just like that!" And she gave a quick snap of her fingers and continued, "Then what would happen? If I thought with my heart as Felipe does, I don't know where we would be now. Martita married a widower, and she is happy. You must not make Luzare wait for your answer. Tell him tomorrow. Plenty of girls younger than you would jump at the chance."

The wedding ceremony was held in Luzare's house, out back on the patio, on Libia's twenty-fifth birthday, June fifteenth, in the year

Figure 16 A

Luzare and Libia

1925. She wore her mother's wedding dress that, many years before, had been imported from Spain and was now a creamy yellow. The fountain in the center of the patio was a gigantic altar of greenery. Around the patio, small tables and chairs were arranged, with groups of friends chatting and dancing in an atmosphere of veritable, idyllic paradise. Flowers hung in sumptuous masses of decorations and were embanked in extravagant walls. Two orchestras, one in the billiard room and the other at the lower end of the patio, furnished music. Luzare spread himself like the proverbial green bay tree. Never had he been more charming, his black mustache waxed to a high gloss. He drank innumerable toasts with his friends, nodded, smiled, shook hands, and enjoyed every minute of his party. The merriment and tinkle of glasses cast out all gloom that, for two years since the death of Esmeralda, had permeated the house.

After the wedding, Libia and Luzare went to Libia's mother's house to wait for Ricardo's wedding, which was announced for a week later. Catalina's motherly eye discerned her daughter's restraint and the bluish circles that had deepened from day to day under her eyes. Poked by her own guilty conscience, she had been overly solicitous of her daughter.

She felt compelled to assure and reassure Libia at every turn, remarking several times a day, "You are going to enjoy that ocean voyage. You'll see. To me, nothing is as soothing as the rock of a boat. And Paris will simply intoxicate you. Every time I think of Paris, I think of opera. Wonderful! At last you are going to hear good opera. All those foreign places will pep you up. One is always tired after one's wedding, naturally."

At the thought of the boat, the bed seemed to rock back and forth. Libia hung on tenaciously, clutching the mattress on either side. She shook her head to drive away the pertinacious, deathly, sickening craziness. There again, the sight of the little bed across the room forced her to push herself up. She slid her feet to the floor and, assured of her balance, swayed to her dressing table and wiped the powder puff across her face to remove traces of her illness. Resolute and determined, she faced the inexorable necessity of an open conflict with Luzare. Dread it, as she might, she must have it out with him before night.

Figure 16 B

Victor's Bed in the Master Bedroom

Figure 16 C

Lorita
iStock.com/PanuRuangjan
https://www.istockphoto.com/photo/red-masked-conure-gm452152181-29809876?clarity=false

CHAPTER THREE

Luzare and Ricardo

1925

LEFT IN THE DINING ROOM, Luzare and Ricardo finished their coffee leisurely. They got up, and, as had always been their custom, they walked over to the billiard room, Luzare carrying his weight along briskly in short steps, Ricardo shuffling along, swaying from one foot to the other in a clumsy, looby gait, like one dispossessed of equilibrium. His clothes were finely cut and of excellent texture. On a hanger there was an elegant display of haberdashery, but, draped over Ricardo, the padding of his coat shoulders slumped and slid down heavily.

The billiard room was Luzare's favorite room of the house. It was a tribute to his providential foresight. The walls were insulated with six inches of cement, a protection against earthquakes, and bulletproof, for although the country had always conscientiously tried to develop a national spirit of progress and enlightenment, one must guard against insurrections and uprisings. But this seemed absurd to Luzare's friends, such a precaution, since no gun of revolution had been shot in the peaceful country. Nevertheless,

Figure 17

The Billiard Room

CHAPTER 3

Luzare liked his idea. Here he kept another black iron safe. This one contained the legal documents for the store. His library of a hundred leather-bound encyclopedias sat cater-cornered on the opposite side of the room.

Luzare picked up a billiard cue and popped a few balls as he chatted with his eldest son. Since his youth, he had always been an excellent player, but today he was interested only in Ricardo, who was more direct than usual in these statements.

"Papa," Ricardo asked, "Do you think it was the better part of wisdom to leave Arturo in Paris? After all, an eighteen-year-old with money in his pockets can get into a lot of mischief alone. Arturo has no sense about escapades."

Luzare nodded but reasoned, "Well, after all, Arturo is no fool. I want him to develop self-reliance. Can you think of a better way? Besides, I intend to send him to school somewhere over there next fall. Let him get the feel of it now."

Seeing he could get nowhere on that approach, Ricardo began again. This time he employed his most trustworthy weapon, indirection, as he continued, "Now don't misunderstand me, I realize Libia is doing the very best she knows. Nobody can expect her to know all about children, but Victor is so sickly-looking, too pale. He needs real motherly care. I am not saying Libia resents him, but after all, you couldn't expect her to have immediate love for a child not her own."

Luzare mulled a moment over the idea of a resentful Libia. He had never sensed it in her nature. Yet often others could see what you yourself could not. He couldn't agree with Ricardo because he couldn't make himself voice any blame on Libia for the boy's strange behavior. "But," he shrugged, "it could be disconcerting for a woman to take a honeymoon with three stepchildren."

The family matters taken care of, they launched into their business. On this one subject they were always completely of one accord.

After Libia left the dining room, little Victor did not wait for dismissal but darted across the hall quicker than the movement of a weaver's shuttle, heedless of his father's voice calling after him, demanding him to finish his food. He pulled at the latch-string that held the stair door closed, opened the door quickly, jerked it closed after him, and started giant-stepping up the steep, closeted steps, two at a time. At that moment, he remembered where his ball was. He had been playing with it the day they left for the boat. The door at the head of the stairs opened into an immense room, long and wide and barren of furniture except for a massive monstrosity: that yellow-lacquered desk standing against the wall in the corner. Victor fell to his knees, ducked his head under the desk, and strained his eyes to see behind the back leg. There, he could see. It was there, caught between the leg and the wall. He poked it out, dusted it off, walked over to the center of the room, sat down, pushed his legs wide apart, and started rolling the ball to the wall. The walls were the favorite playmates of this seven-year-old boy. They never kept the ball. They played the rules exactly right. If he threw the ball hard, they returned it hard. If he pushed it slowly, it rolled back slowly slowly into the fort of his legs. Shifting his position, he played with the three walls, being fair and careful never to show preference. This was a game he had discovered quite by accident one day when, as a small child, he happened to shove the ball, and it rolled back from the wall. He was even fonder of the game now and never tired of playing it. Thus pacified and with his back to the door, he didn't hear it slowly open or the floor creaking behind him. His little body trembled convulsively, and he choked a scream when he felt the black claws fasten into his shoulder and the breath on the back of his head as the whispered-voice, between its short-winded gasps, wheezed at him. Lifting his eyes, he stared, transfixed with terror, into the mask of Micaela, who was more frightening than one of his visions in the night.

Micaela pinched harder into his thin shoulder blade and scolded him, "Now don't look like that. You remember this old woman, don't you? Micaela loves you. Remember, she makes you good platanos maduros. You like them, don't you? Don't be afraid." Victor dropped his eyes. He could not bear to look at the large yellow teeth that bit out at him. The croaking went on, "I know what's wrong with Victor. He's not afraid of this old woman. He knows she is his friend. He is afraid of the intrusa. Victor is afraid the intrusa might poison him or choke him in the night. But don't worry. Micaela has eyes like an animal. She sees everything. She won't let the intrusa hurt you. She will keep watch all the time." Then, because the little boy was stifling a scream, she slinked back across the floor. He heard her thumping down the steps, pausing at the landing, and then finally the bottom door squeaking as she let herself out.

Luzare stopped in the middle of his sentence when the clock on the wall struck two. Time had slipped away from him. He sprang to his feet and clipped up the hall to look in on his wife before leaving. Ricardo stopped for a moment in the bathroom adjacent to the billiard room.

Libia was waiting, her face set, when Luzare opened her door. His hat in his hand, he stepped over to kiss her. Pushing him firmly away from her, she stood facing him with a stubborn defiance in her voice as she spoke, "Luzare, Victor is quite a big boy. You don't realize it, but he is, and this little room," her hand swept toward the connecting door leading into the next room, "would make a wonderful little boy's room. Children notice more than we think, and Victor is such a light, restless sleeper. And even if we closed the door, he could see the lights through the top glass and know that we are nearby. I could still hear him if he should wake during the night." She was talking so rapidly she did not detect the mounting flush in Luzare's face, the tightening grip on his hat brim, or the flash in his eyes. His state of discomposure that he had fought since lunch was touched off like a firebrand stuck to a blaze.

He sputtered, "Libia, I have no intention of letting you pack my baby off into another room simply because you want to get rid of him. I have been overlooking this, but since you brought it up, I must say I do not appreciate, nor have I ever appreciated, your attitude toward my child. If you take some time or trouble with him, you might understand him. He is going to sleep in this room." With that, he turned on his heel and walked out.

Through the window, Libia could see Luzare and Ricardo striding down the walk to drive off in their automobile. She stood for a moment, too stunned to move. Then she half-turned to go back to bed, but instead she whirled about and went across the hall into the living room, which, like the dining room, was as capacious and as architecturally beautiful as a Venetian ballroom. The vaulted ceiling over near the side mirador windows was encrusted with chandeliers that draped the archway like grape clusters, with silver filigreed leaves and tiny bulbs at the tip of each sprig. Around the room was arranged fine French imported furniture.

Seating herself at the expanse of the grand piano, she plunged herself into tumults of trills and swells, softly lifting her voice, sweetly, slowly, again softly, then more stirring, quickening until rapturously the torrents flooding her soul poured out tempestuously through the vibrance of her voice, "*Oh Blessed Virgin, Hear my prayer. Thou, Star of Glory. Look on me! Here in the dust, I bend before thee. Now from this earth, Oh, set me free!*" Elizabeth's prayer from Tannhäuser had never been sung with more fervor.

Upstairs, the little boy, hearing the glorious notes, thought, "She is happy because she has my papa and his house." He did not understand that the last, high, anguished note was a cry that soared to the very gates of heaven, then dropped in crushed dejection back to the earth.

At supper that night, Luzare was again in good humor. While waiting for Libia to finish her food, he talked about the store and the possibilities of increased business from his good contacts in Europe. Afterwards they went into the billiard room, where Luzare took out the farm ledger from the safe, seated himself on the sofa near the lamp, and checked some figures. Libia sat nearby under the full-length portrait of Esmeralda and darned Luzare's socks. Luzare was not a stingy man, but he liked every article to be fully expended of its usefulness before discarding it. After he satisfied his mind on the figures, he placed the ledger back in the safe, locked it, leaned down and kissed his wife on the forehead, and whispered, "Time for bed." She arose, and they walked up the hall together. Victor was already asleep, his black lashes spread fan-like on his cheeks. But as soon as the light was out, he began tossing and whimpering. Then he sat up in bed, flinging and thrashing his arms about fitfully in the air, shrieking and screaming in terror. Libia slipped out of bed and sat

Figure 18 A   The Living Room

beside him, trying to soothe and comfort his disquieted mind. She rubbed his back and murmured endearments she had wanted so many times to say to him. But as soon as he was conscious enough to realize her presence, he was even more frightened and begged pitifully, "Don't choke, please, please don't choke me!"

Libia lulled, "Baby, baby, nobody is going to hurt you; now go to sleep, sweet baby." But he was in convulsions, sobbing, trembling. Luzare came over and held the quaking little figure tightly in his thick arms and talked in a low, compassionate voice Libia had never heard him use before. He held his child until the jerking ceased and the young being was again asleep. Luzare's deepest embrace thus interrupted for the night, he went to bed, turned his back on Libia, and was soon asleep.

After his breakfast the next morning, Luzare came back to the bedroom, opened the desk room door, looked about, and stepped into the middle of the room, his stubby fingers tapping against his stomach expanse or occasionally twitching his black mustache. Finally he tersely remarked to Libia, "I'm going to the finca," and in a moment he was down the hall, traversing the patio, and letting himself out the back gate. His eyes immediately sought and found Enor, the head concho, near the coffee trees where conchos were pruning the tops, standing about the trees hacking with their machetes. Enor was standing by, cursing and sweating, not as to a balking mule, but mildly and naturally as if speaking the only language they understood. Luzare was not ready for Enor yet. He strolled about inspecting his farm. It had been eight months since he had checked this part of his property, and his quick eye was on the alert for signs of carelessness. But every inch met his approval. It was as neat and as carefully cultivated as a botanical garden. Undergrowth and litter, even blooms of the coffee flowers that had shed the day before, had already been raked up. Chicken fertilizer nestled in mounds about the roots of all the trees. The blossoms on the squat, evergreen coffee trees with their small, waxy leaves were healthy white flowers, free of damaging blight evidence. From tree to tree, the berries in their different stages of maturity were a delight to the eye, some a fleshy green berry just out of flower, some a yellowish riper tint, and some red like an artificially decorated Christmas tree, ready for the moment of picking. Under these trees, the conchos were already at work, with their wide wicker baskets suspended from their waists and their great hats sitting atop their bodies like gigantic moving mushrooms. The trabajadores del café, men, women, and children, were catching the slender, flexible stems with one hand and, in a left stroke, shucking down the berries with the other hand. Their arms and hands were sticky, stained, and dark brown. Some already had their baskets full and were walking over to their vat to empty them. There were no laggards at his work because they were being paid by their vat loads, and each worked in feverish haste. Some could even earn two colones a day. The banana trees were just as well cared for. The huge buds of the trees with their tiny, purple flowers were a pleasing aroma in the hot moisture that was beginning to rise from the ground. The old leaves had been cut away; dying stalks were rebudding. The whole farm was without criticism. Luzare stuck his head into Enor's pink adobe dwelling, reached and pulled down the black ledger that hung by a string at the frame of the door, stood out in the brightness of the sun, and quickly checked Enor's crudely drawn figures. He closed the book, stuck it under his arm, and turned to walk back up the lane. The ledger proved what Luzare had long suspected about Enor's character. He had never been duped by the concho's conniving. He had submitted to letting Enor live on the finca because Enor had wanted it and he had wanted Enor. The concho was an excellent and intelligent farmer; where else would he find an intelligent concho? Enor could handle slow workers; he could keep the crops in constant rotation. Not a dead leaf or sprig went to waste. But the ledger was short. The clever are also personally ambitious, Luzare mused. It is the other side of their nature. He didn't want to lose Enor, but he had to control him.

Enor noticed his master and was now standing respectfully by until he was addressed. Luzare looked up and spoke as a man who has just made a spur-of-the-moment decision, "Enor, the lower corner of this lot. Let's take a look at it." Enor, subservient, was always in Luzare's presence, ambled along. Luzare pointed out a strip of land and said, "Now, this, from your house to the back fence, is for your own management. How do you feel to be a landowner, eh?" Enor bared his snaggled teeth self-consciously, then studied his toes. Luzare went on, "Now, in about three years you will start growing rich; how will that be?" Enor twisted his hat in his hand and mumbled his thanks. Luzare then tapped the black ledger, his eyes looking hard into Enor's face as he said, "Let's see if both of us can have prosperous crops." Enor paled under the strong, uncompromising eyes, and he understood Luzare's meaning thoroughly. He knew in business the quality of mercy was strained in this man. With the finca matter thus attended to, Luzare went briskly up the path and through the gate to the patio, down the hall, and out to the street where his chauffeur waited. He rode away in his automobile.

During the middle of the morning, a truck pulled around through the wide back gate that opened from the side street and stopped in front of the garages. The driver walked up to the ironing room, where Micaela was hunched over the ironing board. Seeing her, he inquired, "Where do you want me to put this bed?" Micaela put her flatiron back on the charcoal brazier, then the old sorcerer hobbled up the hall and rapped on Libia's door. Libia stepped down from her dressing stool, which she was using to gain height in order to reach one of Emeralda's pictures. She had started with the corner one, hoping that it would be least likely to be missed. Answering the door with the picture still in her grasp, she listened to Micaela's question.

"Doña, where is the man to put the bed?"

It flashed on Libia, the bed, a purchase. She walked back through the connecting door from her room, opened the door of the desk room out into the hall, and smiled victoriously, "Tell the man to bring it in here." Micaela's asp-eyes glinted from the picture back to her mistress' face, wicked little eyes that they were, full of spite, but she nodded her assent.

Figure 18 B

Enor's Adobe Home With His New Property

Figure 18 C

Costa Rica Flag Ribbon
iStock.com/PeterPencil. https://www.istockphoto.com/vector/costa-rica-flag-
ribbon-set-vector-stock-illustration-gm1337195075-418165107

CHAPTER 3

CHAPTER FOUR

Lady of the House

March 1925

THERE WERE UNDERCURRENTS OF SERVITUDE, but after her first week's stay in the house, Libia felt the servants were reconciled, at least outwardly, to her management. They were orderly and performed their duties on time.

The next Friday night, Rosa stood bent low over the sink, her braids almost touching the hot suds as she swathed the dishes. It was later than usual, and she was worn out. Unconsciously, then consciously, she was aware of another presence, and glancing over her shoulder, she was surprised to see a stranger framed in the doorway. A regal personage she was, with a black blouse drawn tightly to her neck and her hands folded in tranquil neatness at her waist. Rosa hastily dried her hands on her apron and made ready to direct the stranger to the living quarters. But the pragmatic, grave person lifted a restraining finger and questioned in a hollow voice, "Why do you serve that woman?"

Rosa replied stammeringly, "But, but she is the new mistress."

The older woman shook her head slowly and replied, "No, in

Figure 19 A

Esmeralda Constant

this house I am the mistress." With those words she turned, and rustling her long, taffeta skirt, she was gone. The sound of the skirt soon blended and was lost in the wind. Mystified, Rosa stuck her head around the doorframe, wondering, '*Which way had she gone?*' But the wind was suddenly strong, and she could no longer hear footsteps. She finished up in the kitchen, switched out the light, and walked down into the servants' quarters, where old Micaela was already in bed, her enormous white gown swaddling her small, twisted, black body. Lorita blinked sleepily from her perch at the top of the bed.

Still perplexed, Rosa fumbled at her dress buttons and mused absently, "I wonder which way she did go, and there is no one at home in front to keep her company."

Micaela, who never seemed to really sleep, popped up curiously, "Who?"

Rosa responded as she inclined her head towards the kitchen, "The stranger."

"What stranger?" Micaela persisted.

Rosa explained, "The brown lady who stopped in the kitchen a few minutes ago."

"Who did she want?" inquired Micaela.

Rosa shrugged. "She didn't want anybody. Just told me that she was the mistress of the house."

With this, Micaela grabbled herself out of her bedclothes, her eyes afire, her pounces reached up, clawing and pulling at Rosa's shoulders; garbling her words, she begged, "What did she look like? Tell me, how did she look?!" Such a peculiar acting person, Rosa was not likely to soon forget.

She answered readily, "She was middle-aged but straight like a candle and stern-looking, that's all."

Wheezing and clutching at Rosa's arms, Micaela gasped, "Come, come with me!" And half-dragging the taller, larger figure, they crossed the patio and crossed the hall into the billiard room—a part of the house that, until this moment, Rosa had not seen. Snapping on the light, Micaela pointed her white-winged claw to the wall as she demanded, "Now tell me, what do you see?"

Rosa gazed up at the same somber, severe-featured woman who not long ago had stood speaking to her, and she exclaimed, "That's her; that's the one I mean; she was here!"

Gurgling in excitement, Micaela led the dumbfounded Rosa back out into their room, pushed her down on the bed, and perched upon her own while her eyes still bore into Rosa's face and she babbled, "That was doña Esmeralda, my doña. She is back. Did she ask for this old woman? Did the doña want me?" Rosa shook her head, uncomprehending. Micaela went on, "You don't understand, but you shall." Again, she tugged the younger woman after her as her own small, hunched figure floated merrily in the breeze of the patio. Pushing and heaving against the storage door that was heavy with bananas stacked against it, she finally squeezed herself in, then pulled Rosa in. Standing in the large room, she whispered, "Doña Esmeralda comes here all the time to pray. This was her little church. The altar was up there." And she pointed through the dimness toward the other end. "She was so good, so pious, so Catholic, always thinking of the miserable. She always had them here for mass and gifts on Christmas." It was not hard for Rosa to visualize this as a place of worship. The small, high-arched windows let slits of moonlight in through their grillwork casements. The stone floor was cold to her feet as she trailed behind Micaela to the other dark, shadowy end. Micaela was still whispering meaningfully, "Now... now you shall understand."

Rosa's eyes first made out the outline, and then she felt the high poster of a bed. Suddenly the impact of what she had seen and what she was about to see was upon her. She turned to run, but Micaela, strangely strong, held her in her tight little claw as she hissed, "Look at the bed, her bed." She lifted off a large spray of wax flowers lying in the center of the bed, turned down the spread, and revealed a bare mattress with a black stain in its middle. Micaela's voice never stopped its croaking whisper, "Doña is in heaven, an angel. She can come again, as she did tonight. She died right on this bed, having her last baby, a little dead boy. She held my hands, she screamed with the pain, '*Micaela, help me.*' The baby came, and the blood flowed over the floor. My sweet doñita died like that, holding my hands." Rosa broke free of Micaela's hand and fled, half-stumbling, shrieking as she ran across the cement patio and back into her room. Jerking a pillowcase from her feather pillow, she reached behind the door and grabbed her two dresses from the nail, groped for her shoes under the bed, stuffed them into the case, and, crying, sobbing, and gibbering with hysteria, she threw her jacket over her shoulders, wadded the pillowcase under her arm, and went swiftly out the back way. Micaela stood at the door of her room with an evil, sated smile about her mouth. She spoke to her parrot, "Lorita, doña Esmeralda is back." Then, more audibly, she called wooingly into the darkness, "Doñita, where are you? Here I am. Where are you?" The soughing wind blew with a strong gust and rattled and moaned at the storage room windows.

In his own little room now and with a full-sized bed, Victor awoke every morning when the delivery man pressed the doorbell for the diadentro to pick up the fresh bread deposited at the door. The diadentro, who woke up earlier than any of the other servants to set the table and start her cleaning, always fetched the bread. By the time Libia was dressed for mass, Victor was waiting, scrubbed clean, his hair brushed slick from the zig-zag part. The two would walk down the side street together to the cloistered chapel, across from the far corner of their property. The little boy seldom spoke, but Libia enjoyed watching his eyes, as black and dewy as berries, as they looked on the morning's awakening. Although Libia's very nature rebelled and cried out against attending this church, she recognized the social imperativeness of it. It was nearby, and it would be considered a shunning if she didn't go to the chapel founded by Esmeralda. Esmeralda's money had constructed it, and Esmeralda willed the pews and altar from her own private chapel at her death.

Luzare never went with them. Once, in the beginning of her marriage, Libia inquired offhandedly if he were coming along, but he had snapped, "You attend to your soul; I'll look after mine." And as far as she was able to ascertain, Luzare had never set foot inside the small chapel.

After mass, she did her morning's shopping at the pulperías. She always purchased only a day's supply because the servants' thieving could not be coped with otherwise. Then, whatever was left over from the supper, she allowed the cook to sack up and take home to her hungry young ones. However, the servant not only took the leftover provender but also stole the staples. Libia also found it necessary to buy staples daily. First she stopped at the pulpería for her sugar, rice, salt, soap, and tea. Then she went to the verdulería for her vegetables: potatoes, lettuce, tomatoes, corn, and often tacacos. She noticed that when the servant shelled the tacacos, Victor always stood nearby to blow up the flexible membranes of the pods. He was quite adept at slipping the membrane from its prickly exterior, carefully blowing it until it ballooned and, in its expansion, looked like a puffed frog. Sometimes he would accidentally bite the membrane, and its taste, bitter as gall, would make him pucker his mouth into funny expressions. Then they would both laugh together over it.

At the carnicería, she paused for her meat, which hung on ropes suspended from the ceiling. The butcher would ask the measure, reach up, unhook the slab of meat, shoo off the flies with a wave of his long knife, then whack off the amount and cut what Libia desired. Victor always watched with fascinated eyes as the big man threw the meat across the stump and hacked.

Then Libia hired a little boy to bring home her purchases, and she and Victor walked back for breakfast with Luzare. After his eggs and orange juice, Victor would go out to play in the front garden. Libia always looked forward to lunchtime every day. At the tinkle of the bell, Victor would scamper across the yard to the front door, then slow down and walk the length of the mosaic hall and down into the dining room. With Luzare giving his entire days to the store, Libia could have Victor all to herself. She was determined that this child would not be a gobbling abhorrence at the table. Victor did not respond overtly, nor did he resist. He was docile, his earlier petulance toward her gone. She began her lessons by explaining that when children grow larger, they stop having baby habits. They were expected to be careful with their food. Never did they chew too fast. They were supposed to swallow each bit before putting the next forkful to their mouth. Neither did they pack their fork with their knife. During the first lesson, Victor listened, his head bent down, but he ate with less haste. The next day, standing behind his chair and placing her hands over his small ones, she guided them in their manipulations of the heavy instruments, making a sort of game, all the while chanting, "*Load the fork, up the fork into the mouth, now down the fork.*" Victor complied obediently through the next few weeks. As she made up the games, he acted them out. At these times he was the master of the house. He pulled out her chair, helped her to the table graciously, then sat down and executed his lunch according to her instruction, in polished, finished manners. At the table at night he began casting glances at his father's head bent low over his plate, his rapid movements, and his crammed mouth. Once Libia caught Victor giving her an almost empathetic glance.

In cleaning Victor's room every morning, the servant always commented on the clean, good boy. Except for his bed, which was always a tumbled, tangled mass of bedclothes, there was really nothing to clean. He never used the bacinilla placed nightly for his convenience in the bed cabinet. He never touched the glass of water on his table. Entrenched in his own little patterns and ways, he stacked his books in exactly the same order, and they rested at the same angle on his desk. His soccer ball was always put under the foot of his bed against the outer leg. Every morning he put on the clothes Libia had laid on his chest the night before. He never touched the inside of his clothes drawers. The clothes lay in flat layers just as they had been arranged by the servant.

When he started school in March, he walked into the house at three o'clock every afternoon, placed his books on his desk, took off his jacket, reached down for his ball, tucked it under his arm, and walked out into the garden. Libia's heart ached as she watched the odd, lonely little boy out scuffing and kicking his ball, first kicking and then running to receive it. Never having had any playmates for his leisure time, Victor had long since known how to play both sides. As Libia noticed the bare, patchy spots spreading in the grass and sprigs of broken shrubbery, she smiled. The garden had been Esmeralda's particular joy. She had landscaped it with great care.

Here, at least, was one place that had openly defied Esmeralda. At dusk, it was not necessary to call Victor in. He came unbidden, put his ball back under the foot of his bed, went back to the bathroom and washed his hands and face, and then read in his room until the dinner bell sounded. He always presented himself in the dining room punctually. After dinner he sometimes sat with them, or, more often, he went back to his room. And when they passed by on their way to bed, the light was always out.

Sundays were mixed-up days for Libia. She and Victor went to early mass. Luzare always dressed, went over to the barber's for a shave, and then sat in Parque Nacional and watched the Sunday goers. He would sit idly snipping at a tender bough with his rapier, sharper than a razor, which he had unsheathed from his cane. Luzare felt this one object was worth his whole time in Europe, where he had obtained it. It was a slender, shiny, black baton featuring a richly ornamental gold handle, and underneath the crook of the handle was a tiny release mechanism that was cunningly wrought and almost imperceptible. But when pressed, the rapier separated instantly from its sheath. Luzare spent his Sunday mornings admiring his cane, and as he eyed the churchgoers, he sometimes pondered the Biblical meditation: *Thy rod and Thy staff, they comfort me.* This cane, cool and smooth to the touch, light and sturdy, felt his vibrations and, in a peculiar sense, was a part of him. It gave him a sense of security, not to speak of a feeling of elegance that he always relished. He always reasoned very carefully to himself that a man comes by a liking for a cane quite naturally. A stick was the earliest implement in the history of human culture, and primitive man took up a stick to reinforce the natural strength of his arm, either for attack or defense. It was the first weapon and then became a symbol of sovereignty. Even the church dignitaries used a staff, a mace, as ensigns of their authority. And Luzare was uncommonly attached to his emblem of strength and dignity. He never went unarmed. During the weekdays he wore a small, flexible club wedged tightly between his stomach and belt, under his coat, and even on Sundays he carried his cane. At noon he would leave his park bench and walk back up the street for the big meal of the day. He always walked jauntily, twirling his baton rakishly, singing a gay, lilting melody, the words of which he could never remember. Passersby marveled at don Constant's lightheartedness as to the nature of his lyrics. For Luzare always sang in French, and more often than not the only words he could dub in were, '*Son of a bitch, oh son of a bitch,*' which fit any musical stanza he happened to fancy.

After eating his noon meal on Sunday, he always donned his small, black skullcap, which protected the thin spots of his scalp from the pestiferous insects and flies. He always sat down in his deep, comfortable chair near the window in the living room and listened to Libia sing, then he read the newspaper and fell asleep in his leather-covered chair. He always slept with his mouth thrown wide open. Occasionally a fly would alight on his face, and he would wake with a start, swat the fly with a loud "*Caramba*," and in a few moments he would doze back to sleep.

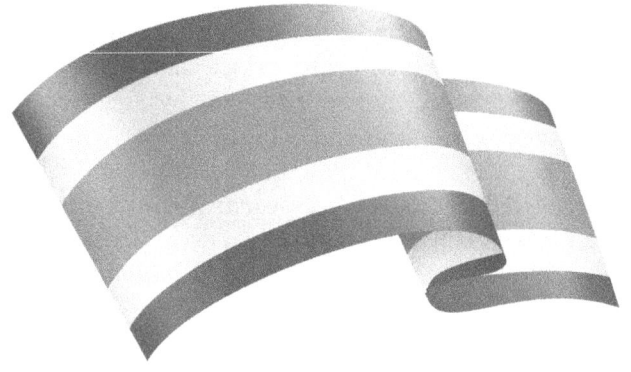

Figure 19 B

Costa Rica Flag Ribbon
iStock.com/PeterPencil. https://www.istockphoto.com/vector/costa-rica-flag-ribbon-set-vector-stock-illustration-gm1337195075-418165107

CHAPTER FIVE

Ricardo, Diana and Arturo

1926

F INALLY, WITH EVERY DETAIL OF the construction meeting with their joint approval, Ricardo and Diana moved into their new house next door. It was as modern as Europe's latest architectural thinking in its simple lines. A long concrete house it was, painted yellow. Though not as wide as Luzare's house, it was the same length and sat in juxtaposition to his on the lot. The floors throughout the house were hardwood and highly waxed, and the walls were in soft pastel colors. The first room to the left of the narrow hall extending from the front of the house to the patio was the deck room; behind it, the living room, large and open with wide-plated windows looking over to Luzare's house. The room was graceful with Diana's figurines from their honeymoon trip in Europe. On the side next to the hall door sat the pianola, a fine self-playing piano that had been imported from Europe. Deep sofas were covered in satin of ivory ground and embroidered in muted, old Mandarin designs shot with gold. On the wall over the pianola, Ricardo had contributed his touch, a picture of his father

Figure 20

Ricardo and Diana's New Home

and mother in their wedding clothes. Luzare at twenty-two had been a handsome, black-haired, mature-looking man. Esmeralda in her high-throated white dress had looked sweetly sedate with a tall comb in her dark hair. Next to the living room, there was a large square kitchen, not unlike Luzare's, except for the stoves. Ricardo fancied electric gadgets and had installed an electric kitchen. However, the electricity was uncertain and often turned off at odd times, so he had a small two-burner charcoal stove to use in case of an emergency. Behind the kitchen were the servant's quarters, and each servant had his own private room. In such perfect settings, it was unthinkable to Ricardo to have imperfect social conditions prevailing. First was Francisco's room, next Micaela's, then Dolores'. At the end of that side of the house, Ricardo had also thought of a playroom for his child, planned so that it would receive sun from three sides.

To the right of the hall from the front of the house, there was a big first bedroom, belonging to Ricardo and Diana. Next was a smaller bedroom for their child; connecting to this was a tiled bath with a low tub and shelves in the walls. Following the bathroom was a large pantry with enamel dry cabinets for staples and a large refrigeration unit. Next, the dining room, which lay across the hall from the kitchen, was a spacious, sunlit room with arched, vaulted ceilings and two sides with nothing but plated glass. The room contained a table of slender, thin elegance, which supported handwrought silver candelabras.

Lying next to the dining room was Ricardo's special showplace, a direct copy of an indoor garden he had seen in Paris. All three sides were walled from floor to ceiling in glass, in front of which cages stacked on top of cages, a veritable aviary of canaries. In the center of the tiled floor was a sunken fountain abounding in rare-colored fishes. Here Ricardo brought his important guests for cocktails and to loll about in the deck chairs.

The patio of Ricardo's back quarters was connected to Luzare's, and their common property was a huge cemented pavilion. The two-door garage, which stood near the side street in Luzare's yard, was shared by both families.

Diana was all over her house, small-boned person that she was; her neat, custom-tailored maternity garments scarcely revealed the protuberance of her enceinte. Her straight black hair was brushed sleekly back from her childlike face, and her big, dark eyes were always round with the eternal wonder of everything. But incongruous with her eyes, her lips were thin and primly fastened together like a well-sewn buttonhole. Primly they pursed in thought, primly they accepted, primly they rejected, primly they kissed, and primly they ate. She purchased the beautiful clothes her prim mouth chose; she selected the expensive perfumes her prim mouth savored. She reflected primly; she prayed primly. Primly she went tripping all about her immaculate house on her eternal safari for dust.

Francisco, brother of Enor, was only a concho but an intelligent, bright-eyed boy, well developed for a fifteen-year-old, short, muscular, and brown with an ugly pug nose. He spoke well and wrote legibly. After he clipped the hedges, mowed the lawns, and washed the windows all day, he would bathe and go out every night with a couple of books tucked under his arm to the opportunity school for the poor.

Micaela and Dolores served unceasingly, basking in their earthly glory under the same roof as Ricardo. They fought nonexistent dirt, scrubbed unsoiled clothes, and scoured unused pots, always busy to please the hypernervous Diana. They often remarked to each other, "Doñita Diana will mark her baby if she doesn't stop fretting so," but then, fearful that any offspring of Ricardo's should be born with a blemish, they would rush about even more distractedly to avoid any such curse. Diana walked from room to room, opening the drawers of silver to see if any tarnish had appeared since her last inspection, glancing into the birdcages to ascertain if Francisco should scrape out the bottoms again, and examining the lawn to decide if it had grown noticeably since she had last looked. Micaela had to manage her time well to squeeze in her surreptitious visits to the other house. New servants would never stay very long at doña Esmeralda's house. She would see to that.

Every facet of Ricardo's being had been brightened with his

Figure 21

Diana Constant

marriage. Diana was indeed his soulmate. He referred to her fondly as "*Mamita*" in anticipation of her coming motherhood, scheduled for the next month. He regarded her with deeper affection now that the time was near to bear his heir. Diana's impeccable taste and her feelings for the subtle and the delicate reinforced his ideas of superiority. The fact that she was well-born, of a background of financial consequence, and that her education had included considerable foreign travel did not lessen his regard for her. They were a splendid couple, he thought. She graced his home and was the very emerald of graciousness when his business friends were brought in.

Now, after two months alone in Paris, Arturo was coming home. Although Luzare had never shown any outward concern at the boy's being so far away, there was a certain relief at the news that he would soon be back home. Ricardo's opinions never seemed important when spoken, but they always stuck in Luzare's mind. Ricardo's judgment in business was almost prophetic, and Luzare did not like to disregard it in family matters. Eighteen was young for a boy to be so long away from home.

On the day set for Arturo's arrival, Luzare arranged with Ricardo for the whole family to be together for supper in Arturo's honor. Libia looked with anticipation to his homecoming. His room, next to the living room, was cleaned, thoroughly aired, and stood waiting. The boat docked at Puerto Limón at sunrise, and the drive through the country was tedious because of the roads. It was midafternoon when the automobile drove up and Arturo hopped out. His long legs strode quickly up the front walk. He was a tall boy with an open face; a long head with hair cropped short, small ears, a high forehead, friendly gray eyes, and a ready smile. His face always put Libia in mind of a satyr, the way his hair formed two short, hornlike swoops away from his forehead. He was warm to her in his greetings, more talkative, laughed easily, and was always showing his white scrubbed teeth while his straight nose twitched as though he had just made a clever remark.

Libia had dreaded the family supper. Ricardo and Arturo despised each other with such vehemence that the very air was

Figure 22

Arturo Constant

always heavy with their hatred. Never, however, had Ricardo been more cordial than he was that night. Seated beside his wife, he again compared the two women. Diana was undoubtedly the better-looking these days. Her Kewpie doll face was as ripe and rich-looking as a plum. Her plumpness was a pleasant contrast to Libia, who, after her second miscarriage, looked sallow and gaunt; her cheeks were hollow and hungry-looking, and there were tired circles under her eyes. Libia's dinner gown was uninspired, whereas Diana was smartly attired, and she knew it. She was bewitching and titillating and kept taunting Arturo about his amours in his travels, laughing often in her high, shrill voice.

After dinner, Libia excused herself from the company of Arturo and Diana in the living room and stepped across the hall to the bedroom for a handkerchief. Her presence surprised Luzare and Ricardo, who blushed as guiltily as robbers caught with their cache. They were huddled over the black safe, Ricardo with a tray of jewels in his hand. Luzare turned, his face still flushed, to explain to Libia, "Libia, since you wear jewels so infrequently, and Diana is so fond of rings, I am letting Ricardo take some of Esmeralda's things." Libia stood, surprised upon finding them there and too confounded to respond. Certainly she had no interest in the possessions and had not even known of their existence. But her silence forced Luzare to add as a thoughtful gesture, "And Libia, these medallions—who could appreciate them more than you? These are for you."

Ricardo, in airy magnanimity, also offered, "And Mama's crucifix. Please consider that yours too, Libia," as he waved toward the wall. "Besides," he added under his breath, "that wouldn't fit into Diana's decor anyway." Libia murmured her gratitude. Ricardo deftly fingered a good-sized diamond and a couple of other rings, chose the diamond, pushed the tray back into the safe, and said, "These other things you can just keep until Arturo and Victor are old enough to have an interest in them, Papa."

Arturo was in and out of the house restlessly during the day, playing soccer in front of the house with a bunch of other teenagers, his shirt thrown open, his khaki trousers and tennis shoes on. Or he competed at throwing knives at the line. But by the end of the first week, he was packing up his warm clothing, his heavy climbing shoes, and his hunting equipment and was making plans to go to his uncle's lodge at the dairy. Paulo owned a vast expanse of woods and dairy land on the side of the volcano, Irazú. Luzare consented to the boy's plan and gave him permission to use his new Buick automobile he had just imported from the United States. It was just a pleasant driving distance, and Paulo would take excellent care of Arturo once he reached the dairy.

Arturo loved driving through the quaint mountain spots where the beautiful village girls stood around in their colorful garments and jumped like startled deer at the sound of his horn. Then they turned and smiled shyly under their lids at his attention.

When he reached the Lecheria, his uncle's dairy, he chatted with interest about the cattle and dairy industry. Paulo was a younger Luzare in appearance and in his thinking. And his speech was identical to Luzare's in its chopped sentences and his mannerism of using his hand like a hatchet blade to hack the force of his words to his listeners. He had been quick to use progressive American methods in his dairy work and employed electricity for milking. To please Paulo, instead of hunting jaguar or puma, as was his desire, Arturo spent the rest of the day walking about admiring his uncle's new ideas. As he bade goodnight to Paulo, he mentioned casually, "I think I will take a look at old Irazú tomorrow."

The next morning Arturo was up while it was still moonlight. The stars were low and brilliant, the air cold and bracing. He slipped out into the stall for a mule and began packing his provender on it. But Paulo had thought ahead of him, and a concho squatted silently smoking beside a mule already waiting. Arturo cursed and motioned the man to stay there. But as stubborn as the mule he was riding, the concho only shook his head and indicated that he was going. The mules padded away from their shelter and out on the trail, which was a gutter formed by years of torrential rains, where now and again the sides rose sheer and higher than their heads. The climb soon became sharply ascending. Every now and then, as they reached a small clearing, they could hear the faraway bark of a dog or voices of the early risers high above who were busy with their syrup boiling. The fresh, clean air wafting down from the heights brought a pungent, sugary smell. The small canyon would no sooner let them feel the brisk morning air than it would close them in to its narrow confines again. After climbing for some time, they emerged from their trail to look down on the whole stretch of the Meseta Central, the central plateau of Costa Rica. Several thousand feet below it stretched from Cartago to the north to Heredia, Alajuela, and down to San José, a distance of seventy miles of spreading grandeur that lay aquamarine in the moonlight. And the little towns sparkled like jewels. Arturo felt exhilarated and full of his own being, a lone conquistador who had just laid eyes on a new land. They started their climbing again. The mules began sweating their warm animal smells, the saddle leather creaked and groaned occasionally, and the rough woven shirt stuck to the back of the silent guide, who looked neither to the left nor to the right but rode half asleep, his head down. He had not uttered a sound during their trek. The moonlight gradually faded and gave way to the hard, glaring light of early morning. At this altitude, moving as they were like specks against the side of the mountain, they could look across to the white-crowned Turrialba. Between the two mountains, layers of clouds floated like lazy splotches of cotton. Arturo felt a chill through his layers of woolens. In this pasture country, with its long ascending meadows, the trees were scant, the meadows rocky, and from the heights above them, the wind blew cold gales down upon them. The two mules leaned sideways against its impact. Small rocks and pebbles crunched and moved and scattered under the feet of the mules. Now daylight was bleakly white upon them. And this was the habituated section of Paulo's dairy where workers were milling around, some mixing cheese into balls and some lugging vats of milk. Arturo waved and passed on by without stopping. Soon they were back into the wooded areas again and began their steep climb through the jungle. Here were the high-level forests, deep, matted, moist, and hanging with fogs. Moss and orchids covered the trees, while creepers and low, tangled lianas hung from the lower branches and crawled over the ground. Buttresses of huge trees and enormous twisting roots snarled the mules' steps, and underfoot little pits and sinkholes sucked at the mules every move. The animals slipped and slogged and squashed about in the boggy mud. Suddenly rain poured down heavily upon them, and the guide took a burlap sack from under his saddle and wrapped it about his shoulders. Arturo pulled on his slicker and buttoned his top collar button. Then, as suddenly as it had come, the rain was gone. The sky was bathed, clear and cloudless, and they were higher than the rest of the world. They were sitting on top of Costa Rica, looking and surveying distant horizons from their altitude of more than eleven thousand feet.

The guide soon motioned for Arturo to dismount. The ground here was covered with scrubby, thorny bushes; myrtles flowered and crowded to the very edge of the crater. Arturo, advancing hurriedly, threw himself upon his stomach and held his hand over the brink. He wished fervently to have this moment alone. Impatiently he shot a look over his shoulder and waved the concho away. The guide retreated a little distance and squatted again. Arturo wanted to be alone with this monstrous power to feel an intimate communion with it. He glanced slowly around the scored sides of the crater, streaked and stained tawny red and orange, a visual delight. It all was strong, bright primitive colors, as if painted by a savage god. Some of the rocks were bronze, some slate or chocolate pink; again, there would be a wave of yellow. The pent-up wind howled and cried rebelliously, and at the bottom of the crater, the mouth of the volcano sat like a cancer. Today the roily old Irazú was restless, bubbling, gurgling, and grumbling low as he sloshed the heavy green boiling sulfurous liquids. Occasionally he belched spitefully his yellow fumes and spray. Arturo felt the thrill of its horror and tossed down some stones, watching them drop far, far below. The concho was suddenly alive with fright. He tugged at Arturo's shoulder and begged, "Quit, don't, please don't. He is mad today, mad! Leave him alone!" At that moment the volcano issued a threatening, ominous rumble and sent a geyser of yellow spray and rocks jetting as high as the rim of the crater, then falling back with a deafening, thunderous roar. Arturo jumped away, weak with fright, and walked over, sat down, and had coffee with the mule boy. He

1926 55

Figure 23

Irazú Volcano, Costa Rica

iStock.com/Mario Sergio Andrioli

https://www.istockphoto.com/photo/irazu-volcano-costa-rica-gm1489587318-514465943?clarity=false

Figure 24

Eruption of Turrialba volcano in Costa Rica seen from the slope of Irazu volcano.

iStock.com/Radoslaw Kozik

https://www.istockphoto.com/photo/eruption-of-turrialba-volcano-in-costa-rica-seen-from-the-slope-of-irazu-volcano-gm1077302382-288562420?clarity=false had seen what he'd been restless to see, and now he'd had enough of it. He climbed on his mule immediately and led the way back down the mountain, pausing on the high clearing to look down on the central tableland again and let his eyes survey the Caribbean Sea on his left and the Pacific Ocean on his right. One moment they were visible, the next they were hidden by this mist.

Back at the lodge, Arturo thanked Paulo for his hospitality and paid him the inn rates as if he were a stranger, since Luzare and Paulo always treated their family relationships as business transactions. Arturo promised Paulo he would come back to hunt with him soon, then packed his equipment into his automobile and headed back home. Like old Irazú, he felt he must keep moving, moving, moving, or he would explode in one gigantic blast.

During the day Arturo played like a youngster with the older boys, while little Victor stood on the sidelines watching. At night after supper, however, he would spend considerable time in the bathroom, showering and scrubbing himself. When he was dressed, complete with a tie, he would head for the front door. Watching him, Luzare would sometimes inquire, "Where are you going tonight, son?" But Arturo was always evasive as he answered, "Oh, to the movies. Maybe to the park."

The following Sunday, after the Saturday torrents had prevented him from going on his hunting expedition in search of entertainment and pleasure, Arturo walked to the Parque Central. It was after 4:00, and Cuerdas was in progress. The band in the center of the park up on its columned kiosco was playing '*Glow Worm*.' A graceful, flowing parade of young people was moving around the bandstand on the colorful mosaic of the boardwalk. Here the social strata of San José mingled almost unrestrained. Conchitas and highborn girls walked at the same time. Conchitas, who had come from the hills and obtained jobs as domestics, swayed along with their comely, voluptuous bodies enveloped in the tight skirts split up the sides to show flashes of their copper-colored legs. Sometimes their dark, rippling hair hung loose; sometimes it was caught loosely with a gay ribbon. Some of the girls tossed dyed-blond hair, and their ears were bedizened with big, jingling earrings. Even young ladies of the refined families enjoyed these walks, their vivacity restrained as their chaperones looked on. The girls strolled in pairs, arm in arm, rhythmically to the music. Girls went counterclockwise in the outer circle while the caballeros gaily marched past them clockwise in an inner circle. If a girl were attracted to a boy, she smiled in a quiet but suggestive way, a motion, a wink, or a shrug of her shoulder to show her acceptance. If a boy were attracted to an unwilling girl, she would make a spitting gesture or turn her head disdainfully. The boy kept walking until he became suitably matched. Pair by pair, as the music played, they walked away and sat on the benches that were scattered throughout the park, which occupied the city block. They might look across to the cathedral, which always kept its side doors open, and they could watch dark-veiled women shadow in to pray. Or they might go across the street for a drink. All around the square, the little shops' windows were hung with foreign merchandise and mellifluous cigars. Conchos cursed their opinionated mules and strolled down the streets with their gay carts.

Arturo was attracted by a curvaceous creature obviously not long from the hills. She walked uneasily in her high heels, but her breasts were thrown high, her head back in an untamed, spirited manner. Her eyes quickly flashed acceptance in response to his glance. Her red-painted, sensuous lips smiled with sultry insinuation and pleasure. Soon the two were coupled, arm in arm, as they made their way across the street to the cantina for a drink. Looking into the swirling darkness of the girl's eyes, Arturo felt drawn by that same strange, horrible power that had made him want to jump into the green, seething cauldron of old Irazú.

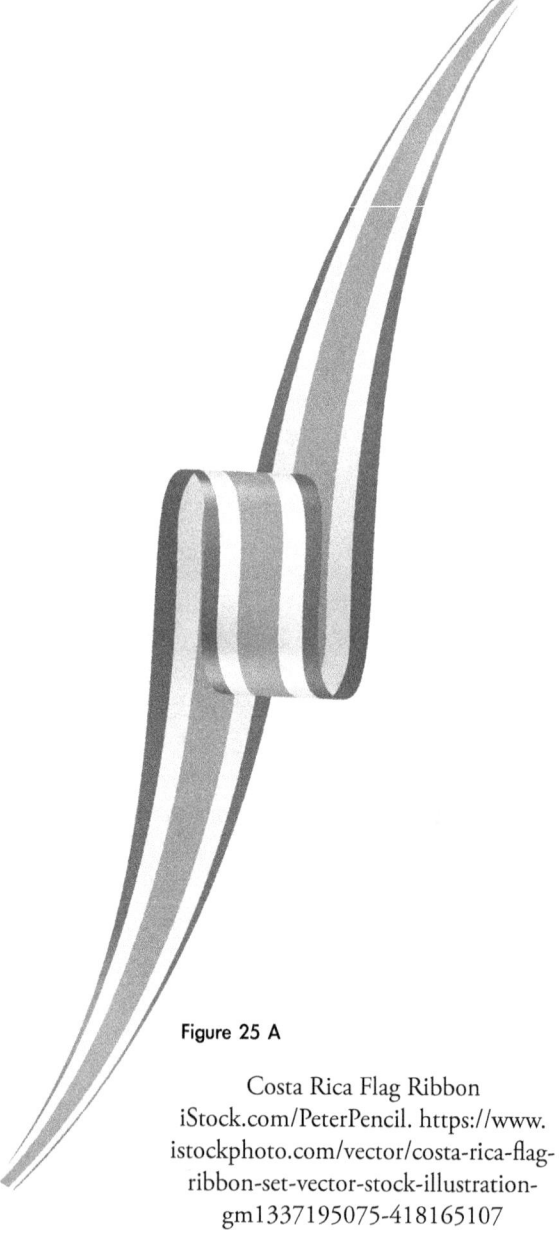

Figure 25 A

Costa Rica Flag Ribbon
iStock.com/PeterPencil. https://www.
istockphoto.com/vector/costa-rica-flag-
ribbon-set-vector-stock-illustration-
gm1337195075-418165107

Figure 25 B

Fiesta

Figure 26

Fiesta In The Evening

Figure 27

More Fiesta Day

Figure 28

More Fiesta Scenes

CHAPTER 5

Figure 29 A

Fiesta At Noon

Figure 29 B

More Fiesta

Figure 29 C

CHAPTER SIX

Arturo's Malady

1926-1927

A S THE WEEKS PASSED, LIBIA was always in the throes of new servants. No sooner would she have a new one trained than Micaela would be slinking about in the corners and go back to Ricardo's, reporting that Libia took no interest in doña Esmeralda's house. Then one by one the servants would be gone, giving their excuse, "Too much work" or "Not enough free nights." It was true she did not give the women servants permission to go out but one night a week, and it annoyed Luzare having the doorbell ring to let them in even though he allowed no servant to have a key to the house. He always grumbled as he came back to bed from letting in a female servant, "Well, she is pregnant. They're like bitches in heat. You can't let them out. If they go out, they always come back pregnant." But Libia knew her servant problem would continue as long as the bloody mattress stood as mute testimony to Micaela's whisperings.

Once, she approached Luzare with, "I wish you would let me get rid of that unsanitary, filthy mess in the storage room."

But Luzare turned livid with fury and bellowed, "You mind your housework. Don't you have enough to do without poking your nose around where it has no business?" So, there it lay. And how could she explain strange noises to dark, suspicious minds when the imprisoned wind, trapped in the patio, shook at the windowpanes and wailed in high pitches to be released? Occasionally she too shuddered, and the screams were so human-sounding!

She sighed as the dust formed on her piano, but she practiced her vocal gymnastics with greater verve, always exercising, purifying her tones, and analyzing her voice. But she went on singing.

On one of his trips through the house, Arturo paused at the living room door, his forehead beaded with sweat, and said admiringly, "Say, that sounds like opera in Paris!" Then he went whistling the refrain down the hall. Libia leaned back on the piano seat, enormously pleased.

One day the new señora de la lavandería came to Libia with a pained reluctance: "Niña Libia, I have never seen this on a young man's undergarments before, but it seems to me unnatural." Libia examined the yellowish pus stains, pink-streaked with blood that was blotched on Arturo's shorts. It was unnatural. She debated with herself whether she should seek Luzare's advice or handle the matter herself. But knowing Luzare's desire to attend to anything that might involve the outside world, she kept the unclean shorts and spoke to him that night after dinner.

Luzare walked across the hall with the evidence in his hand, opened Arturo's door, and accosted him with, "Son, do you have any sores?"

Arturo sank down, glad to find some relief, accepted his father as an ally without looking into his stormy face, and answered, "Papa, it hurts so much to urinate I almost scream!"

Luzare snorted, "Good God, this thing is bad. Put on your clothes." He took the boy immediately to his grandfather, Doctor Muran, who, after a cursory glance at the lesions, nodded to Luzare that the boy had an entrenched disease. Doctor Muran ordered a room in the clinic for immediate occupancy, and Luzare came home alone. Libia was waiting, worried, and her good sense already told her the answer. Luzare entered the house steaming mad, bellowing, "Do you see, you are to blame for this!" As Libia caught her breath, he continued his rage, "You are to blame, entirely so. Not once did you try to stop him when he was running around here at night as wild as a libertine. It's a mother's duty to know what her children are doing when they are out." And as always, when Luzare made harsh accusations, Libia was at a loss for words. How could she explain that Arturo would never listen to her '*new mother's*' admonitions but would only resent her intrusions into his affairs? This was bitter to take. Wearily, she thought of her sister Marie, who is now a nun in France and lives a life dedicated to high spiritual contemplation, leading a rigorous and strict existence focused entirely on her soul's welfare. Sadly, she thought, '*Truly, we walk in vain shadows of what we want to be.*' In frustrated moments like this, she felt as if she were playing an organ. But no matter how sensitively she touched the keyboard of her life, the same rushing sounds as a maddened animal rent the air. The stops would not be manipulated. Her soul yearned to stroke the keys and send forth flutelike flutters and soft, lulling music that pealed excruciatingly sweet throughout the pipes.

Libia knew that Arturo's entrance into the hospital had been handled with the utmost discretion, and she prayed that the servants would not find out enough to blabber to the house next door. However, Ricardo did not seem curious about Arturo's illness. At his house Diana had just given birth to her child, and although it was an effortless delivery and no trouble, Diana must have watched an eclipse of the moon during her pregnancy, because the child was weak and his mouth was open as big as an olla, always crying.

Libia took over the nursing of Arturo herself after his return from the hospital. She welcomed his incumbency as a penance, grateful to God that she could atone for her sin of omission. As she honestly examined her own thoughts, she recognized that her reticence was a weakness and that her fear of being forward always restrained her emotions. In moments that challenged her, she had never been outspoken, no matter how strongly she wanted to be a spiritual influence. It was true that she had always prayed for purity of heart and in so doing had excused herself from seeing impure thoughts in others. But this, she now understood, was simply a blind credulity, and in thinking about other people, she never really wanted to anticipate what might occur.

She kept the servants away from the sick quarters, brought and emptied the bedpans herself, continued Arturo's medicines, and amused him with conversation and books. Arturo flashed her a rewarding smile occasionally, but, more often than not, he was in a slough of black moodiness and self-tormenting thoughts, which made Libia suffer with him. To see his young face, transparently pale, so very young in his disease of the ages, his eyes big and often downcast, made her willingly accept the whole blame. A little more guidance might have prevented this. As she went into the bathroom, she always thought of Esmeralda's unusual architectural designs for this house. Instead of placing the bathrooms near the bedrooms, she had bunched them all together, as if to get the whole obscenity in one place and not stuck around between rooms. There was the first bathroom, which contained a lavatory, a shower, a tub, and the stool. This was used mostly by the boys. In back of it, connected by a door from the one bathroom to the next, was a room with a tub and stool. Behind that room, there was another room with a shower and stool, but it did not have a connecting door. The lavatory for this room was just outside on the patio wall, and the room and lavatory were for the servants' use. In each room, Luzare had placed his fixture, a large clock.

Esmeralda had designed a wallpaper across from the bathroom on the cross hall wall, reaching from the ceiling to the floor, as if to distract attention from the bathroom door—a veritable Eden of flora. In the middle of the mass of flowers, two peacocks with great vanity spread their feathers, a plumage of emerald, gold, and glittering carmine.

One night, during Arturo's illness, after the household had retired early, there was a sudden loud banging and thundering sound. Addled and only half-awake, Libia grabbed her dressing gown, threaded her arms through the sleeves, and scrambled to the door, rushing across the hall toward the source of the noise. Arturo sat in his bed, looking pale and startled, his eyes frightened, while debris was scattered all around him, covering the bed and floor. A big dog, yelping in pain, was extricating itself from beneath the pile of fallen plaster and limping about whimpering. The bitch, Princesa, apparently had been walking about on the balcony upstairs in the unfinished part of the ceiling, which had never been reinforced. Her heaviness on a weak board had caused the ceiling to give way. Arturo was not hurt but was visibly shaken. The suddenness of it had given him a severe shock. Luzare did not even inquire about Arturo but was more concerned with the dog. He grabbed the big animal up under his arm and took it down to the servants' quarters to doctor her. He was fond of the dog, and since Arturo's illness, he had taken the attitude that anything that befell the boy was only his just desserts.

Libia soothed Arturo and finally quieted him enough so she could switch off the light. For a time she had been so busy she hadn't even noticed little Victor standing behind her, shivering in his long nightgown. When she realized his presence, she explained the mishap to him and gently led him back to bed. In a moment of self-forgetful tenderness, she leaned over and kissed him. He whispered in her ear, "Mama, I'm glad it was Princesa. I thought when I heard the noise that you were hurt." The house settled back down again, and as Libia dozed back to sleep, she smiled. What had Victor called her? Victor had said, '*Mama*.' For the first time, Victor had called her '*Mama*.'

In spite of Arturo's weakness, enervated by drugs and debilitated by disease, Luzare had the boy's clothes packed, and on the first of September, he hustled his son off to school. As Arturo was taking his departure, he smiled bravely, but his eyes were bright with tears. Libia wept too; England was far away, and Arturo seemed so terribly young to her now.

The house was quiet during the mornings with Victor in school. Libia sat on the latticed side porch and read or sewed. Occasionally she just sat and looked at the Veranera. Such a lovely flower it was! The petals were separated like butterfly wings, and the stamen was like antennae. In the breeze, the flowers lifted their fuchsia-petaled wings and were wont to fly away from the vines, which held them like chains to the trellis.

In February, Luzare, as was his custom, took short vacations, leaving the store a few days at a time. This time he chose San Isidro de Coronado, where the colorful fiesta on February 16 drew him. All the country people for miles around, and what a tatterdemalion crowd it was, gathered as guests of the priest. Farmers brought their gay, highly decorated, solid-wheeled ox carts to be blessed. There was marimba music, firecrackers, coarse heavy foods, hard liquors, tortillas, and tamales. Victor enjoyed the whole carnival enormously, but Libia was fatigued. Two days of such fast gaiety were too much for her, and this garish carnival only seemed a travesty to her heavy heart. She would soon begin her second year with a man she could not cherish, and the occasion also brought a sense of guilt. St. Isidore, known as the Plowman, had been singularly outstanding in the ecclesiastical history of the church. It was supposed that he had been born in twelfth-century Spain on the site of what afterwards became Madrid. He led such a life of consecrated piety that when he neglected his fields for the sake of his devotions, the angels came down and plowed for him. In the thought of much wondrous singleness of heart, Libia could not bow her head in shame.

Luzare's whole soul and most of his thinking was his store, and he was loath to relinquish his hold over it, even for a day. His whole life had been spent in merchandising, and he could think in no other terms than buying and selling. His passion for justice in business and government was innate, shaped by generations of men who had fed their families with honest bread.

He had the same contempt for shoddy, counterfeit merchandise that Lucien Constant, his grandfather, had felt in 1849 as he lay ridden with cholera in a Paris hospital. The fetid atmosphere of the place reeked from rows of cots with their feverish and delirious occupants. But all the weak faces at that moment had their eyes attentive to the figure who stood in the middle of the room. An insignificant-appearing personage he was, masquerading in a gold-braided, heavy-epauletted general's uniform. His short-legged, long-bodied stance was a ludicrous ape of his uncle. The sick listened to his slow, torturous Germanic intonations of French; his face was like a melancholy parrot. Heavy eyelids concealed eyes that stared with a strange lifelessness. His long, blackened, dyed, and waxed mustache reflected the light as his lips moved. His imperial goatee, like a comic actor's, bobbed up and down idiotically. All the other patients were impressed by the austerity of the moment, and they stared transfixed at the man. But Lucien fell back on his pillow, weak and sickened anew by a disgust that swept over him. Louis Napoleon, President of France, was making solicitous calls on the hospitals of Paris that were caring for victims of the plague. He stood and breathed the sweltering fever air as though he were immune to human ailments. President indeed! France again had an emperor, and this obscure pretender was head of the French state! Lucien was a clearheaded thinker, not given to accepting the common opinions of the street, knowing well that Louis Napoleon was not feeble or disingenuous, as some wanted to believe. Lucien could read an inscrutability, a taciturnity, and an inflexibility in the man's face. This was a man of determination, a man who would create an empire in his own image, and the mockery Lucien beheld was the climax of all his dreams of democracy, a derision of all his years of hope. His spirit for the emancipation of France was now forever blighted. His father's generation brought about the Bastille for a new freedom, and from that time, France bestirred herself time and again with new springs and new saps of liberty. Only the year before, Metternich and his system had been banished, but Lucien now realized that the system did not depend on its founder. His dreams of a new France were forever dispelled by a look in Louis Napoleon's eyes. Lucien stared back contemptuously.

Lucien was but a little tradesman who had never held millennial hopes and only wanted security and a moderate common sense in the government. He was a realist who had been educated on the cobblestones of Paris; every stone had been but a page in a lesson book for him. Although poor, he had attended the museums, gone to the upper galleries in the theaters, read, and spoken with his fellow tradesmen. But as much as he despised the thought, nevertheless it was true, just as Balzac had described it in his '*Human Comedy*.' France was nothing but a struggle for wealth with '*The Ethics of a*

Crab Basket.'

With such an attitude, France would listen to Utopian promises, which she was too eager to believe, and she would yield her rights to a man who would soon take off his pretending mask and reveal his true Napoleonic character. Lucien, as he arrived at that decision, made a pledge to himself and to his God that if he could live to shake off his disease, he would depart this land he could no longer tolerate and seek a country where he could give his heart and place his trust.

As soon as he was freed from the hospital, he began liquidating his small holdings, and in the next year, he sailed for the little country called Costa Rica, which had cast off its yoke of Spain in 1821 and finally, after several adventures with other types of government, set herself up as a republic in 1848.

Figure 30 A

Costa Rica Flag Abstract. iStock.com/khvost
https://www.istockphoto.com/vector/costa-rican-flag-wavy-abstract-
background-vector-illustration-gm1287181758-383457866

CHAPTER 6

Figure 30 B

Lucien's New Home Costa Rica
iStock.com/Mlenny
https://www.istockphoto.com/photo/natural-beach-palm-tree-gm184965831-
19043677?clarity=false

Figure 30 C   Lucien's New Home

Figure 30 D

CHAPTER SEVEN

Annabella and Margarita

1928

I N SEPTEMBER 1850, LUCIEN AND his family landed at the fishing
and trading village of Puerto Limón. It had been this same
month in the year 1502 that Columbus himself, on his fourth
and last trip to the New World, was driven by a great tempest into
the lovely bay of Cariari, at the site of Puerto Limón. Columbus sent
his brother, Bartolome, ashore to scout, where he explored the coast,
sighted mountains fifty miles inland, and returned to tell what he
had seen. Indians visited Columbus aboard his ship, and Columbus
described them as '*handsome and peaceful*' and was impressed by
their trinkets and ear ornaments.

Lucien set out at once to get away from the coast with its
low, murky elevation of only eleven feet. He wanted to escape the
humid climate and the marshlands of the coast, but the mosquitos
found their victim in little Jerome, his younger child, who had no
resistance to malaria. Lucien paused in their journey to dig a grave
in the shifting sand to bury his dead. With each shovelful of mud
he scooped out of the ground, the hole filled with water before he

could place his shovel back again into the mire. The rut-like trail leading inland was often impassable with undergrowth through the swamps, or the carts were mired to their axles when the torrents fell. They had to stop and wait until the swollen riverlets subsided in their banks. They struggled over the crude, rough roads from the low regions, crossed the roaring, frightening, twisting Reventazón River, climbed the tableland, up three to four thousand feet above sea level, and then they gradually descended through a high, timbered, primeval forest to the old capital of Cartago. Above them loomed the volcano Irazú, the smoke from its crater wafting white in the sky. It was October before they finally reached this city of habitation. Wearied by grief, a sick wife, and fearful that he would lose another child, Lucien went into the town, thankful to find shelter and prayerfully hoping to be welcomed as a new citizen. There he made his home and set up his shopkeeping. But in 1859, he moved again, always wanting to be in the shadow of his government. Then, too, he felt it would mean a healthier business, since San José would surely grow more rapidly, being the seat of the government. His only son, Louis, had married Amelia, the flaxen-haired, sweet-faced girl whom he, at the age of twelve, had played with aboard ship on their trip from France. Lucien lived long enough to see his seed sown in five grandchildren on the soil of his adopted country. And he always set his particular eye on Luzare, the oldest, who at the age of twelve, after his father's untimely death, took over the management of the family's rice and candle shop. Luzare and Paulo had always worked. When Luzare was fifteen, being the older, he let Paulo have the whole management of the pulperia, while he went out and found another job to bring in more money. He became a cashier for Dr. Muran, who had earned his money professionally but liked to keep it growing by investing it in small businesses. In this way the doctor became a man of great property and wealth.

Luzare was apt and quick with figures, so Dr. Muran trusted him with the store's cash. When Luzare was only eighteen, Dr. Muran gave him a partnership in the store and sent him to Europe to learn more about commerce and to make connections in trade. Before Luzare was twenty, he had the background of a financier.

But about this time, an old French-born bachelor in San José, who had been a friend of Luzare's father, died, leaving no family. He had watched Luzare's struggle to support his family, and so he willed the boy his own little dry goods store. Luzare was tremendously proud of his new status. At last he had something of his very own. He borrowed money from the good Dr. Muran for business expansion in his store and busied himself with his new proprietorship.

Many an evening he would visit his old friend the doctor, whose delicate, aesthetic features could always be found poring over a book in the library of his home. His daughter, Esmeralda, would always slip quietly in to listen to the two men discuss books. Luzare read avidly, as if he had already wasted too much time and his time from now on would be limited to the realm of literature. His mother, Amelia, was delighted with his advancement in culture. She had always tutored her boys in the fine art of manners and given them snatches of her education whenever they were at home long enough to listen. She was the granddaughter of a duke, and the very thought of her sons growing into manhood without any book education distressed her. Besides, with the rest of her family in and out of the madhouse, it was a comfort to watch the boy study.

Dr. Muran's daughter, Esmeralda, would sit and glare with dark looks of jealousy at the book Luzare held. For two years, Esmeralda sat and glowered until she finally became Luzare's bride and happily began designing the biggest house she could imagine on one of the lots that her father had given her as a wedding gift.

Luzare minded his own business at his store and, in the very beginning, set his aim to reach the average working man's pocketbook, so he stocked his store with clothes for hard wear. Not satisfied with the durability of the clothes, he imported and set up his sewing shop in the back of the store to turn out a stronger work garment. At home, Esmeralda rarely consulted him about her new home, and building the billiard room was an allowance she made in a whimsical humor.

But Esmeralda was a strange woman, with an appearance deceptive of her true nature. She appeared dour-faced and solemn-looking, but in reality, she could have temperamental rampages that sometimes lasted for a week. In these periods, she enjoyed reminding Luzare that one of his mother's sisters was a crazed woman who was mad over the love of her own body and showed it at every social function unless she was restrained. In these distasteful arguments, Luzare would swear and rave, but in a few minutes he would be out of the house. Sometimes it almost drove him insane to think of his mother's family. When he reviewed how his mother's share of the family wealth had been taken over by the ambitious, greedy, older three children, his blood boiled. Always there were the memories of when, in his early childhood, the sisters had driven by in their fine carriages and laughed at the candle shop and at the two little barefoot proprietors, absurd in their shabbiness, busy minding their store.

But as Luzare walked and cooled himself down, he always reasoned that they had already reaped their harvest of evil. Elena, the eldest sister who had waist-length golden hair, was consumed by her own beauty. She once killed a man in her hotel room in Paris while she was on tour in one of her operatic roles. Now she spent most of her time in the asylum, isolated from the outside world and her own wealth, as well as what should have been his mother's money. Helena, too, had turned crazed, though only with greed. After splitting Amelia's money with her sister, she married a Mexican who deserted her after stealing most of her wealth. Albert, the brother, did not fare well with his millions. He was behind the penitentiary walls on San Lucas Island at the mouth of the bay at Puntarenas. He would never spend any more of his money. He was on a desolate island guarded by the hungry, watchful sharks that swarmed the Pacific waters. And there he would remain for the rest of his days, serving his sentence for a crime of violence.

Those three had been the ones who laughed at Amelia's shoeless children. Thank God, his mother had never had to ask them for a peso, nor would she ever have to turn to them. He and Paulo would see to that. But Esmeralda was the woman he had to live with, and she reminded him all too vividly of his mother's sisters.

Thus, they had lived together, Luzare and Esmeralda. She had been a woman of great passions, had borne him three sons, and had died in her fourth delivery when her aging body at forty-nine could no longer endure this supreme demand. After being left a widower for two years, Luzare felt boundless delight in finding a new mate.

For the next two years, Libia felt better than she had since being married. She was slowly regaining her strength; her voice took on more color and drama. Her teacher, Luira, spoke occasionally of Libia's arranging to spend a few months in Italy with an old professor with whom she herself had studied. Libia's voice, she said, was incomparable even with the touring prima donnas who appeared at the National Theater from time to time. With maturity, her timbre was richer, more resonant. But Libia always shook her head, knowing Luzare so well she didn't even broach him on the matter.

Then in August, she realized that again she was pregnant. Luzare was, as always, thrilled over the prospects and was considerate in seeing that the house was well disposed to her nausea. He walked the streets with a look of a new prosperity. Ricardo's child, weak and nervous though it was, was at least a child, while he, a man still virile, had nothing to show for his marriage.

Victor had been eyeing Libia's stomach of late as they sat together on the piano seat. The young boy had an ear for melody and could pick out tunes with one finger. She had been teaching him simple pieces. One day she took his hand and pressed it against her stomach and said, "Victor, inside my body there is a baby that is growing every day. By next April, it will be big and strong enough to be born. And then I will give birth to it." But Victor only blushed, and she realized that again she had begun her sex instructions too late.

As her time drew near, she dreaded her delivery. Her miscarriages had been so horribly painful. Luzare was also worried lest some misfortune again snatch parenthood away from him, and he insisted that Libia go to the hospital to have her baby. But Libia felt confident. Her mother had assured her that she knew a capable midwife who was thoroughly informed on sterilizing instruments and general cleanliness. And this midwife could be depended upon. Besides, it was unseemly, in her way of thinking, for a woman to leave her home to have her baby.

On a rainy afternoon in early April, she felt a strong stab. She called her mother, who in no time had the midwife bustling about with hot water and towels. Libia undressed, put on her largest gown, and sat hunched on the bedside. The contractions were continuous. In an hour she delivered her child, a plump girl, already sucking her thumb ravenously. The midwife finished her parturient details, swabbed the baby, wrapped it in a blanket, and placed it beside Libia in the bed. Libia lay drowsy with exhaustion but experiencing a thrill of able accomplishment. She had coped with nature's demands and had brought forth her baby without harm. Luzare hurried in, leaned over to view the baby, and kissed her forehead with more tenderness and pride than Libia had ever seen in his gray eyes directed towards her. Arturo's old crib was brought in from the spare room under the stairs and placed beside her bed.

Victor was always bashful when he was caught playing with Anabella, but he delighted in listening to her cacklings and gurgles. Luzare would pat the blond, silky hair and bend to caress the cherubic face, but the child would look up at her father with her agate-clear eyes absent of affection, and Luzare found it hard to fondle his little daughter. Aside from the normal attention of a new baby, Anabella was no trouble. She nursed well. She slept well. But Libia was always worn out, and it was with complete despondency that she accepted the fact that again her body would be incubating.

But most pleased of all with the fat baby Anabella, was Luzare's mother, Amelia, who understood her son's great pride in his manhood, in his parenthood. Old and frail and trembling slightly, she rode with the chubby baby in her lap to the church for its baptism. And her delicate, small-boned face leaned close to Libia as she whispered, "Don't be sorry. Luzare wants babies. He needs your babies to complete himself. That is the only way I know how to tell you what you mean to him." And her thin little voice choked a little as she added, "Luzare has his faults, but he is a great man. Since he was a little boy, I always knew Luzare would be a great man." Three months later Amelia died as quietly as she lived, and Luzare's big shoulders heaved sorrowfully for his mother.

CHAPTER 7

Figure 31

Annabella

The following April, Libia answered an urgent ring on the hall telephone. She listened to the news that her uncle, her sweet uncle, was dead. To her mind came the last time she had seen him sitting there so unpretentiously in his office. She recalled how much he had looked like her mother, except perhaps his was a more gentle face, of humble demeanor, accessible to all from the lowest barefoot conch to the highest official; he had lent a listening ear, an incorruptible man, a staunch Catholic. But now he was dead. Costa Rica had lost the president of its seven million people, but she had lost her kind friend. She whirled about and caught a prong of the hat tree. His hand leaned against its marble top for support. She was being tossed about by angry waves. They lapped higher and higher. The dark, cold water seemed to surge and resurge, sucking her under. She uttered a cry and sank to the floor. Luzare's strong arms pulled her up, and Victor carried her dragging feet. They laid her upon the bed. Writhing and raving crazily in high fevers and shock, she was unaware when her baby was delivered, a tiny, premature mass of wrinkles. She was bedridden longer than she had ever been before, dispirited and apathetic, watching Luzare talk about the crib of the sickly baby. He would hold his shiny, balding head down close to the infant thing and seem to derive happiness whenever he could comfort its colic or relieve its pain. He was so occupied with the strange, dark, wizened little gnome that he did not pay any particular attention to his business, only giving it his earnest consideration late in the fall, after these distant rumblings of the Wall Street crash in that year, 1929. He was just a portly fifty-seven-year-old man feeling strong in his body and wanting to somehow give part of his strength to his weak child. He would hold the wee baby upon his shoulder and carry her all about the house. Whenever the baby made faint, mewing sounds of crying, he would pat her body, which was no bigger than his hand. He employed a wet nurse, and he was forever placing the baby to the woman's breast so the tiny mouth could suck. But the little thing would no sooner nurse than she would be spitting up curdled, sour-smelling, yellow fluid. Then she would be whimpering again and would not stop until Luzare lifted her with his stubby fingers and swayed her gently and talked

Figure 32 A

Margarita

to her. The wrinkled little elf that they had given the big name "Margarita Cecilia" would distort her features ludicrously and seem to make pathetic little responses while Libia often lay watching in sheer wonderment. Luzare loved this three-pound mass of redness with deep affection, and she prayed, for his sake, that the little coffin that stood waiting in the storage room would not have to be used.

Figure 32 B

Independence Day 1821
https://www.istockphoto.com/vector/independence-day-in-costa-rica-
gm1337554914-418396210
iStock.com/Andrii Kalenskyi

CHAPTER EIGHT

Edwin

1931-1937

Although it was unexplainable how she continued to live, the baby did, with a stubbornness that must have been far greater than her small being. She lived but was not thriving, and she was afflicted with stomach and kidney disorders, and even at a year, her legs were so weak she never made any efforts to crawl or move by herself. But she was of a sweet disposition and smiled angelically. Her dark eyes were as soft and dewy as a doe's. Libia hired a Conchita to lift the babies for her, and as she sat in the afternoons with her own two children about her feet and Victor running about on his long, quick legs, with his shoulders beginning to show brawn, she thought of all her children. Anabella had been born without anguish. As for Margarita, she had neither known nor cared when that baby made its small entrance into the world. But Victor's birth was one of long labor and pain. And the umbilical cord of love that held Victor to her had not been cut but was constantly growing stronger. Her two children were estranged from her womb and became their own beings.

Then in the late afternoon, automobiles would begin to drive up and park in front of Ricardo's house. Those who had been there before used the back pavilion for parking. The chatter would start with greetings as the chiffon-dressed women floated up the front walk. Libia could hear Diana's high, shrill voice in laughter. These were parties to which she was not, nor had she ever been, invited. However, in a way she was glad. Diana was taking care of a phase of the business she herself could never have done. Luzare never brought his business associates home, and of that she had been spared. If he had any dealings he felt he should attend to personally, he sometimes stayed for dinner down at the Club Union, of which he was a member. Otherwise, he relied on Ricardo, who prided himself on his feelings of Costarricenses and his diplomacy. He was in agreeable relations with the resident foreigners, the consular and diplomatic offices, the local comerciantes and planters, and all the agents of international companies.

On rare occasions, Ricardo would invite Luzare over for a Sunday afternoon to meet his American friends. Luzare took immense pride in Ricardo's magic, his hypnotic trances, and his card reading. Even Luzare felt a weird chill as Ricardo would stare with dilated eyes at his subject and project his power over them. On these visits, Libia always excused herself, saying that she didn't understand English and found it awkward being around English-speaking people. She stayed at home and relaxed in quiet solitude, read or sang, or watched the children as they played.

And the days were contentedly spent. It was, in a way, hard for Libia to realize that four years had passed and Arturo was home again from England. This time he was the person that Libia had first known on the honeymoon, a friendly boy but reticent to talk. He drifted about the house as if he were a stranger to it. To please his father, he spent part of every day in the store; otherwise, he was upstairs in the spare room, reading from the crates of books he had shipped home from school. Four years, however, had not changed him physically; he was somewhat heavier but altogether handsome. At Victor's insistence, he would sometimes take a bunch of the young boys into the empty room next to the ironing room, which he had taken over and equipped with punching bags. In an impressive professional voice, he would explain the fine art of fisticuffs to the youngsters as they waited, eager to try the lesson. All the boys would beat and pound until mid-afternoon, and then they would stop and have tea and cookies with Libia. It was at this moment of the day Libia found the greatest pleasure in her motherhood; she could smile into the faces of her two beautiful sons. And the little girls adored Victor, who teased them only gently.

Arturo went out occasionally at night, but he didn't seem to take social functions seriously. It was something of a surprise when, nine months later, he brought in a tiny dark girl and announced to Luzare and Libia that she was Sara, the girl whom he wished to marry. Sara smiled vivaciously, her green eyes sparkled in her bright face, and she immediately gained their wholehearted approval. After the young couple hurried out on their way to a party, Luzare expanded in his pleasure. He knew the girl's family well, and they were quite influential in real estate and farmlands. Sara had been carefully educated, and if Luzare had been choosing the girl for Arturo himself, he could not have done better.

The wedding was held in Sara's church with Anabella, as train bearer, toddling along in her small blond seriousness. Her younger sister, Margarita, spotting her in the bridal procession, screamed out and flung herself about the pew until Libia was compelled to take her out of the church. Libia understood that Margarita wanted to be a part of the show too, but at two years old, she still couldn't walk or talk. Libia took the younger child back home to check on the reception preparations. It would be a lovely party, much like her own had been. Before the crowd arrived, she let the small Margarita choose a handful of the prettiest pastries on the platter and drink a cup of punch, then she tucked her into bed.

Arturo's honeymoon was protracted, giving Luzare an opportunity to get the young couple's new home in readiness before they returned. It was also built on modern lines, big and white cement. Arturo, suave, smooth-voiced, and diplomatic, would have to entertain a fantastic deal. It was beneficial that both Arturo and his wife were skilled in languages. Luzare bore a love for Arturo, but forevermore, there would be a feeling in his heart of mistrust, as one who has been betrayed. Whereas, to Luzare, Ricardo was like a nail in a sure place to cast his burdens upon.

Margarita's clumsiness annoyed Libia just as it had irked her to watch milk spew from her mouth when she was a tiny baby. The little girl pulled herself around the furniture, gibbered her words backwards, and her eyes sometimes got crossed. She always appeared so plain that relatives looking at the two little girls together would remark, "*Anabella is going to make a beautiful girl*," and then they would shake their heads despairingly at Margarita. Yet she was the more affable child, always smiling her brightest smile at her mother, hoping to banish her mother's frowns. Libia hated her own thinking and often prayed for more patience.

Because of her weak back, Libia stopped handling the children entirely and was using the conchita for all their needs. One day, while the servant and Margarita were sitting at a table on the side porch, Margarita, who was laughing and teasing, fell off. The servant pretended nothing had happened, but Libia noticed the left foot of the frail little body beginning to swell as she examined it. Catalina, as in all such emergencies, was called in and immediately packed the foot in clay, soaked it in vinegar, and took over the child's treatments. She shook her head every day and remarked, "If this child receives another setback, she will never learn to walk." Each afternoon, after the foot began to heal, she would come over and place a bottle under Margarita's foot. Then with Spartan harshness she would force the little girl to roll the bottle to and fro under her instep.

As her foot grew stronger, Margarita at last started walking, and Luzare praised her outrageously, but Libia could only think to herself, "*It's about time*." Margarita was almost four years old when she finally started making excursions up and down the hall, and after discovering that she could take swift steps, she soon began trotting back and forth. One day, as Luzare stood by watching, she ran toward the front door, intent on showing her courage by dashing outside to the porch. She hurled herself toward a patch of light and collapsed in pain. Luzare picked up the sobbing little heap, who was simpering. "Papa, there were two doors. I didn't know which to go to." That afternoon he took her to the optometrist, who fitted her with glasses, finding she was afflicted with double vision. Now Libia had the additional worry that if the child fell, she would smash her glasses in her eyes.

So little Margarita stayed at home until she was eight years old, when her mother felt she was strong enough to start school. Anabella was already three years ahead of Margarita, but despite Margarita's occasional jumbling of words, she was bright and soon caught up with Anabella. For the first time in her life, she hit a normal stride. The little girls would come home every afternoon with their clusters of friends, all of them swinging their shoes in their hands. They always took off their shoes and waded in the gutters that were overflowing with the early afternoon downpour. In the other hand would be a tight bunch of short-stemmed flowers they had picked from various neighboring yard borders. Their voices rang merrily in the afternoon quietness, and as soon as they reached their own walkway, they would break away from the crowd, dash into the house, change out of their school uniforms into dresses, grab a cookie, and head down to Esmeralda's chapel to listen to the rosary while squirming, snickering, and giggling under their breath. At the conclusion, they would sing their little songs to the Virgin and present their wilted, pilfered flowers to the priest to be placed before the Mother Mary. As soon as they were dismissed, they would run and play in the side street until suppertime.

One day, Libia gave strict orders to the little girls to wait on a certain bench in Parque Nacional until she came to pick them up. As she approached the park, she could hear her daughters' voices jibing and taunting, "Look at her. She is loco! Look at that funny umbrella!" Hurrying along, Libia passed the object of their ridicule. She was an elderly lady garbed in outlandish attire, a period costume of long, heavy skirts with a shawl about her shoulders. A big black hat shaded a wrinkled face caked with white powder whose wild eyes were heavily mascaraed and whose sunken mouth was a gush of red. She was wielding her umbrella about threateningly and screaming at the children who ran teasingly close, then fled from her attacks. Libia motioned the little girls over to a park bench and, in an excited voice, scolded them, "Don't you ever say anything to that old lady again. It is true. She is crazy. See how she sings and talks and playacts in the street. Now promise me you won't ever do that again!" The little girls promised not to repeat their actions, but they were puzzled by their mother's nervousness. That night as they lay in bed, Margarita heard Libia's voice talking to Luzare in the adjoining room, "The children were teasing and laughing at Elena today on the street. When did she get out?" Luzare replied shortly, "I don't know. But all her money can't help her. She won't stay out long."

Victor had always been a prompt person, but for the past several nights, he had been late for supper. Luzare was wroth with his son's tardiness and always raved when he had to wait for his food. As the slow-moving boy came dragging in, Luzare would growl inquiringly, "Where did you go, Victor? You left the store earlier than I did? Such behavior must cease!" Libia wanted to save the boy from Luzare's ire, but she knew not to speak. Luzare had always held Arturo up to her as a libertine because of his lack of discipline.

One night as Victor came up the walk, the family was already eating. Margarita, however, sidled out to warn her brother, "You'd better hurry. Papa has his whip out. I saw him get it." When Victor came into the dining room, Luzare began ranting, snapping his words until he was so breathless he could hardly speak. He grabbed up the whip leaning against the table leg and laid the leather-plaited lash over the boy's back until the stripes beaded and bled across Victor's shoulders, and Luzare was too breathless to flog any longer. Victor stood there, a taller, bigger man than his father, and gritted his teeth as the lashes cut into his back.

Then Luzare heaved, "Now, go to your room." Victor turned to go, but as he did so, he glanced over his shoulder at his mother, who sat clenching her fists. Reading tenderness and sympathy in Libia's eyes, he sobbed and ran up the hall.

But Luzare could pick no grievance with Victor over poor grades. The boy had finished high school with excellent marks, and his professors at El Liceo de Costa Rica praised him to Luzare. One morning as Libia was coming out of her room, she noticed the red skirt of Yolanda swish and disappear around Victor's door. Then the door softly closed. Libia stood a moment, waiting for the door to reopen, but it remained closed. More maddened than she had ever been, Libia walked across and flung open the door. Yolanda lay stretched beside Victor, her brown curly mopped head half hidden under his tousled hair. They were so deep in their kiss they did not hear her. Libia screamed, "Yolanda, get out of here! Get out!" Yolanda stood up, shrugged her luscious bare shoulder, and her face, as bright as a copper kettle, sneered at Libia as she swayed past. "So, it had been Yolanda who had turned Victor's fiancée's picture to the wall, and this was the reason." She had initially believed that one of the little girl's pranks was responsible, but now she understood that Yolanda was the reason. Victor grinned sheepishly and went down the hall to the bathroom.

Libia already had just cause to dismiss the girl; her linens had been disappearing steadily since the girl's employment, but Libia regarded these as peccadillos. All servants were eye-servants, to be watched constantly. The game had been to keep her valuables out of the servant's reach. Libia called Luzare and explained the girl's thievery. Luzare sent a detective who ransacked the girl's possessions but could find nothing but several pairs of Victor's silk jersey shorts that had been bunched together to form a knotted semblance of a body with several strands of Victor's brown hair matted in the head, and pins had been stuck in the body of it. Libia did not report the complete nature of the incident to Luzare since he already bore a medieval sternness toward Victor. Only recently had he flogged the boy again when he caught him smoking in the bathroom. Luzare never had a kind word for his youngest son.

After school every afternoon, the girls played in the street in front of the house. Libia sat in the vine arbor at the side porch and listened with pleasure to their noisome whoops and screams. She watched her daughters, one with blue-black hair and the other with flaxen blond hair, as they leaped and danced like nymphs, their short skirts flying and their long legs momentarily dangling in the air while they flitted about playing '*Can*' ball. The girls all lined up on one side, the boys on the other, as they tossed the ball as hard as they could at each other. They were strong, lean, and moved easily on their legs. Compared with some of the squat-legged, fat-stomached girls or the tall, bandy-legged skinny ones, hers were graceful. Anabella was beginning to develop round, high breasts. Margarita was still boyish and straight, but she would grow. Considering Margarita's poor beginning, she was not an unpretty child. People often commented on her beautiful eyes, but at the compliment Margarita would drop her head, push her glasses back up her small nose, and wait until the discussion changed before looking up again.

One afternoon, one of the little girls, Virginia, jumped over close to Margarita and hissed, "Look, there he is, the one I was telling you about. He's an American boy. He comes this way every day. I don't see why you haven't noticed him." Margarita stared. He was not a tall boy, but he walked along in a long stride, as if he were swinging a sandwich wrapped in brown paper. Virginia, a know-it-all, explained, "He goes to take his mother's lunch every day up to the government office. Get Anabella to make Roberto talk to him and invite him to play with us."

Roberto, Anabella's willing slave, did as he was instructed and approached the older boy the very next afternoon with "You are welcome to play with us if you want to" and stood waiting doubtfully for an answer.

The sixteen-year-old boy smiled, and his clear green eyes sparkled as he shrugged offhandedly, "Sure, I'll play with you. My name is Edwin," and with that he grinned widely, showing the pink membranes of his short nose far back into the dark caverns.

Figure 33 A

Parque Nacional. (Present Day)
iStock.com/Eric Broder Van Dyke
https://www.istockphoto.com/photo/empty-play-
area-in-parque-nacional-in-san-jose-costa-rica-
gm664484198-120955195

Figure 33B

Edwin

CHAPTER NINE

Rio Segundo

1938

EVERY DAY AFTER PLAYING, THE youngsters would run over to Virginia's backyard, where the boys had built a rancho. Virginia's mother, glad to have them out of the house, allowed them to play records, dance, and make orange juice. Occasionally, during their music craze, they would lapse into their younger childhood, jump out the clubhouse door, and swing or seesaw in the yard. Edwin showed his preference for Margarita by asking her to dance even though she couldn't and often walked home with her after the afternoon play session. One afternoon when it was time to go home, Margarita sought Anabella, who was still in the clubhouse with Roberto. Virginia was standing on the steps of her house and chanting to the clubhouse door, "Kiss her before I count four: one, two, three, four."

Margarita sprang through the door into the little room, tweaked the bigger girl by the ear, and shouted, "You come home; don't you let that boy kiss you!"

Roberto pulled away from Anabella and smirked, "Oh, it's all right. I kiss my mother; she kisses me. There's no harm."

Margarita's quick response was, "Yes, but for you to kiss my sister, that's different. Anabella, you come home!" Margarita's young soul was possessed by an imp and a saint, and often the saint showed herself.

At Christmas, Edwin gave Margarita a box of stationery, but when she looked up to thank him, he was gone. In January, the four of them were sitting on the side porch in the cool of the vine arbor, Anabella with Roberto and Margarita with Edwin, all with the auspicious excuse of reading.

Edwin climbed over the bench and stood at Margarita's shoulder, tugging at her book. Finally, he snatched it away teasingly. Margarita grabbed for the book; he resisted, and she wrenched it from his arms. But in that moment of her fierce struggle, he kissed her firmly on her lips. She hurled the book to the mosaic and screamed, "Get out of here, you dirty pig." Then she turned and fled into the house, slammed the door to her room, and knelt at her bedside, pleading that the smear of uncleanliness be taken from her soul. After three or four repentant notes from Edwin, however, she relented and consented to let him come back to the house.

One night, after arranging the ruse with Edwin and Roberto, the girls cajoled their mother with, "Mama, why don't you and Papa go to the movies tonight?"

Always appreciative of special attention from her daughters, Libia responded readily, "Why, my sweet babies, how lovely of you to think of it! Luzare, let's go!"

Luzare always enjoyed the luxury of upholstered leather comfort, marveling at the advancements in modern entertainment and often harking back to the days when movie viewers carried their chairs to the old silent pictures. He made a few grumbling sounds, got up from his newspaper and easy chair, and said, "All right, let me take these gray hairs out for an airing." Then he went into the bedroom and brushed his fringe of hair, still as black as patent leather.

Libia looked in on her young girls before leaving. With the covers up to their chins and their angelic faces, as if a benison had just fallen upon them, the girls looked so sweet that Libia leaned over and placed a soft kiss on each forehead. In a few minutes she and Luzare walked out of their bedroom, and as soon as the girls heard the door slam and their parents' steps resounding fainter down the walkway, they sprang out of bed and started brushing their hair furiously. They straightened out their dress wrinkles when the sound '*Cockle-do-oo*' floated eerily through the night air. Then a weirder '*Cockle-do-do*' in a half-bass, half-tenor strain. That was Edwin. The girls pulled their jackets out of their closet and sneaked up the shadowy hall. Outside, the porch was dark; the servant always pulled the front shades down at six o'clock. Margarita sat near Edwin and drew herself up into a chilly little knot. Edwin was talking, but she was not listening. She had her eye on her sister, who was heartily enjoying being kissed by Roberto. Margarita whispered hoarsely to Edwin, "He kissed her twenty times, twenty times. I counted them."

Irked, Edwin replied, "Oh, leave them alone. Talk to me." He pulled a Veranera bloom from the trellis and stuck it in her thick hair, then plucked a Margarita rose and counted his fortune with the petals: "She loves me, she loves me not, she loves me!" Turning to her, he whispered softly into her ear, "Margarita, the rose says '*yes*'." He snatched a kiss from her pouting lips, but Margarita jerked back, frightened! Her promise to the Virgin had been broken. She had promised the Virgin that such an incident would not happen again. Frenzied, she slapped the boy's face soundly. Edwin and Roberto took their hurried departure over the banisters. Their tennis shoes landed with a padded thud, and they were gone in the dark.

Margarita ran down the hall to the bathroom and scrubbed her teeth and mouth with everything she could find in the cabinet. Then she went back into the bedroom to confront a blazing Anabella, who hissed angrily, "Why did you do that?"

Margarita replied gravely, "You are going to hell. You are bad, letting the boy kiss you that way."

Anabella shrugged impatiently, "Don't be stupid. We are big girls now; stop being a silly child." She drew on her gown and was soon asleep. But Margarita tossed in anguish, cried, and prayed while the Virgin's sad, lovely face seemed to look down on her, disappointed and dejected. The young girl begged agonizingly for forgiveness and again promised that the sin would not be repeated. Finally, she sobbed herself to sleep.

Edwin controlled his ardor from then on, content to talk and study with Margarita, who moved her grandmother Catalina's ruby ring over to the third finger on her left hand and considered herself betrothed to him.

One night, something unbelievable happened. With a bunch of carousers, Victor went on a bacchic tear, took his father's new Buick limousine from the garage, filled it with heavy stones, beer, and whiskey bottles, and rode wildly drunk through the town, throwing bottles and stones through the plate windows of buildings, store windows, and even the houses near town. The next morning, Luzare received a call from the jail and went down to pay his contrite miscreant out of confinement and to requite the merchants for their property damages. He did not utter a word of rebuke to Victor, nor did he ever again take up his lash against him.

When Victor announced his intention to leave college and get married before completing his last year, Luzare did not try to stop him. Victor's bride-to-be was a simple shop girl named Olga, whom he had been seeing for several years and whose picture he had always kept hanging on his bedroom wall. Olga was tall and of Swedish coloring, as pink and white as the confections her mother baked in her pastry shop. Her features were plain, but she was always neat and fresh-looking and her body was marvelously curved.

On her wedding day, Olga wore a shawl draped as a veil over her head, a fine hand-crocheted piece of art that had been Victor's gift to her. The ceremony was not elaborate but in excellent taste and included all the traditional rituals. Victor handed the coins to the priest, who in turn conferred them upon the bride—thirteen pieces of coin. The two young people knelt at the feet of the priest with a white cord looped around their necks, the cord that symbolized the yoke of matrimony. Libia's whole being shuddered in emotional pain. Her long labor with Victor was over, and the umbilical cord was now being cut, resting around Olga's neck. The priest blessed the candle and uttered his benediction, and the guests riotously threw rice and danced about the newly wedded ones as they came out of the church. Libia held a reception for them at home. She had spared no expense, and it was a wonderful party. As the evening wore on, the old priest began to feel the heady champagne. He had been invited by Luzare to assist in performing the ceremony because Luzare was fond of the country priest, who was completely self-abnegating in his devotion to his church. Luzare had always remarked sarcastically of the city priests that none of them would ever suffer from the stigmata. Padre Marino stood upon one of the living room chairs and did a little jig, his old shoulders stooped in his mended robes, but he held his glass high as he tossed rice over his gray head and proposed a toast to the young married couple. His voice carried a quavering tone as he spoke, saying, "Young people, it is so wonderful to be young; be glad you are young, especially you two who have just married. It is wonderful, too, to be married. You are so happy, so carefree; you can live in such abandonment of love. I say live fully, fully, to the brim, like this glass. Look at me, an old man who has not lived except for this," and he touched his black sleeve. "Do you think a priest is not human, that he has no feelings? I have feelings too. I..." But he did not get to finish his sentence. Ricardo and Arturo carefully helped him down from his stand, and in a few minutes, he was out in their automobile and being driven away. Libia had been standing in the living room doorway, her hand knotted over her mouth to hold back the screams.

Her young daughters, standing listening behind her, kept whispering, "Mama, why did he act like that? A priest is not supposed to dance. Why did the priest drink the champagne?"

Libia answered as best she could with words from her own sick heart, "Because it is a reception. He was trying to show that he was glad and happy and happy about the mar..." But the tears started flowing, and she stepped over into her room. She listened to the laughing voices and thought hysterically, "Why must time go on and on and nobody wants to go home? Nobody wants to leave. They won't leave."

After Victor went away on his honeymoon, Libia felt within herself a great cleft. Something had departed from her being, and she was lonely, a strange loneliness, as if she were in a dry, barren land, a chapped land, and the pitiless, parched wilderness stretched on endlessly all about her. Her soul was thirsty, and God was far away. Her soul cried out, but God was so far away He could not hear her calling.

In February, when Luzare suggested that she take the girls and go up to Rio Segundo, where he had rented a vacation house, she welcomed the change. The country place was but a few miles off the main highway from San José to Alajuela. It was splendidly situated so that it could be reached in a thirty-minute drive from town. When the girls arrived at their vacation dwelling, they sprang from the automobile with shrieks of hurrahs in the delirious pleasure of exploring the old-fashioned frame house. Libia felt insensitive, as though there were nothing to feel. But in this rustic place she could exist in a vacuum of peaceful surroundings.

Catalina had come along to help with the girls, and as always, she was domination personified. She bossed the young girls to bed or poked around the kitchen with her aristocratic old nose in every pot that boiled over the fire. She was forever demanding the servant open the beehive-shaped oven so she could peek in to look at the day's baking. Catalina's very nature was assiduousness, with every act performed with unremitting diligence. She was ageless, indefatigable, unwearied, and attentive to every detail, and she tolerated nothing less in her servants. Libia lived in an opiate's trance, leaving the vacationing household to Catalina, who, smaller than she appeared with her straight back, was everywhere. Never having forgotten that she had been a Hispanic beauty, she wore black only because custom constrained her. But her dress was always touched with black lacy frills, and she always wore pearls. Her shawl was fringed with deep lace. Her hair, which was as raven black as when she was sixteen, always lay in carefully set waves and was held in place by invisible pins, wiglike in perfection. Her face was lightly dusted with faint-scented powder; her beautifully turned ankles, visible only now and then with the rustle of her dress, were encased in transparent black hose, and on her feet, she always wore small black kid pumps.

After the girls were given their supper in the late afternoon, they could hardly wait for the turquoise evening to close them in. They loved to slip the stumps of candles, soften the tallow, and grab the Abejones out of the little box of safekeeping. Then they would smear the beetles' hard black backs with the tallow, stick a thread in the center of the mound, press and shape the dab of tallow around the thread, and set the thread aglow. They enjoyed watching the slow-crawling living torches march across the floor in dignified procession and then inch their way up the wall. One night an ingenious Abejone got out of hand and escaped into the net curtains. The next moment, the whole window was ablaze. Hearing the girls' frightened screams, Catalina rushed in, grabbed a blanket from the bed, flung it over the blazing curtains, jerked them down, and smothered and stomped them out on the floor. After the excitement was over, Catalina realized she had burned her hands and arms seriously, but the pain of the burn was not as terrible to her as the realization that her beautiful patrician hands with their bluish veins might possibly be scarred. She greased them and walked the floor all night in agony. The next morning, she walked up to Río Segundo, caught a bus into San José, and went to the San Juan Hospital for treatment. The next day she was back, her arms and hands in bandages, but Catalina was considerably relieved that the burns would not leave scars.

Even Libia began to succumb to the spell of natural relaxation and contentment offered by this picturesque old haunt with its pots of fern growing in front and hanging from the eaves. Herbs had been planted around the edge of the backyard by some good country soul with a thought for future sicknesses. Chamomile, dill, and mint grew in little green bunches. Orchids bloomed among the lichens along the roof. Inside the cool, shadowy house, fine wood floors gleamed with hand-rubbed finish, and even the fire-baked red brick of the big oven in the kitchen was colorful.

During the mornings, Libia read. In the afternoons she shook herself into liveliness and walked with her russet-faced, barefoot daughters up to Alajuela. The girls with their overalls rolled up to their knees would sprint and race up the narrow, lane-like country road along which low hedges were heavy with roses and the feathery, delicate leaves of the pink-flowered madre de cafe bloomed. The sun filtered and applied to the earth through the overarching trees. There were ferns as delicate as lace and myriads of waxy scented flowers on both sides of the lane. The ground was covered with soft, powdery, fine volcanic ash, a pale lavender gray. The high hill they climbed just before reaching Alajuela was invigorating, and Libia looked forward to the tall, cool soda as eagerly as the children did. It was an afternoon ritual to look into every store window on their way to the park, and the girls always dashed into the green, inviting park to choose which bench they wanted to sit on. They would seat themselves, squirming, catch their breath, and force their mother to tell them again the Santamaría story. Libia always began the tale by putting the moral in front and stating, "Look at the boy's face; he was not very old, yet he was a hero. And do you see he was an Indian? So, courage has no color. And why is he holding that bundle of sticks high?" The girls never answered any questions because they wanted to hear the story recounted from beginning to end. Libia would take a long breath and plunge into her tale with:

> "This town will forever be grateful to that lowly, simple boy. He was never rich; he was born to the poorest of parents. And when he was a young boy, he was such a mischief maker that nobody knew what to do with him, so they put him in the military barracks. All the soldiers laughed at him and called him "*Erizo*" because his kinky hair made him look like a hedgehog, as you can see on the statue. And since he was only ten years old, he was not big enough to be a real soldier, so he became a drummer boy. In 1856—see, it is written there— President Juan Rafael Mora felt that it was the country's duty to help aid Nicaragua in defeating William Walker, an American politician who was a wicked man. He was nothing but an adventurer, a scheming

man wanting to stir up trouble. So, Santamaría, then a young man, went with the other troops up to the north and into Nicaragua to the town of Rivas. They found Walker and his army had been forced to seek refuge in an armory.

The general of the Costa Rican troops called for volunteers. He shouted, "*Who will help me set fire to the armory?*" Santamaría stepped up first and said, "*I will.*" He took the bundle of sticks and crept forward carefully, dodging enemy fire. He finally reached the building, and pressing as closely to the walls as he could, he ran from window to window, throwing the lighted sticks. William Walker's army was defeated, but Santamaría lost his life."

"Now it's time to go home." Libia said.

At the soldier's glorious death, both Anabella and Margarita sighed sadly and remarked, "Santamaría was brave like Grandmother." In a few minutes they would hop up, ready to be moving again. Leaving the town and turning homewards, the young girls always raced down the now mauve-colored hill and stopped breathless at the bottom to wait for their mother. The sun was already casting long, violet shadows as they made their way back through the lane. When they reached the house, Catalina would be in the kitchen quarreling and fussing over the supper, while the bland, docile cook padded barefoot about the clay floor to do Catalina's bidding. The girls ate their food ravenously, then hurried outside to chase the ducks under the house or poke sticks at the grunting pigs. Time was terribly important to them between eating, washing their feet, and putting on their gowns. It usually required a few scoldings from Catalina's sharp tongue before they stopped giggling and finally succumbed to the sheets and began breathing regularly in the cool night air.

Figure 34 A

Alejuela Church. (Present Day) iStock.com/Gianfranco Vivi

https://www.istockphoto.com/photo/aerial-view-of-the-alajuela-church-in-costa-rica-gm1868401218-552898451

Chapter 9

Figure 34 B

Statue of the national hero Juan Santamaria in Alajuela - Costa Rica, Central America
https://www.istockphoto.com/photo/statue-of-the-national-hero-juan-santamaria-in-alajuela-costa-rica-gm1764690154-545199131?clarity=false

Figure 35

Bronze statue of Juan Santamaría Close Up
iStock.com/Gab13
https://www.istockphoto.com/photo/statue-juan-santamaría-costa-rica-gm1349271017-425948128?clarity=false

Figure 36

Arenal Volcano, Alajuela Costa Rico
iStock.com/MarkGabrenya
https://www.istockphoto.com/photo/arenal-volcano_0086-gm95187090-7028614?clarity=false

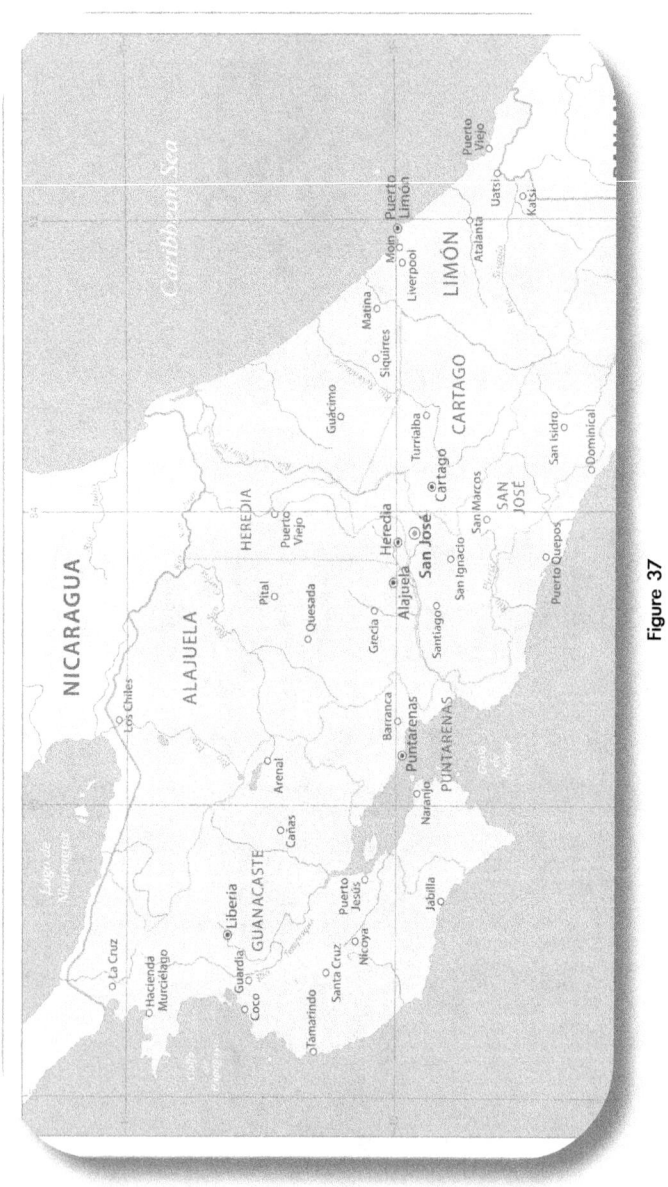

Figure 37

Map of Costa Rica

https://www.istockphoto.com/vector/costa-rica-map-highly-detailed-vector-illustration-gm1497457744-519819294?clarity=false iStock.com/dikobraziy

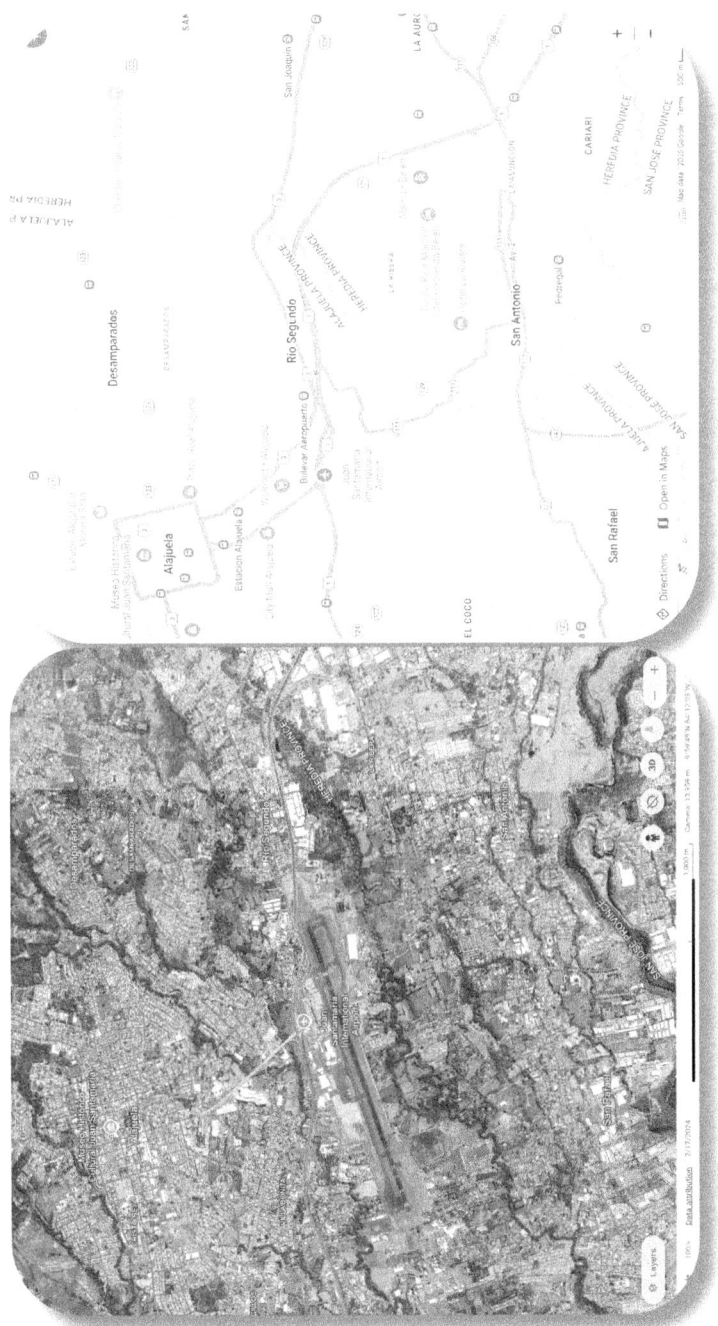

Figure 38

Rio Segundo, Costa Rica - Includes data from Google, Airbus and Google Maps

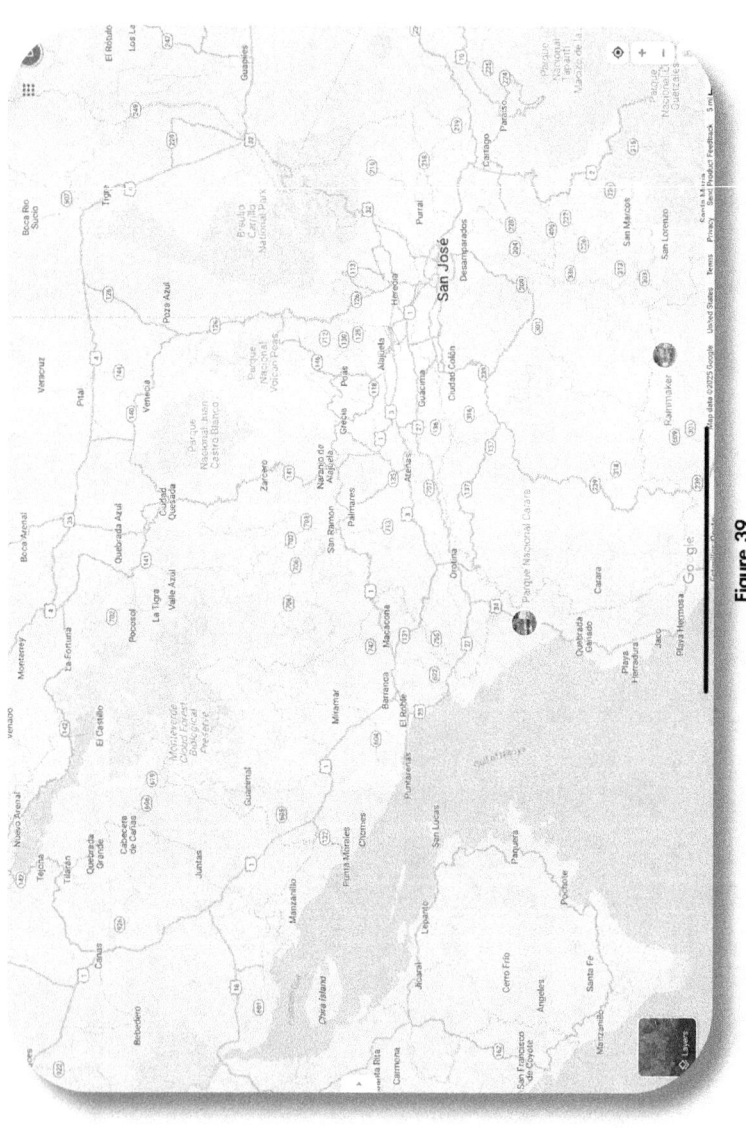

Figure 39

Rio Segundo, Costa Rica - Includes data from Google and Google Maps

CHAPTER TEN

Luzare's Betrayal

1941

Figure 40

Leon Cortés Castro

ON THE WEEKENDS, LUZARE NEVER relaxed for the short time he was with them. His mind was too full of worries, so he walked about the shaded county place cursing under his breath. Since the presidential election the year before, he had mulled, dissatisfied with the man he helped vote into power. The presidential term of León Cortés Castro from 1936 to 1940 had been a strong, sturdy government, completely without any trouble-mongering groups. León Cortés Castro was an able administrator, engineer, and lawyer. He had been an official of the Pacific

Figure 41

Rafael Ángel Calderón Guardia

Electric Railroad before his election and had gone into office with an overwhelming majority of votes and had held the reins of government like an expert rider, sensitive to the emotions of his citizenry horse. Before his four years were up, he had been prevailed upon to succeed himself in office at the expiration of his tenure but squelched the suggestion of ignoring the Constitution with "I will never convert myself into a tyrant." In February 1940, as Cortés was preparing to leave office, he expressed his belief that Rafael Ángel Calderón Guardia would be a good president. Calderón Guardia did receive a majority of votes over Octavio Beeche and went into office a confident man. He had a reputation in San José of being an excellent doctor, having a magnanimous heart for the poor, and having never shown any communistic leanings. But after he was in office, it was not long before the whole country realized its mistake. Calderón Guardia was simply not presidential material. There was something lacking in him for which there could be no substitute. He was ineffectual, had no initiative, and listened to the wrong advisors. And even in the first year, the people started criticizing him with the same freedom that they had when giving him their support. Costa Rica had always fought injustices and pressure with their free, outspoken press; caustic-tongued and cutting as Archer's acid, they told Calderón Guardia his mistakes. Gradually he was turning from support to the committee. They were a minority group—a small union with no strength—but with presidential backing, they would cease being ignored and become dictators. Luzare talked and thought about politics all day. His astute old friends, legislators and thinkers all of them, would drift into Luzare's store, on the presidential residence, to discuss the day's occurrences. They always finished their talks with a sorrowful shake of their heads. For the rest of Guardia's term, they saw no chance of relief. All they could pray for was that he would not go from bad to worse.

On weekends, Libia left Luzare to his own thoughts. She understood him well enough to know any worry consumed his whole mind until he could cast it off, and nothing she could say would lessen the intensity of how he felt.

One morning Catalina brought a neatly addressed envelope in. Surprised at receiving mail at all away from home, Libia gazed wonderingly at the unfamiliar writing before she opened the envelope. Inside, the contents of the letter were even stranger. On a plain white paper were written the words, "Open your eyes. Another woman uses your bedroom for a love nest." At first glance, Libia almost laughed. Who would be so fatuous as to suppose Luzare, a man of sixty-nine years, would be pulling a young man's tricks? Yet Luzare..., Luzare, Luzare had no age. His body was as stout and vigorous as an animal's.

Figure 42   Catalina

Yet, it was possible; it was even probable. Never before had Luzare found a reason to be separated from his family. Here, only thirty minutes from town, it was impossible for him to be with them except on weekends. But who was her anonymous ally? Her own servants at home might be observant enough, but they could not write. Someone close enough to the family, but who? Ricardo? Certainly not! This was not his writing, even disguised; and besides, he would never befriend her, no matter what the circumstances. Libia handed the letter to her mother, who at best never contained her curiosity very well and who, at the moment, was twitching with interest. Catalina read the message and exploded. While she made hacking little strokes with her comb at her hair, she talked rapidly, "Well, don't just sit there. Occasionally you act stupid. Get up and go home. Two months is too long to be away in the first place. What you can find to do in this forsaken place has always been beyond me. Go call Ricardo to pick us up. Hurry, I'll have the packing done before you get back."

Figure 43 A   Renato

Early in the afternoon, Ricardo came in the automobile. Libia had sounded so upset over the telephone he was expecting one of the girls to be sick. His son, Renato, a lanky fifteen-year-old boy, blinked owl-eyed behind his large, horn-rimmed glasses. A fidgety boy, he was constantly scratching himself, stretching his neck, or gnawing his nails. He sat near his father on the automobile seat and rarely turned his head to look at the two girls, who, both mud-splotched from their recent wading for tadpoles in the dammed-up stream in the backyard, were in poor humor. Their fun had been interrupted. Catalina was constantly pushing them back in the seat to make them sit up in a more ladylike manner. She had intended to use this vacation time to teach these girls some niceties. Instead of girls getting ready for their teens, they were more like obstreperous, grubby-handed boys, to her mind. Libia sat upright with a pale, strained look on her face. She spoke not a word of explanation to Ricardo, but his was not unnatural. When Luzare was not around, Libia observed only necessary courtesies in dealing with this stepson.

Upon arrival home, the girls jumped out of the car and scattered over the walk onto the mosaic porch and dashed into the house. Libia and Catalina, approaching at a slower pace, could hear Margarita's voice bursting with warmth and joyousness as she trilled, "Papa, I didn't expect to find you at home!" As Libia was putting her foot on the first step, she felt someone's eyes upon her back. Glancing over her shoulder, she saw Francisco's knurly head, his hair as stubby as the hedge he was clipping. Catching her eye, he nodded his head significantly. Francisco was a trustworthy person. And so it was the truth.

Luzare stood in the hall, arched like an angry bull. His eyes flashed, his short fingers tapped against his vest as he snorted, "Libia, what is the meaning of this? Why did you come home?" "Indeed, and what is so urgent?" Catalina was going from side to side, walking back into the living room, correcting the girls, and shooing them off down to the bathroom. Ricardo stood by for a word with his father, but Luzare was conscious of nobody but Libia as he glared with a bloated, hateful look in his eyes.

Libia's voice began trembling with her mounting anger, and blatantly she made her accusation, "Luzare, in the first place, I don't know what woman would abase herself to become an old man's mistress. But whoever the harpy is, I don't want her in my house."

Luzare spoke sharply, "Shut up. You don't know what you are talking about!"

Libia was not to be stopped. She hissed in a bitter voice, "I say it again. She is nothing but a harlot." Luzare swung his heavy arm and slapped Libia so hard she reeled, staggered, and would have fallen had it not been for Catalina, who caught her. Catalina eased her into the living room and down on the sofa. Ricardo hustled his son out. Not that he hated to see Libia defamed, but there was a look of terrible uncertainty in his tall son's eyes, as if he were going to cry. Disgusted that the boy should see his grandfather's clay feet, he marched Renato across the back patio and over into his own house.

Libia, Catalina, and the girls went to Catalina's house, where Libia walked the floor, her face red and swollen. She blew her nose and wiped her eyes constantly, always half praying, her fingers counting the rosary. Catalina, in her own greatest strength in times of emotional stress, was hard-voiced, trying to make Libia get control of herself.

While one finger twirled and wrapped the pearl strand around and around itself, she kept reasoning, "You haven't had such a bad time of it these sixteen years. At least it beats being a music teacher, which is probably what you would have been doing. He has never denied you anything."

Libia spat out her words of retort, "I want nothing from him but a divorce. I will never look on his face again."

Catalina reached up and combed back her black waves, as if to soothe her own self. Then she softened her voice to a more coaxing attitude as she said, "Libia, you talk like a schoolgirl. Luzare is not better or no worse than the general run of men. They are prone to this weakness, always ravished by strange women. It is up to you to be strong. Besides, he behaves like he has been given a potion. I believe he has. Maybe she drugged him."

But Libia stormed, "I don't care. I can't and I won't live with an adulterer."

In a solemn, reminding tone, Catalina responded, "We live not for this world but for the next, besides," and she paused before pulling her trump card, "Think of the children. You are inclined to indulge yourself in your religion, too self-centered; you must not be selfish with yourself."

Libia's fists beat the pillow in distracted defiance. "Yes, I know, and it was in this very room you told me to marry him." She plunged her head into the pillow and wept bitterly. Seeing argument to be of no avail, Catalina left her daughter to her tears.

As Libia sobbed, she thought of the present as her destiny. '*Why,*' she asked herself, '*must I always be combating this horrible hydra-headed monster that rears itself in my life?*' Sex, to her, was the most loathsome of vices, and it was here to fight.

That night, as Libia slept a fitful sleep, her familiar nightmare came again to her.

Old Juan Quitituy's face was over her; his evil, lascivious eyes were upon her. She could feel his breath hot upon her neck. The repulsive, sinister face came closer and closer, just as it had that day when she was a small girl. The slack-faced stranger had come and poked candy to her through the grill fence of her yard and had half-whispered as he beckoned, "Come with me, little girl, and I will find more candy for you."

As the faithful child servant, Laura, had come leaping over to the fence, he had said to her, "It's all right. I am her uncle." After he opened the gate and let her out, Libia slipped her hand into his, willingly, trustingly. She had left her cool, spicy garden and had walked by his side to the cracked and crumbling adobe where several little girls, dirty urchins, sat around on the clay floor playing.

Laura's skinny little form had stood outside in the squalor and called in to her little charge, "Libia, come here, you know you don't belong in there."

But Libia yelled out to her, "Go away, I want

to get more candy from my uncle." Laura's thin brown legs had carried her as swiftly as the wind back to Libia's mother. Inside the house she ran, panting.

Catalina looked down at her and spoke sharply, "What are you doing here, Laura? You mustn't leave Libia alone."

"But doña Catalina," the little girl burst out, "the uncle has taken Libia, and he won't let me in to look after her."

Catalina bristled, all attention, and queried, "What uncle? Libia has no uncle here." She walked to the front door and cast her eyes about for Libia, then turned in alarm, grabbed and shook Laura, "Tell me, tell me, Laura, what did he look like? Where did he take her?"

Jabbering and pointing, Laura ran on ahead, showing the way, explaining over and over again. "He had no shoes on, but he said he was Libia's uncle. He was an old man, dirty and ragged." Catalina followed, half-running to the mean, low hut. She pushed and flung herself through the door into the room from whence came Libia's shrieks. In the middle of the floor, Libia was wildly fending and fighting, writhing and struggling with old Juan, whose filth-encrusted hands were grappling and pulling at her little white panties.

Old Juan had been put into jail, but his face never left her memory; the fear had never left her heart.

Costa Rica Flag Ribbon
https://www.istockphoto.com/vector/costa-rica-flag-ribbon-set-vector-stock-illustration-gm1337195075-418165107?clarity=falseiStock.com/PeterPencil

Chapter 10

CHAPTER ELEVEN
Rafael
1942

A T CATALINA'S ARRANGEMENTS, LUZARE CAME to pick up his family the next day. He put the girls in the automobile and turned back to call Libia from her bedroom. He stood in the doorway of the room waiting, with a look of letting bygones be bygones. But Libia was equally determined, for once in her marriage, that Luzare should humble himself before her. And so she waited, silently, arrogantly. Luzare's stubby fingers counted his vest buttons; his voice was beseeching with a peccavi sound, but his face was hard and set as he spoke, "Libia, I'm sorry for hurting you. I want you to know that I have never stopped loving you, and what happened had nothing to do with our marriage." Libia stood aghast, stunned, and dumbfounded and wondered how to reply to that kind of reasoning. She said not a word but stepped out of her mother's house and into the automobile with a feeling that she was walking into indescribable chaos.

However, once back at her home, a load was lifted from her heart. She felt lighter, freer than she had ever felt in this house, and more secure. She was no longer the imposter. In some inexplicable way she was the household, and Luzare was the intruder. Luzare, feeling his patriarchal powers dwindling, was domineering with the girls, tyrannical, and unreasonable; without provocation, he would fly into sudden abusive furies. Instead of the silver dinner bell with its tinkle, he brought home a large bell, which he beat with a gong in exasperated gasps as he swore, "*Caramba, Caramba,*" in time with the bell. His bald head would shine, beaded with sweat, and with fury he would wait until the girls took their places at the table. The bell, a mortification to Libia, could easily be heard over in the next block, and she had visions of her neighbors simmering and remarking sarcastically, '*don Luzare Constant is bidding his family to dinner.*' Then when they were seated, he would bang his knife on the table, his face would turn red, and the veins would turn blue on his shiny head as he looked at them and cursed, "*Caraja, Caraja.*" But as soon as the soup was poured, he fell to eating immediately. He growled laconically at Libia's questions, and the girls' gay repartee became mutinous half-whispers at the table. They even developed a system of charade and quick finger talk, which they used while their father's face was down in his bowl.

After supper, Anabella and Margarita, once inside their room, often lapsed into bickering and hot arguments over their possessions. Luzare was an early retiree, and if he were aroused from his slumbers, he would fling open the connecting bedroom door, roar into the room garbed in his large nightshirt, a stocking cap on his head, heavy woolen socks, and knitted bootees; turn back the covers; and lash the girls' legs with his plaited horsewhip that had steel picks in the ends of the plies. Then he would shuffle back to bed, grumbling about the little devils, the '*carajitas.*' The girls would pull the covers back up over their ray-burning legs, which sometimes stayed marked with the print of the lash for three or four days. And the pricks sometimes made sores.

Anabella and Margarita were now attending Maria Auxilia Dora College, where Margarita was in her fifth year at thirteen and Anabella in her sixth year. One afternoon they were standing outside its august portals engaged in a heated exchange of opinions.

Spitting torrents of words savagely at her sister, Margarita was saying, "Anabella, I want to know why you told on me. It was none of your business."

Sneering sanctimoniously, Anabella rebutted, "It was too my business. When Sister asked me if I knew who had given the girls the rape, I had no choice but to tell the truth. It was you who had no business making the whole school sneeze. Why do you pull such stupid tricks?" Margarita, in remembering the whole room full of girls "*choo-chooing*" so hard that nobody could hear the nun's voice, broke into a hearty laugh, and her good humor was returned.

She replied, "Oh, you are just mad because our class got out of arithmetic and you didn't."

But she dropped the debate. It had been the best trick she had ever pulled, she thought to herself. She and Anabella turned to join the six or eight classmates who stood respectfully by until the sisters could end their discussion. They all started up the sidewalk like let-loose children, laughing rollickingly, bumping and jolting each other from side to side. At the corner they stopped before turning into Paseo Colón, and as was their daily ritual, they placed their pocketbooks on the low stone wall and began ransacking them for lipsticks, combs, and powder puffs, which they smeared over their faces in heavy thickness. They topped off their beautification rite by plucking the tenderest roses from the bordering gardens and artfully tucking them behind their ears. They puffed up their starched white blouses and examined each other's neck ribbons critically. Each girl in turn sighed at the deplorably plain, blue juniper, buttoned at the shoulders; the pleated skirts that flared their plump little bodies into tub proportions; and their flat black butcher oxfords! The ensemble was a condemnation of their beauty. Nothing so hideous had ever been worn by their movie heroines. But they sauntered on up Paseo Colón, a quiet old dignified street of some of the finest residences of the city, swishing their skirts flirtatiously as they walked to distract from their ugly shoes. When they reached Avenida Central, Anabella always dropped behind Margarita to watch her flirtations. Very slowly they made their way, careful not to reach the Parque Central one minute before five. At five o'clock, San José emptied its buildings, and all the male office employees and hirelings ogled and whistled ribaldly at the passing girls. The young girls always made two turns through Parque Central, and at times they lifted their heads disdainfully. A moment later they were winking outrageously, then walked up to the corner and split company. Margarita and Anabella always caught the San Pedro Streetcar home and dashed into the house famished for their supper.

One night Margarita read in the newspaper that Errol Flynn, the Hollywood movie actor, was coming to San José, that he was expected on an airplane the next afternoon. That night in bed, she and Anabella made their plans to leave school at lunchtime the next day, play hooky, and go out to the airport.

The plan worked without a bobble. The next afternoon they stood on the balcony of the airport terminal and craned their necks skyward and landward for the overdue plane. Anabella had attracted the attention of an oily, wavy, black-haired boy who kept trailing her about. He followed her through the lobby of the terminal, into the cafe, back out again, and then up the steps. Now he was leaning against the building, a thin boy with white pants and a clean white shirt with the neck thrown open. He was teasing the scornful Anabella, talking to her back, saying, "Why do you wait for that sissy? Movie stars are nothing but sissies."

Anabella slung a retort over her shoulder, "Oh, go away. You are just jealous because he is so good-looking and you are so skinny."

The boy gave a short, jeering laugh and snorted, "Who…me, jealous? At least I look like myself, and actors don't. They wear makeup like a woman. They're not natural." The girls ignored the boy and talked between themselves. Soon a huge plane swooped in, landed, and roared to a stop. Everybody rushed out to the plane. From out of nowhere, throngs of people crowded near. Anabella and Margarita, realizing they could see very well from their perch, just stood and watched. There were a few minutes of hushed expectancy. Everybody disembarked from the plane but the star. Then a handsome horse was trotted out to the plane. There was a loud screaming and squealing. Errol Flynn ducked his head through the plane doorway, swung upon the horse's back, and waved to the crowd. His red hair and mustache shone in the bright sunlight. All the young girls turned mad, wild, and crazy at the sight of him. They jumped about the horse, talking and waving. The dashing figure rode his horse to the front of the terminal building to pose in front of one of the most beautiful buildings in all of Central America. He finally dismounted and stepped into the lobby, a stage-like setting with hand-carved solid mahogany doors and ceiling beams, wrought grillwork, and railings. The perfect man stood in the thick of the crowd and signed autographs. Anabella and Margarita tried to work their way down into the admiring mob below, but it was so thick they were compelled to just stand and wait until the actor finally left the building.

Figure 44   Rafael

The young boy stood on the step above Anabella and leaned close to her head to ask, "Let me take you home."

Anabella shrugged her shoulder and replied snappishly, "No, you are not Errol Flynn. How could I go with you after seeing that beautiful man?"

The boy answered doggedly, "All right then, but I want to see you Sunday in the park. I like you very much."

Anabella lifted her little pointed nose haughtily, "Don't be ridiculous. In comparison with Errol Flynn, you are nothing. You skinny little boy." The two girls went home, cautioning each other not to say anything to Mama. Because Mama wouldn't like it if she knew they had slipped out of school.

But during the week, Anabella's ardor for the movie actor wore off, and the next Sunday she and Margarita went to the park for cuerdas. The boy with the black wavy hair was there and soon coupled with Anabella. They sat on the park bench with Margarita acting as chaperone, and later he walked home with the girls. He said his name was Rafael Valverde. Before they reached home, the girls made him leave them. Anabella explained, not unkindly, "I am sorry, but my mother thinks I'm too young to have a real boyfriend. I will just meet you sometime in the Park."

The next day at school, Ester, one of Anabella's distant cousins and a student there, met her in the corridor and, in her rage, backed her up against the wall. "Why are you trying to steal my boyfriend? Rafael is mine."

Anabella swayed around the larger girl and replied, "I did not steal him. He came to me. But from now on I will see him every time he wants me to see him." Ester shook her curls in fury, but Anabella only laughed, "You will see, from now on."

And it was true. Anabella was not impressed by Rafael. He was no good, and she had an inborn sense of culture. Just ordinary people, his family was low-class, next thing to a concho. She was in love with Roberto, but Roberto, she knew, had another girl. And deep within her, it hurt to realize that Roberto was only using her to make his real girl jealous. She was only a pretty girl to make his girl love him more. But she wondered if she could use Rafael in just the same manner. If she was attracted to Roberto, it would make him mad to see another boy hanging around.

Figure 45 A

Anabella at 16

Figure 45 B

Sunset In Cartago. (Present Day) iStock.com/Dennis Alberto Gonzalez Salas
https://www.istockphoto.com/photo/sunset-in-the-city-of-cartago-with-a-colorful-sky-gm2208911258-626039959

CHAPTER TWELVE
Barrio Escalante
1942

WITH THE DECLARATION OF WAR on Japan on December 8, 1941, and on Germany and Italy on December 11, San José had developed an air of tenseness. The old easy enjoyment of just walking the streets was gone. People pushed their way about in a tremendous hurry, and the President had shown himself openly as to his true nature. In this year, 1942, the communists were a force to be feared. Guardia was giving them all the power and support they needed. Their fighting banner was '*The Social Guarantees*,' a labor code using as their appeal paid vacations, social security for workers, and health insurance to gain and spread their propaganda.

Guardia openly gave conchos government employment, ousting those who voiced any criticism of his regime and replacing them with handpicked communists to fill important government seats. The citizenry retaliated in every way it could. When President Calderón Guardia appeared at public functions, football games, or bullfights, the crowd stood, whistled, and jeered at him and his official entourage. Calderón Guardia only turned his big-jowled face away from the crowd and engaged himself in amusement with his own group until the entertainment began.

The Declaration of War on Germany, December 11, had given his predatory designs all the liberty they needed to confiscate German-owned properties and large, rich holdings. German-blooded families who had adopted Costa Rica as their home and who had lived their lives as loyal, patriotic citizens, building their fortunes up from her soil, were uprooted, routed, run off the country, or sent to concentration camps. Like the monstrous tyrant he was, he despoiled them of their wealth, their beautiful homes, fine automobiles, and plantations and turned them over to Guardia devotees. He and his special group of communists formed a Calderó-Communist Party, which had as its focal point of interest taking money from the government and spending it lavishly upon themselves. On the giant lot behind the Constant property, Calderón Guardia bought the entire expanse belonging to Esmeralda's sister Lina, whose married name was Escalante. A sprawling new section sprang up known as the '*Barrio Escalante*,' gorgeous homes of Spanish Colonial architecture, with screens in the windows, a startling innovation. Vast gardens were luxuriant with flowers, and wide streets separated them from the rest of the city. All of Calderón Guardia's favorites and kinsmen were set up like kings in their own palatial estates, and they wallowed in their own opulence.

Anabella and Margarita stood on the balcony of their house in the late afternoons and watched men from the customs house check huge boxes and vats of building materials being cleared through the customs house: cement and wrought grill iron imported from Spain. All this could be used in building homes. Tales of the fantastic luxuries enjoyed by Calderón Guardia's chosen were always in the air. Stories that told of whole rooms being paneled in mirrors and how a person could mire up in the carpets that spanned the tremendous floors.

At night, Libia permitted the girls to see their novios from seven until nine, provided they sat in full view of the open living room window while she and Luzare sat in the living room. Luzare, however, scowled at the arrangement. First, he didn't trust the boys. Second, times had changed. One didn't feel safe even in his own house. Every day he heard reports of brutalities inflicted by Guardia's bloody '*Brigades de Choque*.' These storm trooper henchmen of Calderón Guardia operated in the true communist sportsmanship. They went in groups of threes or fours with their blackjacks under their coats. Stalking down a free-speaking citizen on a deserted street, they would mob him and leave him half-dead to be picked up by his relatives or friends. But they never dared attack citizens in bunches. The Brigade was never apprehended because the police had also been replaced by Guardia's own men.

One night at the supper table, Margarita heard her father say there was going to be a communist in the streets that night. "Please, Papa," she begged, "Let me go. I want to see one. Please, I would like to go; take me with you."

Luzare gazed hard at his daughter and answered, "I hadn't planned on going, but maybe I will. I have to teach you some way that you must be more careful." After he finished his food, Luzare left the table, went up to his bedroom, and reached to the side of his gild-trimmed clothes cabinet, where he had a special hook for his baton. He drew the cane down and walked back to the hall to wait for Margarita to put on her wrap. Anabella thought the whole expedition silly. She said she would rather stay at home and sit on the porch with Roberto.

The streets of San José were a multitudinous, clamoring rabble that night, packed with a half-drunk mob talking loudly. Soon a parade of men came down Avenida Central bearing torches, and the crowd started shooting torpedoes and screaming. Communists all around Margarita and Luzare were waving their hands and screaming filthy words, vulgar words Margarita had never heard before. Back and forth they called, "*Cortés has a sick liver. He needs to drink Sal Uvina so he won't have bile. Then he won't be sick with bile.*" The rough crowd made up a chant as they screamed, "*The mother of Cortés is a son-of-a-bitch. Cortés is a bastard.*" Margarita became swept up in the maddening throng and screamed out loudly in the next lull, "You devils, you shut up. He is a good man! Don't you say that!"

A big man reeking of guaro, behind her, leaned over and said threateningly, "You had better shut up, little girl. Somebody might hurt you. You never can tell."

Seeing the man too close, Luzare lifted his cane, tapped it against the man's chest, and muttered, "Move on. Move on." The man showed his toothless gums in an animal sneer but moved away. Luzare took Margarita's arm and guided her out of the main crowd, back into the quieter streets.

Margarita kept raving, "Papa, I want to go back and fight. Why do they say those ugly things?"

Luzare shook his bald head. "No, the fighting is not yet. But there will come a day when that bandit thief Guardia will eat his own dung." He tapped his cane hard against the cement, and gripping the gold handle, he snapped his words along with the noise of the cane, "There will come a time. There will come a time."

Luzare's nervousness was heightened by another occurrence not long afterwards. Guardia had tried to place a communist woman as head administrator in one of the main colleges in the city, the Colegio Superior de Señoritas. The students demonstrated and refused to attend school. They were threatened, but still they refused to accept the woman as principal. One day the girls left the school en masse. '*Brigades de Choque*,' with their blackjacks and whips, charged against the defenseless girls and tried to drive them back to the campus, beating and scattering them until they took refuge. That same day, newspapers blazed the news of the infamy perpetrated against the finest of Costa Rican womanhood. After this fracas, the public was so enraged Calderón Guardia passed the word to his brigade to take it easy for a while.

But Luzare stayed uneasy. If his daughters were a little late to the supper table, Luzare no longer sat and beat the table with his knife. He would walk to the door and wait, or he would take his cane and stroll up and down the sidewalk outside. Shortly after the girls in the public college were assaulted, the Maria Auxilia Dora College held an Ejercios Espiritules, three days of intense spiritual concentration. No regular classes were held. The girls were instructed to examine their consciences, make special sacrifices in food and enjoyment, ignore everybody as they came and went to and from school, and strictly obey the rule of silence for the three-day period. The nuns felt this would bring down upon them a spiritual manna to strengthen their beings in this time of stress. The students were also put to the task of composing a general confession, remembering all their offenses against God all their lives, writing them down, and having them ready at confession for the priest to hear.

Luzare worried all the more. He was afraid this spiritual concentration might be construed as a subtle knitting together, a retaliation against Guardia and his politics. During the first two days of the Ejercicios Espirituales, he was home early to see that the girls arrived safely. Over and over, he would inquire, "Did anybody speak to you on the streets? Did anything unusual happen today? Are you sure nobody said anything?" Anabella and Margarita could keep their vows not to eat special foods, especially since they ate lunch at the college and those foods were not provided anyway. The rule of silence was a vow they were compelled to adhere to as long as they were within the college walls, but just as soon as they stepped onto the streetcar, they found various urgent reasons to convey a few words to each other, and by the time they reached home, their tongues were loose at both ends. After two days of anxiety, Luzare decided the girls would stay in the college the whole third day and night and for several days thereafter until the atmosphere seemed less ominous and frightening to him.

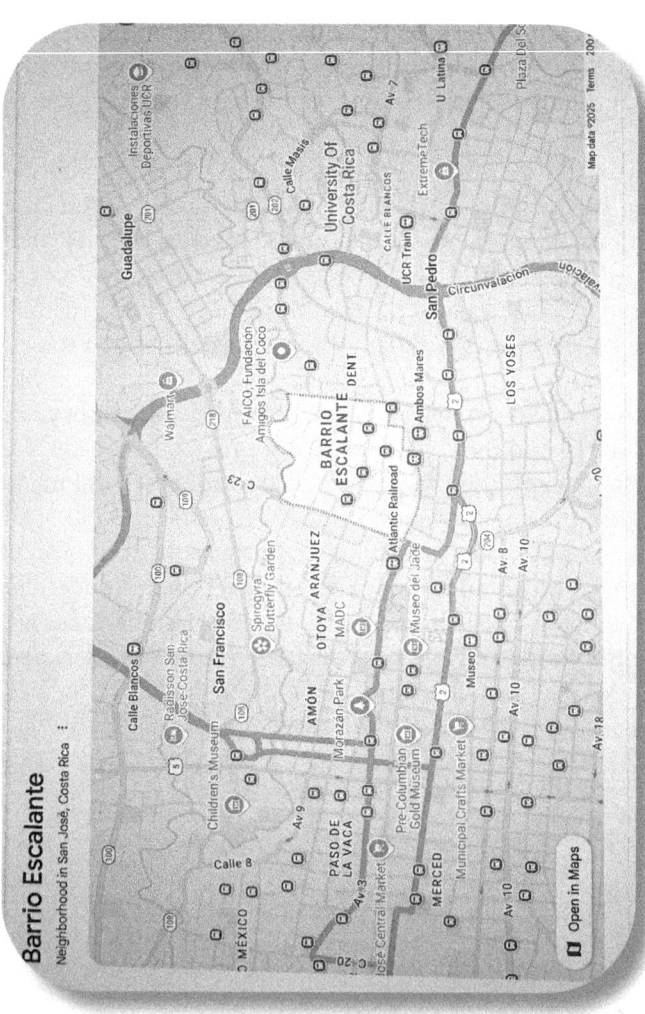

Figure 46

Barrio Escalante
Google Maps

CHAPTER THIRTEEN

Christmas

1942

I N A FEW DAYS, THE Christmas holidays began, and the girls were at home all the time. On Christmas Eve night, the girls begged to be allowed to see their novios in the Parque, but Libia refused, and that night she and Luzare walked Avenida Central with the girls. All the streets were packed and surging with masses of people, confetti was in the air, and balloons were blown and popped. It was a magnificent celebration. At the Parque Central, the crowd was so large the boys walked clockwise in the streets, while the girls strolled counter-clockwise on the sidewalk to form their cuerda. Roberto and Edwin were there, but the crowd swept them on, moving, moving in the opposite direction, and every time Edwin approached Margarita, he was so short he had to jump to be able to catch a momentary glance of her before he was gone again to walk around the entire block. Anabella and Margarita again begged to be coupled with their novios, but Libia shook her head. "You are still too young, even though it is a celebration," she repeated. And that ended it. On the way to the church, they talked to each other about how nice it

Figure 47   Christmas Eve at Parque Central

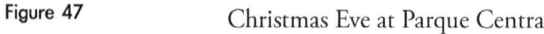

would be if they were allowed to invite their boyfriends to their big supper. But this would never be considered, so they just keep their whispers to themselves. Libia sang gloriously throughout the mass, just as she always had since Margarita and Anabella could remember.

After mass, the family went home. This Christmas supper was a very personal midnight meal and observed in a personal manner throughout the whole country. Each family sat at its board. Even Catalina ate alone in her own house and did not join her daughter's family. The table was loaded with food, including tamales, thick and almost as long as the platter itself. They had been made by Catalina's own hands with her own secret recipe of combining chicken, pork, rice, peas, garbanzos, raisins, pimentos, carrots, and condiments. Each ingredient had been cooked separately, then placed in separate little mounds onto a thin pastry that had been rolled out of fine cornmeal. The pastry had been rolled tightly, then wrapped in banana leaves and tied with a string. After all the rolls had been prepared, they were stuck in a huge vat of boiling water and cooked until they steamed in their own juices. The whole ritual always required three days of preparation and cooking, and each tamale was a meal in itself. There was a fish platter, a chicken dish, coffee, fruit, a great pile of apples, which were a rarity and a high favorite with the family during Christmas, as well as nuts, pears, and grapes. There were homemade sweet breads, pan dulce served with the main dishes, and red wine. Then there was champagne, cakes, and ice cream.

After the family ate, they went into the living room, where Libia had made a portal. She said all during the Christmas season that it seemed more than poor taste; it was sheer mockery to decorate a Christmas tree when there was so much sadness and grief in the world. So she had busied herself preparing the manger scene with '*must go*,' a matted, dried grass, and she formed the hills and ground. With pieces of dyed wood, she constructed the manger. The scene grew more elaborate every day, with every purchase she could find. There was the Mother Mary, the Baby, and Joseph in the open manger; a star hung overhead. Wise men offered their rare gifts as camels stood patiently by. Shepherds knelt with their humble gifts, and all the earth stood in an attitude of worship and adoration. The complete portal covered half the room.

Quietly the family wrapped packages for each other, and then each one placed the packages beside the portal and went to bed. The next day, they unwrapped their gifts and giggled in pleasure. On Christmas Day it was the custom for some of Luzare's country friends to pay him a visit. People whom he had befriended in times past and who had not forgotten to be grateful came bearing their simple gifts. One old fellow always brought a bowl of tomalasado, a baked corn dish. Another brought a sweet corn pudding called mazamorra. And he always complemented his gift with a jug of chicha, a drink brewed by the country people with pineapple or corn juice, crude sugar, water, and levadura, a strong cheese. This concoction they put in earthenware jugs and corked. Then they buried it in the ground for three months until it was properly fermented. Luzare chuckled that it had a kick like a mule's, but he enjoyed it and was never without it during any celebration season.

One night not long after Christmas, the girls asked to be allowed to sit on the curb. Luzare flatly refused, but Libia begged, "Oh, Luzare, you are going to make them nervous, always thinking something is going to happen. Let them be as normal as they can. These are not happy times at best."

Luzare grumbled, "I don't understand why they even bother to ask; they always do what they want to anyway." He took his cane and walked down to his club for a few beers with a friend.

The group of young people sat under the streetlight: Margarita with Edwin, Anabella with Roberto, Nena (the girl who lived across the street), and another girl cousin were gaily singing, talking about movies, and enjoying the night. Suddenly, from across the railroad tracks, a man came running, passing in a quick swish behind them on the sidewalk. They turned to watch the fast-moving figure with a bundle clutched under his arm. Margarita whispered, "I bet he is a thief." Just as the man reached the other corner, he flung the bundle as hard as he could over into some hedge and kept running.

Edwin said, "See, he threw it away. Maybe it's something good if we can find it."

But at that moment a policeman came hurrying up and asked, "Kids, did you see a man running this way? With something in his hand, maybe?"

Edwin pointed and replied, "He just threw something away over there."

The policeman waved the girls back with, "You'd better stay here, girls. This man is dangerous. He has just killed three men." Anabella and Margarita felt themselves break out in goose pimples, then they darted up the walk and into the house.

Figure 48 A

Roberto

Edwin and Roberto went with the policeman to the spot where they thought the package had landed. Beating around in the bushes, they brought out a coat wrapped tightly around a pistol. The sleeve of the coat was bloody. The policeman muttered, "This is proof; now all we have to do is catch him." He straightened up, gave a strong blow on his whistle that pierced the stillness of the night, and in a few minutes six or seven policemen were gathered around him. The first policeman pointed the way down a dark street, and shortly, they were all gone.

Anabella and Margarita stood in their doorway and watched. Their consciences hurt because they had, not long before, watched their cousin take that same dark street, and neither of them had offered her boyfriend to walk home with her. They were both too jealous to let the boys go off alone with another girl, but now they had visions of their cousin lying in a gutter with a bullet through her breast. The policemen rapidly overtook the girl, who was in a loping panic, stopped her, and tried to calm her down. The lead policeman asked the same question he had asked the other young people, and she nodded, '*Yes,*' her eyes starry with terror. The policeman patted her on the shoulder and inquired, "Did you get a good look at him? Did he just pass?"

Again, she nodded. '*Yes.*' But feeling safe at last, she sobbed out, "He just ran by; he said to me, '*If anybody comes and asks for me, say you haven't seen anybody.*' Then she burst into tears and ran the rest of the way into her house. The policeman turned up the side street where she had pointed and soon found their man.

The next morning the newspapers were full of Beltran Cortés, who had confessed to the murder of three men, giving his reason to kill as revenge. Long ago, he said, Doctors Echandi and Moreno Canas had done him a hurt, and he wanted to even the score. The newspapers called it a communistic plot; Beltran Cortés, they said, was but a tool. He murdered because he had been instructed to murder. Dr. Moreno Canas had been a surefire candidate for the next presidential election to be held in February. He stood justly and upright, being the director of San Juan de Dios Hospital. He had fallen at the hands of the communists who wished to remove him from the political picture.

Beltran Cortés, with a maniac's pride, told how he had committed his acts of violence. He said he'd gone to Dr. Echandi's house and rung the doorbell. When the doctor stepped to the door, he shot him in the head three times. Then, he'd gone to Doctor Moreno

Canas' house and done the same thing. He rang the doorbell, and when Doctor Moreno Canas came to answer the ring, he fired and shot him through the head. He said he turned to run but saw a man across the street; being careful to have no witnesses to the deed, he ran across the street and fired on the man, and the man fell.

The newspapers spoke of the shame that such a dastardly act would bring to the country's name. The witness had been an American businessman, influential in trading circles, who'd married into a fine Spanish family. Dr. Moreno Canas, they lamented, could not easily be replaced. He was a man of outstanding character and abilities whose fame was widespread as a physician and was always giving unstintingly of his time. Even the poor in the hills had regarded him as their family doctor. Never had a man been more sorely needed in the affairs of his country. The communists had indeed struck a mighty blow, and sending Beltran Cortés to San Lucas Island for the rest of his life to be sealed in a cement hole, never to see sunlight or visitors again, did not in any way make amends for the loss.

The whole incident struck close to home for Luzare. Not only had his daughters been involved, however inadvertently, but the American was the husband of Diana's sister.

Figures 48 B,C,D

The Police Chase

CHAPTER 13

CHAPTER FOURTEEN

Winds of Change

1944

IN THIS YEAR, 1944, TEODORO Picado Michalski was the official candidate for the National Republican Party, the party of the government, and León Cortés Castro was the opposition candidate. The people knew and loved Cortés, remembering his successful tenure in 1936-40. On February 6th, Cortés held his rally and had his force day. All of San José turned out. From all over the country, followers of León Cortés Castro streamed into the neat capital. It was such a movement of men and a demonstration of loyalty, with the parade lasting four and a half hours. Horses, flags, trucks, and a show, such as had never been seen before by the people, took place. A float showed communists hanging in effigy. More than 25,000 people jammed into Plaza Cleto González Víquez to cheer in a political frenzy. It was a peaceful rally, an opportunity for the people to publicly acknowledge their political affiliation. But on that same day at five o'clock, just as they were disbanding, the communists with blackjacks and knives came into their midst, fighting and assaulting the dispersing mass.

On February 13th, Picado, the official candidate, had his parade of Vanguardia, the left-wing party that supported him, his government employees, and the rabble. Their parade lasted only thirty-five minutes and was a riot of drunks.

On February 20th, the big election was held with a majority of the people voting for León Cortés Castro, their old standby. But when the votes were counted in the presidential house, the totals were changed. Picado was announced as the president. Everybody was wroth and wanted to fight. Mad and wild, they walked the streets begging to fight. But they had no arms. The government had cached away all the ammunition granted from President Roosevelt's aid in the war effort, and nobody could get to it. The communists went about their gangland tactics in earnest, parading the streets in groups of five or six and attacking defenseless citizens. León Cortés made a statement to the people through the newspapers that the life of one of his countrymen meant more to him than the presidency, and he implored them not to resist at this time. From semi-retirement on his farm, Cortés made yet another gesture against communism. He issued a statement saying he'd rescinded his lawyer's diploma and declared he no longer wanted to hold such a title since his barrister friends had shown communistic leanings toward Picado.

His *Gone With the Wind* dynasty over, Calderón Guardia left the country in the hands of feckless Picado and went up to visit his good friend, Somoza, the blotched, freckle-faced dictator of Nicaragua. Otilio Ulate, a strong public-minded citizen and owner of the highly popular newspaper *Diario de Costa Rica*, in retaliation to the presidential fraud, stated that he no longer wanted to exist in this deepest chicanery. He announced that as an act of protestation, he was closing his newspaper. A group of young college students called '*El Centro para el Estudio de los Problemas Nacionales*,' boys of fine families, asked Ulate for the use of his building and machinery. Ulate left the entire newspaper property in their hands and went to London. These students of the *Universidad Nacional de Costa Rica* operated and published the newspaper, setting themselves about the task of offering constructive criticism to the government.

The people looked upon them as sort of political scientists and commonly referred to them as '*Glosteras*' or glamour boys. Picado began his regime as a puppet for the communist chieftain Manuel Mora Valverde, who pulled all the strings, and the "*Brigades de Choque*" was abolished.

One night in early March, the girls sat on the porch with their novios. Libia sat at the piano and played in her desultory manner, with her back to the window. Luzare, however, never trusted the arrangement and always sat over near the window listening to the radio or reading the paper. He had always leaned near the window so he could hear his daughters' voices. He always sat fully dressed with every hole buttoned on his vest, and every now and then he would glance out onto the porch. Once when Libia accused him of not trusting his daughters, he responded, "Even between saints, a strong wall!" The girls were being unusually quiet tonight, and Luzare finally got up very casually and stepped through the hall to the porch. Both girls were completely enraptured in their young lovers' kisses. Luzare raged and swore, "*CARAMBA!*" The boys vaulted over the balustrades into the rose bushes as he roared, "Get out of here, get off my property!" They blundered off into the dark. At the front door, Luzare bellowed, "And don't ever come near this house again!" The boys were long gone, but Luzare was still wild. He got out his shotgun and trod up and down the front walk, waving it about and cursing. Margarita and Anabella stood trembling inside, leaning against the hall wall, awaiting the ugly horsewhip, which seemed to them inevitable.

But when their father came and stood before them, he was more like a bald Jeremiah, with a face grieved over a Jerusalem that had been laid asunder by sin. He threw his heavy shoulders back, looped his hands behind his back, and his penetrating eyes pierced down into their pleasure-stricken eyes before he spoke. He shook his head regretfully. These are broken cisterns that would hold no water. Lamentingly he seemed to be thinking like the old prophet, "I planted noble seeds, but these are degenerate plants of a strange vine." His eyes clouded over in sadness as he searched sorrowfully into the deepest pits of their shameful beings. Then he spoke quietly, all the while shaking his head, "These are not señoritas who behave in such a manner." He turned on his heels, went into his bedroom, and closed the door.

Thus chastened, the girls sometimes met the boys and walked home with them in the afternoons, but the boys did not come near the house at night. Rafael was on the corner of Parque Central nearly every afternoon to catch a glimpse of Anabella as she came swishing up the street from school.

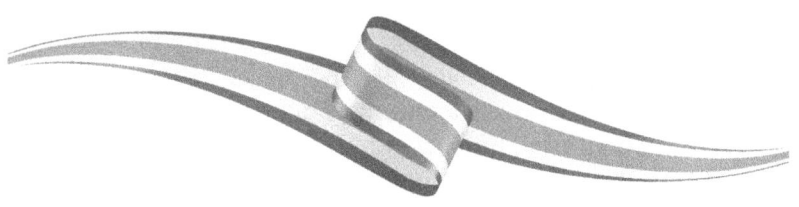

Figure 48 E

Costa Rica Flag Ribbon
https://www.istockphoto.com/vector/costa-rica-flag-ribbon-set-vector-stock-illustration-gm1337195075-418165107?clarity=false
iStock.com/PeterPencil

CHAPTER FIFTEEN
Sacred Heart College, Cartago
1944

W ITH HER ALL-IMPORTANT FIFTEENTH BIRTHDAY approaching, Margarita besought her mother to broach her father on the subject of her party. Libia called her aside the next afternoon and imparted the news that Luzare had consented; custom also prevailing heavily upon him, he could not easily refuse.

On the momentous April day, the young people busied themselves since early morning. Edwin and Roberto beat eggs for the cakes while Margarita and Anabella wove ropes of Margarita Roses to be garlanded throughout the corridors and porch. They wreathed the entrance to the billiard room and made it stage-like with the wide folding doors pushed back. Margarita ran excitedly about, talking of musical selections for the orchestra or inquiring if her dress was ready yet. Libia brought a seamstress from the store to the house so she could personally supervise every stitch. At seven-thirty, the house was heavy with the aroma of exotic flowers, and enormous jardinières of floral exhibitions lined the hall and back into the patio.

Margarita stood before her mirror arranging her mother's cream-colored, lace wedding veil about her hair. She touched the front of her dress, uncomfortably aware of the low, rounded back she was wearing for the first time. At eight o'clock the house was overrun with young people, and as the orchestra struck up the lead-out number, Margarita, flustered, cast about for Edwin. But rather than hold up the procession, she started walking solemnly across the wide space with Roberto. She walked in her usual boyish stride, her hands swinging at her side. Libia slipped on ahead, and as the couple passed through the dining room door, she looped Margarita's hand through Roberto's arm. Out the side dining room door onto the side porch, around the front porch, and back down the mosaic hall they came, and then halted like a cat that has caught its tail. They waited until the floor had been cleared and the orchestra drifted into a waltz. Edwin, waiting by the hall wall, led her onto the floor and glided her about. But she stopped halfway through, overcome with timidity, and called the others to join her on the floor.

The stone fountain of the patio sparkled with colored lights reflecting on the cascading waters. The lower patio was decked with coffee and banana leaves, colored lights, deck chairs, tables, and candles. Late in the evening, Luzare, always suspicious of dark corners, poked about in the garages and surprised young couples in their embraces.

After the party was over, Margarita, dreamy with happiness, heard her father in the next room rumbling to Libia, "It's your fault, arranging the tables too far from the house. You might have known this would happen. Won't you ever learn?" Libia lay in her bed and shuddered; her bête noire, the many-headed monster, again! So insidiously and relentlessly did it snake its way through her life! And where did two hundred people come from when she had only invited a hundred? Even though Luzare's preaching, "*Man is fire, woman is kindling, and the devil comes and fans!*" was tiresome, the truth was there. There were elements in youth with which she was at a loss to cope. She recalled couples, unobserved by their mothers, as they had broken away from the picnic crowds and drifted arm in arm into the shadowy darkness. She always glanced about with

The Fifteenth Birthday Party

Figure 49

frightened eyes until she was assured her daughters were there safe. *"Oh God! How to keep her little girls good, as good as they were at that moment?"*

One afternoon shortly after her birthday, Margarita, still basking in the glow of her party, burst into her father's office. A tall Jamaican woman was leaning over his desk, her glittering eyes hard, like an eagle on its prey, her décolletage dress revealing half her high, tight breasts. The woman turned her sharp, chiseled features upon the

young girl. Luzare's voice was prodding her with, "Margarita, you must thank the newspaper lady for printing such a nice account of your party. Your picture was so big too, wasn't it?"

Margarita hung her head in a way she knew irritated her father and flashed beams of hate at the woman. This was the same face she had seen in an automobile at the side of her house on the horrible day when her Papa had slapped her Mama. She turned and, without answering, ran out of the store.

In three months, Luzare made arrangements for the girls to attend Sacred Heart College in Cartago. Libia had no objections since Cartago was only twelve miles away and the Sisters there would certainly keep the girls safe. Margarita felt this was her father's revenge for her rudeness to the woman, and she sulked through her preparations to go. She had an enlargement made of Edwin's snapshot and pledged her eternal love to him.

Figure 50   Luzare's Mistress

And now, after being in the school for three months, Margarita had not adjusted herself to waking at 5:30 to the tinkling of a bell, gripping the covers high with one hand while she held her head under and tried to pull on her panties, her long, thick, black stockings, and elastics. She was forever losing one of the stockings in the bed or sitting on the elastics. Now and then she would stick out her arm to fish more clothes from her hair. All the while she sleepily mummered the rosary that the Sister had often emphasized was dedicated to the joyful, sorrowful, and glorious mysteries. Following the rosary came the response to the litanies, the Oraciones de la mañana, led by the nun. At the completion of the litanies, the girls lined up for the laboratory, each girl with her coarse white shower gown over her left arm. This was a feat Margarita had not yet mastered. The gown stuck to her wet body and felt ugly. She always locked the cabinet door and enjoyed the deliciousness of the water on her flesh. Luckily, she had always escaped detection. Upon finishing her shower, she always wet the gown thoroughly, put back on her clothes, opened the door, and walked out, holding the wet gown. At the completion of their ablutions, the girls formed their line again, all of them dressed in their long-sleeved, cream-colored blouses and dark blue, cashmere skirts. Their hair was brushed neatly back, their faces scrubbed and shining, and with their wet shower gowns over their arms, they filed back into the dormitory, made their beds, and formed their line again to go down into the dining room. Margarita, being rather tall, stood near the back of the line.

At this time of the morning, since the Dora incident, Margarita, in some inexplicable way, always felt guilty and was always restless to get out of the dormitory, down the steps, and into the dining room, just to get away from remembering. All because of Dora. Dora was a hunchback concha, loose-walking in her long, dark uniform, an orphan who had been in the school all her life doing servant's work for her keep. A lowly person she was, barefoot, but almost pretty because of her beautiful blue eyes looking out, sad and misty, upon the world. Her twenty-six years had held nothing but drudgery.

Margarita had first begun to notice the servant girl because she always gave her extra big helpings on her plate. To show the servant she appreciated the attention, Margarita rummaged about and brought an old pair of Oxfords from her drawer, which she took down to the kitchen and gave to Dora. Since that time, Dora had not stopped doing favors for her. Dora did the daily marketing for the school and always brought back a flower for Margarita.

Because the girls were only given changes of undergarments twice a week, on Thursdays and Sundays, and a change of uniform only once a week, regardless of how wrinkled or mussed they became from handling under the covers, one day Margarita asked Dora to bring her an extra pair of panties. She explained to the servant that she didn't like putting on the same underwear she had just taken off.

The next morning, while Margarita was busy with her prayers and dressing with her head in the cave of covers, she was surprised to feel a tug on the sheet. Then the cover was pulled back, and standing above her was Dora, who, with a quick motion, slid the garment from her apron bib under the cover to Margarita. But instead of giving back the sheet to Margarita, who was straining to cover herself, the girl just stood and kept whispering, "You look nice like that. You look so beautiful."

From the middle of the floor, Sister Carnación's eyes witnessed the scene. She stopped her praying and called sharply to the servant, "Dora, what are you doing in here? You don't have any business slipping in here; go back to the kitchen." Dora hunched her loose-jointed way out. The nun called to Margarita, "Come, Margarita, show me what Dora gave you." Margarita handed over the panties, and when the Sister saw the nature of the garment, her whole face was inflamed with anger, but in a controlled, terse voice she scolded, "Margarita, wait until you are supposed to change. Don't ever ask for extra changes again." And looking around to the other girls, she admonished, "Let this be a lesson to everybody. You never ask for anything from the servants." After the girls lined up and started out to breakfast, Sister Carnación laid her hand on Margarita's shoulder and drew her from the line. She spoke in a low, private voice, "Margarita, what I am going to tell you, you probably won't understand. But you see," and her eyes searched all around for the

Figure 51

The Basilica of Our Lady of the Angels and its surrounding neighborhoods on a cold winter morning in Cartago, Costa Rica. (Present Day) iStock.com/ Dennis Alberto Gonzalez Salas https://www.istockphoto.com/photo/aerial-shot-of-a-cityscape-of-the-basilica-of-our-lady-of-the-angels-and-its-gm2187780757-606341313?clarity=false words, then she went on, "you see, there are girls who like only girls. And there are boys who crave only the company of boys. This is not good because these people are not normal. Such a girl as Dora can do bad things to you. It is better for you not to have anything more to do with her. Now you may go down to breakfast." Margarita blinked uncomprehendingly, pondered it briefly on her way downstairs, but unable to solve such an intricate riddle, she soon gave it up.

However, she heeded the sister's admonition. She had stayed away from the kitchen and Dora. No matter how hungry she got in the afternoons for bread or cookies, which Dora always kept in her big pocket for her, she didn't go near the servant. One day, however, Dora chanced upon Margarita leaving the dining room alone. She pulled the young girl out into the storage room, and staring into Margarita's eyes, she said wistfully, "You don't ever come to see me anymore. I can't come to see you. I am forbidden. I would be put out on the street, and then where would I go? I have no home; nobody loves me. But you don't care. Do you understand that I love you, Margarita, that I am in love with you?" The servant patted the girl's arms and started stroking them upward. Cold chill bumps rose on Margarita's arm. She smiled uncertainly and edged her way back out, promising to come the next morning to get her flower, which Dora would bring back from her marketing. But from that day on, fear kept her away from the servant, even though she did not really understand why she was scared.

And the nuns did not have to scold her to take the flower from her hair. It had even become a habit for one of the nuns to say, even without lifting her head from her desk, "Margarita, take the flower from your hair and put it in the chapel for the Virgin."

Ever since the Dora incident, whenever Margarita lined up to go down to breakfast, she somehow always expected the nun to reach out and pull her from the line. She always half expected it. She did not know why. And as she went down the stairs, she always wondered why anyone could think evil of such a simple girl as Dora—such a kind, hardworking girl, a girl so willing to do favors.

In the dining room, the sun was beginning to reflect on the long, bare tables as the girls stood before their places at the benches, their heads bent, thanking God for their food. The great Red Heart in the middle of the wall seemed to perpetually shed its sacred blood. Sister Rosario clapped the palm of her hand on the table, and the girls sat down to the meager, humble fare of coffee, an orange peeled and stuck by the fork and eaten as if it were on a stick, and two pieces of heavy, coarse bread. Luzare always thoughtfully provided his daughters with butter and honey to heighten their provender, and even Sister Rosario, with her small, white face and large, fawn eyes, always smiled gratefully when the honey reached the head of the table. After breakfast there was another pause of grace for the bounty just received, and Margarita always thought ruefully, "They are thanking God for Papa's honey." The girls then lined up and passed into the hall, gathered their veils from their cabinets, and went to mass. Margarita, heretofore conscientious in her devotions, these days found her thoughts straying to Edwin, and she wondered if he missed her too. As she prayed, she absently plucked at the string under her neck that secured her veil. Over and over she wondered if Edwin could come Sunday with her mother.

The sight of greenery before the altar brought fresh remembrance of the day when Edwin had climbed the tallest tangerine tree. His puerile figure intrepidly walked along the limbs, tossing down the yellow balls to the waiting hands of the youngsters. One of them yelled, "Edwin, throw it to the girl you like the most." And he threw the tangerine to her. She recalled how she had just stood there, her mouth open, so surprised she let the tangerine fall through her fingers, and the others taunted her for her shyness.

After mass the girls filed to their cabinets, hung up their veils, and then went into the long, white-coated dormitory to tidy up the room. Afterwards there was a brief rest period in which, encircled by her friends, Margarita would hold them spellbound with accounts of her romantic career. They were especially fond of the tale in which, after she had refused to allow Edwin to kiss her, he acquired another girlfriend to make her jealous. One day while playing ring, it became her penalty to kiss the one she loved the most. She leaned over Edwin and smacked him quickly and whispered, "I like it now.

I won't be mad anymore."

But he flaunted her affection and remarked tartly, "What changed your mind? But I don't care. I have another girl now I like just as well."

At this point, all the girls sighed dolefully over the unrequited love. "It is true," they said, "virtue is indeed its own reward." Often the girls would be so enthralled with Margarita's amorous adventures they would not hear the soft-padded nun as she approached, and it was only the younger ones loitering nearby within listening distance who gave coughing warnings. The entrepreneur would then switch the subject by altering the tone of her voice and would not be caught. In line for the classes, Anabella was always petulant with Margarita. She could never rouse herself an audience no matter how often she mentioned Roberto's name. Outside the classroom, the girls would wait respectfully until the Sister had seated herself and signaled them with a hand clap before they advanced to their desks and then stood beside their desks for a moment of prayer. Margarita would be of a devout and sincerely concentrated spirit as long as she had her eyes closed, but she would no sooner be seated than she would be engaging the nearby girls in quick glimpses of the tilt-nosed vestige of Edwin, which she had pulled from the leaves of her book. Edwin was doubly illustrious, attractive because he was an 'older' boy and notably so because he was an American.

Geography, History, Philosophy, Physics, Chemistry, Arithmetic, Astronomy, Latin, French, and Home Economics: they ran the formidable list of eighteen subjects until they completed their cycle of hour-long classes during the week. After the first three hours every morning, the bell tinkled for a rest period in which Margarita would dash by her cabinet, toss her books in, and head for the lavatory. There she would draw forth her bottle of castor oil she always kept well secreted behind the toothpaste. She would then proceed to anoint her eyelids, heedful to coax the lashes upward with every application, always lamenting the absence of a mirror at this time because she couldn't tell by feeling if her lashes were increasing in their growth. Then she would carefully stroke her brows with her pencil, extending their lines as prescribed by the latest movie magazine she'd read before leaving home. After this secret ritual, she would whisk back through the hall and motion her cronies into a classroom with her. In a moment's time she could depict on the blackboard an enormous map of the hand with spatulated fingers. While the girls waited with their heads averted, she would print on each finger: LOVE, HATE, MARRIAGE, KISS, ADORE. Each girl, without looking, was allowed to choose the finger of her future. Upon turning, the girls always stifled an amazed shriek, but they thoroughly enjoyed Margarita's little game of prognostication because each day she changed the future of each finger.

After one more long hour of class, Margarita spent the following thirty-minute rest period in the chapel. Having gotten her morning's restlessness and mischief-making out of her system, she always felt as if she had an empty stomach, as if she were the most miserable of sinners and deserving of the most terrible of punishments. But at the thought of retribution from on high, her heart contracted in fear, and she would read voraciously all the religious tracts on hand. Afterwards she would line up for lunch. Lunch was never gleefully anticipated because of its drab sameness. Meals here were to sustain life, not to placate whimsy. Rice with onions, black beans (always black beans), a small piece of meat, which was usually steak, potatoes, and platanos. Thus usually ran the menu of the repast. Followed by a few minutes of relaxation after the noon meal and then mass again. Sewing always climaxed the three-hour afternoon lessons. The girls at this time of day felt giddy and in a playful, half-free mood. One day of the week was spent mending their wearing apparel; on the other days, the nun liberally granted that the girls might sew on whatever they chose. Most of the girls pulled and plucked with infinite patience, extracting strings in preparation for hemstitching luncheon cloths. Even Anabella thought kindly of her mother and was painstakingly whipping lace to the square of linen for a handkerchief. Except Margarita, and here the black-robed Sister always contained her consternation as she watched Margarita pull forth the fuchsia crepe material, which she had cut out into a snug-fitting dinner dress to be sewn with gold sequins. After the class, the girls again hustled for their veils for rosary at five, and then they went up to the lavatory to wash up for their last meal of the day. After supper they were allowed a brief moment to let their food settle, and at six-thirty they went into the chapel for Oraciones de la noche, to bid goodnight to God. After their prayers they enjoyed a twilight playtime, running, playing, and talking. At seven o'clock they retreated to the dormitory, brushed their teeth, washed their faces, undressed under the covers, spread their blouses and skirts upon their chairs, slipped their large white gowns over their heads, and said their prayers. At seven-thirty, their day was over, and Sister Carnación bade them goodnight and switched off the lights.

One day after the lunch rest period, Margarita and Flora, the oldest and tallest girl in the school, were throwing a lemon Flora had "borrowed" from the kitchen. Sister Rosario apprehended them in their sport and held forth her hand, requesting, "Girls, give me the lemon."

Refreshed with lunch, Margarita was her impish self again, so she answered, "No, no, Sister, catch it if you can," as she volleyed it over the small nun's head to Flora. Caught up in the spirit of the play, Sister Rosario leaned and jumped about for the lemon. Suddenly Mother Superior was in their midst, and Sister Rosario, standing between the two younger girls, looked as helpless, as guilty, and as contrite as they.

Figure 52 A

Sister Rosario

Figure 52 B

The plaza and Basilica of Our Lady of the Angels in the city of Cartago, Costa Rica (circa mid 19th century). Vintage etching circa mid 19th century. iStock.com/powerofforever. https://www.istockphoto.com/vector/plaza-and-basilica-of-our-lady-of-the-angels-in-cartago-costa-rica-gm106140187 6-283739421

CHAPTER SIXTEEN

Irazú

1910

Margarita and Anabella always stood self-conscious and important when Libia looked them over on her thirty-minute Sunday visits. Victor, who always drove his parents to their visit, grinned amiably, and Luzare sat, puffing short-winded, and counted his vest buttons. He interrupted the conversation periodically to ask, "Apple Cheeks, are you getting enough to eat?" This Sunday Margarita could not repress her disappointment. Edwin had not come.

Libia cradled the young chin in the palm of her hand as she consoled, "Margarita, I'm sorry too that Edwin couldn't come, even though it would've meant I would have had to lie about him to the Sisters. But you see, Baby, he left this very week to go to the United States to fight. Aren't you proud he's going to be a brave soldier?"

Margarita sobbed brokenheartedly, "Oh, Mama, he is gone. And I didn't get to tell him '*goodbye*.' Please, please write to him for me and send him a gift. Some memories he can keep forever, so he won't forget me. Get him a medallia, a medal of St. José." Libia promised and wondered fleetingly how one went about composing a love letter. This would be her first one.

Libia always looked forward to the Sunday afternoon drives after her little visits with her daughters. Her sentiments for Cartago were deep because she had been born here. Cartago was but a small San José with low-built, neat, fortress-like concrete buildings, reinforced for shock. She leaned back and half-closed her eyes, reminiscing. This was not the Cartago she had known and loved, for that Cartago was no more. It had forever lost its flavor, its simplicity, and its piety, and it was hard to even imagine that this new-looking place was actually the oldest city in the country and, until 1838, had been its capital. Founded by Juan Vázquez de Coronado, the first governor of Costa Rica in 1563, who had been called the gentle conquistador, a visionary who could see the land peopled by peaceful homesteaders from the mother country, Spain. Cartago would be a Spanish

Figure 53

Juan Vazquez de Coronado statue, Central Park, San Josè, Republic of Costa Rica
Paolo Reda - REDA &CO/Alamy Stock Photo

Figure 54

Park inside the ruins of an old church destroyed by earthquake, in the historic center of the city of Carrago. iStock.com/ Salvador Aznar

https://www.istockphoto.com/photo/park-and-ruins-of-cartago-in-costa-rica-gm1440772311-480662074?clarity=false city, with its settlers, livestock, and European vegetables. So, just as Coronado envisioned, the city had survived, and Spanish art, culture, tradition, and religion had perpetuated, with the old city nestled like a trembling bird against the foothills of the volcano Irazú.

On her kaleidoscope of memories, Libia could see a little girl skipping up and down its smoothly worn cobbled streets, peaceful streets they had been with grass growing on either side. The little girls played with her brother, peered into the dark caverns of the adobe shops, and paused to watch the blacksmith with his forge and chimney, while a horse stood patiently waiting, whisking away the pesky flies with his tail. Old Colonial houses with their deeply curved, red tiles shining in the sun bordered the streets. Her own spacious home stood behind its grille gate, where one could look into an inconscient garden with its twisted blossoming vines, smell the orange trees, and look upon the quaint rock fountain. The heavy door stood with its strange escutcheon shield. Libia's eyes could see all these pictures; they were still vivid and colorful in her mind. This had been a gentle, somnolent city, drowsy and graceful for a little girl to skip and hop only on the pink tile of the walks while her

Figure 55   Irazú Eruption

brother hopped only on the blue, as away they would go out to the edge of the town where the stone walls were always blooming with a profusion of wild roses and blackberries growing and entwined in the stones, and the fragrant-smelling maize fields ladened the air with their sweet, fresh perfumes. Here, she and her brother frolicked, climbed, and ran the length of the walls, then turned, half-losing their balance, and ran back along the wall again.

That late afternoon of May 4, 1910, she and her little friend had been playing jacks in front of her door. Her mother called her in for a wrap. She could still hear the impelling voice: "Libia, come get a wrap; the air is too chilly. It's getting too late for you to be out anyway; come in." She had come dragging, though she hadn't wanted to come at all; however, she came because she could never disobey her mother's insistent voice. Just as she stepped into the corridor, the tiles beneath her feet started making crazy patterns. In the twinkling of an eye, her mother jerked her out of the hall, back to the patio, and into the rancho, which had been built for this moment. Libia remembered how the earth had shuddered in one violent convulsion and trembled with the detonations of a gigantic crack of thunder that filled and rolled in the sky. There were only a few seconds while chaos prevailed outside. Inside the bamboo rancho with her mother

Figure 56   Irazú Eruption

and her sisters, she crouched while the flexible cane structure swayed and cracked and banana leaves fell on their heads. They were tossed up and down and tumbled over each other. And then there came the deathly silence, save for the incessant roar. They waited, crouched and huddled together, straining their ears, listening, listening, and trying to hear beyond the roar. Finally, Catalina straightened up, smoothed out her skirt with a fastidious pat, and stepped out of the bamboo rancho. Libia could still remember how tightly she clutched her mother's skirts as they pushed their way out. All the children were clinging bewilderedly to Catalina, who lifted her face to survey the black sky heavy with ashes. Before them, their beautiful home with its massive protective walls lay in smashed pieces of brick and carmine tiles. Working their way out into the stifling hot air, into the twilight of smoke and cinders, they beheld their front wall as it had been hurled with its terrible weight and impact down upon the little friend whose small hand was sticking up through the rubble, still holding the jack ball.

One tremble and crash had leveled the city. It was no more. Sodom and Gomorrah had not been more utterly desolate, more wholly leveled. It was a deserted city, buried under its stones and the dust of its own abodes, a complete disaster. Not a building in the city stood but the unfinished cathedral. Andrew Carnegie's Peace Palace, almost completed, lay in ruins. Here and there, the greedy earth had opened and sucked in its victims, its red, gluttonous mouth not bothering to completely swallow them. A head, an arm, or a leg was left grotesquely dangling in the cracks. Dante's visit to hell had not been more horrendous. And the venomous, boiling mud crept along, feeling its way, scorching and searing and burning, licking its tongue on its destiny of devastation.

In this limbo, people walked about with hypnotic stares, crazed by suffering and anxiety, numb with a horror that was too terrifying for human beings to comprehend. The very air was heavy with the shrieks of the shocked and the moans of the dying. In the darkness, people were groping over debris, listening to the cries of the entombed, and clawing with bare hands at the earth to release the imprisoned. Many were trapped themselves by falling

Figure 57

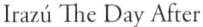

Irazú The Day After

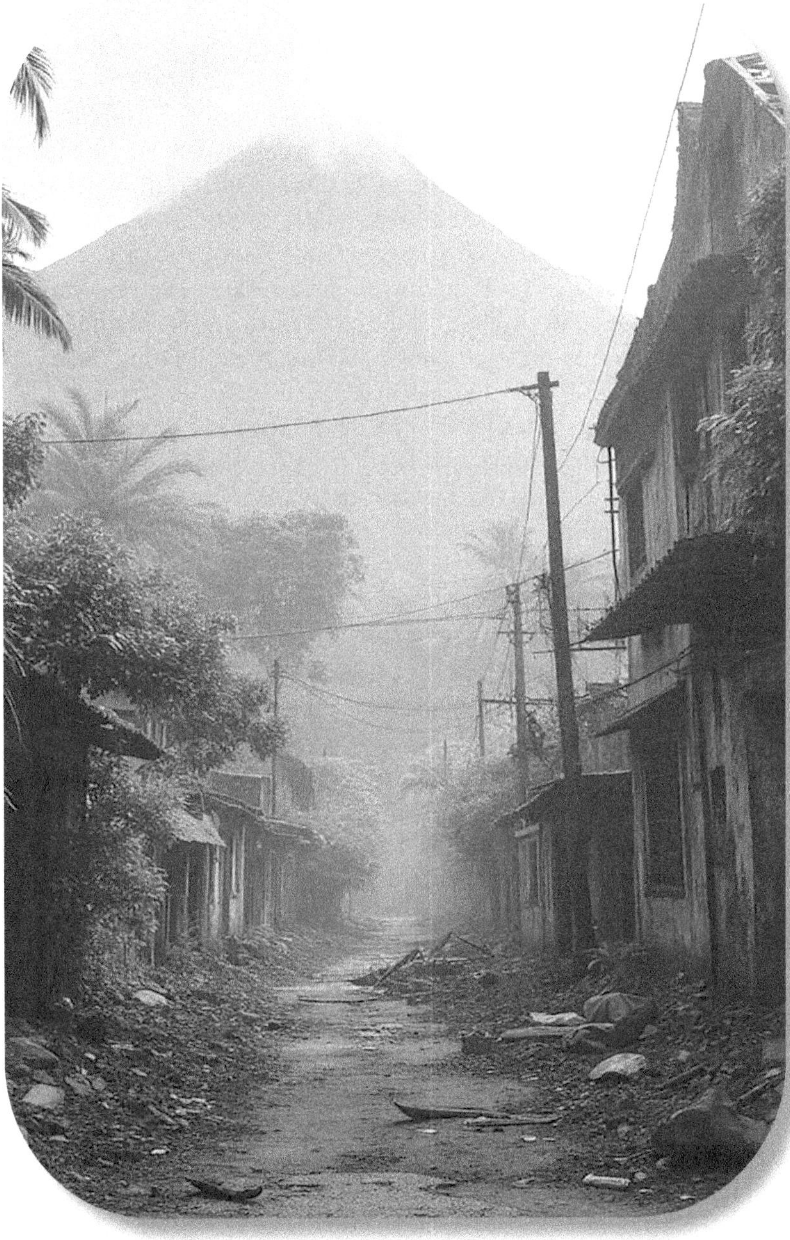

walls, or in the darkness they stumbled into earth cracks. Through the blackened fog, every face that met another peered hopefully, pitifully, seeking their missing ones. Through the black dust and ashes toward where the bakery had stood, Catalina saw a small dark figure advancing out of the twilight of smoke. Little José had been sent to buy a loaf of bread. So heavy was the air he almost passed before she recognized him. Catalina clasped him in her arms, sobbing, thanking God that all her children were now safe.

The little boy struggled for coherence, but babbling, he kept repeating, "Mama, as I was buying the bread, I kept feeling someone pull me by the coat, pulling, pulling me until I was outside in the street. But when I looked, there was no one there. Mama, there was nobody there!"

Huddled together, they looked up through the blackened haze to Irazú, a boiling, seething mass that lit the sky an eerie red and puffed foamlike clouds, like monstrous petaled blossoms, unfolding and unfurling their wreaths into the very heavens in wondrous splendor and beauty.

Felipe lay in front of where his dental office had stood, his eyes staring, a vacant, imbecilic expression on his face. They led him back to his backyard, and there he sat, motionless, apathetic, and listless.

The next morning, in the clearness of the day, horror was even more terrible to behold. Rescue parties were organized to search for the dead and to carry them to the plaza for identification, a scene too grisly to ever forget: the carts with their loads of torn and dismembered bodies while loved ones stood by, sometimes unable to identify their unrecognizable dead.

In the next few days, more than 1,500 bodies were pulled out of the shattered ruins, victims of the monster. Irazú had not given them a chance. Hundreds of injured went about looking for their missing ones, and the park was packed with the seriously wounded and the dying begging for care. The railroads lay twisted and distorted, and no trains could be sent to San José.

Catalina, with Libia trailing after her, went tirelessly from tent to tent, nursing the sick and injured and aiding the priest as he gave unction to the dying. She stood by the grieved at the burial of their dead, and each time she gave thanks to God again for sparing her own family.

However, it had not been mere accident that Catalina and her family were saved, for Catalina had heard the voice of God as clearly as she could hear her own voice as the voice had spoken, "*Build a rancho in your patio, Catalina, for the day of destruction is upon you.*" And when she picked up the Bible, it always fell open to the same place. Her eyes always fell upon the sentence, '*And desolation shall come upon thee, which thou shalt not know.*'

Catalina called her servants to her and instructed them to cut down the heavy trees around the patio and leave it bare. In the center she wanted them to build for her a rancho. A small shelter she wanted, made of bamboo cane tied with hemp and covered with banana leaves. The servants did as they were bidden, but the neighbors looked on and laughed with faces like those who jeered Noah's building of the ark. They remarked, "Catalina, if you want a rancho, why don't you go to the country?"

But she only held her chin up more firmly and responded, "Do you think I'm an animal or a peon that I should go to the fields? I will not leave my house. But I will be prepared."

With the word '*prepared*,' the neighbors laughed all the more scathingly and said, "Prepared? Do you call a few canes erected against old Irazú being 'prepared'?"

But Catalina had gone her way, never ceasing to pray that she would have time to get her family into the rancho. For, from the beginning of the year, disaster seemed inevitable to her. The whole four months were full of perturbation, a strange, unnatural beginning when, on January 25, Poás, up past Alajuela, became strongly activated. Gray smoke rose from the crater in thick columns like giant trees flourishing their boughs into the heavens, a beautiful and frightening spectacle. Everybody was struck with fear at its rumble. Ashes fell like rain and lay like gray, powdery salt over all the sidewalks and the streets, over the floors and in every crevice of the houses, strong as potash, wilting and killing plants and sickening animals in the fields. People from that time went about their business with smoke burning their eyes and a sour, acidic taste in their mouths. Catalina could no longer allow her clothes to be hung outside on the line, for the ashes ate holes in them even as they hung. And her gorgeous begonias, geraniums, gladiolas, and bushes of dahlias wilted and hung their heads, too heavy with the fine powder to stand upright.

But to Catalina, even the heavens portended ominously. Halley's Comet had shone brightly in the sky night after night, and the weather was terribly hot in the daytime and cold, too cold, at night. Then, right above their heads, Irazú awakened on the morning of the thirteenth of April and stirred, trembled, and groaned as if in answer to Poás. From that time on, Irazú and Poás talked in grumbling, roaring voices. In the headquarters of the president's house in San José, scientists hovered anxiously over the seismograph that was recording the tremblings and movements.

And on that night of May 4th, that night of death and ashes, the glass plate of the seismograph jumped from its place and broke into two pieces, writing the end to old Irazú's threats. In the sky above Cartago that night, Halley's Comet shone with unaccustomed brightness, and its tail sparkled and glowed blood red. So they, the family of de la Esprilla, moved to San José, departing Cartago, after having abided there as a continuous family since 1573.

As Libia rode along on her quiet Sunday afternoon outings, she tried to remember only the sweeter days, the days when she and her little twin brother, José, had played their little games and talked of their wonderful futures. José always wanted to be a doctor, but he had grown up inattentive to his books and given to wandering about in idle daydreams. Once, he received a kick from a horse he was trying to saddle, and people often whispered that it had done something to his mind. But Libia, who understood her brother, knew that José had always been the same. José would always remain childlike and simple in a world that baffled him.

Figure 58 A

Irazú Eruption

Figure 58 B

CHAPTER SEVENTEEN

La Negrita

1944-1945

O N SUNDAYS AFTER MASS, THE dormitory girls of Sacred Heart were shepherded across town and out into the Potrero, the government-owned cow pastures. Here the girls spread their cold lunch, ran, played tag, and talked. Margarita told them of Edwin's letters to her, transferred verbally through her mother. Always they were sorrowful and full of devotion.

For the past few Sundays, Sister Rosario had observed Margarita and her little clique sitting apart from the others, interested in their own little stories. One Sunday Sister Rosario seated herself in the shade of a wide-spreading tree and called the girls to her.

"Girls," she said quietly, "would you like to hear a beautiful story?" All the girls nodded, not really knowing what to expect. "The story I am going to tell you happened right here in the city of Cartago, and it is true. It's a wonderful story of purity and holy thinking. This took place a long time ago in the 18th century when Cartago was not as free and as open as it is now. At the time this happened, there were zones in the city through which Indians were not permitted to pass.

And this was awful, because the girl I am going to tell you about was young, no older than you are, and lovely, but she was just an impoverished Indian. Her name was La Negrita, and she lived back in a miserable hut in the woods with her family. One day as she was going about through the woods gathering sticks for the fire, she was seen by a very wealthy boy whose family was in governmental circles. From that day on, Carlos often came to see the strange, beautiful girl, and although La Negrita loved Carlos, she was shy and afraid of the noble young man since she knew such love could never be fulfilled in matrimony. She was lowly and despised while he was high, yet she loved him. On this particular day, as she was going along, she noticed on a rock a brilliant light that shone more brightly than the sun. She was strangely attracted to the rock and stepped closer to look. There on the rock she found a little image, dark like herself. She picked up the little thing and cradled it in her arms and said, "Oh, little doll! I will take you home with me so you won't be lonesome out here by yourself in the woods." She held and fondled the small statue until Carlos came, and she showed it to him. Her face was bright with happiness as she explained, "Look, Niño Carlos, see what I have found, a poor little doll, all alone."

She wrapped the doll in her shawl, took it home, and there she carefully tucked her in a trunk. The next morning she eagerly opened the trunk to look again at her doll, but what she sought was not there. Distraught and crying, she looked all about the miserable little hut but could not find her doll. Then she ran through the woods again to the spot where she first found the little shape, hoping she could find it again. The light was shining just as brilliantly above the rock as before, and she stepped forward quickly and snatched up the image that was again lying there on the shelf of the rock. Over and over, she exclaimed as she hugged the doll to her breast, "I have found my little doll! Why did you come back to the rock? I love you. Don't leave me again. I hope you will never slip away again." This time when she

Figure 59

La Negrita

reached her hut, she wrapped the doll carefully and put it at the very bottom of the trunk, then locked the box and put the key in her blouse, saying, "Now you are safe. You will stay and wait for me until I come back from my work." As she was busy gathering sticks in the forest, she met Carlos. Bursting with the news, she told him, "Niño Carlos, my little doll, remember my little doll? I took her home, but she came back again all by herself. I put her in the trunk, but when I looked for her, she was gone. Then I came back here, and I found her again."

The boy listened and knew that, indeed, some strange phenomena had taken place. He said to her, "Go look again for your doll and see if she is there." The girl ran through the woods to her house. She took the key, opened the trunk, and behold! The doll was gone. In tears she ran back to Carlos, who said, "Don't cry. Go to the priest. He can help you."

The girl ran with her story to the kind old monk who listened and spoke, "Go again, seek the doll where you found her before. Perhaps she will be there again." And for the third time, there was a light above the rock, glowing and shimmering. As the young girl picked up the black shape, she looked curiously at the key that she drew from her blouse.

She whispered, "Oh, why did you leave? How did you come here all by yourself? Now that I look at you, I can see that you're a little angel, and I believe you belong to God. But I don't want you to go away again! I love you." The simple girl carried the image to the old monk, who looked at it, cast his eyes toward heaven, and began counting his beads, for indeed he knew the Mother of God was present. Tenderly he took the image and placed it high upon the mantel in the next room. Then he returned and sat down to talk to the mystified La Negrita.

Thinking half aloud to himself over this discovery too wonderful to believe, he mused to the sweet young face, "This, I believe, is a sign from heaven to make peace for the two classes. He sighed sadly, "God must be grieved that Indians cannot dwell in peace here. They are banned from the city and treated shamefully. And this sign coming to a girl, so simple, just a poor little Indian?" He looked closely at her. "What is the matter? You look sick."

La Negrita told him of her love for Carlos, but she sobbed, "We can never marry."

The old monk patted her head and instructed, "Bring the boy to me." Quickly La Negrita found and brought Carlos, and the priest inquired, "Carlos, why don't you talk to your father? Tell him you love this girl and tell him it is no ordinary girl who can see the light of God."

At that moment, there was a knock at the door. In came the governor with the boy's father to see the priest. The priest told La Negrita's story, emphasizing that the rule of segregation must be abolished. But the boy's father did not believe the story, and he said, "It is impossible for such a thing to happen. I can't change the rule. I don't believe this lying Indian." The priest reached toward the mantel, but the image was not there.

Quickly La Negrita said, "I know where I can find her." Leading the way, she took them to the woods, just off the road over which was hung a large sign, '*Indians Do Not Trespass Farther.*' But there was no light over the now familiar rock. La Negrita dropped to her knees with tears flowing from her eyes as she prayed. Suddenly, a glorious heavenly light shone over the rock, which everyone saw. It was a light so bright and dazzling, it almost blinded the onlookers. In the light, butterflies fluttered and lifted their yellow wings in the glow of it. There, in the midst of the light, stood the dark image. And with the light, the sky was filled with voices like angels, singing so that all the country people heard in their fields and were drawn by the glory of it. The monk reached for his rosary, and all the people fell to their knees. La Negrita covered her head with her shawl, folded her hands as in prayer, and walked up to get the little virgin.

She smiled sweetly and said, "I have found you again. Don't ever leave. They all believe in you now."

The tearful crowd heard, and the boy's father stood up and took La Negrita in his arms and spoke, "You are welcome to my family, for you are so good. You are a little angel, and you have made me understand." The governor rose from his knees and stood with bowed head before the priest.

Humbly he said, "Everything will be different. You will see, I will make everything different."

Carlos' father called to the boy, "Carlos, this is going to be your wife."

The monk accepted the virgin from La Negrita's hands, saying, "Thanks to you, little virgin, everything is going to be all right. We are going to build you a church."

And so they did, a magnificent church right on that spot, a sanctuary that you know well. It is called the '*Lady of the Angels*,' and from the rock where the virgin is enshrined, there flows natural water with healing powers. People take pieces of the rock home with them, but the rock never grows smaller. It is all part of the miracle of Our Lady."

The girls were unusually quiet that Sunday on the way back from their outing.

One Sunday, as the nuns were leading their flock of sequined-garbed girls back through the town, picking the quieter streets, Margarita was so bored with her usual cow pasture visitation, she yearned so desperately to see human form that she became emboldened enough to implore Sister Rosario's permission to let them walk through the park. Sister Rosario, not really fooled by the

Figure 60 A   Basilica of the Angels in Cartago, Costa Rica. (Present Day)
iStock.com/manx_in_the_world
https://www.istockphoto.com/photo/basilica-of-our-lady-of-angels-
in-carthage-costa-rica-gm1161604232-318355593?clarity=false

young girl's innocently lifted eyes, yielded but not before procuring numerous promises from her roguish countenance that she would be good. All the boys throughout the park rose to the occasion, whistled, caterwauled, and waved.

They heaved manfully heavy sighs at Sister Rosario and taunted, "Grandmother, take your veil off; let us see your pretty face." From the corner of her eye, Margarita caught a glimpse of Sister Rosario suppressing a pleased look and replacing it with her mask. Ushering the girls quickly off into a side street, the nuns walked one before and one after the girls to supervise the way.

But there was a persistent escort on a motorcycle who swerved and swooped up close to the sidewalk and called softly to Margarita, "I want to see you again."

Margarita shook her veil vigorously, hissing, "Go away, I have no chance."

The boy concluded with, "I'll be outside the windows anyway." And he went putt-putting loudly down the street.

That night Sister Rosario summoned all the girls before her. Her voice was serious as she demanded, "Girls, I want a confession from the girl who attracted attention on the street this afternoon." Her eyes questioned each face, and Margarita felt the eyes. Did they linger longer on her face? Still, she did not move. The nun's voice was edged with a provoked note as she continued, "An offense must not go unpunished. If the girl doesn't acknowledge her guilt, then the whole school must pay for it."

Still Margarita, with her mouth dry as cotton, did not speak. Anabella pinched Margarita's backside hard and hissed, "If you don't, I'm going to tell Mama." But Margarita didn't move or lift her face.

All the girls were ordered to turn facing a blank wall, and Margarita could feel their accusing glances as they, one by one, chanced a glare in her direction. Later that evening after the mass punishment, Sister Rosario called Margarita aside. She shook her head and spoke quietly, "Margarita, I'm disappointed in you. I hoped you would admit your guilt." The young girl did not, could not, look up. In a long eternity of an interval, Sister Rosario's voice sounded again as she inquired, "Have you missed any of your personal possessions?"

Margarita's eyes blazed as they shot up at her. "Yes, my picture, somebody stole my picture of Edwin."

Sister Rosario again shook her lovely head and corrected, "Nobody '*stole*' your picture. I have it."

Margarita implored, "You, you, Sister? Please give it back to me!"

Sister Rosario smiled compassionately, and her face beneath the Sacred Heart Emblem on her headband was as divinely sweet as the Virgin's herself, but she refused, saying, "No, I mustn't give it back now. Your mind is too much in the air. I'll keep it until you leave the school, and then you may have it."

With her picture gone, the girls were sullen toward Margarita for making them accept her punishment, and she was completely ostracized as they ignored her coldly. She felt she had to contrive some method to regain their good graces, and so she resorted to Flora, who, being the oldest and biggest girl, commanded prestige. Margarita allied herself with the older girl and listened, compelled but repulsed by her filthy jokes.

One day Flora motioned Margarita into the lavatory, opened her clamped fist, slipped her a cigarette, and pushed her into the cabinet with "Come in here, nobody will see us."

While Flora was showing her how to light and puff, the curling smoke wafted above the cabinet and out into the lavatory. Suddenly, there was the Mother Superior's voice screaming '*FIRE!*' and beating on the door. Out stepped the two culprits, with Margarita slowly revealing her cigarette from behind her back. The Mother Superior was horrified! Filled with righteous indignation, she rustled her flowing self toward the telephone and spluttered as she talked to Libia over the line. Her voice was tense as she stated, "Doña Constant, I cannot keep Margarita any longer. It is impossible, and today is the end. My tolerance has ended!" Harassed and worried, Libia was in the principal's office within the next hour. Learning of the offense, she felt somehow relieved and reasoned with the Mother Superior to give her daughter another chance since the term was so close to the end. The wise old Mother calmed down and allowed herself to be compromised into another chance for Margarita. The girl was, she felt, essentially good; however, Flora was older and had the manner of a Jezebel. She had been guilty of undermining the morals of a younger person. That was an offense that must be purged, and Mother Superior expelled Flora that very day.

Margarita kept her tearful vow to her mother and to the Superior and didn't transgress again, saving only once. She attended her prayers with a heart of contrition and considered instructive religious works during her rest periods. She read aloud in the dining room with earnest concentration during lunch and supper meals and didn't grumble when she sat down to cold beans. She even, at risk of further ostracization by the girls, became Sister Carnación's helper, taking down names of noise makers in the dormitory.

At the pageant for the end-of-school exercise on November 15, Margarita stood in place at the back of the line. Stealthily she pulled a bit of red crepe paper from her wrist sleeve, moistened it with the tip of her tongue, and applied it to her lips. Next, the stubby, soft lead pencil was drawn across her brows, and the last touch, the rose, a gorgeous red, she pulled from under her collar and tucked it behind her ear. Obeying an instinctive impulse to take another look at her charges, Sister Rosario espied Margarita in her adornment. She commanded Margarita to the lavatory to scrub her face. Margarita turned and fled down the hall crying, "I won't be in the play looking plain!"

In the last few minutes before Margarita would walk away from the place of a year's internment, Sister Rosario took from the folds of her robe a picture and pressed it into Margarita's hand. Then she tenderly patted the young girl's fingers. Her gray eyes were lucid with unshed tears as she bade, "Please come to visit me whenever you can." At the sound of the little nun's low, soft, entreating voice, Margarita wept more at leaving her confinement than when she had entered it.

When she and Anabella got back home and unpacked their belongings in their old room, they could hardly wait to see each other in their nakedness. They took off their clothes, and Margarita motioned, "Come on, Anabella, let's look at ourselves in the mirror." They stood and stared at their own young bodies and at each other and still could not figure out why there was all the secrecy of dressing and undressing at the school. Margarita gave herself another good look in the mirror, then snorted, "Huh, I don't see anything so wicked about my body that the sisters are always talking about. They must be silly, that's all." She slipped back on her dress in a more satisfying frame of mind.

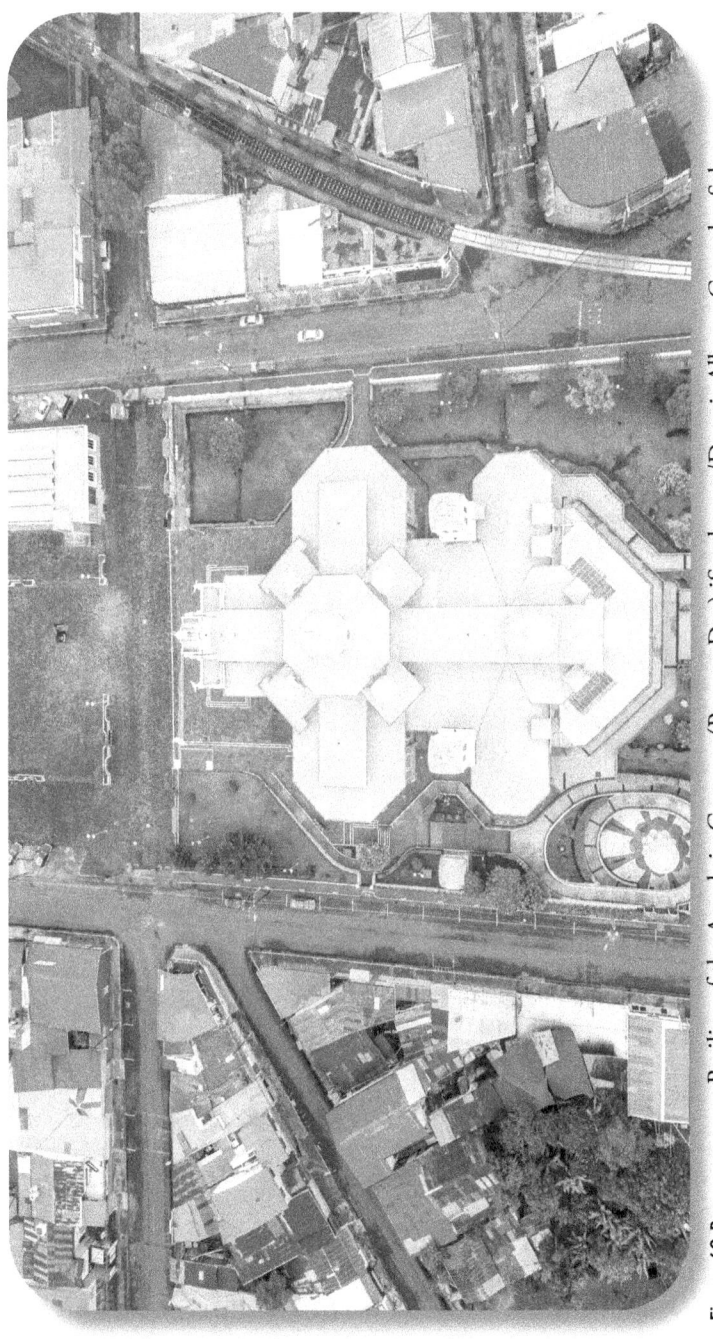

Figure 60 B   Basilica of the Angels in Cartago. (Present Day) iStock.com/Dennis Alberto Gonzalez Salas
https://www.istockphoto.com/photo/aerial-view-of-the-basilica-of-our-lady-of-the-angels-on-a-cold-winter-morning-in-gm2187780771-606341322

Sacred Heart College

Figures 60 C,D

CHAPTER EIGHTEEN

Nastalia Mora
1945

O N THE MORNING OF NOVEMBER 22, quite early, even before Luzare left for the store, there was a ring at the door. Shortly, Luzare came into Margarita's bedroom, cursing, "Margarita, that woman, Mora, is at the door. She's looking for you. Be careful what you say. She has a long tongue."

Margarita stood surprised. She had never had any social dealings with Eddy's mother before. In protest she replied, "But Papa, I can't help it. I didn't tell her to come here."

Luzare snapped, "Well, she has a cake for you. Why did she do that?"

Nastalia Mora, a buxom woman with her black crepe dress pulled tightly across her heavy breasts and fat buttocks, stood waiting to be received. Reluctantly, Margarita approached her. But as soon as the woman caught sight of Margarita advancing, she called out loudly, "Hello, darling, How are you?" Her high voice with a concho tinge and with accents like an affected stage actress carried throughout the whole house. As soon as Margarita was near enough, the

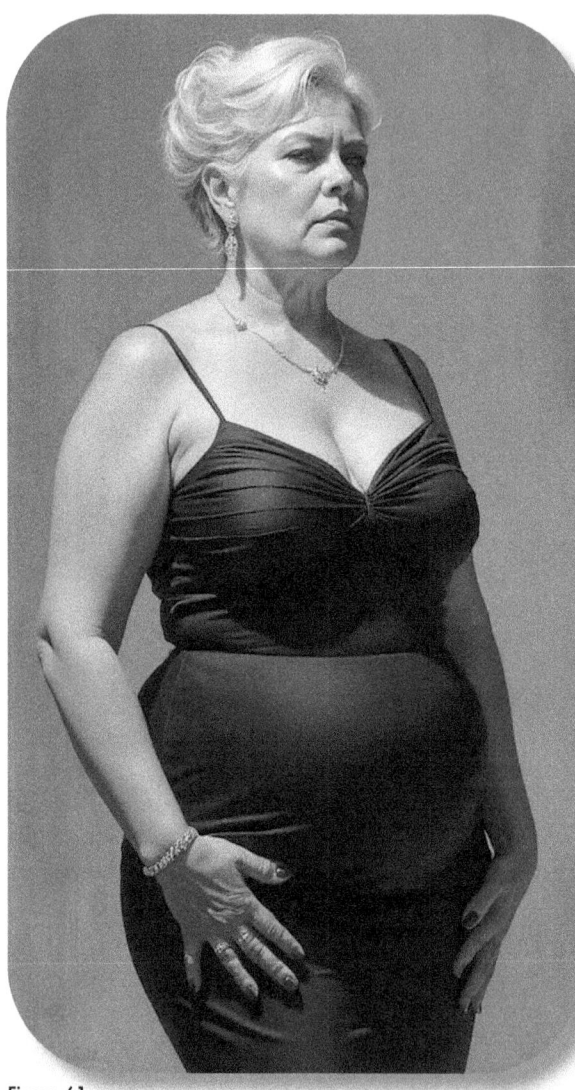

Figure 61

Nastalia Mora

woman patted her forearm in warm familiarity, saying, "Margarita, I brought this for you. Did you think I had forgotten you because I never came? I don't forget you; see, I even remembered your humanístico."

Quickly it flashed on Margarita: today was her saint's day. She was named for Saint Cecilia. The woman's busy tongue went on, "Look at this cake. I paid too much for it, but I wanted it pretty for you." Margarita looked. It was a beautiful cake, big with white icing, and decorated in green were two palm branches crossed. In the center of the cross were written the words "*Love Forever.*" At the top of one branch was the name Edwin. At the tip of the other, Margarita. Margarita stood, just looking. She didn't hold out her arms to receive it but was paralyzed with fear, wondering wildly what she would do with it. She didn't dare take it into the house, but the woman was pushing her into the hall and forcing the cake in her arms as she guided her down the corridor. Margarita paused at the living room door, but the woman urged her on, saying, "No, no, take me to the kitchen; don't put me in the living room. Just treat me like one of the family. You're almost my daughter-in-law." Margarita could think of no answer. In the kitchen, Libia was giving the servant instructions for the day. Nastalia Mora stepped up to Libia as if she were her warmest friend and spoke, "Hello, Libia, how are you?"

Libia stood and glared at the woman for a long second before she replied, "Hello, Señora," and turning on her heel, she said, "Excuse me," and left the room.

The Mora woman looked at Margarita and simpered, "Your mother is," and lifted her nose high in the air in a mock snob.

At that moment Margarita had an idea. She inquired, "Do you want some sweet lemon? Come, I will get you some." Luzare, who had not left for the store since the woman's arrival, sat on the porch sunning. As soon as the two were gathering lemons, he stood up, strained his eyes to see them better, and cocked his head to listen. Glancing over her shoulder at her father on the porch, Margarita knew he was swearing. Frantically she kept picking lemons to keep the woman occupied.

The woman was still talking, but Margarita paid no attention to what she was saying: "I have a house for you and Eddy. I am going to give it to you the day you are married. And I want to come and live with you." She smiled warmly, brazenly at Margarita, and continued, "You are going to be my daughter-in-law; I will like that."

Margarita stammered, "But we're not engaged, not serious; we have no plans."

The woman brushed away the words with "Oh, don't be shy."

For want of something else to say, Margarita imparted, "I sent Eddy some cigarettes. Did he write to you?"

The woman answered, "Oh, that was all right. It didn't hurt you to buy them. You have money."

When the sack was so full it was ready to tear, the woman took the lemons in her arms, turned to go, and then said, "Thank you. But aren't you going to have a party?" Then, nudging Margarita, she went on, "A rich girl like you, I believe you are going to have a little party."

Honest-faced, Margarita replied, "I have no plans to throw a party."

The woman insisted, "This is your day. I brought a cake because I want to come to your party."

Margarita answered in a wan voice, "I don't know, all right. Maybe I will have one."

"Good," said the woman, "I'll be coming back in the afternoon. Goodbye, I'll see you later today."

When Margarita stepped up on the front porch, Luzare growled, "What did she say to you?"

Margarita answered in a very noncommittal voice, "She didn't have much to say." She knew her father would be wild if he had any idea of the woman's intentions to return. She went back to the kitchen and said, "Mama, I want to have a party this afternoon."

Libia glanced up with a knowing face but replied, "Well, you may have a party, but don't invite that woman. I don't want her around here." Margarita went immediately to the telephone and invited her grandmother Catalina because Catalina always expected to be issued the first invitation to any little function.

Catalina, always curious-voiced, inquired, "Why didn't you tell me your plans yesterday when you were over here? But I will be glad to make suspiros and cremitas for you anyway." During the morning, she sent the manservant with a platter of suspiros, fluffy whites of eggs that had been beaten with honey and filled with blanched almonds and then browned; she also sent a large sandwich tray of cremitas and dainty creamed cookies. Catalina came early in the afternoon to look at the tables and add touches here and there.

Soon the living room and garden were full. Some thirty people in all, both young and old, Margarita's young friends and some of her aunts. Her grandmother had also invited a few old women to chat with, but Margarita could not feel the charm of the occasion. Her whole body was filled with dread; her throat was dry with it. Catalina was sitting in the living room with the older ladies having their coffee and cakes when the doorbell rang. Luzare had decided to stay at home that day and so sat with the ladies in the living room. The doorbell rang, but Margarita didn't hurry to answer. She piddled with the napkins until her grandmother gave her an impatient wave of her hand. As soon as Margarita started up the hall, the voice sounded out, "Hello, darling, I'm sorry I'm late, but the bus!" Catalina walked out into the hall, her body like a ramrod, her face like stone.

Nastalia Mora twisted up to the old lady and spoke casually, "Hello Catalina," without the respect of '*doña*.'

Catalina drew herself up and responded in a frigid voice, "Hello, Señora."

The woman pushed her way into the living room, where the older women looked on, their cups held midair in astonishment. They listened to what the woman's tongue was saying: "I am making plans for Eddy and Margarita when they are married. I want to take Margarita to the United States to marry Eddy." Without pausing, she glanced around at the opened mouths and said, "Introduce me to your friends." There was a moment of terrible silence. Catalina crossed her arms and said nothing while Margarita waited for her grandmother. After a moment, the woman said with a flourish, "I am the future mother-in-law of Margarita."

Luzare was standing nearby, getting his breath in short gasps. Swelled fit to burst, he cut in, "I never knew my daughter was serious about your son. She is just a young girl, and I make her plans for her. Excuse me." And he left the room. Catalina turned and walked out, and Libia, who had heard the last few words, came in to be with the women.

Nastalia took Margarita's arm and directed her from the room and into the hall as she gushed, "You want to put me with the old ladies. I like to be with young girls." She took Margarita's elbow and led her to the garden where Anabella and Margarita's friends were seated, waiting for Margarita's return; then they looked up and saw her approaching, being pulled along by the twisting woman.

As soon as the woman was in loud-talking distance, she began, "Oh, you pretty girls!" And as she drew closer, she patted Margarita's arm and remarked, "Listen, girls, do you know I am the mother of Margarita's boyfriend? She is my future daughter-in-law. She is engaged, girls." The girls cast glances at Margarita, accusing her of withholding a secret.

They all murmered, "We didn't know about this." One by one they sidled up and pinched Margarita and whispered, "Why didn't you tell us?"

The woman continued pointing to the cake. "It is true; do you see the names on the cake?" The girls looked, and their eyes condemned Margarita all the more for being selfish with her secrets.

Nastalia Mora was the last to leave. As she departed the doorway, she called out, "I want to come one of these days to take your picture to send to Eddy. I have a good camera."

The family was waiting when Margarita came into the dining room. Luzare sat drumming his knife and cursing. As soon as she sat down, he spoke, "Listen, if you think you're going to marry that boy, you're not my daughter." His arms waved her away. "You will be nothing to me."

Libia implored, "But Luzare, she's not in love with Eddy. That woman, don't blame her for that crazy woman!"

Luzare turned on his wife. "Do you see! While they were sitting on the front porch, you were always telling me, '*There is no harm; they are just kids; he is a good boy.*' Now look! See what it has led to."

Margarita batted away the tears and protested, "Papa, you know I'm not in love with that boy."

Luzare raved on, "Well, let me open your eyes. She is nothing but a puta, a plain whore, that caraja woman!"

Libia quickly motioned Margarita out of the dining room and took her to the bedroom to explain in nicer words what Luzare was storming. Libia sat down on the bed and said:

"What your father wanted to tell you is like this: That woman married a good man, an

American, with a little money, and he took her on a honeymoon trip to the United States. They lived for a while in New York, where Eddy was born, but the man developed T.B. and was put in a sanitarium. Nastalia was left alone with her young baby, and so she started her whoredom, but unfortunately, her husband got well. He found out what she had been doing and even doubted if Eddy were his son, so he left her and got a divorce. When Eddy, poor boy, was six, Nastalia brought him back here, but by that time, she was known as a prostitute. Her whole family and the others are nice, a good family, so they turned their backs on her, and nobody would speak to her. She has been in that profession ever since and has had every important man in the country, ALL the men." There was a stern look on Libia's face as she emphasized the word "*ALL.*"

But she continued, while Margarita sat wide-eyed, listening, "A few years back Nastalia even took her niece, a simple country girl from San Ramón, a young innocent girl who had just come to San José. She took her and told her she wanted to introduce her to a rich man and explained that maybe the girl might meet one who would want to marry her. Nastalia made plans with the man beforehand, who gave her 30 pesos, and she took the girl to the man's hotel room and said, "Stay here; this rich man is coming very soon. I will be right back." She left the girl there and locked the door. The girl was scared. Soon the door opened and the man came in, locking the door behind him, and the girl screamed, but he said, "It won't do you any good. Your aunt isn't coming back. You belong to me." He forced her that night, that innocent girl, so cruel. So the girl was scared to go back to the country after her sin and stayed with the Mora woman. She had a baby, but she didn't want anybody to know, so she gave it to Nastalia because she said, "It was your fault." The wronged girl was sorry. She confessed to the priest, put on the Abito dress, and now you see her with a brown dress and rosary. She has come back to God. But still she has nothing to do with her own daughter because it reminds her of her sin. Now you see why you must try to stay away from that woman. She would do anything for money, even sell her own family."

In a few days, Nastalia Mora came back. This time she had her camera and a little girl, a lovely curly-haired child whom she called Eugenia. She explained to Margarita, "I adopted this little girl because her real mother left her, poor child. I want to be good with her like a mother. Do you know a good school I could put her in? I want her to grow up to be good." Margarita looked down with pity at the little girl and offered her hand for the small fingers to take as they crossed the street. Across the street, Margarita posed for a few pictures while Luzare stood on the porch and watched.

After the woman left, Luzare reproached Margarita again with, "You tell that woman not to come again. I don't want people to be talking about my family. Your reputation will be on the floor, ruined. Next time she comes, I will tell her to get out!"

But the woman did come again. Margarita watched from the window as the Mora woman came up the walk, but Luzare headed her off, and Margarita saw her father say a few words, then the woman turned and walked away. When Luzare came back into the house, Margarita said, "Papa, what did you say to her?"

But Luzare only smiled briefly and replied, "I'm sure she will not be back," and Nastalia Mora never did come back again.

CHAPTER NINETEEN

Jaime Aragon
1945

O N NEW YEAR'S EVE, IN the gorgeous million-dollar Renaissance National Theater, the loveliest Joséfinas in Costa Rica were dressed in their exquisite bouffant dresses. They glided over the shining floors, floating up and down the pale, solid marble staircases, past gilded paintings and enormous mirrors fluted with gold edging. The girls walked over red velvet carpets to form their beauty court. All the august corridors were ablaze with beaten and bronze decorations, shining in the glow of chandeliers. On this night, all the young girls, who had just turned sixteen and were from good families, were making their formal bows to society. Luzare sat grandly in his new tailored suit. Libia, always full of graciousness, smiled and nodded her head at passersby. Catalina, stiffly regal in her black brocade, luxuriated in eliteness and looked more like the habitué of the original Paris theater than its mere copy. At this moment, Catalina was complaining that these affairs, although sumptuous, lacked the culture and fineness of the parties of her own youth, when the presentation was held in the home

Figure 62

New Year's Eve Party

Margarita At The New Year's Eve Party

Figure 63

and only a select few attended. Now with such crowds, how could one tell who was at her elbow? Bereft of an escort, Margarita sat between her mother and father; her young face beneath her high, sophisticated coiffure was sullen, her eyes red and puffed. Anabella, more ingenious in her wiles, had not lingered around to wail her own stranded plight but had winked wickedly at a few roving young men and was not lost in the dancers. As the party grew gayer, Catalina thawed perceptibly, especially after her second glass of champagne, and even rallied into sociability after the president of Panama treated her with such singular courtesy. She agreed that the party did compare favorably with others she had attended, and she occasionally jibed the sulking Margarita with "Stop making such ugly faces. You scare people away!" Libia watched Luzare's face turn in its attentiveness to Margarita. There was an expression of warm tenderness as he looked on his child's eyes, bright with swimming tears. Through the years, so seldom, too seldom, had Libia caught a glimpse of this hidden man.

When Luzare, like an old courtier, said to his daughter, "I crave the honor to dance with such a lovely girl." Margarita grabbed up her skirts and fled through the foyer to the powder room.

Libia followed, and glancing into the blue-plated mirror at her daughter's absurd little swollen face, she felt her heartstrings plucked with sympathy as Margarita sobbed, "Mama, I want to be a nun. I hate the world. I want to be a nun." Libia smiled in loving consolation; so violent and raging a storm would soon pass.

Ever since Victor's marriage, whenever Margarita felt a special yen to speak with her brother, she always visited him at the store. Although he lived just around the corner and down at the edge of the lot in a bright little bungalow, Margarita never went there. She felt an estrangement, as if he didn't belong to her; however, when he was on the back balcony of the store, carefully, meticulously cutting out work pants to be sewn by the women workers, or when he leaned over a piece of material with his mouth full of pins, he was the gentle, painstaking Victor who, all her young life, had picked her up whenever she stumbled, brushed off her legs, and washed her bleeding, bruised knees.

CHAPTER 19

One day Margarita came rushing up the wide back stairs all out of breath. She patted Victor's shoulder up from his cutting and panted, "Victor, listen, I want to know who the man is that I saw."

Victor's fine, chiseled face smiled whimsically, and he inquired, "Who is it you saw where, Linda?"

Margarita jabbered on, unconscious of the sewing women's pricked ears who sat around at their machines, as she said, "On the street, I saw him as I was coming out of the movies, and he looks just like you. He was walking along the street with an old, devil-looking woman, an ugly old black-painted face with black-looking dyed hair. She should know she is too old to have such hair. She was hanging on to his arm just like this," and Margarita pulled fiercely on Victor's elbow while she mocked the woman's possessive clutch. Victor looked around at all the listening faces, walked his half-sister over to the side balcony, and leaned over with uninterested eyes, staring at the shoppers on the floor below.

He spoke carefully, "Linda, that fellow you saw does look something like me, as you said. It is because we are kin, and he's a fine man, a doctor here in town. There is nothing wrong with him, but the woman you saw is his mother. She is Helena, your grandmother, Amelia's sister. And your grandmother's sisters were strange-acting people. This Helena you saw is not as bad as her sister, but she is crazy enough. She married a Mexican who took a lot of her money and had this boy, and she never lets him go with girls. She goes along everywhere he goes except to his sick calls. No girl wants to have anything to do with him because of his mother, and that's the reason Papa never said anything to you about those relatives; they're crazy. So you might as well go along as if you still don't know."

Margarita nodded her head comprehendingly, giggling a little, "OH HOH! I've seen her, the other sister. I remember when I was a little girl. She is really loco, that one is."

Victor grinned, "It isn't funny. But you might as well laugh about it." He shrugged his shoulders and turned to go back to work as he added, "There isn't much else you can do."

One afternoon Margarita received a call from one of Eddy's

aunts, who had just been notified that Eddy had died in an American hospital from wounds he received in action. Margarita found herself offering the family her condolences, but she felt no grief in her heart for the death itself. After she went back to her room, she felt a rather heavy melancholia, a sorrow for a lost age, and nostalgia for a time of childhood enchantment that was gone forever. She folded her hands and sat hunched on the bed, thinking of joyful times that now were only shiny spots in her memory. Edwin had wanted to be a clean, decent person in spite of his mother. She remembered once, before she knew about his mother, as they were sitting on the porch, he said, "Margarita, someday I must tell you some things you need to know about me and my family, but I am not going to tell you now. You are too young." And so theirs had been a friendship that had not really been touched by his mother's sordid life. Margarita sighed to think that only a few days before, the newspapers carried on their front pages his mother's latest illicit endeavor; this time, she had been caught with it. Nastalia Mora, the papers printed, had taken a bunch of servant girls with her down to Panama and set up her prostitution business with them. When some of the girls discovered their betrayal, they somehow managed to get back home. Others were not so fortunate; who knew what their fate would be? The United States government expelled Nastalia Mora from the Panamanian territory and forbade her to ever come back. Margarita sighed again and got up from her bed.

On Sundays it was the custom of the young people to meet at the airport terminal for refreshment. Everybody came after the soccer games, which were played on the smooth plains of La Sabana. The orchestra played from 11:30 until 2:00, and there were tea and dancing. On this Sunday, Margarita and her American friend, Claudia, sat sipping their sodas and waiting for the boys to start drifting in. As Margarita sat chatting, a waitress tapped her on the shoulder and whispered confidentially, "You are wanted in the office." Margarita got up and followed the white-clad woman.

As soon as the office door was closed, the woman said, "There is a fellow out there who wants to be introduced to you; stay in here, and I'll get him for you." But frightened by this encroachment on decorum, which was next to religion with her, Margarita simply followed the woman back out and stepped quickly to her table.

There was a man sitting at her place; her very own pocketbook was balanced loosely in his hands. He sprang up at her appearance and stood tall and arrogant as a conquistador as he explained, "You see, I asked the waitress to introduce us because she was once my nurse, but you wouldn't wait." And, noticing her wide eyes, he continued more softly, "Little one, you need not be afraid of me; I'm not going to bite you."

Piqued by the '*little one*' address, Margarita drew herself tall, shrugged her shoulders bizarrely, and huffed, "Oh, I'm not afraid of you."

Then the man said, as he turned to Claudia, "I had just introduced myself to your friend when you were coming out of the office. I am Jaime Aragon, a doctor in town. I was sitting at the table over there and just happened to see you two sitting here. Would you care to dance?"

While they were dancing, Jaime's voice above her head was saying, "This is not the first time I've seen you, and I've wanted to meet you for some time. I've watched you from afar. Will you let me drive you two home?" This was such a new and drastic decision for Margarita to make, it required consultation with Claudia in the restroom.

Margarita twittered and gulped as she talked, "He wants to take us home in his car!"

Claudia, always self-contained and cool, more seasoned in these mundane affairs, nodded her neat, blond head in consent and replied, "It's all right. I'll be with you." The younger girl needed no more urging, and they soon climbed into the tall man's convertible and glided away from the Terminal Building. The clear air was sparkling, and it felt soft and caressing to Margarita as she bared her face to it. Across this great flat stretch of meadowland on the edge of town, boys met to play football, golf, or occasionally polo. And here, Lindbergh, long ago, had landed on his flight from Managua. On all sides, like an opera backdrop, the velvety, deep-furrowed, dramatic mountains with their bright, crumpled peaks walled in the vast plateau. The lower sides of the mountain were checkered about with pasture fields and slashed with brilliant blue ravines. It was a brisk moorland, and Margarita always delighted in riding here. Only now and then did she steal a glance at the driver, who was chatting pleasantly with Claudia, who responded to all the questions easily and naturally. At that moment he was commenting that being a doctor had its drawbacks in the way of social life, and he hardly had any time to call his own but felt he had to get away from the hospital every now and then. Margarita did not speak; she could think of nothing to say, so she pretended to be preoccupied with the scenery. Closer into town, they passed small bungalows with their front gardens full of pink and white flowers. The sight of these little homes always made Margarita wonder if the people inside were as ideally happy as their cozy houses indicated. Then suddenly the automobile was nosing its way back into the

Figure 64 A

Jamie Aragon

industrious, go-ahead city, down Central Avenue, halting behind the streetcar every now and then. Claudia gave directions to her apartment, and in a few minutes they were at her front door. She hopped out and was gone.

As the automobile started again, without turning to look at her, the man spoke, "Do you want to go to the Sesteo tonight about eight o'clock? I will be waiting for you there." Margarita held her breath. She had never gone to the plush cocktail bar called "Sesteo," and to think of going with a real date! That had been one of her dreams in her far-away future of grown-up years.

She stammered, "I, I don't believe that I can."

The voice went on, "Well, I will be waiting there anyway."

As the automobile stopped in front of her house, Margarita slipped from the seat before the man could open the door and was gone without so much as a goodbye. Swifter than a bird to its mountain nest, she flew across the walk and into her door. Breathless inside, she flung open her mother's bedroom door, blurting, "Mama, a doctor wants to take me to the Sesteo tonight, Mama; please say you will go with me."

Libia looked up from her reading, all attention, inquiring, "Who, linda? Who wants to take you? What doctor? How do you know he'll be there?" Her voice was only a shade calmer than her daughter's. Margarita explained her morning's meeting with the man, describing in full detail his dark face with the big black mole near the left eye.

Later in the afternoon a corsage of gardenias was delivered to don Constant's residence with the card enclosed on the back of which was scribbled in green ink, '*My dream has come true.*' Margarita held the card before her mother's eyes, providing visible proof that she had not been hallucinating, and stated, "Now, you see, Mama, he does want me to come."

That night at the leather-upholstered Sesteo, Margarita, Libia, and Jaime Aragon sat smiling amiably over their drinks. Jaime talked mostly with Libia and was inquiring jokingly, "And how does it feel, Señora Constant, to have daughters of dating age?"

Libia smiled into her drink and answered pensively, "There are two stages in a woman's life when she has enjoyment. When she goes out as a girl and then again when she goes out with her daughters." Margarita sat and felt somehow terribly immature, even though she was wearing her fuchsia dress with the gold sequins that had been planned for such an occasion.

At breakfast the next morning, Libia made several comments on the previous evening. She praised the young man to Luzare; she said she thought he was a splendid fellow and that she had enjoyed the evening thoroughly. Margarita was abashed to tell her mother that the splendid young man had not asked to see her again.

Two days later, as she was walking down the street, there was a loud screeching of brakes, and the recognizable convertible with the splendid young man who sat grinning and saying, "Ah, little one, I forgot to ask you when I could see you again. I have been hoping to see you on the street. Come, take a ride with me." This time, before letting Margarita out of the automobile, he obtained her permission to see her on Thursdays and Sundays and whispered as he left her at the door, "I am looking forward to meeting your whole family Thursday."

Thursday night finally came. In the living room Luzare, Libia, Anabella, and Margarita sat like children at a tea party around the small central table with its stiff chairs. Margarita fingered the crocheted macramé doily, tracing the star design up and down each point. She wondered uneasily if her father would approve of her suitor. When, at last, the doorbell rang and Jaime made his entrance, she saw at once that her father was taken by his charming manners. Jaime spoke to Luzare of his work, remarking that he was on the staff of the San Juan de Dios Hospital.

In the meetings that followed, Libia was more impressed with Jaime each time she sat and watched the two young people at the movies or when they danced. Lately, however, in the afternoons, Margarita had been slipping to meet Jaime without her chaperonage. At her father's insistence, Margarita started a commerce class at Castro Garazo, taking Spanish, typing, and shorthand. But the typewriter frustrated her; she hated sitting and wiggling her fingers, and shorthand baffled her. So she loved slipping out to meet Jaime, and at night, if they didn't go out, they sat on the porch in front of the window, listening to Libia's fantasia of song. Margarita could feel the echo in her heart to the vibrance of Jaime's warm, sincere voice. He often spoke of his family, his career, his struggle through medical school in Mexico, and his poverty-stricken younger years.

Margarita's days were so sublimely happy she hardly dared to speak to Anabella, whose delicate pale face somehow seemed more porcelain these days. Ever since the night when she was sitting on the porch with Roberto and the fight occurred.

It had been a bright, moonlit night. Anabella, Roberto, Margarita, and Jaime were all sitting in the patch of light from the living room window. Anabella wore a rapturous look of enchantment that night, for, as she confided to Margarita earlier that day in an excited whisper, "I believe Roberto is going to propose to me. I heard he is mad at Olivia. And don't you think he seems to like me more these days?"

Margarita agreed. She was in love, and she wanted her sister to be happy in love too. And as they sat and sang and teased, a figure walked up the front steps and called to Roberto, "Roberto, I know you are here. You don't love Anabella; come out here." Roberto stepped forward toward Rafael's slighter figure. In a moment they clinched together and started rolling down the steps onto the lawn, flinging their arms and thrashing at each other.

Then Roberto, who was the larger, disentangled himself, stood up, pulled Rafael up by his shirt, and said, "Stop acting like a fool. I don't want to fight. You can have Anabella. I'm not in love with her. I love someone else. You are welcome to Anabella." And with that he strode off down the street, leaving Rafael sitting on the steps, catching his breath. Anabella stood for a moment watching Roberto's departing shadow. There was a strange, dead look on her white face. Then she slipped inside the door and never once mentioned the incident to Margarita again.

Figure 64 B

Costa Rica Brush Stroke Flag
https://www.istockphoto.com/vector/costa-rica-brush-stroke-flag-vector-
background-hand-drawn-grunge-style-costa-rican-gm1488973381-
513993575?clarity=false
iStock.com/Ivan Burchak

Chapter 19

CHAPTER TWENTY

Rafael and Anabella
1946

F OR SOME TIME, MARGARITA NOTICED quick pains in her stomach after meals. However, recently the pains have become more severe and cramp-like. Often she couldn't finish a party if she accepted refreshments during the evening. It was at a wedding party that she collapsed. The evening was wonderful; she drank champagne for the first time and danced sensuously close to Jaime's lean body. But suddenly, she experienced cramps that tightened her stomach into hard knots. Jamie took her and Libia home immediately and wanted to give her medical assistance, but she demurred. It seemed unfitting that Jaime should touch her in a professional way. The pain diminished, but she was still too weak to make efforts to dress the next day. That afternoon Jamie took her and her mother to a stomach specialist he had contacted and who, after his examination, consulted Libia. "Your daughter is very sick. Her condition should have been given attention before now. She has an ulcer at the mouth of the stomach that could easily be aggravated into a tumor." He cautioned Libia that under no circumstances should Margarita be let out of bed within the next two months, that she must drink a glass of milk every hour, and that she should avoid any excitement whatsoever.

After Margarita's confinement to bed, Jaime came every night with magazines for her next day's reading. Sometimes he also brought flowers. Libia, who always felt proximity to be a breach of decorum, placed Jaime's chair at a satisfactory distance from the bed, while she herself always sat in the desk chair. Nor would she be uprooted; regardless of the urgency of the errand, she always dispatched someone else. In the adjacent bedroom, Luzare would listen to the hourly news reports over the radio, then he would get up restlessly, pace through the open door into Margarita's bedroom, chat for a few minutes, make his round out the door, into the hall, then back up the hall into his bedroom for more news.

This arrangement had been going on for about two weeks. One night in early May, the four of them were talking. The chill in the air prompted them to close the two bedroom doors. Luzare, as was his manner when a matter lay heavily on his mind, struck while the iron was hot. He stated his business without preliminary trimmings to the suitor, "Jaime, I wish to tell you what I have planned for my daughters. I have decided a couple of years spent in the United States is necessary to complete their education. Then when Margarita returns, she can marry if she wants to."

Jaime nodded in complete accordance, adding, "Margarita does need finishing. She is too immature in many ways." Margarita felt resentment towards Jaime for readily accepting the idea of her departure. But the thought of traveling exhilarated her in spite of her petulance. At this moment, while the cloistered four were discussing plans, Anabella finished packing a trunk that Rafael had brought over in a taxi. She pushed the trunk to the front door, where Rafael waited in the shadows outside, and then Rafael rode away with the trunk to his home. After Jaime had gone, Anabella came back into the bedroom, prepared herself for bed, and lay down beside the excited Margarita, who, in her mind, had already purchased dozens of pretty dresses and had arranged and completed plans for the trip. Brimming over with the news, she whispered their future to Anabella. But Anabella only listened. She said nothing.

The next morning, Anabella got up early, dressing for six o'clock mass. Afterwards she came back strangely elated, with a secretive, malicious smile about her face, saying she had taken communion. Margarita and her mother exchanged questioning glances, for neither Margarita nor her sister had partaken in the communion sacrament since their last heated quarrel when they both avowed that they hated each other. Ignoring their surprised looks, Anabella shrugged casually and retorted, "Why shouldn't I take communion? I no longer hate you. I can't carry a grudge forever." Margarita shed tears upon the restoration of her sister's affection. Later in the morning, Anabella walked out of the house, remarking that she was going to the dressmaker for a fitting. But long after lunch she had not returned. Feeling unsettled and sensing foreboding, Libia could no longer contain her anxiety and went in search of her daughter. Anabella had been in such a peculiar frame of mind for the past several weeks. At the dressmaker's, Libia learned that Anabella had not been there all day. A worried Libia returned home. Following her mother's uneventful search, Margarita, acting on a hunch, threw back her covers, crawled out of bed, and padded across to her sister's clothes closet. It was empty! Everything was gone! At that moment, Luzare walked back into the house from a checkup with his doctor. On the way there, he was hailed on the street by a friend who mentioned that he heard Rafael boasting in the cantinas, saying he would soon have some of the Constant money to spend.

Luzare sat down heavily in her bedroom, drumming his stubby fingers against his vest, his face harassed. Libia quietly closed the empty closet door, trying to think of some way to tell Luzare of their missing daughter.

At two o'clock, Mr. Patterson, Libia's aunt's husband, high in the consul department, stood at the front door. He said he wished to see don Luzare on business of a personal nature. Margarita carried the message to her father, and Luzare snorted and hissed "Caramba" under his breath. He abhorred this oily, unctuous, diplomatic man and had never experienced a visitation from him before. It was too unusual. Luzare crossed the hall with a clouded brow of anxiety.

Standing behind the corridor wall, Margarita listened as the bland, pitiless voice spoke. "Don Luzare," he began, then hesitated, awaiting further persuasion. Luzare, however, waited in silence. Mr. Patterson continued, "I don't like to be the bearer of bad news, but your daughter was in my office this morning and asked that I please tell you that she is going to be married to Rafael Vargas." Luzare's hand shook violently as he grappled for the arm of his chair. He made utterances in his throat, which Mr. Patterson accepted as dismissal, and he retired from the house. Luzare's thick bulk slumped to the floor. His face was a blackish red.

Seeing her father fall, Margarita looked for a moment at his throbbing face. Her eyes sought desperately for her mother, whom she knew had slipped out again looking for Anabella. She ran to the hall telephone, called the doctor, and then called the store for her half-brothers. Hysterically, she sobbed, "Ricardo, Papa is on the floor and sick; please come!"

Within minutes, the three men gathered around their father, hoisting his heavy body up and placing it on the bed. Ricardo kept demanding impatiently, "Where is the doctor? Why doesn't he come? Are you sure you called him?" Then, without waiting, he trotted to his automobile to bring back the physician. A few minutes after he was gone, the old family doctor came panting in, fumbled an ammoniated pellet from his satchel, and broke it under Luzare's nose. Once he regained consciousness, Luzare snorted, shook his head, pulled like a dray horse, broke free from his sons who were restraining him, stood up, and struggled to reach the desk drawer. He drew out his pistol, and with his mouth lathery with a lunatic's froth, he stood and fired at the ceiling, sprinkling plaster with every bullet. Then, like an estrous animal, he started out of the house screaming, "I'll kill him for taking my daughter; leave me alone." The sons, all talking at the same time, tried to soothe him, but he strode out into the garden and shouted to the policeman on the corner, "I'll kill you too if you try to stop me." Barefoot and coatless, Margarita trotted behind her three brothers as they implored their father. Then, as suddenly as a tempest that has passed, Luzare dropped his arms dejectedly; the pistol fell from his limp fingers, and his eyes were locked in a daze, uncertain of his original purpose. He acquiesced meekly as they guided him back to bed. Depleted of energy and under the doctor's ministrations, he soon fell asleep.

At three o'clock, the telephone rang. Rafael's father, with his concho voice, was ingratiatingly announcing, "Your daughter, Señora" (and he rolled the '*r*'), "has just married my son." Libia stood for a moment, too stunned to hang up the receiver. Then she placed the instrument on its hook and turned wearily to the back of the house to moan in private.

At eleven o'clock, the priest who had performed the ceremony was at the door. Roused from his opiate by the bell and the mummerous indistinctness of the voices, Luzare bellowed, "Who is it?" Not receiving any answer, he supported himself by holding on to the furniture until he stood facing the priest.

The church representative, feeling the tenseness of the moment, immediately stated his mission: "Don Constant, I have come to get your blessing on the marriage I performed today. You mustn't stand in the way of these two young people if this union is for their happiness."

But Luzare interrupted him with, "You can talk, but I won't change my mind. My mind is made up. You are wasting your time."

The priest continued, "But this is for your daughter's future welfare; maybe it would mean her ruin if she didn't marry." The priest's face grew more concerned as he implored, "Listen to what I'm trying to say." But Luzare was not listening.

Instead, he took a long, deep breath and, with a voice controlled and resonant, spoke coldly, "Don't interfere. Mind your own business. This is a family matter."

The nervous priest, mopping beads of perspiration from his brow, continued speaking, "Don Constant, I do not marry couples when they are underage, except under one condition. This couple came to me. They said they had to marry; they *HAD* to." But Luzare did not hear.

He leaned very close to the priest's face, and his voice, which had always carried so singularly clear and firm, began quivering.

The vein in the center of his forehead stood cord-like and deep blue as he thumped his thick chest in suffering throbs, "You cannot know what my heart feels, because I have lost a daughter. When she married that boy, she became dead to me." Between great sobs he continued, "She is dead. Look at this tie. Do you see it's black? I have lost my daughter, and for the rest of the time I live, I shall wear it. I shall die wearing it." The old man ceased his sobs, drew a long breath, squared his magnificent shoulders, and held his stance until the priest bowed out the door. Then he stumbled blindly across the hall and fell on his bed.

The next day one of Rafael's cousins came to call. Only one generation removed from the hill concho, the woman stood simpering in her cheap, gaudy getup. Her arms were loaded with trinkets and bracelets, and her old black hat, which sat askance on her head, gave her flat-featured face an idiotic expression. A sleazy pink dress, a green coat, and green shoes completed her showoff attire. But malapert in her new importance of being lifted from low to wealthy brackets overnight, she, in her concho patois, presumed to chat with her in-laws. When she entered the room, Libia, Margarita, and all the sons' wives turned like mechanical puppets, as if controlled by fantoccini, and remained frozen with their backs to her until the self-styled parvenu took her departure.

For a week Luzare ate nothing. Always an honest and very able thinker, he now sat in his room, staring into a maelstrom of darkness. Every now and then he would take a deep breath, hoist himself up on his unsteady feet, and begin a distraught rampage, cursing and shaking his fists in defiance of God and man. Weakened by the activity, he would then sink back down into his trance-like grief. He heeded no one and moaned as one who has turned sad, dragging steps away from a newly dug grave. One morning he went down to his office and took legal precautions that Anabella could not touch another penny of her money in his lifetime.

The more Luzare thought of Anabella's blighted future, the more attentive he became to Margarita. He would look around frightened if she left the room for a moment, and often, during the day, he would cup her face in his stubby hand and beg her, saying, "You will

Figure 65   Rafael's Cousin

never do what your sister has done, promise me you won't!" And without waiting for reassurances, he would go into his lamentations, pounding his square fist against his heart, exclaiming, "You can't understand what your sister has done, marrying that common son-of-a-bitch concho. He doesn't even have a job." Margarita would always pat her father's arm, her voice soothing him momentarily.

Jaime waited in the background, never intruding too deeply into the family's emotional upheaval. He sometimes sat down and spoke with Luzare of impersonal matters. His voice was always sincere, low, and understanding. One day, and as naturally as if he were discussing the weather, he asked Luzare's permission to marry Margarita immediately so he could take her to the United States with him, explaining that he had plans to study another phase of medicine. Always fearful now of that shape in the future that had snatched one of his lovely daughters, Luzare saw Jaime as Margarita's salvation and a rescue for his own sanity. It was a lifting of his spirits; he felt revived. Calling Margarita to him and placing Jaime's hand over hers, he said, "I have just given Jaime permission to marry you." Margarita, still sick and weak, was hilariously happy. She began shopping trips to town, bought an enormous trousseau, and talked of a big party.

But Libia could see that both Margarita and Luzare were too overwrought for more excitement and so made reservations for them at the resort hotel in Alajuela. Margarita was too thin. The pneumonia she caught while running barefoot on Anabella's elopement day had sapped all her strength. They both needed quiet and special foods, and Libia prayed that a change of scenery for Luzare would mean a change of heart.

At the resort hotel, Luzare and his daughter lazed about. Margarita listened to her father when he felt expansive or rested in her room when he felt tired. Luzare's old friends from the nearby coffee plantations and cattle ranches gathered when they heard he was there. After seeing Margarita with Jaime, they took a lively interest in the courtship. One by one, the friends brought stories to Luzare's ears, all dealing with Jaime's dishonesty and his instability. They said they knew whereof they spoke because Jaime's brother lived right there in Alajuela. In one account, Jaime had been making one of his quixotic trips to Mexico and had taken a fur coat to be exchanged but had neither brought back another nor returned the coat to its too trusting owner. Another told of Jaime being given 5,000 pesos to buy a war shortage refrigerator in Mexico, but neither the refrigerator nor the 5,000 pesos were forthcoming to its rightful owner. Others related stories in which young girls had been accosted in Jaime's very office. But worst of all the inflaming tales were Jaime's politics. Jaime was a known communist and had been a close friend of Calderón Guardia, who financed his last few years of medical school in Mexico. Sick at heart already, Luzare pondered why he must proceed from evil to evil and why in his later years his soul must be so tormented. Vexed and bruised, he felt inside, wounded and filled with putrefying sores for which there could be no mollifying ointment. As Luzare listened, he was always more infuriated with Jaime's exploitations in business and his friendship with Guardia than he was with the immoral issues. Still, his friends bore down on him with advice. The air was alive with rumors and warnings. Disgusted and disheartened, Luzare held Margarita's face between his trembling hands and besought her with, "Margarita, open your eyes. This dishonest, corrupt man cannot make a good husband. I'm disappointed in him too. I beg you, here and now, stop the relationship. Don't see that man again. I can't bear to see you take the same road your sister did."

Margarita lifted her dark eyes to her father and answered, "Papa, I love him, and whether these stories are true or not, I don't know. All I know is that I love him." And dropping her eyes, she added, "I know I can't stay here without seeing him. But I'm scared. Send me away! Send me to the United States."

In spite of her solemn promises to stay away from Jaime, she found herself slipping down to meet him whenever he waited in the lobby. At her last meeting with him, the hostess took it upon herself to inform Luzare of the visitor, describing very accurately Jaime's cavalier features.

The next morning, as Margarita was fluffing up her father's pillows, he caught her hand. She felt herself under the spell of his gaze as he inquired, "When is he coming again, my child? You must tell me." In answering, Margarita spoke as one not possessed of her own will as she replied, "He will be here again Thursday."

Thursday night, Luzare sat in the lobby waiting with Margarita when Jaime, quick of step and facile of manner, walked in. Fresh and smiling, he stepped to meet his beloved. Luzare rose and faced the tall young man. He had thought his words over many times; now they came out in the concise order he had wished. "Jaime, you must not come here again. My friends whom I trust have told me too many stories of your exploitations, and I have good reasons to doubt you. Do not come again." Jaime opened his mouth to speak, but at the sight of Margarita's pale face full of concern for her father, he executed a stiff little bow, turned, and walked back through the door.

Margarita wept silently and scolded her father, "Papa, it was wrong to do that." However, Luzare remained unwavering once he made up his mind.

He shook his head and said, "No, my child, I can tell with my eyes. You could never be happy with him." And stroking her dark hair, he added softly, "Another better one will come along. You will see. Now promise you will not consider marriage with that man or see him again." Margarita nodded her denouncement.

Barely audible Luzare whispered, "Thank you. God will bless you for it."

CHAPTER TWENTY-ONE

Los Angeles
September 1946

BACK HOME FROM THEIR STAY in Alajuela, Margarita could not step out of the house without the convertible following her. Her love, stronger than her will or her promise, forced her to meet Jaime on the university campus for a few breathless words. Lost in the anonymity of the bustling campus, yet she was always fearful of being seen. Ricardo, obeying his father's instructions, made arrangements for Margarita's passport and cleared all her travel credentials.

Two days before the date set for her departure, she met Jaime for a hurried moment. She pushed a photograph of herself into his hand. He pressed her close and begged with a lover's ardor, "Don't go, please don't go, Little One. Don't leave me!"

But Margarita shook her head and answered, "I have no choice. But wait for me. Wait for me a year."

At the airport terminal, only a few minutes before the departure time, Margarita was paged to the telephone. At the other end of the line, Jaime's intense voice was making his past pleas. "Please listen to me," he begged. "I have my mother and father here beside me to talk to you. Listen to them if you will not believe me."

In a moment an older, thicker voice was beseeching, "Do you love my son? If you do, why do you go away? I want to convince you to stay. My boy loves you. I know. You don't stay because your family disapproves of my boy. He has done nothing wrong."

Margarita interrupted in a high, nervous voice, "No, no! I'll be back."

And again the voice of Jaime was crying bleakly, "Wait for me. Wait for me. I'm coming. I'm only a few miles away." Standing nearby watching the changing expressions of her daughter's face, Libia knew who the caller was. At that moment, like a hideous nightmare, the loudspeaker was blasting the announcement for the departure of the airplane.

The voice of Jaime sounded thinly into Libia's ear as she took the receiver from her daughter's hand. "Wait, wait, don't go!" the voice called. Libia spoke coldly, "Leave her in peace. She is going." And she placed the receiver on its hook. As she walked out and boarded the airplane, Margarita's eyes remained fixed on nothing.

Figure 66

Type of plane used to leave San José, Costa Rica. iStock. com/MMADIA https://www.istockphoto.com/photo/old-turboprop-airplane-gm92407836-8340026

The great four-engine airplane made such a smooth takeoff that Margarita was not aware she was airborne until she glanced out the window and saw below her the city of San José lying like a checkerboard that drowsy players had left while they napped on that quiet Sunday afternoon. The plane made its outbound swoop and nosed northward, climbing higher and higher above the gigantic rumpled northern mountains and then over Nicaragua with its deep green forests. The seventeen-year-old girl soon became adjusted to the feel of the pull of the plane and its occasional trembles, and she began looking around the interior of the airplane. She was idly pondering why Jaime could not come with her. Something he said at the last meeting kept flashing through her mind. His jaw had been so set as he had answered her question, "I can't tell you, little one, why I can't see you at Christmas." Noticing the stationery provided on the back of the seat in front of her, Margarita took a short pencil from her purse and began a letter to Jaime. She dated it '*September 12, 1946*' and began, '*My Dear Jaime,*' but suddenly the plane was rolling, shuttering, dropping, then rising, lurching,

Figure 67

Mexico City (Present Day)
iStock.com/Joel Carillet
https://www.istockphoto.com/photo/
mexico-city-skyline-at-dusk-gm511609492-
86740271?clarity=false

and pitching. The steward stood in the cabin door requesting smokers put out their cigarettes. He walked the aisles checking seat belts, and all the while, in a calm, reassuring voice, he spoke of the little roughness usually encountered at this juncture of their flight. Clutching the arms of her seat until the knuckles shone white, Margarita closed her eyes and prayed. Her lips moved silently in her white face as she said, "God, if you won't kill me, I promise not to write Jaime again."

Night came on, and there was nothing below but a blink of lights from time to time. At last the plane landed in Mexico City to remain overnight. Margarita stood outside the terminal looking for transportation into the city. Finally, she hailed a cab and stuck her head inside, but when she saw two men already seated as passengers, she hesitated undecidedly. The taxi driver's sarcastic voice strained, "Oh, come on, lady, we don't have all night." She crawled in and drew herself into as small a knot as possible in the corner and watched her companions.

One of the last warnings her father had given her was, "Always keep your eyes open, think, and don't get into a taxi in which there are already passengers, especially men. One could hold you while the other one robbed." The frightened girl pressed her purse containing the $300 tight against her stomach and wondered if the men knew she was carrying so much cash. She thought of her beautiful new trousseau being rifled. The man sitting next to the driver turned to speak to his companion in the back seat, giving him a broad wink. Margarita swallowed. Were they signaling? She watched the man's hand and sank back relieved when the two men only laughed and went on talking.

In the hotel room, with her door safely locked, Margarita walked into the bathroom, glanced behind the door, picked up the hem of her bedspread, and peeked underneath it. Satisfied, she pulled off her blouse and reached down to bring her skirt up over her head. But instead, she yanked it back down with a snatch. She walked over, jerked open the closet door, and peered into its bareness, then looked again all about the room. Finally, she completed her change. She lay down and immediately dropped into a tired sleep on a bed that seemed to move and tremble like the airplane under her. Suddenly she was awake. There was someone knocking at her door and asking in a shushed voice, "Señorita, do you want anything?" Margarita's frightened eyes dilated in the darkness. She listened, but the voice didn't speak again. In a moment, soft steps shuffled on down the corridor. Margarita sprang out of the bed, pulled on the light, and fumbled about in her suitcase until she found the small virgin she had packed. Placing it on the pillow beside her head and feeling fortified by its presence, she dropped again to sleep.

The next morning at eleven, the plane swooped down and dispatched its load at Los Angeles. Climbing out of the airplane and into the brightness of the California sun, Margarita felt oppressively, breathlessly hot. She walked into the terminal lobby and sat down to wait, as her mother had instructed her to do. She looked into every face, not knowing who she was seeking. Her mother had wired a cousin to meet her. Loudspeakers blared announcements

Figure 68

Los Angeles Today
iStock.com/Joel Carillet
https://www.istockphoto.com/photo/los-angeles-california-drone-aerial-
gm2191776144-610084720?clarity=false

of arrivals and departures, while outside, the planes landed and took off. Crowds rushed in and out. The hours began dragging. Margarita began squirming about in her seat, restless with hunger but not daring to leave her waiting post lest she miss her cousin. As the hand of the clock drew up to click the number five, the tired girl jumped up and went behind the ticket counter to the airline's office. Sobbing unrestrainedly and with wild gestures, she tried to explain that she wanted someone who spoke Spanish. The employees looked at her frightened face with sympathy, wondering about her distress, and finally sent to find one of their mechanics out on the line who spoke Spanish. The boy came in and listened for a moment to the distraught Margarita's story; his greasy fingers took the slip of paper she handed him. He pawed through the heavy directory until he located the name, dialed a number, and soon was explaining to someone that there was a girl just in from Costa Rica waiting at the airport, expecting to be met. He hung up the receiver and began instructing Margarita how to take a cab to the address on the slip. He said the woman at the address said she had received no telegram. The mechanic and the taxi driver efficiently loaded the girl's eight suitcases, transporting Margarita to an unknown destination once more. To her anxious mind, they seemed to ride for hours. She plucked at the weave of her suit and wondered what the driver's intentions were. Maybe he couldn't find the right address. Maybe he would never find it. She wanted to turn around and go back to the airport. She only knew she wanted to catch the next airplane back home.

Finally, the driver drew up in front of a large, white frame house, and an old man limped out to the cab and pointed to the front door. He, however, made no indications of welcome or any attempt to lift or carry a suitcase. He just watched while the driver placed the baggage on the porch and received his fare from the girl. Toughened by his daily carloads of troubles, nevertheless the driver shook his head as he drove away. There had been no sign of greetings, no friendliness at all for the new foreign girl. And there was a terrible, lost look on her face.

A small, emaciated woman with yellowish skin and gray hair came out into the hall. In plaintive Spanish, she explained, "Please understand that my relationship with your mother is only that of a distant kin. I run a boarding house here for twenty-five girls from the Southern Countries. All these girls pay in advance." She held out her palm but then added with a flourish, "I can wait for you to pay me until you get your things put away." She turned and led the new girl upstairs to a large room with five cots. She pointed to a cot and walked out, closing the door behind her. Margarita stood glancing about. The only closet in the room was already so stuffed with clothes and boxes that the door hung open, itself a

Figure 69   Amelia

sagging hodgepodge of shoes, sashes, hats, and a few slips stained with sweat lines that swung on the nails. Shoes of all sizes, conditions, and colors lay under the cots, the bureau, and out into the floor. The bureau was open in steps of half-closed drawers on which draped unfolded garments.

    Too tired to think or move, Margarita sank onto the cot the woman had indicated and decided she would just leave her clothes in the suitcases. She walked to the stairs, intending to ask for something to eat, but from the top of the staircase she could hear the woman's voice whining up to her, and she knew she didn't have the courage. She slowly descended the steps. At the bottom, a bunch of girls huddled about her, and before she really accepted the invitation, she found herself on the way to a skating rink. After her skates were strapped on, she pulled herself around the sides, feeling faint from hunger. Each time she passed one of the girls, she hoped they would suggest buying refreshments, but they never talked of food, and she couldn't bring herself to approach them. So she rolled around endlessly until the girls were tired too. Then they all went back to the woman's house. But standing again in the hall, she realized she couldn't climb the stairs again on her empty stomach, so she walked over to the woman called Amelia and asked, "Please, may I have something to eat?"

The woman inquired, "Didn't you have any dinner?"

"No," responded Margarita, "no, I didn't have any dinner or any lunch either." While the hungry girl wolfed down her pieces of bread smeared thinly with sandwich spread, Amelia took the ledger from her kitchen cabinet and listed under Margarita Constant's name, "*Meals, September 13, 1946.*" Margarita took her purse, peeled off three five-dollar bills, and paid the woman in advance for a week.

The next morning, Amelia was in the room early, fussing and sniffing, "Girls, you must keep your room neater. And I mean it." All the girls laughed as soon as the grumbling woman left the room. They finished their dressing and went down to eat. After breakfast, they went back upstairs, and Margarita cast about for a starting place to clean. The top of the bureau was cluttered and stacked with jars and boxes of powder. She walked over, made a mark through the powder dust with her finger, crossed back to her cot, spread the cover, stooped down and took from her suitcases what she needed at the moment, and then left them unlocked for her convenience. After she finished dressing, she went downstairs to study the telephone directory and to set about the task of finding a school. After numerous difficulties, not being able to read English, she finally registered at an opportunity school not far from where she was staying, which one of the girls had mentioned to her. After a few days, she rather enjoyed the school. Many of the other students were Spanish newcomers, and they were more friendly than the girls at the house.

She had only been attending classes for two weeks when Amelia's son was killed in an automobile accident. The whole house was thrown into an upheaval of condolences and laments. Amelia sent all the girls to mass every morning to say prayers for her dead son. In the afternoon she, herself, expected Margarita to come in and say the rosary for the boy. She sacrificed food and was disinclined to cook, or else hurriedly threw together cold concottic for the girls' consumption, a mess too unappetizing to eat. Margarita and one of the girls in her room started buying their own groceries, cans of beans or soup, and on the girl's little burner, which they kept hidden under the bed, they warmed their meals. One day when Amelia was sniffing and snooping about, she happened to find some cracker crumbs. She attacked Margarita with, "If you don't like my food, you can get out! After all, I do the best I can on the little sixty a month you pay me."

The other girl was older and not intimidated by the old woman's whines, and so retorted, "We are leaving just as soon as we can find a place to move." After Amelia left the room, Margarita sat down and took out the stationery folder. In her frightened, distressed mind, it always brought her mother closer. She wrote the words "*Dear Mama.*" Today she begged, "*Please, I want to come home. The old woman here is crazy. My life is impossible. I have to pray all afternoon. I am not allowed to go anywhere, and the girls have taken all my clothes.*" She left the unfinished letter on her bed while she answered one of the girls yelling to her from downstairs.

When she returned, Amelia and her daughter, their eyes smoldering with hate, were waiting, with the unfinished letter in Amelia's hand. The old woman's voice was menacing as she answered, "I see you don't appreciate kindness. I am not crazy. You don't know anything about death."

Margarita stuttered guiltily, "I, I didn't mean to say that."

But the old woman snatched away Margarita's words, saying, "You're a liar. You never did like me." Attracted by the discord, all the other girls gathered around the murderous faces. The woman straightened up and walked out, saying over her shoulder, "I will take this letter; I am going to write your mother a true report." A few days later Margarita received a troubled letter from her mother that read, "*Margarita, have you no respect for other people's homes? This woman has befriended you. I expect you to behave yourself while you are there.*" Margarita read the letter and sobbed. She knew she couldn't continue in this bedlam of torment. Again, she grabbed up her stationery folder. A card with Claudia's New Orleans' return address dropped out. She accepted the card as the intervening hand of God and wired Claudia that she was on her way. Then she secured reservations at the airline ticket office, paid a visit to the consulate office, and stopped in a store to purchase two pairs of panties. From her entire trousseau, all the underclothes she had were the garments she was wearing. Claudia was immediate in her cordial reply, "*Come ahead, wire, and I will meet you.*"

Margarita went back to the house and rooted about in the clothes closet for her hat. While she was crawling about on her hands and knees, Amelia came in inquiring, "And just what are you looking for?"

Emboldened with her own secret, Margarita snapped, "My hat."

The old woman sniffed, "Well, you have lost it if it isn't here. We are not thieves."

Margarita got up, pulled ten dollars out of her purse, and in a stronger voice than she had ever used with the woman, she stated, "This is your money for the rest of the week; I'm leaving." Amelia's yellowish eyes blinked in astonishment. Her mouth hung open in shock. But Margarita did not bother to explain. She picked up her bags, carried them downstairs, and in her best broken English, she ordered a taxi over the telephone and was soon on her way to the airport. When the airliner circled the field, winging its departure, she looked down, relieved, and thanked God that at last she was on her way, nor did she ever wish to return.

At the airport in New Orleans, Claudia, as cool and immaculate as always, was waiting. She took Margarita into the cafeteria. Margarita, seeing the quantities of delicious, beautiful food within arm's reach, filled her tray until she staggered under its load and ate until there was not a scrap left.

Claudia was attending a Catholic college out near Tulane

University and was boarding with an old Costa Rican lady who kept her spacious house as clean and quiet as a nunnery. Every night after the great hall clock struck ten times, Sara Williams could be seen strolling down the hall in her billowing white gown, a Virgin-shaped candle in her hand shining wanly in the glow of artificial lighting from the lamps. But Sara Williams, good and pious and interested in her girls and her God, carried her candle to seek and burn out all lurking evil that might be crouching in shadowy corners.

Claudia soon had Margarita enrolled in her own college, and the young girl's days were a happy arrangement. Also, she struck up a friendship with a girl from Honduras. And from her own struggling few English words in the classroom, she could lapse into her easy, effusive Spanish with Estrella as soon as they met in the halls or out on the campus.

Figure 70 A

New Orleans (Present Day)
https://www.istockphoto.com/photo/aerial-view-of-jackson-square-along-decatur-st-new-orleans-louisiana-usa-in-summer-gm2167456005-587518505
iStock.com/Jeremy Poland

Figure 70 B

Claudia

CHAPTER TWENTY-TWO

New Orleans to Atlanta
Christmas 1946

IT COULD BE SAID OF Margarita's grandmother, Catalina, that she needed no cloud by day or the light of fire by night to show her this way through life. Life to her was either clean or unclean, and she always picked her way carefully. Her lifted skirts never touched the mire. She often quoted her favorite biblical motto, "*And that doth the Lord require of thee, but to do justly, and to love mercy, and to walk humbly.*" On the other hand, it must be said of Margarita that she could not divine the clean from the unclean. If an evil befell her, she regarded it as a type of carnival monstrosity and not likely to be encountered again by chance. How could she eschew evil men when she did not even recognize them? She was simply unaware of evil as a force, and therefore the dark places of the earth were not habitations of cruelty to her. If Catalina had been God, after her first five days of creation it would never have been written of her that she looked on her highest creation and, "Behold, it was very good." For Catalina would have perceived that an extra squeeze was needed here and there, a little more patting off of dust.

A fleck of sand would have marred its perfection in her eyes. But to Catalina's granddaughter, Margarita, all people were perfect. And all people were alike. She possessed no culler, no winnower, no means of discrimination, and she was therefore incapable of conceiving sordidness as such.

Catalina always divided children into two groups: those who could afford school uniforms and those who wore their own shabby clothes. And the fact that Margarita's entourage was always the barefoot conchos led Catalina to make the statement once, "Margarita, you have a taste for trash!" The statement in itself was not altogether true. It wasn't that Margarita actually craved trash; it was just that the conchos never gave her any resistance. They never seemed to notice her glasses. They never made any remarks or snickered when she sucked her milk out of a nippled bottle at school. And they never laughed when she jumbled her father's name into '*ion Cuzare*' instead of '*don Luzare.*' Instead of waiting for her turn like the uniformed bunch, she enjoyed being the first in all the games.

Estrella's friendship came easily, requiring no cultivation. It was in full bloom the very first day they chatted. Estrella's lips spread easily into a sweet, confidential smile, disclosing her small, closely set teeth. She affected simplicity, and her darkness always provoked the onlooker's eye to search for jewelry, which she never wore. She complemented her severe suits with a white shirtwaist, the collar of which she neatly folded over them. In the next two or three days, she told Margarita her whole background. She had been in the United States only three months herself and said she had come from the very jungles of Honduras, a horrible place, practically inaccessible except by airplane. It had been her father's stupid idea to dig for minerals and petroleum, and all she ever saw back home were dirty, filthy workmen, her father, and her poor mother. "And," she emphasized, "I can't understand my mother giving up her whole life just to be with my father. He's coarse and simple, not in the least diplomatic, and always dirty and working. While my mother is beautiful, she always lived in the city before she married my father, and how my mother hates those wilds! But there she stays, only getting into town once a year. What is a town but a few houses? My mother wanted me to come to the United States to get away from the whole thing. She hopes I will meet somebody with money and get married so I won't have to go back there. My mother is so sweet, but my father is stupid, plain stupid!"

Figure 71

Estrella

In the next few weeks, Estrella's warmth dimmed Claudia's self-containment and book-spoken Spanish. Margarita spent all her free time with Estrella, whose personal problems were always overwhelming her. Margarita regarded Estrella's cozen ways as fitting her mother's description of a naive girl, "a simple girl," and she felt increasingly stronger, more protective, and more pleased by Estrella's confidences.

Shortly before Christmas, Margarita received a telegram from Costa Rica that read, "*If all works out, will see you on Christmas Day. Love, Jaime.*" Margarita wondered how Jaime had found her address and also pondered if she would be glad to see him. Finally she decided that she could not even imagine him in New Orleans. He was part of the earth she had left behind when she rose from land in the airplane and looked down on the city of San José. Now he was as unreal as the land below her had looked. She was relieved

Christmas 1946   229

when she received another telegram on Christmas Day that stated, "*MY PLANS CHANGED. WILL SEE YOU LATER. LOVE JAIME.*"

In January, Estrella did not re-enroll in school. As she explained to Margarita, "These girls here are discriminating against me because I'm foreign. I want to go to Atlanta, where I can be sure of better treatment. But," and she gave a woebegone gesture, "it's no use. I have no money right now, and it would take a lot to get us situated."

Margarita considered her own dwindling bank account and inquired weakly, "How much?"

Estrella's small eyes wrinkled and squinted, pinching invisible pennies. "I'd say $200, at least." Margarita consulted her checkbook. There was less than a hundred dollars balance, but she would have to find a way. She must not fail Estrella. Her mind gnawed over a name her father had written her in one of his letters since she had been in New Orleans. A moment of concentration brought the name to her. Mr. Bonette, an affluent sugar refiner and one of her father's old friends, was someone her father had wanted her to look up to as soon as she could.

Behind his shiny expanse of desk, Mr. Bonette listened to the young girl's pitiful story of running out of money and needing enough to enter her second term of school. He chuckled and said he would be glad to oblige. Luzare was a good friend, and there was no risk in lending money to one of his children. Luzare always paid his debts.

Once again outside, Margarita tucked the $150 into her purse and felt ingeniously clever. Estrella need not worry a minute more.

No sooner did Estrella behold the flourish of bills than she was making plane reservations, sending a wire, and packing clothes. By midafternoon, after telling Claudia about the unsuitability of her present arrangements, Margarita and Estrella were on their way to Atlanta, Georgia. During the flight, Estrella kept reassuring Margarita of Roy's reliability. She seemed to relish speaking Roy's name, and each time she rolled the 'r', she smacked its very sound. "Roy," she said, "is my only friend besides you, of course, Margarita. I met him on my flight from Honduras to Atlanta; he was a tall, good-looking steward. Wait until you see him. You'll see how good-looking he is. Anyway, when I reached Atlanta, I was completely lost and didn't know how to get to the school in Milledgeville. Everything was so strange, so different. You can imagine how I felt, but Roy was so sweet. He went to Milledgeville with me to get registered in school and came down every weekend while I was there. He was the only one who understood how lonely I was. And the girls there were so hateful to me. They discriminated against me just as the girls in New Orleans had, and you know how ugly they treated me!" Margarita nodded sympathetically, although at that moment she was unable to recall any incidents of that nature ever occurring. But Estrella went on, "And when I couldn't stand it any longer, Roy suggested that I go down to New Orleans. And that was a lucky break because otherwise I wouldn't have met you."

At the airport in Atlanta, Roy, a wiry blond man with a clipped brush of canary-yellow mustache, was waiting. He kissed Estrella warmly, led the girls to a rusty-looking old automobile, lifted the creaky back lid, placed their baggage inside, and introduced the girls to his brother, who was sitting in the car. After driving a few blocks, Roy stopped again, took the bags out of the back of the car, and went into a house. In a few minutes he was back and drove them into the city.

In the hotel room on the eighth floor, Roy and Estrella sat in intimate closeness on the bed. Every now and then, Estrella would pull herself out of Roy's grasp, make a few protesting squeals, and roll her eyes in mock shock. Then in a moment she would melt again in his embrace like wax before a fire. In trying not to stare at the couple, Margarita turned her attention to the floor and studied the pattern in the carpet. The baggy-panted man, Roy's brother, came in the door bearing drinks, and a convivial feast soon began. Margarita kept sipping along on the sweetened whiskey water. The hour was late, and she was tired. She eyed the bathroom door longingly, wondering how she could make it into the little room without being noticed. But as the hours dragged on, the fest-making grew merrier. Roy and his brother were knee-slapping and telling jokes, while Margarita was so sleepy she dared not lean her head against the back of her chair. She managed to catch Estrella's eye and made yawning motions.

But quick-eyed Roy saw the gesture and commanded, "Margarita, go to bed. You're sleepy!"

Figure 72 A

Roy

Margarita looked confounded and asked in English, "How do I go to sleep? You're here."

Roy tossed his blond head and replied, "Well, go undress. I'm going to stay here tonight."

And the bleary-eyed brother, with a big swoop of his hand, grinned and said, "Move over, Margarita, I'll be with you."

Margarita's eyes snapped open, and her voice quivered on the brink of hysteria as she cried, "Get out! Get out!"

The older man backed out the door stammering, "Oh, I'm sorry. I had you confused. I guess I didn't understand what Roy told me." He beckoned to the cozy Roy and called, "Come on, Roy, let's get going!"

But Roy only shook his head in disbelief and replied, "Not me, I'm staying here." Margarita watched the door close behind the baggy man before going into the bathroom to take a shower. Having no clothes to change into, she put back on her wrinkled slip, and while Roy was deep in another kiss, she eased into the nearer bed, pulled the covers about her neck, and peeked out like a curious baby at the embracing couple.

With his mouth still on Estrella's face, Roy cocked open one eye in Margarita's direction, broke the kiss, and scolded as to a child, "Margarita, go to sleep. Estrella is going to be my wife." Too frightened to disobey, Margarita turned her back on the lovers, and with her face to the wall, she listened awhile to the stillness but soon fell asleep. Much later she was awakened by a familiar hiss. Turning over, she looked into her friend's dark-faced, disheveled countenance and her drowsily satisfied eyes, and she listened as the troubled, confiding voice whispered, "Margarita, look, what am I going to do? He is asleep."

Margarita, remembering, popped up in bed, her eyes big and half afraid, half shocked, as she asked, "Did he do anything to you?"

Estrella drew her full lips down into an insulted denial, "Of course not!" And inching into the narrow bed, she lifted up the covers, hoisted her slender body, and replied, "Look, there is no blood!" Knowing Margarita's ideas of a virgin union, this was unquestionably conclusive evidence. She then raised a slim, smooth leg, flexed the muscles luxuriantly, and pointed her toe daintily, dimpling the dark marks in the calf of her leg, where, as she had often explained to Margarita, a dog had bitten her when she was a small child. She always ended this story by sighing that it was a pity that the blemish marred her otherwise perfect legs.

Due to Estrella's restlessness, Roy flung his arm over her breasts, yawned, crawled out of the bed, drew his pants up his thin legs, pulled on his shirt, tightened his belt, and tugged on his tie until it was straight. He glanced at the watching, silent Margarita, placed his finger over his neatly chopped mustache, and said, "Don't say anything. It's all right. You are just a little girl, and you don't understand. So don't say anything." Then he combed his yellow hair with his small black comb, slicked it down with his hands, pulled on his coat, turned to the girls, and commented, "Got to go make a dollar. See you this afternoon. I'll take you out to eat." He winked slyly at Estrella and walked out. Margarita stayed most of the day in the room. Her suit was rumpled, and her underclothes were drying on a hanger in the bathroom. Although she had taken two baths, she somehow felt uncouth. She showered again and ate the sandwich Estrella, who was in remarkably fine spirits, brought back to her from downstairs. At six, Roy was back. He took the girls to a café and treated Margarita in such a paternal manner she felt like a small child tagging along.

Figure 72 B

Present Day Atlanta Skyline Over Piedmont Park
https://www.istockphoto.com/photo/iconic-view-of-atlanta-skyline-over-piedmont-park-gm1482238845-509279640
iStock.com/Marilyn Nieves

CHAPTER TWENTY-THREE

Maurice, Barton and Barr
1947

AFTER THE FIRST NIGHT, MARGARITA accepted Roy's presence in the room at bedtime, but each morning she awoke questioning Estrella, who tossed it off in amusement, "Of course not, Roy is nice. He did nothing to me." Margarita's big problem was no clothes, and Roy found it too inconvenient to fetch the clothes at night, and so for three days the girls had no change. On the third night, his brother came, lugging the suitcases in, and on the fourth night, Roy sat with the telephone directory between his thin legs, looking for a place for the girls to move. After making several telephone calls of inquiry, he finally turned and relayed that he had found a place on Piedmont Avenue, a church home for girls at $7 a week, which included food, and that he would take Margarita's references over for the woman to see first thing the next morning.

The next day, with Roy's help, the girls checked out of the motel. Roy bigheartedly paid the bill and took them by cab to the brick dormitory building with its expansive bay windows looking across

Figure 73

Piedmont Park, Atlanta Georgia (Present Day)
iStock.com/mphillips007
https://www.istockphoto.com/photo/atlanta-gm183801340-16205283?searchs
cope=image%2Cfilm

onto Piedmont Park. While Estrella and Roy unloaded the baggage, Margarita spoke with the housemother and paid rent for both of them for two weeks. As soon as she settled herself in the dormitory room, she sat down and, using the house stationery, wrote to her father where she was, emphasizing the strictness of the rules. This was a feature that would appeal strongly to Luzare. She also requested some money, and, acting with more prudential foresight than was her usual wont, that very Sunday morning she placed her remaining $100 in a bank to be kept for future school fees. Looking in the telephone directory, memories of her old school attracted her to Sacred Heart, the church where she would attend Mass the next morning, her first Sunday in Atlanta.

A big, husky fellow with a head like a shaggy blond Saint Bernard sat on the pew next to her. Their eyes chanced to meet several times during the service, and afterwards, outside, he passed her on the street, smiled courteously, paused, and inquired if she were not

Figure 74

Maurice Du Clerc

foreign. She nodded, smiling. He went on chatting in Spanish, strolling along beside her. He himself was of direct French descent, although he had been born in New York City and was only in Atlanta to attend school at Georgia Tech. He explained in a pleasant little accent that he was in his junior year and his name was Maurice Du Clerc. Margarita was so delighted to hear her own language she almost forgot to tell him her name. They caught a bus at the corner and got off in front of the church home, but the day was too gorgeous to go inside, so they walked over into the park, enjoying the January sunshine.

The next Sunday Margarita again met Maurice at Mass. That afternoon while walking with her in the park, he talked of his future as an engineer and his high ambitions, and he asked permission to see her during the week. Margarita took him to meet the housemother, who beamed her approval.

So the first several weeks passed serenely for Margarita in Atlanta. One night, however, just after she finished her dinner at the home, she was surprised to look up and see Estrella coming in. It was Roy's routine to pick Estrella up after he got in from the airport, take her out to eat, and bring her back at the curfew hour. At this moment, Estrella's face was downcast, her heavy lips dropped into a pout, and her voice was troubled and low. She confided in Margarita, who, acquainted now with the symptoms, mentally counted her money. Estrella leaned closer. "Margarita, I hate to ask you, but I wonder if you could lend me some money? I'll have to pay my tuition in advance to get in school, and if I don't register by the weekend, my passport will be revoked. The time is running out, but the school will extend my passport if I'm a student. But how can I? I have no money, and my money from home is past due. It will come, you know that, and then I'll repay you."

Margarita hesitantly inquired, "How much do you need?"

"A hundred dollars" was the quick response, which, by some stroke of accuracy, just matched Margarita's bank account. Always obsequious to Estrella, Margarita drew out her hoarded money and handed it to her the very next day.

Two days later, Margarita awoke aching and was too miserable to stir out of bed. Roy suggested that night to Estrella that Margarita should go see a doctor, and he wrote the name of one on a slip of paper. The next day, Margarita dragged herself downtown to the appointment. In a bristling voice of alarm, the doctor instructed the sick girl to go straight to the hospital. Margarita had no money, but Roy promised the hospital registrar he would take care of the matter, and she was allowed to be admitted. For two weeks, her pneumonic condition was critical, and afterwards for days, she lay in a febrile kef, a languorous tranquility, too weak even to be interested in the magazines Maurice left at her bedside with every nightly visit. The lonely girl depended on his big, comforting presence at the end of the day. Upon leaving, he always puttered about the room, adjusting the shades and the windows while waving his hand, feeling for drafts. Then he would go to the end of the hall and bring back a pitcher of water to put beside her bed. If he were leaving a box of candy with her, he would always shake his finger in a forbidding manner and say, "Mind you don't eat too much. You will make yourself sick." As he was about to walk out, he would always pat her arm affectionately, and his gruff voice would say, "Be a good girl. I'll see you tomorrow." Next, he would stoop down and delicately caress her forehead, chin, and cheeks, creating the symbol of the cross.

Maurice felt entertainment was essential to his visitations. The nurses and doctors walking past the door grew accustomed to seeing the big man illustrating his gymnastics, sometimes doing push-ups between the chairs or walking on his hands across the length of the floor while Margarita lay looking on admiringly. And Maurice thrived on people, too. As the weeks passed, to enliven the evenings, he often brought his friends so Margarita could feel she had really been visited by company. Once he brought one of his instructors from school, and another time he brought a Costa Rican couple whom he had located through the Latin American Club.

One night after the visitors had gone, Maurice sat near Margarita's side, stroking her hand. He lifted the hand to his cheek and asked, "Margarita, would you consider yourself engaged to me? We could be married in June next year after my graduation. You are such a wonderful girl, and I feel very close to you. I want you to say you will marry me."

Ensconced in her covers, wrapped in warm contentment, Margarita glowed at the thought of being in Maurice's custody. Softly she whispered, "Yes."

Even though Maurice felt officially entitled to kiss her, the touch of his lips was as cool and clean as mint and even Edwin had kissed her harder and with more ardor when she was only thirteen.

After five weeks, during which it was necessary to wire her father for $500 to evacuate her from the hospital, Margarita went back to the dormitory. Too weak to do little more than just sit, she whiled away her time in a state of "*dolce far niente*," delightful idleness. Like a lotus eater, in dreamy indolence she spent hours in the park, and at night she occasionally went riding with Maurice. Later, as she grew stronger, he took her to the American Legation, proud to introduce her to his friends there. Once she attended a masquerade ball at the home of one of his French friends. Dressed like a doll, she tied a wide, pink, satin ribbon under her chin, flounced the frills on her big bonnet and encircled her dark hair, and whirled her short skirt, which was sprinkled with flowers. The fluffy skirt flounced teasingly away from her legs. Upon beholding her, Maurice picked her up in his arms, oblivious of the housemother, and carried her to his automobile, saying, "See everybody, I have a little doll who can't walk alone."

And as much as Maurice enjoyed being in crowds, he was somewhat priggish about his personal life. He abhorred dormitories, and when he first started college at Georgia Tech, he found himself a quiet apartment, furnished it to his taste, and employed an old woman to do his cleaning and cooking for him. His clothes were always immaculate, and he was fastidious about little things. If a candy wrapper fell in his automobile while they were driving, he was not at ease until the paper had been picked up and taken out of the car. He was of a perfectionist mind. He searched the city for a proper engagement ring, found nothing to his liking, and decided he would rather wait until he went home on his vacation in June before purchasing one.

One day Margarita received a telegram from Ricardo in New York saying that he had come to get Renato from the university and that he would be stopping in Atlanta to see her on his way down. Margarita, who had only visited Ricardo once or twice in her whole lifetime, even though he had lived next door, was in high excitement in anticipation of his visit. On the following Sunday morning, Ricardo, Renato, and Diana stood in the small lobby of the church home and awaited Margarita. Down she rushed, greeting them effusively, for they were home to her heart. Turning last to Renato, she reached to plant a kiss but stood staring instead. Renato's long, skinny frame was hunched forward like an old man's. At twenty, he was the picture of a medieval alchemist. His lanky dark hair hung shoulder length with swooping curls that lay on his swarthy hollow cheeks; his eyes burned with strange intensity behind his thick horn-rimmed glasses. A loosely fitting frock coat swathed his bony figure, and a large black ascot tie was looped carelessly at his chin. Suspecting a joke, Margarita giggled and looked teasingly into his eyes, but Diana, her arm encircling Margarita's waist, pressed a warning squeeze, and her eyes bade the young girl to make no remarks. For a moment Margarita stood in shocked suspension as she realized that Renato, gentle, brilliant Renato, was mad!

Hurriedly Diana put in her high, shrill voice, "Margarita, have you noticed my purse and shoes?" Margarita followed with her eyes the tiny, beautifully turned shoes of soft tawny brown and the bag that was pouchlike and had patches of longer, darker hair. Diana laughed and questioned, "Do you know where I got them?"

Margarita shook her head dully. "Remember the puma that Ricardo downed with a single shot, the one prowling about in the patio one night? I had these made from the hide. Wasn't that clever of me?" Then Diana laughed again shrilly.

They stepped outside to the sidewalk and waited for Maurice to pick them up in his automobile. And as soon as Maurice hopped out of his car, Renato turned from the others, walked out, and crawled into the vehicle. With his usual insight, Maurice gave no hint of being aware of Renato's stage-like garb. He answered Ricardo's questions conversationally as they drove along, pointing out from time to time the dogwood trees along the streets. The trees were in rare beauty this spring. Like slender young girls, Margarita and Diana waved their pretty pink and white Sunday dresses in sprightly, frolicsome gaiety.

Diana listened and only spoke in her high voice during the dangerously quiet moments. Once she called out as they passed a sidewalk fruit shop, "Oh look, the pineapple, so comically little!"

Parking the automobile downtown, the five people sauntered along the sidewalk. Diana became absorbed in the Easter finery displayed in the shop windows. Ricardo peered into restaurant windows, his meticulous eye searching for just the right atmosphere. But Renato was magnetically drawn to a used bookstore, and he started pounding on the glass door, screeching in his thin falsetto voice, "Open the door, open the door!"

Ricardo's low and cajoling voice said, "Son, it is Sunday; the stores will be open tomorrow." But that only excited Renato all the more. He rattled, kicked, and banged on the door with intensified vigor until the proprietor, who was in the back of the shop listing merchandise, peeked around a row of bookshelves to see what was causing the commotion. When Renato caught sight of the man, he put the weight of his thin body against the door and banged again with all his might. Then he stepped back, pointed to the proprietor, pulled two bills from his pockets, and held them high, pointing again to the man as he made a gesture of giving. The old man shrugged his shoulders defeatedly as if to answer, "*Who can refuse money?*" and opened the door. Once inside, Renato crawled about on his knees in the darkest corners, now and then pulling a dusty volume from the shelf and thumbing through the aged leaves. The others, left standing in the patch of light from the window, chatted with the owner until Renato had completed his search. Then he plunked his three finds on the desk, paid the amount the merchant stated, handed over the extra two bills that had opened the door, turned, and led the way out.

In the muted Sunday atmosphere of the restaurant, Ricardo attempted once or twice to make sociable comments, but these were interpreted by Renato as innuendos, and he lifted an insulted voice and flung his hands above his head as if to implore the gods to rain down punishment on his enemies.

Maurice calmly laid his heavy hand on the boy's thin shoulder, pointed to the untouched plate, and with the authority of a prison warden stated, "Your food is getting cold, Renato; you had better eat." Renato immediately relaxed, and in docile meekness he ate like a child in his nursery. Margarita had always thought of Ricardo as a sort of Dives and her family as the Lazarus of his rich table, accepting the crumbs of his attention and his iron authority on all matters that her father did not rule. Now she looked on Ricardo's face and felt a great pity for him.

To finish their afternoon's entertainment, Maurice invited them to the sumptuous Fox Theater to show off its magnificent interior. Renato was totally unimpressed by the dissonant, harsh jarring of the Spike Jones orchestra, which was making its stage appearance. He lifted his notebook above his shoulder to catch the faint backlight. While the audience listened to music that might have been composed by Loki, he made scratchy notations on mass psychology in his little black book.

Afterwards, in the new coldness of late afternoon, he left the others standing in front of his newly acquired treasures; he couldn't wait another moment. He did not relinquish his bed, even for meals, during the five days that his mother and father spent in Atlanta. Ricardo and Diana left Margarita, promising to give a good report of her situation to Luzare. And Ricardo jokingly nudged his stepsister and said, "Make sure you don't let that boy get away. He's very nice."

Margarita always attended mass with Maurice, but during the prayers her eyes were frequently attracted by the pretty headwear and the colorful hats that even the old ladies paraded. To her, it never ceased to be pageantry to come to church, but Maurice would catch her eye and whisper in a severe voice, "You're supposed to be praying to God. Stop looking around like that!" She would duck her head, but from time to time she would forget again and become engrossed in the festival of high vivid colors.

On Good Friday, with Estrella's help, Margarita cleared off the dressing table of the dormitory room, draped it in black, placed the Virgin's statue and the Crucifix in the center, then lit a candle and prayed. The other girls kept milling in and out during the ritual, whispering loudly, "Look, they're making black magic." Estrella listened to a few of their slurring remarks, finally got up from her knees, and began ironing a dress for her date. Scenting out disturbance, the housemother walked in upon the scene. Her sensible eyes under the tight gray curls understood Margarita's nature of worship. She wheeled around, facing the girls, and used her tongue like a lash: "Shame on you girls. Get on with your business. It wouldn't hurt some of you to be doing a little praying yourselves; I've a mind to say. Now get on." After the girls scattered, she consoled the trouble-hearted Margarita, "It's all right, child. Pay no attention to them." And as she bustled out, she called over her shoulder, "Just watch that candle. Loose fire like that could burn the place up!"

Margarita, however, found her mood of worship shattered. Her soul was too disquieted for her to remain in the house. She sought her refuge across the street. It was three o'clock, and the noise and din of the city continued unceasingly, and Margarita found herself running into the park away from the clang and roar. Her mind kept asking, "Don't they know? Don't they care that God is dead?" Away from the clamor, she sat down by the still waters of the pond and stared into its cold depth. Like the waters of Siloam, they soothed her soul, and she thought of home. There were no automobiles moving in the streets today, and even the buses and trains were not running. All the stores would be closed. Black-garbed people had gone at eleven o'clock to the church to hear a sermon on the betrayal of Jesus. An image of Christ with the Cross was carried through the streets, and along its predestined route, the Samaritan Woman offered Christ water. Magdalene groveled at His feet and anointed them with precious oils. Veronica wiped his pathetic, blood-sweated face, and its imprint stained her handkerchief. The Virgin Mary and John had met their Lord.

Then in the afternoon there were two long sermons, and at three o'clock the image of the dead Christ was eased into a glass and gold sepulcher, and the doleful dirges of the procession began. Throughout the procession, little girls, dressed in white transparent wings, were borne on small platforms and jostled along on strong men's shoulders. In their hands, they carried mottos bearing the seven last sayings of the Cross. Veronica had been carried back along the platform, sitting beside a deserted cross, and Magdalene, the Samaritan woman, and a hundred men, thus highly honored in somber black suits, carried the sepulcher. Last came the priests, the image of John, and the sorrowful Mary. Along the way, the streets were lined with emotional and tearful onlookers, fingering their rosaries and thinking of that cruel day and of their crucified God.

Margarita's heart was too full, and it felt ready to burst. She looked about the park, found a barren tree, dead of all leaves, and there she knelt and stretched her arms to the imaginary cross and mummered the thirty-three Credos. Close by, a dogwood stood resplendent in its pearly white and pale pink-tinted petals. And to Margarita's blurred eyes, the trees were the Madonna, lovely, gentle, swaying in her immaculate garments. This was indeed hallowed ground.

Easter that year, the first week in April, was a gloriously mild spring day. After Mass, Maurice took Margarita to dinner, and in the afternoon they shouted and yelled at a ball game at Ponce de León Park.

The next two months were a wonderful dream for Margarita. She felt strong. Maurice always took her into crowds and never lacked money. They danced at nightclubs and went riding in his automobile. Maurice was always optimistically speaking of his bright future once he was over his senior year hurdle. His English grew more fluent and articulate, while Margarita's was still broken and inexact. As they took their rides, Maurice would say, "Now take out your mirror. Watch your mouth and say these words," and once he began an English lesson, he never stopped until Margarita grew too inattentive to even look in the mirror.

Early in June, they exchanged photographs; Maurice gave the eighteen-year-old girl his New York address, and they promised each other they would write often. Maurice again rehearsed his itinerary with Margarita to make sure she understood. He was first going to Cuba, and then he would be at home in New York until September.

But after Maurice left, Summer took his place in Margarita's affections. She heard from him only occasionally, and she wrote a card every now and then. She went swimming with the girls in the park, took sunbaths, and began a convivial dormitory life, carefree and easy. Whenever she thought of Maurice, it was like a well-remembered movie. More often, it was with a certain relief that he was not there. Whenever she thought of Maurice, she invariably thought of her grandmother, and if she thought long enough, Maurice assumed her grandmother Catalina's black dress. But the remembrance of his unruly hair made the whole picture untidy, and she often had the impulse to say, "Brush your hair, Maurice; my grandmother never lets her hair fall down." The more she thought, the more ridiculous it all seemed until there was no sentiment whenever she remembered.

Except for the Italian lady, there were now no prods in Margarita's life whatsoever. The Italian woman had taken such an instant interest in her ever since she met her at the American Legation. The woman was always popping in to visit her and asking her what she intended to do for the future. It was upon her instigation that Margarita went to school in March, over at the Central High School for a night course in English. But on the first night there, after registration, a cocky, muscular boy in a red plaid shirt and blue jeans had pestered her. So she hadn't gone back. As they sat in the classroom, the blond-haired boy asked her name, but she and the Italian lady ignored him and refused to answer. However, the Italian woman supplied him with answers. The woman loved the idea of promoting romance and volunteered Margarita's name and her telephone number and even added, "You be sure and call her because she has no boyfriends."

The boy doffed his white, blond head toward Margarita and said, "Good, now I can call you."

But Margarita replied archly in her best English, "It won't do you any good. I don't go to the phone, and I don't talk to strange men."

The Italian woman nudged her and winked, "Now why are you mad? It's all right. You're like an old woman. Have fun. Let him call you!" For a couple of days afterward the boy telephoned, but Margarita had not gone near the phone, nor had she gone back to school, afraid that she might see him again. Then when summer came, she forgot the whole incident.

Then there was a space of more than three weeks when Margarita did not hear from her father. She always depended on at least four letters a week from him, but for a time there was nothing, nothing, no matter how urgently she wrote inquiring. Finally, her father sent a long letter explaining the situation:

> "My dear daughter," went the big scrawl, "I am sure you have been worried. Not being able to hear from me. But affairs have been such here that it is just as well you missed them. My friend Ulate, who owns the *Diario de Costa Rica*, asked Picado to set up an electoral tribunal. He suggested He suggested that a council of three men be established to count the votes. (We expect Otilio Ulate to be our next president). Ulate was looking ahead, trying to avoid what happened in the last election. But Picado refused. Our whole country went on a general strike. All businesses remained closed. No food came in from the country; nothing moved. It was like Good Friday.

It was our only way to show our power.

On Roma Ida, August 2, the streets were filled with women of all kinds, including teachers and schoolgirls—such a sight as we have never seen before. They went to the Presidential House asking for the electoral tribunal. Picado spoke from his window, in his sarcastic voice, "Ask for a miracle from the Virgin of the Angels." But the next day he gave in. "In February, there will be a different system for running things. Don't worry about anything. We needed nothing during the strike. Our side was well-organized; nobody went hungry. But your mother stayed in the billiard room all the time. It was strange times."

The Italian woman wouldn't leave Margarita alone to her lazy peacefulness. She next suggested a beauty course for her. As the woman explained, "A young girl never knows these days when she might have to support herself. You might as well be learning something you can use in the future. Why don't you become a beautician? Good English isn't necessary in that profession." So Margarita wrote to her father for $200 for the tuition, and she went down to the Powder Puff Beauty School to enroll.

That night as she lay in bed, she thought of her first tonsorial experience. She could see old Lola, the lavandera, as she stood over the tub scrubbing clothes. Her coarse black hair, straight as a horse's mane, lay in one heavy plait down her back. The ends were webbed and dotted with tiny white eggs, and often live, wispy, spidery nits fell from her hair and onto her shoulders and back. She could see herself as she had been at that time, a long-legged ten-year-old child. She remembered how she had brought out a stool and a large pair of shears that were hidden behind her back, then stood behind Lola and said, "Lola, let me even up the ends of your hair." Unmindful of the young girl's endless chatter, Lola nodded her consent, and the little girl climbed onto the stool and began clipping. The scissors slipped and slid, but she held tight and tugged on the queue while the shears blistered her fingers, but she didn't stop until, at last, she held a long switch, now like a horse's tail. Lola glanced over her shoulder and screamed. Then she ran to Esmeralda's full-length mirror in the servant's room. Her short hair, cropped into weird zigzags, stood straight out from her head. Lola flew up the hall, shrieking for Libia, flinging her hands toward the culprit, and pointing. Libia scolded Margarita and tried to calm Lola.

That night, Lola's man refused to let her out of the gate when he walked by to pick her up from work. He preferred to believe that Lola had spent the day with another man during one of her drunken sprees and that a different lover had cut her hair out of revenge. He slapped her face soundly and walked away. Left While standing there, Lola turned to Margarita, who was watching, and said, "Do you see? I lost my man because of you!" The next day Lola asked for a day off to go to the barber shop to have her hair cut again.

But once Margarita started her beauty course, she found she was more interested in beauty culture than she had ever been in any of her studies. She spent every day from nine to four there and didn't look for excuses to skip classes. Another one of the students, Evelyn, asked her to move into her boarding house with her since she needed a roommate. Besides, as she pointed out, it would be more convenient for Margarita too. The boarding house was only three or four blocks away from the beauty school, within easy walking distance of her new Washington Street home. The building, a big, rambling, five-story structure, stood on a street where pretentious, fronted rooming houses crowded both sides. Each was a relic of a grander era, with filigreed and fluted woodwork, some with austere columns; the paint was flecked off in spots, on which *FURNISHED ROOMS* signs were tacked. Each night, the light reflecting through the stained-glass borders above the front doors shone weirdly onto patches of lawns that were bordered by scrubby, scratchy hedges. The wind had blown litter, boxes, and papers up against the wire like prickly growth. Here and there, a porch held a ghostly, contoured bulk of half-moved furniture, a refrigerator, or a washing machine. Windows from the second floor, bare of curtains or shades, were lit with the yellow glare of a drop cord light.

Margarita had not left her forwarding address with the church home on Piedmont Avenue, mostly because she didn't think to do so at the time of moving, and afterwards, every time she thought to call up about the mail, she was either too busy or she just let it slip her mind.

At school she made the highest grade in her first examination, and Barton, a tall, feminine-faced student with golden red hair, arranged her hair, massaged her face, manicured her nails, and every day in some different way attended her like a handmaiden. Although Barton seemed harmless enough, Margarita still had qualms about unchaperoned dates, but she sometimes double-dated with him.

The daytime was fine. She was in school. But at night, the other girls in the boardinghouse went out. Margarita found her nights too dull. Her thoughts turned back to school, especially after the relocation of Central High School from Pryor Street to Washington Street. She passed it every day, and besides, every time she encountered the Italian woman, it was necessary to have a ready excuse as to why she didn't go back to school.

Figure 75   Barton

One night she decided she would try it again. As she went up the hall, her green dress flipped from side to side with the swerve of her rounded hips. Suddenly, behind her there was a meaningful whistle, and then he was striding beside her. The same boy was still here, and his hair shone like platinum silk under the artificial light. His eyes, which were green and filled with tormenting glee, sparkled as he exclaimed, "You again! Where have you been all this time? I hope you've come to stay a little longer than you did the last time!"

Margarita propped her finger on her chin in an attitude of pondering a decision. Her eyes were a display of mirthful, impish lights as she sassily replied, "DApends."

The boy, not much taller than she, hopped about her excitedly as he questioned, "Which class are you in?"

"I'm in the beginners," she answered, then turned and questioned him, "Which class are you in?"

He responded, "I'm in the same."

Feeling teased, Margarita remarked, "No, this is not your class." But he preceded her into the room and sat at the next desk to hers.

As the teacher passed by the desks, she inspected the boy's application and noticed that he was scheduled for the 12th year class. She demanded, "Go to your own class. You don't belong in here!"

Flatly refusing, he retorted, "No, I want to stay here!"

In her stern, didactic voice, the teacher explained, "You will only be a disturbance in here. This is for beginners," but glancing at his stubbornly set jaw, she sighed resignedly at the ways of foreigners and replied, "All right, if you stay in here, you will have to have your card filled out again." After leaving the room, the boy returned and proudly displayed his corrected card that now read "Room 101— Beginners Class." He was beyond the simple prodding rudiments of the others and so sat in the back of the room reading funny books or drawing cartoons. For the first few nights, he advanced only to asking for the privilege of spending rest periods with Margarita, but after a week, he asked to walk her home from school.

At the corner of her block on Washington Street, they always stopped into a small café for a cup of coffee. Barr would take out his little notebook and trade languages with Margarita. She would write Spanish in his notebook. Often she sang in Spanish for his amusement.

Figure 76 A   Barr

Figure 76 B   The Corner Café

CHAPTER TWENTY-FOUR

Barr
1948

FOR A NINETEEN-YEAR-OLD, THE BOY'S face was a hard, hewn-in-stone study. There was fierce bitterness and defiance about his eyes. His features were dabbed on with rough, irregular carelessness, and over the whole terrain, emotions shifted, one moment a scowl, the next a winsome smile. His eyebrows lent a whimsical attraction, bleached white on his bronze skin. But more often than not, the complete face was cynical, resting in a quiet sneer. Margarita soon learned that he prided himself on his toughness. He fought his own way since he was thirteen, living with his big family—three older sisters and two younger brothers—in a drab, dingy flat in Dublin. He sold vegetables in a marketplace there. At fourteen and a half, he enlisted in the Canadian Army and fought more in the barracks than he ever did on the African sands during the war. After his dismissal from the army, he returned home. But he was forever in a brawl or picking a fight in the taverns. Weary of his waywardness, his widowed mother appealed to a married daughter in America to send him fare for his passage to the United

States. So Barr came to Atlanta and worked for his brother-in-law in a garage. To keep the boy out of mischief, the brother-in-law suggested that he go to night school. At first Barr rejected the idea. He still remembered the painful memories of his black and blue legs, which were inflicted by the Christian brothers in Dublin; they often tried to impart knowledge through physical punishment when they could not reach the stubborn child's mind. The fear of the school, and all schools, remained etched in his memory. For that, school was like prison once the gates were closed for the day. The children remained isolated from the outside world until the afternoon, when the gates reopened, allowing them to return home. Despite the fact that it made her wince to look at Barr's striped legs, Lucy Tully felt she had to see that Barr got some education. Barr's intelligence and alertness were too strong to allow him to roam freely.

Figure 77 A   Barr

So Barr agreed with his brother-in-law, and he went to school with expectations of having a fight with the teacher. Instead, he was amazed at their lax rules and felt so free at first that he ignored all discipline, refused lessons, and read the newspapers in class. Then when the teachers seemed not to notice or care and disregarded him altogether, it nettled him that he was being neglected. He threw himself into a lather of intellectual activity and was soon placed from elementary into 12th grade.

Night after night, as Margarita listened to Barr talk in his thick burr, she often compared him with Barton. Barton's hands were long and covered with fringe-golden hair. The nails were pale and beautifully kept. This boy's grubby, short fingers were big-knuckled, and small white scars shone in little crescents when he knotted his fists. His nails were a gnawed, blackened unsightliness. Barton always smelled of strong disinfectant soap, and his uniforms were as unwrinkled at five o'clock as they had been at nine. Barr's hard, barrel chest caused his tight-fitting crew shirts to pull and split at the ribbing. His rough, dried pants were turned up at the cuff. But when Margarita considered Barton, he seemed niminy-piminy in comparison, too mincing, too refined.

One cold November night as they sat on the street, arching themselves turtle-backed against the icy wind, Barr was talking along. Suddenly his voice thickly rolled out the question, "Margarita, will you marry me?"

Softly came the answer, "Yes."

He turned in amazement and faced her with, "Do you understand what I mean? I mean, be my wife."

Still she nodded and said, "I understand; you mean we go to the priest and get married. Yes, I will marry you."

The boy stood up, himself surprised over this turn of events. "Holy cow! We are engaged. This calls for a celebration!" Hand in hand, they skipped back to the café for a beer. Barr made plans rapidly over his suds. "Tomorrow," he said, "we will buy an engagement ring." The next day, Margarita looked up to see Barr asking the school instructor permission for her to leave early. They walked downtown and entered the store with the blinking

1948

advertisement that read, "*SEE BRADSON, WEAR DIAMONDS.*" A little later they walked out with Margarita wearing the biggest cut-glass diamond on the $7 rack. Then they caught a bus and went over to Margarita's familiar haunt, the Piedmont Park. There, on a secluded bench, they began their serious lovemaking.

Later, as the betrothed girl was repairing her smeared lipstick, Barr was explaining, "Honey, you understand what engagement means, don't you? It means you're not supposed to go with anybody but me. Everywhere you go, you go with me." Margarita understood, and she nodded. However, she cut the conversation short because she was anxious to get home to roll up her hair for a few minutes. Barton was going to take her dancing to a new place, and he always noticed her hair.

The next few days passed, but one day at beauty school, Margarita forgot to take off her ring. Through the suds of the lavatory, the big glass danced and twinkled. Barton, who was standing nearby, pulled her hand out of the bowl, snatched off the ring, and demanded, "What do you have on your finger?" Then, sneeringly, he added, "I trust this isn't an engagement ring."

Always subservient under pressure, Margarita murmered, "No, no. It is just a ring."

Barton held it between two long fingers and glared at it contemptuously. "Well, don't wear it. I will give you pretty jewelry you won't be ashamed of. But don't wear glass." He hurled the ring under the sink. As soon as he turned his back, Margarita stooped down and stuck the ring into her pocket.

Sometime during the Christmas season, Margarita was passing around a picture of Barr. Barton made sure he personally got a look. His only comment afterwards was, "I hope you aren't thinking of marrying that boy. He is so tough and so ugly, and you are so cute and little."

Christmas Day was a gigantic feast for Margarita. First there was a turkey dinner at the boarding house, and Margarita was particularly impressed with the small individual favor cups filled with colored mints and nuts. Somehow, they reminded her of fiesta and home, although she had never seen anything like them before.

Then Barr took her to his sister's house for a family dinner at three o'clock: turkey and chicken. Later they went to a relative of the brother-in-law for Christmas supper. Barr brought her home at ten-thirty, so full and happy she fell asleep immediately, listening to the small green portable radio he had given her for Christmas. Every day thereafter she carried the radio flung by its strap over her shoulder as she went to and from school, and every night she met Barr after night school.

Early in January, Luzare sent Margarita $200 for a vacation check, instructing her to take her roommate with her on vacation. Luzare had always written letters to her friends too, whom she mentioned in her letters to him. As he always explained to Margarita, "I like to write to the people who are being good to my baby when she is far away from home." Margarita took her roommate, and together they spent every penny of the money in a week on the beach in Jacksonville, Florida. Margarita had just returned when she started hearing tales of Barr's stepping out. She confronted him with the information, which he did not deny. "Fine!" she sniffed. "If you can go out, I can go out, and I'm going whenever I please from now on too." She frequently accepted Barton's invitations, ignored Barr at school, and did not answer when the girls called her to the hall telephone.

One night at the boarding house, Barr sent word up that he was waiting downstairs to see her. Margarita went unresistingly with him to the little café for a cup of coffee. Barr's hand gripped like a steel vise as it clamped itself over her wrist, and he muttered, "You must not see that sissy, beauty, again. Do you hear?" Margarita promised. Her arm hurt. Walking back to the boarding house, she wondered why she let this low, mean, jealous boy see her. He never complimented her like Barton did. He was intolerant of any of her suggestions and was utterly without manners. When he left her at the door that night, he said, "I'll call you again when I'm ready to see you."

Margarita finished the beauty course on the fifteenth of January and received a large diploma with her name inked in scroll lettering stating that she had successfully completed six months' training at the Powder Puff Beauty School. The next day she went to work beside Barton at a swank Buckhead Section salon where Barton, who finished his course a week earlier, had already obtained a job for her. A green pleated nylon uniform was waiting, and her drawer was well stocked with supplies. The morning went quickly. She felt completely at ease. It was almost like being at school. For lunch that day and the days that followed, Barton took her across the street for a full dinner of vegetables and meat.

She had been working for about two weeks when she got a call one afternoon. Barton, who was answering the ring, called out in his tenorish voice, "Pretty girl, it's for you." Margarita placed the phone to her ear. The timbre of Barr's voice resounded clearly as he asked, "Do you want to marry me tonight?"

Margarita was content for the moment and so responded, "NO!" quite firmly.

"Why?" came the insistent voice.

"Because I'm too tired to marry tonight, and besides, how can I marry without thinking?" inquired Margarita.

Barr's voice came back in nasty, querulousness with, "Make up your mind. What's the answer, 'yes' or 'no'?"

Margarita drew the receiver from her ear, saying, "Wait a minute," and lifting her voice, she asked, "Barton, this boy wants me to marry him. What should I say?"

Immediately tense, Barton straightened from the hair he was combing. He faced her and said, "Say NO."

In the same voice, Margarita spoke into the telephone, "NO."

But doggedly, Barr kept talking. "Are you sure? I know that Beauty, Sissy told you. Okay, marry him. You don't want to marry me because I ain't got no money. Well, go ahead. But you can't say I didn't try. I had the preacher ready and everything." Margarita hung up while he was still enumerating his preparations.

Barton, who was listening all the while, waved his hairbrush and comb in whirling motions of exuberance. His voice was high with excitement as he exclaimed, "Wonderful, now Margarita, you are going to marry me! We are going to celebrate tonight. He is too ugly, too crude for you. We'll first have a big dinner at four o'clock.

That will give us time to go look for a ring." Then he shampooed Margarita's hair, arranged it in a heart-shaped plaited bun over each ear, and sprinkled brilliantes on the glossy black finish.

But even as Margarita was selecting the biggest diamond shown her, her perfidious mind was imagining a priest and a couple standing before him. And the groom was Barr. After giving the jeweler a deposit, Barton drove Margarita to her boarding house, and as she sat talking in the car with him for a moment, he said, "Now, I will meet you every morning up on the Peachtree corner, you know where I told you I catch the bus, and we can ride out to Buckhead together. I won't mind riding the bus anymore with you along. I can stop driving the car to work every day. Run along now, and don't forget to put a net on tonight."

Margarita was tired. This has been a long day. She kicked off her shoes, worked off her dress, and was reaching for the net to slip over her hair when one of the girls called her to the telephone. A male voice was soon explaining that he was a friend of Barr's and, in dramatic overtones, stated, "Margarita, Barr wants to talk to you. He must talk to you in person. We are just a couple of blocks away. Please let him see you."

Then Barr's voice interrupted with, "Baby, I'm sorry I was rough this afternoon. I was just mad, that's all. And disappointed, because I had everything ready."

Margarita stopped him with, "But I don't want to marry you."

Barr slipped into his nasal voice again and asked, "Why not? You love me!"

Margarita blurted angrily, "Do I?"

Barr's voice was again lazily confident, saying, "Sure," then raising it again and demanding, "What the hell's with you? I want to talk to you. Come downstairs."

Margarita protested, "But I'm getting ready for bed."

Barr's voice then came pleadingly, "Can you come, please? Just for a minute."

Margarita had gradually weakened under his barrage of insistence, and she succumbed completely now with his meekness. "All right, but you will have to wait. I have to put back on my dress."

1948

She went back to her room, slipped back on her shoes and dress, and without even looking at her face, she went downstairs. Barr was already there, with the friend to whom he nodded and said, "His name is Jack."

Outside, in a dilapidated jeep, a girl slid out and gave her place to Margarita. Barr motioned Margarita to sit down. He placed himself beside her and began his grilling questions with "OK. Now answer clearly. Do you love me?"

Margarita felt herself closely surrounded with hostility. The girl, May, who, in a sloppy lumber jacket, propped herself against the car door, popped her gum, and eyed Margarita hatefully. Jack sat under the steering wheel and drummed his fingers impatiently. Barr, his strong fingers already making Margarita's wrist ache, tightened his grip. In a small voice she answered as they desired, "Yes."

Then Barr went on in a voice as grave as a judge, "Do you wanna marry me tonight?"

Margarita felt smothered; they were all so close, so frighteningly close. Her mind was screaming for release, while her voice was begging for more time: "I'm not ready."

Barr squeezed her wrist harder, and his voice hissed accusingly, "You love that sissy beauty guy." Margarita looked around helplessly for escape, for freedom. Numb with nervous fatigue, she forced her legs to make an effort to extricate herself, but Barr pushed her back against the seat and pinioned her with his shoulder as he muttered hoarsely, "I love you. Everything's ready. If you love me, there is nothing to stop you. If you don't marry me tonight, it means you love that other guy."

On the other side of her, Jack, feeling her silent sobs, spoke up soothingly, "Margarita, you know May and me got married a couple months back, and we're happy."

Barr was saying testily, "If you don't marry now, I'm not coming back again. This is goodbye forever." Still, he didn't release his grip on her wrist. As he felt Margarita's entire resistance collapse, he let out a deep sigh and said, "OK, go upstairs and get your rings and nightgown." Margarita went as one bidden, but her mind was so frozen into thought she couldn't find a gown, so instead she pulled out a slip and stuffed it into a paper sack she grabbled out of the wastepaper basket. Not even bothering to shake out the apple cores, she rolled the sack tightly and stuck it under her arm, then went to find the housemother. She told the woman she wanted to spend the night with May, who was nearby writing her mother's country route address in the sign-out book. The two girls bade goodnight to the kindly woman and ran out to the boys, who had moved and reparked down the block in the shadowy darkness.

The two girls hopped into the jeep. For the occasion, Barr had exchanged coats with Jack, whose coat looked cleaner. May took lipstick from her cracked patent-leather bag and shoved it into Margarita's hand, saying, "Here, dike yourself up a little. You don't look so good."

Jumping out of the jeep in front of the minister's study, Barr took account of his cash, finally counted up the four dollars, and with that they all advanced toward the door. After ringing the bell and waiting a few minutes, the door was opened by a tall, earnest-looking man who greeted them and arranged them before the fireplace. The glare of the bright overhead lights blinked on his glasses in peculiar, elongated patterns as he read the service, now and then nodding to give emphasis to his words. The minister's vigorous handshake and heartfelt "Congratulations, Mrs. Tully!" startled Margarita out of her somnambulist daze.

He filled out a certificate for Barr and extended an invitation for them to attend his church. Barr awkwardly fumbled around for the four loose dollars and placed them in the minister's palm.

Once again outside, the two couples ran and leaped into the jeep, with May and Jack pretending great hilarity as they drove out to the highway to an open-all-night drive-in stand for barbecue and beer. Barr and Jack put their heads together, plotting where they would spend the night. Jack finally thought of his granddaddy's house, remembering that the old man was out of town at the time.

The gas had been disconnected, so the house was cold. Standing in the middle of the dark living room, Jack assigned one bedroom to the bridal couple and another bedroom for himself and Margarita. Barr, holding Margarita's hand, jerked her roughly behind him into their bedroom and closed the door. He quickly shucked off his clothes and jumped into bed. Margarita stood shivering for a moment in her slip, her teeth chattering. Then she slipped between the icy sheets to join her impatiently waiting young husband.

Later, after Barr was already asleep, she lay staring into the darkness. The covers under her nose smelled musty and old. Barr groaned and turned restlessly in his sleep, and with a sudden kick he sent her sprawling onto the floor. She picked herself up, pushed Barr over, crawled into his side of the bed, and went to sleep herself.

The next morning they dressed quickly. Jack locked the house, and then he and Barr went to a café for breakfast. Afterwards, Jack drove Barr and May to work and let them out. He turned and asked Margarita where he could take her in town to catch her bus. Margarita thought quickly and said, "Please, put me out on Peachtree Street. I will show you where."

She got out a couple of blocks from where she knew Barton would be waiting. As she approached the corner, she could see him standing there, his hair glinting in the early morning sun, a freshly pressed suit on. There was an anxious wrinkle on his brow, and his eyes were on his wristwatch. By lifting his face to see her, he smiled warmly, and the two dimples in the hollow of his cheeks deepened. He drew a relieved breath and said, "You're a little late, but we can still make it." Upon noticing her more closely, he added, "Your hair is a sight! You didn't change your dress. What's the matter? Didn't you sleep well last night?" His eyes dropped down to her hand, and catching up her wrist with his slender fingers, he held it up with the inquiry, "What does this mean? Don't tell me you did." His voice sounded shrill, and for a moment, it seemed like he might sob. Then the tone sank low and weary-sounding as he spoke, "I thought something funny. I called several times last night. The housemother said you were spending the night out. But I couldn't think of anybody you knew that well." Then with a sick groan he added, "And so you are married!" He gave a short, bitter laugh, but his voice ended with a note of despair as he asked, "What have you done?"

They climbed on the Buckhead bus, but on the long ride

out to the suburb, he said nothing. As they neared the business section, he turned his distressed face to Margarita and said under his breath, "I can't forget what you have done to me. And after you just promised me last night!" During the day, neither spoke to the other. Occasionally Margarita caught him looking at her in the mirror. She had taken off her rings as soon as she slipped on her uniform, but every now and then, Barton's eyes would stray to her bare hand.

That night in the boarding house, Margarita hid her rings in her cosmetics box before going into the dining room. At the table the housemother scanned her with concern and inquired, "Margarita, you look peaked! Didn't you have a good time last night?"

The young girl swallowed a lump and found it hard to lie to this sympathetic person. She answered, "Yes, I had a good time, but we have to get up so early to get to work!" The housemother nodded understandingly. The girl did live quite a way out, according to the address on the register.

During her working hours, Margarita rarely spoke to Barton. She only saw Barr at school, a frantically possessive Barr now, who moved from the back of the class to the desk across from her and expected her to keep her eyes on him instead of the book. At nine o'clock after school, Barr walked her home. On the fourth night after their wedding, Barr could hardly wait until the rest period to tell her his news: "I have found a room, and if you like it, we can move in tomorrow." After class they took a bus to the address, which was in a good neighborhood, a fact Margarita did not even notice, and near a shopping center, but the room itself was no bigger than a dressing closet. Its total contents were a bed, two chairs, and a small bedside table.

That next night after school, Barr went in with Margarita to tell the housemother. Margarita rushed and stammered through the introductions as ungracefully as a Conchita might have, "I wan' to introduce my husban'. I married him five nights ago. This is Barr. Barr Tully."

The stout old woman stood for a moment flabbergasted but managed to question, "Why, child, why didn't you tell me?"

However, she pumped Barr's hand warmly, punctuating each stroke with a phrase of admonition, "Take good care of her. She's a good kid."

After moving all of Margarita's belongings, including various suitcases, boxes, a radio, and clothes, the tiny room of their new abode was so crammed that Margarita couldn't even move about the floor. She sat in the middle of the bed and undressed, peeved that it should take Barr so long to go to his sister's on his mission of telling the story of his marriage and picking up his clothes. Barr came back at 11:30, explaining the reason he was so late was because he didn't know how to go about telling his brother-in-law, and they were plenty put out with him about it when he finally did tell them.

After two weeks of marriage with Barr, Margarita felt desperately tired. Barr's tempers, fractious and sudden, were disturbing and frightening, and they argued constantly. Every time she made a purchase at the drugstore or bought some trinket at the ten-cent store, they bickered. Her new life of being pinched for money and of not buying whatever she wanted, whenever she wanted, was irksome and humiliating. In every disagreement, she always defended herself with the hot taunt, "You are so miserable, so poor. You can't geeve me anything."

One morning her distress weighed on her intolerably. She talked to Barton's white-frocked back. "Barr is not bad, but he has a terreeble temper and besides, he can't support me." She glanced at his back for a response, which came immediately. Barton whirled around, grabbed the telephone, and in less than an hour, he had Margarita stating her grievances to a lawyer.

The lawyer was questioning her for necessary information in the legal procedure. "Mrs. Tully," he asked, "how long have you been separated from your husband?"

Margarita looked up from her hands, baffled. "Separated, what does that mean?" she inquired.

The lawyer explained with careful patience, "I mean, I must count the number of days you have not lived under the same roof, that is to say, lived in the same house with your husband."

Margarita's heart contracted in fright. "Did they mean she could no longer know Barr's passionate, tempestuous love, not to sleep with her head on his shoulder? They couldn't mean that!"

But reading the distress on her face, Barton spoke comfortingly and reassuringly as his hand patted her shoulder. He said softly, "Don't you worry. Everything is going to be all right. You'll get used to being alone, and in three or four months you'll be free of him forever." Barton reassured the lawyer he would find a satisfactory place for Margarita to stay and that she would be moving very shortly. Margarita said nothing more to Barton for the rest of the day, but on the bus home she was thinking in quiet panic, "I must quit that job. I can't leave Barr!"

The next morning Barton greeted her with a look of "*guess what*" and said, "I have already found a room for you to move. You can go to see it after work today."

Margarita responded weakly, "I'm glad. Now I can move!" But by midafternoon her stomach began cramping in painful knots of worry, and as always when she was under strain, she looked up helplessly. Trembling, she spoke to Barton, "I am soiree but I feel sieck! I wan' to go home."

Disbelieving and scornful, Barton shrugged, "I hope you aren't lying again, but I wouldn't be surprised. You will probably change your mind."

Margarita answered in her little girl voice, "But it is true. I feel sieck."

At home, Barr, in one of his rare sweet humors, was waiting and hurried her to get cleaned up. He wanted to take her out to a good dinner and maybe to the show. During dinner he explained to his wife, "Honey, I've been thinking maybe it wouldn't be a bad idea if you found another job. I'm jealous-minded. I can't help it. I'm just jealous-minded." And with this he threw her a disarmingly charming smile.

The young wife agreed eagerly, "I'll quit tomorrow. I can find another job."

Four days later she was in another beauty shop downtown. Sometime during that very day, Barton looked Barr up at the garage and gave him Margarita's hairpins and a book she had left at the beauty shop. He laid her possessions down with the remark that he didn't suppose Margarita intended to come back to work.

Barr came home that night crowing with amusement, "So that was your boyfriend! When he shook my hand, it felt like a woman's. Ha! I won't ever be jealous of that anymore." And with Barr's vanity appeased, life slowed down to a walking pace for Margarita. Barr got a six-dollar-a-week raise, and she made thirty-three dollars a week herself. At night they were like lovers again. They went to the neighborhood movies or sometimes just walked around. Margarita's blood sometimes bubbled to dance, but Barr didn't know how, and he held in contempt men who could. Feeling the need for elbow room, they moved into a one-room apartment over on the boulevard, and now, at last, Barr felt completely married. He could have breakfast the way he craved: fried potatoes, leftovers of the last night's dinner, beans, tomatoes, and lots of bread. He liked to go off to work with his stomach heavily loaded. Their union involved possessing each other every night and letting the world possess them every morning.

Figure 77 B

Pennant with flag of Costa Rica
https://www.istockphoto.com/vector/3d-realistic-pennant-with-flagn-gm1153505418-313313921?clarity=false
iStock.com/grebeshkovmaxim

Figure 77 C   The Downtown Beauty Shop

Chaos In Costa Rica

Figures 77 D, E

CHAPTER 24

CHAPTER TWENTY-FIVE

Revolution in Costa Rica
April 1948

B UT IN THE COUNTRY OF Margarita's birth, the right of possession had not been as simply worked out. At the February election, the right-wing editor Otilio Ulate had been the winner by electoral votes, but figurehead President Picado, a weakling for communistic leader Manuel Mora, refused to recognize the majority. Prodded by Mora, Picado turned the vote over to the communistic Congress, who annulled the election and called in Calderón Guardia. But this time Costa Rica had been expecting the fraud, and quietly José Figueres Ferrer had been working behind the scenes. An archenemy of Calderón Guardia, he had been deported by Guardia during the Guardian regime because he had gone to the radio stations and stated to the public the exact figures of robberies in the government. He was thrown into jail, and the next day, without any personal possessions save the clothes he was wearing, he was put out of the country. But the Spanish-nurtured Figueres could bide his time. An engineer from the Maryland Institute of Technology in the United States, he was a man of powerful strategy and wit. During the administration of Picado, Figueres came back into the country and started a

Figure 78

Otilio Ulate

cooperative farm, *San Cristobal,* which soon flourished with far-reaching results as a sociological study. His money established a hospital, schools for workers, and a little community. On March 12, Figueres, at his farm, *La Lucha,* organized his army of liberation. With a handful of volunteers, seven shotguns, and some festival rockets borrowed from a church, he started action. He commandeered TACA DC-3s and made 19 trips to Guatemala for guns and ammunition. Out went his appeal over the radio to his countrymen, "Don't pretend you have no weapons. In the humblest kitchen there is a knife, and in every farm an oxen prod". Out of San José went every young man able to fire a weapon. Into the

Figure 79 A

José Figueres Ferrer

dense brush and thick forest, they went with sacks over their heads to protect them from insects as they moved camouflaged through the undergrowth, stalking their prey. An hour from San José on the '*Hill of Death*,' young Ticos moved in the brush, hacked their way with machetes through entanglements, and squatted behind rocks. Overhead, low-flying planes tried to follow their actions. The government was using TACA airplanes that carried dynamite-filled cans, which were rolled out of the cabin's side door after the bombardier activated them, igniting their fuses. All over the mountain echoed the radioed voice, '*Nothing will stop us*.' Figueres, a small, square man with elevated soles on his highly polished boots, moved from camp to camp, intent on using his head instead of his men's lives, anxious that not a bullet would be wasted.

In the capital, Picado sat protected in his red-roofed Casa Presidencial while Mora, the communist boss, ran the show. Mora controlled the guns and sent campesinos and volunteers to fight the rebel army.

From Nicaragua, Somoza, helping the Costa Rican communist-backed government, sent guns, ammunition, fighter planes, transports, and 400 well-trained National Guardsmen. At the La Sabana airport, they were met by trucks and carried to the front. It was a matter of business with "Tacho" Somoza, and if Calderón Guardia lost, he stood to lose. He had been selling Nicaraguan cattle in Costa Rica, contrary to the laws of both countries.

During these days of strife, the streets of San José were half-empty, and people moved by stealth. Anybody suspected of possessing a weapon was seized by the government and put into jail. From government circles came word that the President was sick: "It makes him feel bad to put so many of his friends in jail." But inside their homes, the women prepared beans and bread that could be sent to their men, and at night they carried their provender to their waiting fighters.

Figueres sent his messages via Western Union in code, using the names of flowers as keywords. The telegram would be delivered in the city to a worker who passed it around from palm to palm until everybody understood the message. Once the desired number of men was secured, they would be spirited away, under the cloak of darkness, to the spot where they were needed. Many women followed their men into wild areas that had, before that time, remained inaccessible, sealed by their steaming hot breath, their dank sinkholes, their serpents, alligators, and slithering, creeping things that repulsed and expelled human beings. Anabella's fair face, for four weeks, sweated over boiling pots and suffered the ravages of the jungle so she could be near Rafael. One day Rafael was wounded, captured, and carried back into the city, where he was placed under guard. It was a filthy confine, so crowded the men had to take turns lying down on the floor for their sleep. Over five hundred prisoners had been herded into the small city jail, and for twenty-one days Rafael's wound puffed and rotted and formed proud flesh as he sat in the mass of men.

Humorless and sour-faced, moody Manuel Mora, shrewd and clever in his own prodding, persistent way, daily visited the same cottage on the edge of town. Mora had never married. He had struggled from a humble beginning as a carpenter's son, up through school to get a law degree. He always fought in Congress for a communist program and was an unyielding man who refused to even imagine defeat. "I will not compromise or throw away anything I have fought for these twenty-five years. The people must seal their social gains with blood," he said. Every day he brought his problems to gray-haired Carmen Lyra, who sat in her parlor and gave him advice for his next move against Figueres. But Figueres was not a man who could be outfigured in a woman's parlor. Weaving through the jungles and surrounding Cartago, he forced the hand of the communists, and when hope was futile, Manuel Mora left the country. Calderón Guardia also made his hurried departure, but he did so with a red gash in the shape of an "*L*" carved into the center of his forehead. The "Latron," thief, would wear the scar of his infamy and become a hunted, despised man for the rest of his life, an outcast to his own country.

After the five weeks of civil war, José Figueres, with his small brunette American wife beside him, became head of the ruling junta until a new arrangement could be worked out to put Ulate into his rightful presidency.

Figure 79 B

Revolution In The Streets

CHAPTER TWENTY-SIX

Embarazada
1948

Not long after Margarita and Barr moved to their Boulevard apartment, one afternoon as they were walking down to the grocery store, a tall, well-dressed figure with a great shock of hair blowing in the breeze advanced, and in sight of Margarita, he held out his hand. Maurice. It was Maurice! "Did Barr feel her tremble?" Margarita wondered as she recognized the big figure. But standing directly in front of her, observing her flint face, her downcast eyes, and the cocky man's flexed muscles standing beside her, Maurice dropped his hand to his side. He spoke slowly, "I'm sorry. I must have mistaken you for someone else." He swerved and passed rapidly up the street. Margarita's theatrics at times were most convincing, but Barr had never ascribed cleverness as one of her assets. And the smile she turned up to him was completely dazzling.

Margarita had never written to her parents about her marriage, hesitating, not knowing how to break the news to Luzare, who conscientiously wrote to her four or five times a week. With Barr's stiff argument that her father might stop sending her allowance if he knew of her marriage, Margarita drifted along and pushed the bothersome thought back in her mind every time it cropped up.

When Barr was born, his mother debated between naming the red mite "*Begg*," meaning "*tiny*," or bestowing upon him her own family name of "*O'Barr*," which was a derivative of the old clan name of "*O'Barrie*," a good, solid old name, originally from the Gaelic word "*bearrgacht*," meaning "*diligence*." That particular family in Iverossa, in the barony of Kenry County, Limerick, had furnished chieftains to the clan even back in the tenth century. The motto of the coat of arms was old French and read, "*Bourex En Avant*," "*Drink First*," a gesture of liberal hospitality. Lucy Tully had always held a fierce pride in her ancestry. It had, through the years, dwindled into poor channels, yet was still a name to keep, so she had called the baby "*Barr*." The Gaelic words "*maol*," meaning servant or devotee, and "*tholl*," meaning "*will*," formed Tully, another good name. It meant "*descended from one devoted to the will of God*." Barr had never really listened to his mother's prattle on family names, but he fulfilled the "*Barr*" motto admirably: "*Drink First*." Since his marriage, he discovered a source of wealth that he had not been aware of, and he was privately very pleased. He felt like a prospector who has finally hit pay dirt but keeps his discovery to himself; however, it was not long before Margarita had to keep her marriage a secret.

One day a letter came from Libia announcing that Luzare was coming to the clinic in New Orleans and was making plans to come to Atlanta. Margarita realized her day of reckoning was at hand, so she sat down and wrote to Luzare of her marriage, stating that she had been fearful of his disapproval and for that reason had not written sooner. Luzare's letter back to her was congratulatory. Ricardo had spoken so highly of the blond boy; Ricardo could find absolutely no fault with him. He was ambitious, with a fine, professional future, and apparently of a good family background. Luzare said he was pleased with the match. Now doubly hard to backtrack, Margarita wrote home again, explaining that her husband was not the same man Ricardo had met. This time, Luzare made a cautious inquiry into the boy's education, focusing intently on specific questions regarding his profession and his family. Husked of all the fantasy that she had built around Barr, Margarita stated the bare, unadorned facts. She wrote that Barr had no education, no property, nothing, but that she loved him. Luzare still expressed his desire that she would be happy, but he also mentioned that since she was married, he would cease the allowance. He believed that every husband should provide for his own wife, and it was his responsibility to do the same. Margarita read with concern. She already noticed that her $150 to $200 a month went alarmingly fast since she was married. Barr lived in a riotous manner, not reminiscent of a vegetable peddler, out two or three nights a week playing poker with the garage boys, and his drinking was becoming more frequent.

One afternoon not long afterwards, as she was reading her father's letter postmarked from New Orleans, the doorbell rang. Dashing down the two flights of stairs, she opened the screen door. The ponderous bulk of her father had flumped in a rocking chair. His florid face was beaded in perspiration, and his mountainous stomach was heaving in a gasping struggle to breathe. He glanced up, still wearing his gray hat. Margarita squatted herself beside him and, in rapturous tears of happiness, kissed his short hands and jabbered, "Papa, I didn't know you were coming. I had just found your letter in the mailbox. I haven't even finished reading it, see!" The old man grunted while nodding, his eyes appraising her figure as she wore a simple cotton housecoat.

He puffed between words, "That's all right, but I was wondering why you weren't at the station. But you don't look too good, too pale." And then, fingering the fabric of her dress, he inquired, "Are these your clothes? Have you no more dresses than this?" Margarita laughed and started pushing her father ahead of her while Luzare strained and pulled his weight up the stair rail, step by painful step, and at the top he stood too breathless to speak. Margarita motioned for him to enter her one-room apartment. Luzare stood on the threshold, mopping his throbbing red face and neck, his eyes taking in the mare's nest, darting about the poky little room with its greasy oil burner, lumpy bed, and two unsteady chairs. He turned his questioning eyes on his daughter. "But Margarita, what is this? Where is your house? Where do you live?"

Suddenly Margarita found herself just a tired little girl weeping to her father, "Papa, this is my house; this is it." The old man's eyes filled with tears. He blew his nose hard, then walked over to the chair and sat down, heaving for breath while looking around. Margarita hustled down and up the stairs, bringing up her father's suitcases and arranging them stacked against the wall. Then she busied herself with the table, first pushing all the furniture tightly

Figure 80 A

Margarita and Barr's Apartment

into corners so she could pull the table into the middle of the floor. She quickly heated some chicken soup and poured tea. Luzare turned up the bowl and gulped down the soup, snorting that he was hungry. He hadn't stopped for supper in town. After consuming the soup, he leaned back to enjoy his tea. Margarita sat, taking inventory of her father's vest, remembering from childhood all the pockets with their various contents. There was the same little leather case, inside which she knew fit the sharp blade of a knife Luzare used for cleaning and cutting his nails. He always kept it in his upper right vest pocket. A pen and pencil set sat snugly in the other upper pocket. The big gold watch on its heavy hand-wrought chain was pushed tightly into the small watch pocket, although Margarita noticed her father was now wearing a wristwatch too. Reading her eyes, Luzare explained that it had become so hard to pull the watch from the pocket that he needed a quicker way to tell time. Then he jokingly patted his large stomach. He had always grumbled that he carried everything he needed in his pockets because he could never find anything in the house.

The gray suit was new. Luzare had always possessed a penchant for suits and always kept twenty or more on hand, but he never wore more than two, sending one to the cleaners while he wore the other. Luzare would hang the other suits from season to season without wearing them, as long as he enjoyed the ones he was currently wearing.

At that moment, Barr came in. Without changing his position, Luzare surveyed his son-in-law and inwardly sighed that there was no accounting for taste. However, he greeted Barr cordially, shook his hand, and patted his arm but continued to chat with Margarita in his rapid Spanish. Bratlike, Barr kept butting in, asking Margarita what the old man was saying, and Margarita, to keep Barr from becoming sulky, turned from one to the other in quick succession.

After Luzare talked himself down, he told his daughter he was tired and wanted a hotel room and rest. Margarita sent Barr to the telephone to make a hotel reservation and to call a taxi. A little later, Barr was back. He helped Luzare down the stairs while Margarita, two steps behind them, was reminding her father to come early the next morning. She wanted to talk with him, and this time she would have a good dinner for him.

The next day, Luzare sat down at Margarita's morning work, clearly touched by what she had done. In addition to the plate of fried chicken and potatoes that she prepared, Margarita remembered to include two big bananas, which were one of her father's favorites and always present at home, along with a glass of milk that he always drank with his meals. Luzare had never tasted fried chicken before, but after the first bite, the obese epicure chunked his mouth full of its greasy substance, smacked, and made gestures of pleasure at its deliciousness. Replete with the meal, Luzare sat with Margarita and talked. But as dusk drew on, he began shivering with the chill and started coughing. "I can't stand this climate. I had intended to stay longer, but I see I can't. I'll take the train in the morning. You must ask Barr to let you go with me as far as New Orleans to help me on the boat. I don't like to travel alone."

The next morning, Margarita was with her father in the comfortable Pullman. Occasionally she pulled a banana from the paper sack for him or poured tea from the thermos she had brought along. Every now and then, Luzare would pause his conversations of home to look at his daughter and say, "You are pregnant. You don't look well, too sallow!" Each time Margarita shook her head in emphatic denial.

The day and night in New Orleans were a wonderful treat for her. It was a marvelous luxury to have the whole bed to herself. Barr's ardor was constant and always left no time for her to speculate whether she was enjoying it or not. She found it good to be by herself, like visiting with a familiar friend whom she had not met for some time. Before she bade her father goodbye, he handed her a $50 check and said, "This is for my grandchild. I want to be the first to give a gift to my grandchild." Then he kissed her lovingly.

She in turn kissed her father gratefully and promised, "I will save it, Papa, just for the baby." After leaving him, she promptly went shopping, and before the afternoon was over, she had spent all the money. Then she stopped in one of the restrooms and vomited.

She went back to Atlanta and for a week listened to her mother's voice on records her father had brought to her. Her mother's gloriously appealing voice grew more mellow, more tender with the years.

Margarita worked for two more months before she finally yielded to Barr's insistence that she see a doctor. Dreading the truth, she didn't want to go. After the pelvic examination, the doctor sat behind his consultation desk and said, "You are a little more than three months pregnant."

Margarita's eyes stung with tears, and she screamed back, "NO, NO, I am not."

The doctor's calm voice reiterated, "You surely are."

The young patient sprang up and started toward the door, retorting over her shoulder, "I'll see you next year. I just cannot move my bowels; that is all."

The doctor smiled in faint amusement and replied as she walked out, "You'll be back. You'll see."

All the way home she argued and pouted with Barr. Blaming him, in a hissing voice she said, "Remember the thing you used with the middle hole that you said didn't matter? See, now you see. You are always so smart. You think you know so much." Barr laughed at Margarita's hand-flinging and called her "stubborn" for not listening to the doctor. But inwardly Margarita knew she was fighting the truth, and in desperation she was thinking, "Poor baby, now I have no money for you."

The next month she felt even worse. Moreover, her stomach, always swollen now, made her clothes fit tight and ugly. The fifth month she went back to the doctor, who chuckled at her entrance, "Ah hah, I knew you'd be back," but aware of her downcast countenance, he added comfortingly, "You'll be glad it happened." Each week she went back for exercises, but she still felt sick all the time. And she ballooned in size from 110 to 160 pounds in weight.

At her mother's request, she already sent her Protestant marriage license to be used in the newspaper publication in San José. When Barr finally received his birth certificate and they were at last married by the priest, she sent this too to be printed. Libia liked to have written proof that her daughter was not away living illicitly, and this was a sure way to stop tongues wanting to wag.

Figure 80 B

Margarita's Pregnancy

CHAPTER TWENTY-SEVEN

José Figueres Ferrer
1948-1949

O N CHRISTMAS EVE, MARGARITA ATTENDED mass with a heavy heart, convinced that some terrible evil had overcome her family. Since the twelfth of the month, she had received but two letters from home, and these were so clipped by the censor that they made no sense. The Atlanta Newspapers briefly mentioned that a revolution was in progress in Costa Rica, but the details were so scant that her imagination ran wild. She could close her eyes at night and see her whole family massacred, the house and store in flames.

But these times were so strange and different in the little country of Costa Rica, it would have been impossible for the native daughter to imagine a true picture. On the night of December 11, under the luminous light of a full moon, a band of invaders crossed the border from Nicaragua and battled their way five miles into the small town of La Cruz, located high in the Guanacaste region, where the locals commute by saddle. Soldiers in new uniforms with shoulder patches reading CCCR (Constitutional Commando of Costa Rica) grappled with the hearty-spirited, pleasure-loving cattle herdsmen and had been held in combat until the heartbeat of the Republic, San José, had been notified. The next morning, shrill sirens in San José brought people to the streets to hear the news of the sneak attack on their land. Bright-eyed, hawk-nosed, dapper Figueres spoke to the people and immediately reactivated his army of liberation.

All day organization went on; Figueres was calling in his 1,000 well-trained army, his police force, and his well-disciplined coast guardsmen. He greeted them all, shook their hands, and said, "Let's get down to business." All night Saturday, truckloads of men rolled out of the city up to the north, where the invaders were crossing over the Nicaraguan border and had already come in from the Pacific coast into the town of Liberia, thirty miles inland. Young boys and women left in the city began a mobilization action, filling sandbags and setting up first aid stations in case of air attacks.

One of the most active members of the organization for defense was Father Benjamin Muriz, a priest who had been educated in the United States and who was Figueres' Minister of Labor. Father Muriz explained to the people, "Self-preservation is one of the principles of Christianity, and with Divine Guidance we shall turn back the invaders of our soul, but we also need machine guns."

Figueres had not expected this reprisal from Calderón Guardia. On December 1, in a big public celebration, he had turned the keys of Bellavista Fortress over to the Minister of Education. He had picked up a sledgehammer and smashed stones from the bastion of the fortress, saying, "The many hundred thousands of dollars we save from having no army will be used for public schools and education." He stated that it made him heartsick to see so many "swaggering militants" taking over the other American democracies. From now on, the parade grounds will be a lush tropical garden with a national museum.

Figueres went with his army up to cope with the exiles and followers of Rafael Ángel Calderón Guardia, who was urging his men on, saying, "With absolute faith in the triumph of our course, I call upon my fellow citizens to follow me. My aim is to restore the state of things destroyed by a group of insensate men led by José Figueres, a legal and spiritual adventurer." Figueres surveyed his real enemy. There were 800 to 1,000 men, of whom 100 were genuine Costa Rican exiles. The remaining forces consisted of communists and troops from Nicaragua's National Guard, who were actually Nicaraguan but posed as exiles. And this meant real war. However, he would not launch a major counterattack because he wanted to spare lives, so he appealed to Somoza to recall his troops, who replied blandly, "If my National Guard had invaded Costa Rica Friday, they would be in San José by now."

Figure 81 A

Troops Invade

The wires were hot with flashes between Washington and the two Central American countries. Costa Rican Ambassador Mario Esquivel in Washington called a special meeting of American states and presented its case. He denounced Nicaragua as pulling a '*Pearl Harbor*' attack on Costa Rica and reminded the States that as such, it invoked the newly ratified treaty of Rio de Janeiro for hemisphere defense. It was in direct violation of the "Inter-American Treaty of Reciprocal Assistance."

Upon hearing the term "war-maker," Somoza displayed a surprised expression. He remarked, "I'm told Calderón Guardia invaded Costa Rica, but that this is his affair. We are guarding our frontier."

The organization in Washington sent telegrams to Costa Rica and to the Nicaraguan government saying that it was counting on their fullest cooperation to preserve order and maintain peace. And the tinderbox that could have lit all the Central American countries let their sparks fly wildly, then subside into a quiet ember.

Figure 81 B

Costa Rica Flag With Brush Paint Texture
iStock.com/OnlyFlags. https://www.istockphoto.com/vector/
costa-rica-flag-with-brush-paint-textured-isolated-on-png-or-
transparent-background-gm1472932570-503160543

CHAPTER TWENTY-EIGHT

Home Again
April 8, 1949

I N January, Margarita was forced to give up her job because the shop owner found it unwise to depend on her since she came to work too irregularly. Therefore, Margarita quit her job and stayed at home in her dingy room, where she made handkerchiefs. The other beauticians had given her a surprise baby shower in December and had supplied her with all sorts of baby clothes. They also tossed in $5 for diapers. She bought a dozen diapers and spent the change on groceries. Luzare never sent her another check, but Barr kept right on living as if the checks were being received. He was easily riled and flung temper tantrums whenever Margarita suggested that he stay in at night.

One day a letter arrived from Luzare inviting Margarita and her husband to come home. Libia wanted to meet Barr, and she was worried about Margarita being so far away during her confinement. Margarita took the tickets and went to New Orleans to get her passport straightened out. She had not renewed it at the end of her year's stay in the United States, and it was now two years past its renewal date.

After attending to the business arrangements in New Orleans, Margarita again spent a luxurious night alone, without being mailed or annoyed. She thought with her cumbersomeness Barr would leave her alone, but now she wondered if he ever would. Returning the next day, she told Barr that everything was in order, and then she busied herself giving away the heavy equipment they had accumulated: her iron, vacuum cleaner, and record player. They packed their bags of personal belongings, went to New Orleans, and spent the day pretending they were rich. The next day Margarita marked on her calendar as an important date in her life, April 8, 1949, when they sailed on a small United Fruit Liner tourist boat.

Figure 82

Tourist Boat To Costa Rica

It wasn't long before the twelve passengers found convivial ways to amuse themselves. On the second night at sea, Margarita was pained with cramps. One of the passengers, an old lady who had been a midwife in bygone years, came in and punched about on the sick girl's stomach and agreed that it was possible for Margarita to be in labor. The motion of a boat, she had heard, would sometimes bring on sudden birth. All the other passengers gathered in the captain's quarters to decide a name for the child. "*Mar*" for ocean would be a good name, they thought, if it were a boy, and "*Marina*" for a girl. The captain, a tall, spare Englishman, declared in generous eloquence that if the baby were born on his ship at sea, it would be entitled to free passage aboard for the rest of its life. But the pain passed, and the next morning Margarita came into the dining room and ate the heartiest breakfast of anybody in the room.

The next three days were spent as the first two, playing cards, having little parties in the captain's room, and making little jokes about La Misteriosa, the strange, mysterious woman who would give no answer in inquiry to her name and, in a voice like brambles crackling in the fire, maintained she was Spanish. But she reminded Margarita strongly of the Jamaican woman in her father's office, though the Jamaican woman had the finer figure. This personage wore her dresses opened almost to her waist, revealing half of each low-sagging breast. She was hawk-faced, with a jaded, tired expression, and always wore a black scarf thrown over her greasy, kinky hair. The rest of her was garbed in garish yellows and reds. Always secretive and apart, she sat at a table by herself to eat, seeming not to understand the English being spoken all around her. However, one time Margarita chanced upon the woman and the captain in one of their little chats, and the mysterious one was speaking in very fluent English. Another time, in the late night, Margarita had seen the black figure making her way to the captain's quarters. During the day the captain showed the strange creature deference by patting Margarita's shoulder in the dining room and, in a very audible voice, saying, "Are you treating Trinita good? Be sure to treat Trinita good!" And over at the table to herself, Trinita would smile a secretive, pleased smile.

Abel, the Cuban boy, who was one of the crew members, afforded the passengers much gaiety with his charming nonsense. Always immaculate in a white shirt and pants, he would dance around as he was setting tables and sing Spanish songs in his strong, beautiful voice. He seemed to fancy rhumbas and risqué words, and with every meal he would sing, '*Bad woman, bad woman, I don't know why I love you like I do. Bad woman, bad woman, I don't know why I think of you.*'

The food was delicious, and the tablecloths were always clean. In the late afternoons, the passengers would stand on the upper deck and watch the sunset. There was always the quaint old man who was there first in his chair and who always offered everybody candy. Down below on the lower deck, the crew gathered, and Margarita looked down and listened to Abel sing and strum his guitar while the islanders hummed. Often, overcome by the music, he would get up and dance alone around and around with the rhythm.

On the morning of the sixth day, Margarita watched the sun come up over the rippling horizon. A million jewels, each one matchless, danced glimmeringly, shimmeringly for a moment, then, like fairy ornaments, they would disappear into the emerald deep only for millions more to take their place. As her excitement mounted, Margarita wanted to awaken Barr but kept restraining herself. Sleepy Barr would only look with surly eyes at the small green sentinel of an island they were passing. La Uvita, shimmering green and bright, was like a toy soldier guarding the entrance of the port of Limón. The dock was quiet. Six o'clock by Margarita's watch was only five there, and there was nothing to do but wait until the Customs and Inspections offices opened, perhaps at eight.

Margarita's spirits soared. She wanted terribly to share the glory of the moment. She was home again! This was her own soil! She ponderously helped herself back down the narrow stairs and awoke Barr, who was in a surprisingly good humor. He pulled on a sweater and his pants and reached under the chair for his shoes.

Back again at the rails, she pointed out the chattering monkeys that at the moment were the only movement ashore. They both laughed at the agile little animals climbing and swinging about in the Indian laurel trees. A big black sloth was flinging himself from branch to branch, rustling the polished leaves. Colorful birds, some ruby and some topaz, flashed now and then like enchanted beings in the sun, and the quetzal soared bright green with its scarlet breast, a bird breathtakingly beautiful, which only lives in freedom and dies in captivity. As the sun rose higher, brilliant green bananas hanging in heavy hands were beginning to be loaded into fruit ships. Giant, strapping workers, stripped to the waist with their bulging muscles molded in ebony, lined themselves up from the freight car to the loading machine of the ship's hold. As one hoisted the banana from the car, he would hand it to another who carried it over his tremendous left shoulder to the machine; back and forth they worked, an endless cycle.

People were beginning to mill about now. Someone ashore kept waving and motioning to them. Feeling happy and carefree, Margarita returned the wave, but as she watched, she recognized the person. It was Rafael, a much heavier, stronger Rafael. Rafael was sweating, and he kept lifting his hat to mop his brow. Surely he had not been sent to represent the family! But now she was being jostled and hurried, and she had no more time to consider it. The passports were in good order, and they passed through the Customs and Inspection Offices quickly, but their heavy suitcases, along with those of the other passengers, would have to be inspected at a later time. Taking only their handbag, they scrambled through the crowd and met Rafael, who reeked of beer. The three started up the back streets for the railway station, but the only train for the day left Limón at nine. Margarita, cumbersome and clumsy, handed Barr their handbag and clasped both her arms about her stomach that jostled and pained as she quickened her pace. The boys kept running ahead, then stopping and waiting for her burdensome advance. At the railway ticket office, Margarita changed their money into pesos, and they rushed to board the narrow train on which there was standing room only. Margarita stood with her feet wide apart, bracing herself against the chugging motion of the locomotive. Her feet were beginning their midmorning swelling, and the stench of islanders blended into a sickening smell in the depressingly close, tropical lowland hotness. To distract herself from her queasy stomach, Margarita stared out the window at the changing panorama. The train seemed to be going through a well-laid-out garden. There were rows of palm trees, some stately and majestic, some with leaner trunks, and others colossal with wide branches into which *Barba de Viejo,* '*Old Man's Beard*,' hung in silvery, wispy veils. Now they were away from the ocean flatlands and into the sweltering swamplands of banana plantations and the workers' dwellings. Some of the dwellings stood unpainted and rickety beside the railroad, while others stood out with a startling, prideful whitewash. In front of all these habitations, the islanders

Figure 83

Train To Cartago

stood waving and grimacing while their naked little babies squashed and sloshed about in the warm morning rain, which was falling heavier now, hot, steaming, tunneling the train in a sheet of green. After a few torrential moments, it waned into a polite drizzle, and the sparkling mist reflected and caught the sun in gorgeous rainbows. There and again clusters of bright flowering trees hung like vivid nosegays among the foliage.

When Margarita thought of this railroad, she could recall her father's description of it: '*Every cross tie of that railroad is a human body.*' When she was quite small, she envisioned bodies lying neatly across the rails and the train rushing across them. She could remember how she asked her father so many foolish questions about the bodies until one day he sat down with her and told her the whole railroad's history. He described, with a feeling so peculiarly his own, how the people inland had been shut off from the coast for many, many years. Their only communications with the Atlantic coast were with mules and carts. He told how an American, just a young man by the name of Minor Cooper Keith, who at the age of twenty-three came to Costa Rica to help his three brothers who were trying to construct a railroad from Puerto Limón to San José. But fever in the malarial swamps was an enemy too strong for them. The first twenty-five miles out of Puerto Limón cost 4,000 lives, mostly white men, even Keith's three brothers. Minor Keith had taken over the contract to finish the railroad, and at the same time, he included Black, White, and Brown workers who went without any pay for nine months. Luzare, in telling the story, stressed that it had taken nineteen years to complete that 102-mile stretch, and looking at its cost in human lives, it was probably the world's most expensive railroad. It was not until 1890 that San José was directly connected with the Atlantic Coast.

A scrawny Indian girl, noting Margarita's hugeness, got up from her seat by the window and motioned Margarita to sit down. Margarita did; she was grateful. Now she could breathe easier. The train was ascending, leaving the banana country behind, and the air was becoming cooler. They were now in the Reventazón Valley, where the truculent Reventazón River wound clear and was dancing, jumping, and gurgling its way to the sea. At Devil's Elbow, Margarita stuck her head out of the window and looked far down into the frightening precipice where the river swirled, roared, and rolled. Twisted rails, mute victims of the river's last torrential joust with the railroad, lay half submerged. Margarita tried to get Barr's attention, but he and Rafael were having too good a time teasing with some oily-haired local girls near the front. The bridges that spanned the precipices were more thrilling than flying had been for Margarita. One moment they were on the ground, the next suspended in midair.

After another steep ascent of stony tracts and prairies and another gradual descent, the train pulled into Cartago. Margarita felt faint with hunger. They had eaten tortillas at eleven o'clock at Siquirres, but now it was three o'clock, and her baby was leaping and kicking with hunger. She wanted to point out spots of interest in Cartago to Barr, but instead, she bought a cold drink that was stuck up through the window by girls who were pressing their wares on passengers.

Another thirty minutes of riding, and the surroundings were as familiar to Margarita as the lines of her own hand. Streets she had known all her life swished past her window. The train wheels began screeching with applied brakes. Margarita and Rafael made as much haste as possible on the rocking surface of the moving conveyance back to the observation balcony. As the slowing train passed Margarita's house, real, almost too real, they stood there: her family, her father, Anabella with a small girl standing beside her and a bundle in her arms, an aunt, Diana, and Sara. They were all there waving. And the peacocks were as outstanding as the people, framed by the length of the hall, bright in their colors of paradise.

The railroad station sat beside the tracks like a little boy under a man-sized hat. As Barr helped Margarita off the train, Rafael hailed a carretón driver with his somnambulant donkey. The driver heaved their suitcase into the back of his latticed cart, pushed back up its back gate, and lashed at the balking, flap-eared animal who preferred rather to stand still.

When she first started walking, Margarita's legs and feet felt numb and clubfooted as she clumped along, but the circulation started them tingling, and soon, she was over the two-block distance between herself and her family and was being caught up in warm embraces and chatter. Finally breaking away from the front yard group, she met Catalina, who in her brittle voice greeted her, squeezed her hand, and patted her back. But the old lady's body never leaned closer than arm's length. She stood straight and thin as a needle in her best black dress and pearls. Margarita started through the house. How cool and fragrant with flowers and how inviting it all was! Each room seemed to speak its own peculiar greetings, and each remembered her in its own way from out of the past.

Margarita went as far as the kitchen, walked out onto the patio, and cast a searching glance in the direction of the servants' quarters. Then she started back up the hall. Finally, she softly pushed open the door to her mother's room.

Libia was just sitting there, waiting, too full, too overcome with emotion for other eyes to see, waiting alone for her daughter. Tearfully they drew each other close. Libia had her cry, subsided, and powdered her nose, and then she patted and kissed Barr warmly when Margarita fetched him into the room.

Luzare hustled them all down the hall and stood at the bottom of the stairs awaiting their return while Libia led them on an inspection tour of their new quarters. The big spare room upstairs had been changed into a three-room apartment, snug, clean, and charming. The blue-colored walls still smelled of paint. A bassinet, gauzy with a net at the top and caught with a gigantic pink ribbon, stood beside the bed. Catalina peeked her thin nose into every corner and finally nodded her wig-like head in acknowledgement of a job well done. Downstairs, Luzare stood eager to hear the comments and inquired again and again of Barr when he descended, "Do you like it? Are you sure she is going to like it?" Margarita remained upstairs to unpack her suitcase and change her dress. She felt extremely tired. Anabella lagged behind to watch her sister unpack. Her voracious eyes were on every article of clothing Margarita pulled out.

Insidiously she began her questioning, "And how do you like Rafael now?"

Figure 84 A   The Way Upstairs

Preoccupied with her unpacking. Margarita answered, "Rafael? Oh, he is fine. I like him now." Everybody was kind to her at that moment. Her mind was wandering in a labyrinth of happiness.

Again Anabella inquired, "And how did he behave on the train?"

Margarita answered unthinkingly, "Oh, he was all right. He acted fine." But the picture of Rafael and Barr flashed to her mind, of how they had laughed and flirted. But to say Rafael had misbehaved was to say Barr had misbehaved, and she did not like to think of Barr being anything but good. Again she replied, but more quietly, "Yes, he was all right."

Anabella's fingers stroked Margarita's nylon panties lovingly. "I don't believe it, but I hope he was good." Unable to bear her sister's greedy eyes, Margarita found herself giving what she had enjoyed as her best underwear. She couldn't wear them now anyway, so it didn't matter. She was home again.

Figure 84 B

A neighborhood in Cartago. (Present Day) iStock.com/DennisAlbertoGonzalezSalas
https://www.istockphoto.com/photo/landscape-overlooking-a-neighborhood-in-cartago-costa-rica-at-a-beautiful-sunset-gm2187780759-606341312

April 8, 1949

Figure 84 C Scenic overlook of present day town of Cartago in Costa Rica. iStock.com/alexeys. https://www.istockphoto.com/photo/town-of-cartago-in-costa-rica-gm1131840226-299824816?clarity=false

CHAPTER TWENTY-NINE

Charlene
1949

A T DINNER, IN HONOR OF the occasion, the whole noisome family was together. Ricardo, Arturo, their wives, Victor, his wife, and his three children. They were all there but Catalina, who had excused herself from dinner, saying that she existed on a special diet. However, Libia had long understood that her mother was offended with Luzare's table manners. Later, after the meal, Libia sent one of the servants through the back way with a tray for her mother. In her mew of correctness and formality, Catalina lifted the napkin on the gratuitous tray, took a bite of the cake, and laid it down. Just as she suspected, Libia always stinted her cakes of eggs. She herself would never mix a cake batter without at least eight eggs. Then, as was her custom, she drank a glass of milk, placed her good pearls back into the jewel case, undressed, and put on her white gown pleated at the yoke.

She sat on the foot of her bed and lifted her eyes to the space on the wall above the head of her bed. A magnificent black rosary hung from the wall above her bed. Each bead was as big as a finger joint. The five stations and the crucifix were in hand-wrought silver. Originally from Spain, the symbol of everlasting and continuous love was draped on three hooks, and the crucifix itself, as long as the hand, had been etched with minute precision—a delicate and intricate work of art.

Catalina's heart was heavy. As she kept count of the beads with her fingers, her lips were mummering rapidly, but her mind was praying a fervent prayer of deliverance for her daughter. For her shrewd old eyes had beheld a violent force that wanted disruption and destruction. Catalina had never put her trust in a man. There was no help there. She always turned to her God. He was all majesty and all powerful, and He would not be mocked.

But Catalina was not particularly missed at the Constant house. After dinner everybody gathered in the living room, talking, laughing, and making jokes. Luzare, proud of his daughter's thoughtful gift brought from the United States, kept showing everybody the ribbed cotton socks Margarita had purchased for twenty-five cents a pair for him to use as nightcaps. Nervously, Margarita kept an eye on the liquor consumption, and in a little while she sent a servant out to the pulperia to replenish the fast dwindling supply. People kept coming, gathering in, curious to see Margarita's husband. Barr stood leaning against the back of Margarita's chair, his muscles flexed. He was not sure all the glances and smiles were entirely admiring. But the women raved and simpered to Margarita that he was a perfect husband.

Margarita dreaded seeing her mother take her second drink because Libia always became another person, a person hard for Margarita to recognize as her mother. She always went into a little act of imagining herself a witch. She would go and rummage about for an old hat, stick it comically cocked on her head, pull her curls out until they stood bunched over each ear, and then she would remove the bridge of her two front teeth, grab a walking stick, and go stalking about the room, throwing her guests into hysterics of laughter. But Margarita was always terribly ashamed. Seeing her mother sticking her tongue through the front spaces revulsed her. Why did her mother enjoy making herself ugly when she was such a beautiful woman? Yet Margarita had seen her mother enact the witch scene many times.

As the guests kept coming, the servants were busy washing glasses. Once Margarita looked up and stifled a giggle. A very proper neighbor matron was sipping a drink and commenting on its delicious contents. And the glass was her father's gold-rimmed one he had always kept on his bedside table for his teeth. Every night the teeth were put into that gold-rimmed glass. Every morning they were scrubbed well with one of Luzare's several toothbrushes before he stuck them back into his mouth. The entire family recognized the glass, and many a smile was suppressed until the guests left.

The next few days, Margarita sewed baby clothes from materials Libia had gone to town, selected, and sent to the house. Libia was forever thinking of more little jackets or dresses that the baby might need and the closet with racks of small garments. Each visitor had to be conducted upstairs to view the small garments and preparations. And as they sewed, Libia and Margarita tried to catch up on their talking, scarcely noticing Anabella's lithe fingers lingering in the background. Libia explained in hushed tones, "Pay no attention to Anabella's attitude. She feels estranged because Rafael has no job. And the boy drinks all the time. Anabella has her hands full with her poor sick baby. I wish she would let you get a look at it. Imagine, it is two months old now and only weighs five pounds."

Margarita could hear the weak whines whenever she passed the billiard room. One day she excused herself early from the table and slipped in for a look at the baby while Anabella was still eating. She peered into the folds of the covers to look at a wrinkled head no bigger than a doorknob, a hideously grimacing creature like one of the monkeys in Bolívar Park.

Anabella's voice behind her apprehended her in her actions. Margarita blubbered out the best compliment she could think of, but Anabella, hot with bitterness, only snarled, "You are just being kind because the baby is so skinny. You think you are going to have a big boy. How do you know what it will be like?"

Though resentful of Margarita, she was in and out of the little apartment upstairs on the most trivial of pretenses. Each time she would cast her eyes about enviously, then toss her shoulders haughtily and remark, "It is pretty, but I don't like it because of the stairs."

Libia mumbled out Anabella's story piecemeal while Anabella went back and forth minding her babies. She tried not to ramble, and for the most part she kept a continuity of the events that Margarita had missed.

> She began with, "I wrote you that Anabella went to the Pacific Coast after her marriage. Rafael had located a good job in Puntarenas doing office work, translating English for a banana company. And as much as I hate to praise him, yet you have to give the devil his due. They say Rafael's English is absolutely pure. Well, anyway, Anabella got sick in that low, hot climate, and she is so frail. She just couldn't take it. She caught malaria, and they had to come back to San José, to Rafael's father's. But that man doesn't make enough to support anybody but himself; he's only a clerk in one of those little cheap stores. Besides, he had no living accommodations for them either. There they were, all sleeping in the same room. After two weeks of it, he was forced to tell them flatly he couldn't feed them any longer. He sent them to Grecia to Rafael's aunt's place. That woman is just a farmworker herself. But at least she did the best she could for them, keeping them six months."
>
> "Then one day she and Anabella had a big spat because Rafael wouldn't even go to the job they had found for him. He is too good for manual labor, you know. The aunt got mad and told them to '*get out*.' So, there was poor Anabella with her suitcases, her husband, and her unborn baby on a bus. By some hook or crook, they found out we were staying in Alajuela. Luzare's heart was

acting up so badly I talked him into renting a place there for us. It was a way of getting him out of the store. Well, anyway, one day I went to the door, and there stood Anabella, poor child, miserably skinny. She was crying and begged me to take her back until after the baby was born. But Luzare was absolutely stonehearted. When I told him Anabella was at the door, he said, "Well, tell her to go away. This is what she wanted. Let her be hungry."

"But I begged, tried to reason with him. I said, "Luzare, she is your daughter, and she is going to have your grandchild. After the baby comes, we will see what we can do. Go look at Anabella. She is in no condition to leave now. Besides, where would she go?" Luzare didn't say "yes" or "no," so I took Anabella to the back bedroom, and before I could bat my eyes, Rafael moved their suitcases in, and they were there to stay. And I tell you Rafael didn't lose any time finding a job either. He knew this was his last chance. I kept nagging Luzare until he found him a better one in one of the government offices, and Rafael latched right on to it. And we couldn't stay in the same house, eat at the same table, and speak. I must say this for your father: he tried to be tolerant with Rafael and even told me a little secret. He said, "If that boy proves himself worthy of helping, I'll forgive him. I'll even accept him as one of the family."

"Then one night after dinner, Anabella started her labor pains. I was afraid with it being her first baby she might excite and upset Luzare, so I had Rafael bring her to the clinic. The baby was born that night, and she was back home again in three days."

"All in all, things were going along smoothly

in Alajuela, but we couldn't just live there. I was always worried about the house. It's not good to leave a place unoccupied. So, before the year's lease was up on the house in Alajuela, we moved back here. I told Anabella to take the billiard room for their bedroom. It is farther back than these front bedrooms, and if the baby cried, it would disturb Luzare. We brought the old Esmeralda bed out of the storage room. At last I had a good excuse to burn that filthy, rotting, mildewed mattress. Anabella polished up the bed until it was perfectly beautiful. It is a fine piece of furniture anyway, hand-carved. I wanted to use the opportunity to take Esmeralda's picture down from the wall, but I was scared to stretch Luzare's good-natured streak too far. However, Victor solved that problem for me when he asked for the picture the other day, and Luzare gave it to him."

"But back to Rafael. His new job didn't suit him. He soon became restless and started drinking again. About that time came the revolution excitement. He was in jail twenty-one days on nothing but bread and water, except for what Anabella could slip in to see him. It's a wonder all the prisoners hadn't died; they were so packed. After Rafael's release, he was so thin and listless. He didn't even make an effort to find another job, even after the new baby was born."

"So he spends most of his mornings down in that old room next to the ironing room. He has a big islander come every day to be his sparring partner while he practices boxing. I don't mind because when he's in there, at least Anabella knows where he is. She worries so when he's drinking. He turns into such a devil; she never knows what's happening when he's away from home."

"Ricardo never did interfere with Rafael because, over there at their house, they were having their own troubles with Renato." And here Libia always dropped her voice a tone lower to confide, almost whimpering when she even as much as mentioned Renato. "Poor Renato. After Ricardo brought him home, the poor boy closeted himself in his glassed playroom and dared anybody to come near him. A couple of afternoons a week I would see Ricardo drive him away in the automobile. Luzare said Ricardo was taking Renato to a psychiatrist, so I suppose that is where they went those afternoons. And that went on for several months, with Renato growing worse. Sometimes you could hear him raving and screaming over there like a cornered animal. Francisco told me over the hedge that Renato did that every time his parents came near him. So finally Ricardo just gave up. He bought a big farm up near Alajuela. Your father said it was a beautiful place, and Ricardo hired one of his old servants to keep house and cook for Renato. So, he just put the boy away up there, but the most surprising thing happened! Renato stopped reading all those philosophy books and started studying agricultural pamphlets. The next time Ricardo and your father went up there, they found him in khakis and sandals. Ricardo could hardly recognize his own son! He was as brown and simple as a concho out working on his tomato plants and hoeing his maize. Luzare says it's a strange thing how those conchos feel about Renato. They don't feel he is their master but instead feel he is their friend, and there isn't a single one up there who wouldn't die for him." Libia chuckled as she concluded the story with,

"Not only that, but Renato is producing some fine crops now, making money!"

As Margarita seemed completely uncertain of her baby's possible delivery date, Libia called in a midwife, the same one who attended Anabella's second delivery. The strong, rawboned woman in her starched white uniform came on Saturday morning to look Margarita over. She kneaded around with her heavy hands on the girl's monstrous stomach, listened to the heartbeat with her stethoscope, then patted Margarita reassuringly and remarked, "Everything looks good, nothing to worry about. You can expect labor in two or three days." That night, strained and tired from bending too long over the sewing, Margarita went to bed. Barr was out, but he promised this would be his last good time until after the baby was born. From now on he would save his money for the baby. Not that they needed anything at her mother's, but the money Barr earned in the garage was gone the day after he was paid. Margarita wondered idly how Barr would make out for enough food during her confinement. Since they'd been home, she was slipping up early, frying potatoes on their hot plate, or warming up a bowl of beans and toasting platanos as bread. Afterwards Barr would go downstairs to the breakfast the servants had prepared of two eggs, coffee, and bread. Libia used more than a dozen eggs for her omelets at the noon meal, and she made several distressed references as to the number of eggs consumed daily in the house. So Barr got along on two eggs at the table without asking for more, and at night she prepared him an extra snack before going to bed. She bought chorizo, a long sausage purchased by the yard. It could be sliced and eaten with bread, butter, and tea and made a pleasant little repast before retiring. Margarita sighed that her husband would just have to get along with the house meals until she could be active again.

She was awakened by Barr's stumbling feet bumping up the staircase. He lurched in, switched on the light, glanced around with red-rimmed eyes, pulled off his clothes, dropped them to the floor, switched off the light, and fell beside her into bed, too tired to touch her. Margarita breathed a relieved "Thank God" and listened as in a moment he was snoring heavily, his breath stinking of cheap guaro. She tried to go back to sleep, but little quick pains kept her from relaxing. She shook Barr and talked into his ear, "Barr, wake up! I feel sick!"

Barr roused enough in his pillow to mutter, "Maybe you ate something. Take some soda. Let me sleep." Margarita felt her way around the room to the small niche of her kitchenette, stirred a tablespoon of soda in a glass of water, and downed it. But back in bed, the pains attacked again, with greater force. Then there was a great grasping pain that held her in its clutch and finally released her weak and sick from the grip of it. She felt cold and shaken from the tremendous pressure that was around her, upon her. She was afraid and terribly alone and in a panic.

Unable to hear the terror of her aloneness, she shook Barr hard and cried, "BARR, get up! You'd better get up!" But this time he was too far under the layers of sleep to even hear her.

Changing her position, she had an urgency to urinate. She got up and groped down the stairs to the bathroom, but she would no sooner pull herself back up to the top of the stairs than she would be compelled to go down again. On the last trip she stood at the bottom step and realized she could not pull herself back up again. The pain was now so intense, so upon her she wanted to walk, to keep moving. She went through the living room, down the hall to the dining room, and back up the hall, quickening her pace, running in her heavy, awkward way. Hearing noises in the hall, Libia stepped out of her bedroom, pushed Margarita into a chair, turned on the light, and peered anxiously into the girl's strained face as she inquired, "What's the matter with you, linda?"

Gripping her stomach with both arms and drawing her knees up toward her chin, Margarita panted, "I have pains. My stomach, my stomach, my stomach is killing me!"

Always thorough, Libia's eyes took account of the clock, then asked, "How long has this been going on?"

Margarita gasped, "Since the clock struck two. Since Barr came in."

Libia talked in a very conversational tone as she stepped to the hall telephone, "I'm going to call the midwife now." But she soon learned that the woman was out on another case and could not be reached at that moment. Libia left a message and returned to comfort her daughter. Placing her arm strengtheningly about the girl's back, she led her upstairs, rustled Barr roughly out of his sleep, and shoved him into the small apartment living room, where he flopped over on the sofa and continued his snores.

Placing Margarita in a chair, Libia went about her preparations efficiently. She changed the sheets on the bed and placed cotton, water, and alcohol in readiness on the bed table. Margarita sat in anguish. Her long nails tore at the flesh of her arms with every pain. In an hour the midwife was there. Her tired, sleepless face showed concern as she placed the girl in bed, pressed about her stomach, shook her head at Libia, and stated, "I won't have time to give the enema." Spreading Margarita's knees apart, she rammed her strong finger into the vagina and ruptured the membranes of the waters. With a piercing pain, Margarita felt the gush of warm liquid as the fluid bags released their contents. The midwife handed two large men's handkerchiefs knotted together to Margarita and showed her how to pull them over the knee and strain. The woman repeated constantly as she showed, "PULL, pull, pull, hold on, strain with the pain. Downwards, strain downwards." Standing by the bedside, Libia poured black coffee through Margarita's swollen lips to strengthen her. The agonized girl wobbled her head around crazily. Her eyes were large and glassy with the intensity of the agony.

Libia mopped the sweat-stained face while Margarita, mad and delirious with pain, screamed, "I want to kill myself. I want to kill myself!"

Still half-drunk but unable to sleep through the commotion, Barr sat smoking, his head between his legs. Every now and then he would lift his head long enough to mutter, "Take it easy! Take it easy!"

Thrown into a heightened frenzy by the sound of Barr's voice, Margarita shrieked all the louder, "Don't talk to me. I hate you. I hate you! I want to kill you. I hate you."

Watching the full dilation, the midwife spoke firmly, "Push down as hard as you can. The baby has a large head." There was a great strain downwards, and Margarita's breathing was interrupted with catches in her throat as the head crowned. As the midwife looked on, she threw up her hands excitedly, "I can't take it. It's too big. The baby's head is too big! Do the best you can. It's up to you to do it!" The terrified girl sobbed brokenly. The excruciating pain did not release her now. A gigantic wave of contraction rolled down upon her, increasing in its power, growing stronger and stronger. Libia poured whiskey into the corner of Margarita's mouth and tied a handkerchief around her jaws to keep in the lolling tongue. In its engulfing intensity, the pain seemed to paralyze her. Margarita felt herself rip, tear, and give way to the pressure of the expulsion. The midwife held the baby's head with one hand, reached for a pair of scissors with the other, raised her eyes heavenward, and quavered, "God help me! I'm going to cut it. The cord is too short. I can't wait. It will choke the baby." In a moment the midwife held up a wrinkled being by its ankles, gave it a resounding spank, and handed it to Libia's waiting arms. Margarita was bleeding profusely. The midwife pressed her hand down heavily on the stomach, and with a mighty yank, she reached and pulled forth the afterbirth. Taking a needle and coarse thread for suture, and with no thought at that moment of sterilization, she stuck the needle in and out through the torn, bleeding flesh. Four times there was an inhuman scream, shrill enough to be heard by God. But Margarita's travail was over. She felt herself slipping away into the dark peacefulness of utter exhaustion.

The next morning Libia was up early, and she tiptoed up the stairs to look in on Margarita, who was still sleeping, and the little red thing, snug and still in its bassinet. Afterwards she went to Mass. Back from church, as she stepped into the front door, a servant sidled up to her. The poor, distressed girl wrung her sodden, dirty handkerchief and asked in a halting, embarrassed voice, "Let me speak with you, doña." Standing just inside the little desk room, the servant dropped her crimson face and, in low tones, explained, "The young man, doñita Margarita's husband, came into my room last night. I was asleep. He woke me up when he lay down by me, and he wouldn't let me scream. I'm going now because I can't stay in this house any longer or look at him again." Libia listened dumbfounded.

Weary from want of sleep and overly tired, yet Libia suddenly felt strong, exhilarated by her anger. She drew a deep breath and girded herself against another battle with the many-headed monster. This time she was determined not to be the loser. As Barr walked into the dining room for a late breakfast, Libia beckoned him back up the hall, and standing where his accuser had just stood, she, with fierce vibrance in Spanish and the few English words she knew, blurted, "Barr, in your stupid drunkenness last night you went into one of my servant's rooms. Do you think I will tolerate that in my house? I would put you in the penitentiary this very minute if it weren't for Margarita. She is too weak to worry. But for the rest of the time you are in my house, you will be watched. If you try another trick, I will put you in the street." Barr did not make any reply but walked into the dining room.

Libia turned and went upstairs to show Margarita her baby. She placed the chubby, short nursling near her daughter's pillow so she could examine every feature thoroughly. The little, round face was puffed until the eyes were mere slits. The body was perfect, as plump and round-chested as a pigeon. But the shape of the head was like a reflection in a distorted mirror; one side was pushed in, the other pulled out into an oddly curved peak.

Libia sponged the baby with oil, dressed it in a long, lacy dress, and offered it to Barr, who came in and stood watching. He stared at the baby indecisively for a moment, then shook his head and said, "I'm afraid I might drop it."

Figure 85 A

Charlene

Figure 85 B   Beautiful aerial night view of the Basilica of Cartago in present day Costa Rica
iStock.com/GianfrancoVivi
https://www.istockphoto.com/photo/beautiful-aerial-night-view-of-the-basilica-of-cartago-
in-costa-rica-gm1433653854-475500637?clarity=false

CHAPTER THIRTY

Estrella
1949

A ND SO THE HOUSEHOLD SETTLED down again but seemed to pivot around the new occupant. In four days the midwife had Margarita walking in her room, but the girl's discomfort made it necessary for the midwife to request that a doctor be called in to treat the infected stitches. Libia trotted up and down the stairs all day. Dulce, a sweetened water for energy, one of the country people's treatments that Libia put great faith in, was given often. Four large glasses of milk were carried up every day; oatmeal rich with cream, meat, eggs, cod liver oil, and calcium tablets were loaded on trays and brought to Margarita. With Libia's careful supervision, Margarita was downstairs in a week, enjoying visitors who dropped in to see the baby. The baby's head was so ugly; Margarita hated for people to look at it, and also it was a fretful baby. It had been born with thrush. The mouth was so infected that the nipple hurt its mouth. The whole family, including Catalina, who stopped in every afternoon on her way to have tea with one of her six sisters, thought the baby looked "*polaca*," and to be Polish was, to say the least, not a compliment.

Anabella always had a ready excuse whenever people inquired to see her baby. She was always asleep. But as a precautionary measure, she always hid the baby in the servant's room until the visitors were gone. In a few weeks, Anabella took her baby to the clinic for plasma transfusions. Between her visits to the hospital, she did not bother to hide her contempt for her sister. Often her smirking remark was, "Charlene is too fat. I think fat babies are ugly." Margarita, however, was proud to exhibit her baby, although she admitted to herself that the child was ugly. Yet the baby's coloring was ruddy and clear, her cheeks fat and pink. And Margarita hoped the child would grow to look like the little nurse for whom she had been named, the one who had been so nice to her while she had been sick in the hospital in Atlanta. The two sisters argued and sniped at each other constantly. Anabella had a friend who visited her almost daily, and in the presence of Margarita, they would carry on a fatuous conversation of pretense. Anabella would lean over expansively to her companion and inquire socially, "Do you remember the wonderful old palaces we visited in England?"

And continuing the dialogue, the other girl would add, "Yes, and those heavenly days in France. How I do love to travel!"

Margarita always tossed it off with a snorting laugh, "Why do you two pretend such things? It's silly." Then with unaccustomed generosity she would add, "Maybe someday you will have a trip too. Who knows?" With the friend gone, however, the two sisters would grow sullenly agreeable, and by afternoon Margarita would be treating Anabella to a movie. Anabella wore Margarita's clothes better than she herself could because she was still ungainly. Barr and Rafael became great drinking partners, frequenting the cantinas and bars, but Barr's constant antagonizing of the other workers at the garage, and more notably the fact that he sought out known communists as his friends, led to his soon being fired from his job. About this time Rafael found a position befitting his intelligence, and he took it. Capricious fate had changed her allegiance. Rafael and Anabella were now the ones who could go, spend, and buy, so Margarita often sat at home. Rafael found other friends for his drinking bouts too.

Margarita complained to her mother about Anabella. Every now and then she went to her mother with "Mama, Anabella treats me as if I were dead or just not even here. She never asks me to go with her anywhere, not even to Mass." Libia disbelieved the situation was quite as Margarita colored it. Both girls, to her thinking, were guilty of spiteful, hateful words.

So she mummered the Psalmist's admonition, "Pleasant words are as a honeycomb, sweet to the soul and health to the bones." But Libia's words only galled Margarita all the more.

Luzare saw to it: there was never a spare peso around the house. He would feed his girls to keep them from starving and feed their husbands too; the situation was that he had no other choice. He made it clear, however, that he was not going to furnish them with easy spending money.

As Margarita sat alone in the afternoons, she often thought of Estrella. The more misgivings she held for her family, the more she could see Estrella in a clearer light. She could remember expressions that had played across Estrella's face from time to time. She recalled once when, in the middle of the night, Estrella received a long-distance call from Florida. The housemother came bustling in, worried and disturbed over the thought of bad news for one of her girls. But Estrella only smiled a strange smile and went to answer the telephone. When she returned, she whispered in the dark to Margarita, "It was Mario. He is in Miami. He wants me to come down to visit him for a few days, just for the time he is going to be there. He just flew in."

Margarita remembered that she had never heard Estrella mention Mario before, and she inquired, "But who is Mario?"

And Estrella whispered, "He is an engineer with my father's gang. Mama was scared that we were getting too friendly, so she wanted me to come to the United States. I'm not in love with Mario, but I'd like to see him again. I think I'll catch that plane tomorrow." The next afternoon, just when the two girls were ready to walk out of the dormitory, the telephone rang for Estrella, and with that same strange smile on her face, Estrella said, "You answer it, Margarita. It's Roy, I know. Tell him I'm not here. Tell him I've gone to Milledgeville for the weekend. Say, I've already gone."

And Margarita could still hear the hurt expression in Roy's voice as he said, "Why didn't she let me drive her down to Milledgeville? She didn't say anything to me about wanting to go. I would have gladly taken her." Then Estrella's voice sounded in the background, and Roy heard it. He said, "Margarita, I believe you are lying. I hear Estrella. She just doesn't want to talk to me. I'm coming out there right now."

Margarita recalled how she had gone back and told Estrella the whole conversation. But Estrella only laughed and said, "Let's get going. It's time we were leaving anyway." And as they were riding the bus on their way into town, they met Roy's car with Roy driving at a fast clip. She and Estrella ducked their heads, and he passed, unaware of their nearness. Estrella only smiled and said, "Poor sucker. Roy is such a fool." While Estrella went to Florida, Roy came out and talked with Margarita.

There was a harassed, haggard look on his face as he pleaded with her, "Tell me the truth, Margarita. I know she didn't go to Milledgeville. She hates that place. Where did she go? I love her, but I don't trust her." And he clenched his thin fists as he went on, "That's the trouble. She knows I love her. And I sleep with her because I love her. I want to marry her. I wonder if she will ever marry me. I just wonder."

Estrella came back from her little holiday refreshed and gay, and there was the same little secret, strange smile on her lips as she inquired, "Did Roy say he missed me?" Then she laughed, a peculiar little mirthless laugh, and said nothing more about her trip.

Just as suddenly as Estrella had done everything else, one day she packed, and the next day she left. Neither Margarita nor Roy ever received a word from Estrella again, but the memory that incensed Margarita was the smile. Estrella wore that same smile the night she took the hundred-dollar loan. And now, as Margarita thought of it, she realized the trickery of the girl's mind, the subtlety of her methods, and the very insidiousness of her being.

Figure 86 A

Estrella

Figure 86 B

3d realistic pennant with flag of Costa Rica. iStock.com/ grebeshkovmaxim
https://www.istockphoto.com/vector/3d-realistic-pennant-with-flagn-
gm1153505418-313313921?clarity=false

CHAPTER THIRTY-ONE

A House Of Their Own
1949

O NE DAY MARGARITA BECAME so stirred up in her thinking she wrote the old address she found on a Christmas card that Estrella's mother had sent to her in the United States. She wanted the letter to be friendly so Estrella would reply. She also wanted it firm so Estrella would understand her meaning. So she wrote,

> "Dear Estrella, It has been a long time since you left the United States. I hope you and all your family are doing fine. What about you? Are you married now? And how has everything been? I am married and have a little baby girl. She is very cute and has blond hair like her father. We like it here better than the United States. But it is still too hard to live. I wonder if you could send me some money. I really need it now and would really appreciate it if you would repay part of the loan

I made to you. Sincerely, Margarita."

She posted it with a prayer that she would get some results.

The house was quiet during the daytime, but at night it was lively with visitors. One night, a group of young people gathered on the patio, dancing and singing. Craving the complete attention of the crowd, Barr and Rafael tied on their boxing gloves, cleared the center of the patio, and started a friendly showoff match. The crowd joked, throwing jibes first at one and then at the other. Then some started yelling, "Rafael!" Others, to make the match interesting, started chanting Barr's name. Rafael was known to have no competition in all of San José, but the stocky stranger was strong. They could see his muscles drawn tight and hard in the moonlight. The laughing ceased. Tense and excited, the crowd looked on as the impact of the gloves sounded harder and harder. Rafael was a powerful fighter who had learned to make his fists obey his mind. Barr was a born fighter, swift, quick, and mad, defending and holding his own, boiling with a bitter hatred that rankled and poisoned and purified his being since he had been in the land of jabbering people. They were perfectly matched. Breathing hard, they stepped and darted about, dodging blows, swaying, and inflicting whenever they found openings. Barr rolled Rafael's heavy lick off his jaw, cursed under his breath, and went in to kill Rafael, pounding Rafael's swollen cut lip and eye. Rafael's next blow on Barr's nose brought blood that splattered over his face. Luzare roared, "Stop those boys. The party's over! It's too rough." Friends hovered over Barr and Rafael and led them away to their separate quarters. However, they forced the boys to eat together the following day. Fearing a scene of slaughter at any moment, the whole family ate in hurried gulps.

Whenever Rafael met Barr in the house, he flexed his arm and smiled slowly, maliciously in Barr's direction. Barr spent his days on the patio exercising and swinging on a bar he had constructed for himself. In odd times he walked about with a rifle under his arm, taking bead on a bird in a tree and downing it, then looking and catching Rafael's eye. On the streets the two men vied for attention.

Barr strutted like a gamecock, expanding his chest until his pullover shirts were skintight, while Rafael strutted the streets like a god.

The air was too taut with strain for Luzare. Glancing about at the glowering faces, he would jump to his feet with every meal. In a volcanic rage, he would curse and pound the gong of his dinner bell as he would rave, "I can't stand this place. If I can't have peace in this house, I'm going to run everybody out. This has to stop." Then he would clip up the hall at as fast a pace as he could force his body. Luzare was no longer his virile self. After every outburst he would be so tremblingly weak that once inside his room, he would stagger across the floor and fall across the bed. Also, he had changed his lifetime custom of early rising. He now pulled himself out of bed at about ten o'clock every morning, ate breakfast, and read until the dinner meal, and then in the early afternoon he would call and have one of the boys from the store come and pick him up in the automobile. When he reached the store, he would walk up and down the aisles examining all the new merchandise and the displays and passing his opinion here and there. He would work his way into the office, where he would sit down with the books for a while. His keen brain, with machine-like rapidity, would add the day's accounts. Occasionally he would point out some dissatisfaction or error. Other times he would close the books with a grunt, stride back through the store, and nod to a son to take him back home.

With a heavy voice, Luzare talked with Libia one night. "I hate to see Margarita leave, but, God help me, I have no choice. She brought her own undoing with her. I can't endure that cocky bastard another day. You know what he's doing now? He's going around town pawning himself off as an American. Not only that, but the other day somebody told me they saw him with some of the Guardia sons-of-bitches. Rafael is a credit to him, concho devil that he is. At least he has some ability; he's clever with business books. He's a drunkard, a damned drunkard, but otherwise he measures up to what's in him." Luzare walked the floor, sweated, swung his heavy arms, and writhed with his conscience. He nodded toward the billiard room and continued. "Listen to that puny baby. I can't turn it to the streets. Dragging it around would kill it. But

Margarita's baby is strong. You will just have to ask them to get out. I can't stand this any longer. I don't care how, where, or what, but get them out!" And he swung around with ire in his voice to add, "And mind this. Not one peso of my money is going to support that carajo. Don't you forget it!" Libia nodded her agreement. She had borne the secret of Barr's misbehavior and in doing so grew to hate the boy more every day. It was her one intention to get Barr out of the house.

The next day Libia talked to Margarita about finding a little house of her own. While the picture still appealed to Margarita, the two of them went house hunting. On the outskirts of town,

Figure 87

A Home Of Their Own

Libia found and paid the first month's rent on a three-room, scanty house, a simple place with a dirt floor and a smoked dark interior. But Libia did not want to contract for more than the couple could pay should Barr find a job, nor more than she herself could manage out of her household funds should she be compelled to keep up the rent. Above all, Luzare must not know she had helped in any way. Neither did Libia look upon the arrangement as merciless. Although her cross had never been poverty in marriage, she had been forced to bear all her marital grievances without the balm of love. She endured Luzare's tempers and bore his children, conceived without passion, while Margarita's marriage, she knew, was one of tremendous passion. And with such abandon of affection, one could easily forgive, forget, and live. Libia intended to spare Margarita as much as she could without indulging Barr a morsel.

On the first of July, Margarita moved into her small house, whitewashed all the walls, and repainted the furniture her mother sent out for them. Libia paid for and sent a Conchita, Gabriela, to help Margarita with the baby. She herself brought fruits every week and arranged to have a credit account for the baby's medicinal needs at the drug store with the stipulation that she be called to verify the amount and item. It was a precaution she took to guard against Barr's ever making a purchase.

But all the assistance her mother could give still left Margarita doing her own washing. The conchita was too little for that chore. The diapers that at her mother's house had stayed bleached white by the lavandera soon became a stained yellow. And it was not long before Margarita's hands were cut and raw from handling the acrid black hunks of charcoal that fed the little stove.

Ineffectual and totally at a loss about housework, Margarita never finished from sunup until sundown. Barr puttered about, stuck a sign outside as bait for the conchos that read "*ENGLISH LESSONS,*" and waited for conchos who were eager to improve their status in life. The sign brought inquirers, and for a few weeks six or seven students spent two hours a week striving with the unknown tongue. Margarita taught the beginners their alphabet while Barr, the professor, pedagogued the more advanced. Gabriela, too, was a godsend to Margarita. As much as Margarita despised the tall, thin, old, meddlesome woman, she could not have managed without her. The drab-figured, bony creature in her heavy, black cotton stockings was always up early, hustling her daughter's five children off to school, doing her big daily washing, and as soon as her work was finished, she was over to look in Margarita's house. Always an intensely curious old being, she would point to the table or chair and comment, '*I'll take this if you don't need it.*' Receiving no donations, she would attack the dishes, washing them with her gnarly, work-worn hands, and she would soon have the washing on the line. It was her curiosity that brought her to Margarita one morning when, not seeing movement about Margarita's squalid abode, she poked her head into the bedroom door. Blind with dizziness, Margarita was lying in bed. Seeing the old woman, she struggled to stand up, but as soon as her whole weight was on her feet, there was a sudden expulsion. On the dirt between her legs lay a horrible, sickening sight, like bloody chicken entrails. Frightened by the unsightly pile, Margarita shrieked, "What's that?" Gabriela calmly pushed the girl back down into bed, pulled the pillows from under her head and propped them under her feet, and then went off about the business of digging a hole in the back of the house and burying the fetus.

Afterwards she returned and said, "It's nothing to worry about, just a miscarriage. Didn't you know you were pregnant? But it's no matter now. Just stay in bed until you stop bleeding. That's all."

Margarita sighed and thought, "Pregnant again and the baby only five months old. Will I always have such luck?"

She thought at once of her mother, but even as she thought, she realized that Libia was not at home. She had gone to New Orleans the week before to have an eye operation. Wildly, Margarita wondered where she would get help. She trotted the Conchita to the drug store for the medicine Gabriela told her she needed, but the little girl came back empty-handed. The man would not sell unless doña Libia Constant said, '*yes,*' and where was doña Libia Constant? Barr was not there. He had gone to Puntarenas to look for a job.

In her need, Margarita's mind turned to Jaime, but it was

useless. She remembered hearing somebody tell how Jaime Aragon had gone to Mexico after the revolution. Unlike many known communists, Jaime Aragon did not face exile; an alternative route existed. For months after the revolution, he kept his office open, waiting for clients who never came. A doctor cannot run an empty waiting room forever. And he took his whole family with him. Jaime's brother wed Paco Guardia's child, a daughter born to a servant and raised by Paco's wife. Paco, Calderón Guardia's brother, was an engineer. The whole Guardia family lived in the wealth and luxury they had taken with them out of Costa Rica.

For a week there was no relief for Margarita. Gabriela kept the baby, bathed it, and fed it whatever milk the other neighbors brought in that they could spare from their own children. The old woman often went without her own meals to bring them to Margarita.

As Margarita lay on her sickbed, she often thought of the very irony of living. Here she was presumably rich. Her father had so much wealth he founded a whole little village, complete with its church. And as a commemoration, the village was known as "San Luzare," yet she, his daughter, and her child must depend on alms from the hands of the most humble and wretched. What strange and devious turns one's life can take! But to be honest in her own thinking, Margarita had to admit to herself that Luzare never indulged his daughters in luxuries or in too much free money. Until the day she left for the United States, she still went to her father with her palm outstretched for him to place a single peso. She recalled how she used to say in exasperation, "But Papa, how do you expect me to go to the movies and have a soda on half a dollar?"

But Luzare would never give in. He was always absolutely firm about money transactions. He would always shake his head emphatically and ask, "My child, what are you in need of? You have beautiful clothes, shoes, good food, and a big home. It isn't meant for one to have too much. Money spoils and destroys when it is in excess of its need. Think of the miserable people and be ashamed of yourself. Now run along and stop asking for more. I will never spoil you."

1949

And about the automobile. It had never done Margarita any good that a long, sleek Buick stood in the garage. When she reached sixteen and begged to be allowed to learn to drive, Luzare refused. Margarita remembered how she had whined, "But girls in the United States are allowed to drive; why can't we?"

Her father only growled, "It makes no difference. You are not in the United States, and if you don't like to ride with the chauffeur, you can take a taxi or, better still, you can walk. I don't care how you get there." On their Sunday drives, the chauffeur drove as if he were on his way to the cemetery, and Margarita and Anabella always harangued. Luzare only puffed and said, "You know, it makes me nervous to go fast. Very well, if you don't enjoy these rides for the sake of the ride, I'll just get rid of the chauffeur. I'm not going to ride like I'm going to a fire." And that was exactly what he did. He dismissed the chauffeur, and the Buick sat unless Victor would take pity and come to drive them occasionally.

One day a letter came postmarked from Honduras, and Margarita tore it in her anxiety to get it open. It was from Estrella, and it read:

> "Dear Margarita, I was pleased to hear from you. Really, I was glad. I am married now too to an American boy. He is like your husband, blond, and his name is Johnny. I have a little boy. He has a dark complexion. I call him Ricardo because it is Papa's name.
>
> "We have our home, and Johnny has an airplane; even so, it is too hard for me to send you any money now, but a little later on I will. I will never forget what you did for me. You helped me, and I will help you now that you need it. Write soon. Love, Estrella. Mama and Papa send their love."

CHAPTER THIRTY-TWO

His Last Breath
December 1949

FINALLY GAINING ENOUGH STRENGTH TO walk to the pulperia, Margarita called Ricardo at the store. He listened to her story and finally said, "All right. You may go home provided Barr stays away." Dismally, Margarita pondered what she would do about Barr, who had returned from Puntarenas jobless and hungry.

She wailed, "But what can I do? He has no money to feed himself. I can't leave him to starve." Ricardo finally relented to the point of telling her to send Barr down to a small hotel where there would be a week's reservation waiting for him. He also made it plain that the main reason he was allowing her back home was to help look after Luzare, who was in bed. He finished the conversation by saying he would have a truck come out and pick up the furniture. Later during the day, Victor drove the automobile up in front of the shabby door, Margarita and her baby, with its bundle of clothing, got in, and in a few minutes she was back home again.

Once again in her apartment, she felt infinitely lighter of her burden. However, her father remained confined to his bed and kept

December 1949

bellowing for her attention all throughout the day. He had always relished taking frequent baths, and he was not going to be denied the pleasure of them now. He didn't want a strange nurse touching his body and demanded that his daughter scrub his whole body thoroughly and completely every morning. After his bath he would take an end of the towel in each hand and pull the towel across his shiny bald dome until its thin, clear skin glistened. Afterwards he wanted his complete attire put on him, his suit, with each buttonhole buttoned, and his socks and shoes. He liked a sponge bath in the middle of the day to refresh him. In the afternoon, Margarita would slip away to Barr with a sack full of food from the kitchen. Since the responsibility of grocery shopping had been turned over to her, she had to pinch and scrimp to keep the rent paid on Barr's hotel room. No scrap of food was wasted. The cook was sullen with her because doña Libia had always allowed her to take the leftovers home to her children.

Nothing seemed to help Luzare. He was losing strength steadily. Ricardo wrote to Libia to cut her own convalescence short and come home. In New Orleans, just released from the hospital, Libia was elated over contacts she had made. Radio City New York had wired her after listening to her recorded voice and requesting an interview. But the next telephone call was from Ricardo telling her to catch a plane and come. Luzare had reached a state of hallucination, and Margarita was baffled as to how to care for him. When she attempted to feed him soup, it looked like rice to him. The rice became bread, and when that didn't taste like it looked, he felt there was some trickery afoot and would have none of it and would shove away the tray angrily. Anabella rarely came into her father's room. She had made her exodus, as Ricardo requested, back to the ironing room with her crying babies. But she was furious because Margarita had not moved also; she was directly overhead her father's room.

In the first place, Margarita had no intentions of giving up her cozy little recluse upstairs. In the second place, she had also been terrified of the servants' quarters since the chicken rescue mission. Even now, every time she thought about it, she shuddered. The memory was still too fresh in her mind.

One night, shortly after she and Barr arrived from the United States, there was a terrible commotion in the servants' quarters. A hen squawked loudly. Libia turned to Margarita and said, "Go see what's the matter with that noisy chicken, will you, linda? Something's disturbing her. She's nervous anyway, back there trying to set." Margarita went to the bare, empty room, which had fallen into disuse since Libia had discharged her male servant. On a wide, low shelf in the semi-darkness, Margarita discerned the old hen as she wriggled and squawked obstreperously.

She walked closer and slipped her hand under the warm softness of the hen's body to feel the eggs. Her hand felt the hard smoothness of two eggs, then gliding her hand over, it rested on a cold, hard, rough surface she had never experienced before. She drew her hand back quickly and went back up the hall to tell her mother, "Mama, the hen is still upset. There is something in the nest. I don't know what it is."

Libia replied, "Take Barr with the flashlight." When the circle of light lit up the distressed hen, it also caught the glistening body of a snake, the end of its tail still in the nest under the hen. Its body was slithering between a crack in the wall, and at that moment, Barr pulled a machete from the wall and lifted it to strike the snake. The round body of the large reptile writhed, slid down through the crack, and vanished. Barr crushed two unhatched chicks, causing their shells to crumble into their bodies. So even with the mention of servants' quarters, Margarita could still feel the rough coldness of the snake's body as she had fumbled her hand into the nest.

One day, Margarita took a big jar and caught a bus to Cartago to visit the shrine of Our Lady of the Angels. She sat in the shadowy coolness of the beautiful church and waited her turn at the fountain while others filled their jars and splashed the healing waters about their bodies, their heads, their faces, eyes, and arms. All around the wall there were hung gold and silver objects, even including cheap trinkets, given to the church as thankful tokens by those who had been helped by the waters. Finally she was able to fill her jug from the spring bubbling through the circular stone. Margarita took the water back to her father, thinking that soon he would be free of his

December 1949

Figure 88

La Negrita
KsenQO/Shutterstock.com
https://www.shutterstock.com/image-photo/virgin-mary-figurine-known-la-
negrita-1802828080

pain. Cautiously she approached his bedside. "Papa, I have brought some water from La Negrita. Please drink it. It might make you feel better."

Luzare leaned forward with a sudden grateful movement and said, "Give the water to me. I believe in that little virgin. I'll drink it." He gulped a few deep swallows and then had the nurse save the remainder for him.

On the day Libia was to return, the whole family went to the airport to greet her. With the news of the expected return of his wife, Luzare's mind was suddenly alert and lucid. He demanded a bath, had himself dressed in his newest suit, and brushed his fringe of black hair until it lay in a soft little mound about his head. Between them, Victor and Arturo supported their father's imposing weight

CHAPTER 32

on the automobile. Ricardo drove the family over La Sabana to the airport terminal, and there they helped the heavy man out and seated him in the lobby. He sat sprawled in the chair, half fainting from time to time. The flight in at noon was a disappointment. Libia was not aboard. The sons asked their father if he wished to go home and wait the two hours until the next plane was due, but Luzare, with sick perspiration beading on his forehead, shook his bald old head. When at last the two o'clock plane swerved in and settled and the passengers disembarked, Ricardo waited until he saw the figure of Libia before he awakened his father from his drowsy, sick sleep.

Standing on the balcony, Anabella and Margarita could hardly recognize their mother. She was wearing a hat with a half-veil, and even from afar there was something oddly strange about her appearance. As they rushed downstairs, Libia walked in to greet Luzare. The old man took his wife in his arms and embraced and kissed her openly for the first time in the children's remembrance. Over and over he declared, "Oh, it is so good for you to be back. The children were good to me, but they could not take your place." There was a quaver in his voice as he added, "I was afraid I would die before you came back," but reviving himself with the sight of his wife, he would breathe, "You look so beautiful, so good!"

Looking on, the girls observed that one side of their mother's face was like the Mona Lisa's. It was fair and drawn free of wrinkles on the one side as a young girl's, but set and without expression. Even the eyelid did not move. The other side, however, was Libia, smiling and crying, generous and open in all its fleeting, lovely expressions.

The children held a small tea that afternoon at the house in honor of their mother's homecoming. Libia stayed right beside Luzare to keep him from struggling to follow her around. He was constantly reaching for her hand to touch and stroke it while commenting to anyone nearby, "Look, isn't she beautiful? So wonderful! I have such a beautiful wife!" And his dimmed, cataract-filled eyes, with the glory of her being, could not see her face, not yet healed of its operation.

December 1949

Libia realized at once the whole chaotic condition of the household. This was an abattoir for Luzare. True, there was a nurse on hand at all times, but she could not control the incessant coming and going of relatives. The three boys were in and out all during the day, taking turns leaving the store. Babies wailed from the back of the house, and Margarita and Anabella screamed at each other in their high-pitched, angry voices.

Tired and exhausted by her trip, Libia called Ricardo aside and asked that Luzare be moved to the resort hotel in Alajuela. Within an hour, Luzare was bundled off to a quieter resting place. Once at the hotel, Libia ordered special foods for her husband. For two weeks, the two lived as they had never before, relaxed and content in each other's company. And in some strange way, Libia was aware of a happiness that he had never had before. She was at last on her honeymoon. In this late hour of her life, she had found in Luzare the man she had sought but had only caught glimpses of through the years. His harshness and tenseness vanished, releasing a great tenderness and devotion to her. Instead of passion, they shared love. They awoke to a leisurely midmorning breakfast and strolled through the park to the fruit market, occasionally stopping to sit and rest. Or they sometimes just sat and chatted with old friends who chanced by. Libia, too, was regaining her strength. And the doctor who came every day from San José to check on Luzare was delighted with the change and improvement in his patient.

But on Tuesday morning of the next week, Luzare sat up in his bed and muttered to Libia, who was already dressed and was brushing her short, iron-gray hair. "I feel so strange; I don't think I'll get up for breakfast." Libia ordered the breakfast sent to the room, and when the tray arrived, she sat nearby and helped her husband with his food. But Luzare shoved the tray away with annoyance and began talking in riddling, half-finished sentences. He turned again to Libia and in a mysterious tone of reverie remarked, "I had a strange dream last night. I dreamed a priest came to see me for confession, but I told him to get out." Then he half-turned his head in an intent listening attitude and answered, "Yes, yes." He listened a moment longer. But vigorously he rejected his speaker. "NO, no, NO!" And then in a frightened, lost voice he called, "Libia." She touched his hand soothingly. He sank back on his pillow coughing, "It is nothing. It is nothing at all." But he soon roused, trembling, begging, "Libia, Libia, pray, pray the rosary with me." Libia complied at once, reaching for the rosary she always kept hanging over her bedpost. But there was amazement in her voice. She had never heard Luzare pray before.

He awoke from short naps in the afternoon, dazed and panting, always frightened until he heard and was reassured by his wife's voice. Again in the night he screamed and drew himself up into a cramped fetal position. But afterwards he pulled himself straight and fell back to sleep. The next day the doctor bent an anxious face over the old man, who panted breathlessly. After making his check, the doctor shook his head gravely at Libia and whispered tersely, "He is very, very sick. Complications. Better get him back to San José." Libia called Ricardo to bring an ambulance for Luzare, but by afternoon the doctor thought it would be better if Luzare made the trip the next morning. Libia asked Luzare if he wanted a priest. His mind seemed to be in such turmoil. Luzare's mind appeared to be in a state of constant turmoil, fighting, resisting, almost accepting, but again rejecting a voice that only he could hear. But at the suggestion of a priest, Luzare only shook his head glumly. The next morning the ambulance drove the, ordinarily, thirty-minute span in two hours. Renato sat over his grandfather, sweating in the heat and closeness of the slowly moving vehicle.

As Luzare was being wheeled through the patio into his house, he looked about with perplexed eyes, turned to Libia, and inquired, "Where am I?"

Ricardo responded in a tender voice, "Papa, this is your house. You're back home."

But the old man shook his head vehemently and demanded to be taken to his right house, crying wildly. "This is a strange house. Take me home! Take me to my house!" They put him in Victor's old room, and immediately medical service was all around him. An oxygen tent, a consultation by doctors, and a transfusion were in progress. Nurses stood against the side of the wall awaiting orders.

December 1949

People came and went until late, peeking over the bed, pausing to pray with Catalina and Libia, who knelt in the hall with their hands piteously uplifted, beseeching heaven to intercept death. Candles flickered, and footsteps tread back and forth.

At eleven o'clock that night, Luzare fell asleep, and the household retired. But everybody was up early the next morning, moving in and out of the rooms. Luzare was still gasping, but his face was more placid, more relaxed, and he seemed much stronger. However, in the early afternoon he began struggling, panting, and turning purple. The veins in his forehead became blue, knotted, and ropelike. The old women standing about recognized this symptom of encroaching death and began whispering excitedly, "Oh, he is going to die! He is going to die!" And the family watching, listening, grabbed candles of the Virgin and walked about crying from room to room.

Libia touched her mother's elbow, and they went into Libia's bedroom to closet themselves in prayer. Upon just returning from the pulperia, Margarita felt the hush and the new presence in the house, and she burst into her father's room. The doctor was at that moment facing the brothers and shaking his head, saying, "I cannot lie. He is very badly off. Everybody must get out."

But Margarita dropped into a chair and whimpered, "I want to stay here. I can't leave." Every eye was on Luzare, who in his last hour grew darker and struggled as valiantly with his invincible foe as he had fought in his life. The doctor held on to the old man's wrist, counting his pulse. A nurse had the other arm from under the tent, giving a transfusion. There was a long gasp and a slow exhalation, and the word "Libia" carried sweetly, distinctly, trailing softly away in the last breath Luzare would ever take.

CHAPTER 32

CHAPTER THIRTY-THREE

Laid To Rest
December 1949

T HE DOCTOR PULLED AWAY THE tent and looked slowly from Margarita to the three sons, one by one. He spoke slowly, "I'm sorry. I did everything I could; he is gone."

Victor sprang to his father's side, lifted the square, old hands, and kissed them in a flood of tears, sobbing, "Little old man, don't leave us. Don't leave us, little old man."

And Ricardo, stunned with grief, shook his father roughly and shouted, "Wake up, wake up, don't leave us now. Breathe." He broke down crying, "All I have is gone." But immediately he straightened himself and motioned the nurses to strip and bathe Luzare. While the nurses carefully scrubbed the legs, Arturo tucked a towel about his father's shoulders, stuffed the mouth with cotton, and set it at ease, almost in a gentle smile. Then he lathered and shaved the face and soaped and scrubbed the ears and bald head until it shone. He shook sweet lilac tonic about the fringe of hair and coaxed it down. He pulled the sheet up to Luzare's chin and sat down to wait for Margarita to bring the fresh linens for burial.

Not having been told of Luzare's death, Libia rose from her prayers, crossed the hall, and walked over to the bed, surprised that Luzare should seem so refreshed and revived. She approached the bedside, patted his arm fondly, and murmered teasingly, "Luzare, you are better." But her grasp tightened. Tearing back the sheet, she shook the flaccid body and screamed, "Luzare, Luzare, listen to me, open your eyes." Slowly she released her hold. Neatly she pulled back up the sheet while her face turned into a horrible working distortion, one side moving with motion, the other side still. Her voice was as cold, as lifeless, as dead as Luzare's own body as she spoke again. "You are dead. It is no use. You are dead." The brothers, standing silently by, led her out, and someone gave her a stimulant.

Upstairs Margarita grabbled and dug out the fine, bleached, hand-embroidered linens that had been packed deep in the chest she once started for Jaime. Tucking them under her arm, she hurried back down and into the death room. The brothers placed a crucifix on Luzare's chest, crossed the solid old hands over it, and wound his body tightly, mummy-like, until nothing but his head was visible. They placed the body in the coffin that had just been delivered, a box lined with white satin and covered with gray velvet outside. About the pillow on which his head rested, Libia arranged fresh flowers and pinned religious medals on the sheet over his chest.

Mourners sat about singly or in little huddled black groups, praying, talking about Luzare, and even addressing him as if he still heard. Muffled, quiet voices filled the house, broken only by an occasional unsuppressed sob from one of the family. Other people were drifting up and down the hall on their way to the kitchen for fresh coffee. All the servants filed in to pay their respects, all dressed in black. Enor slouched over to look at Luzare and then turned and smirked at Libia. Already he was sneering at the knowledge that there would be no restrictions on him anymore. And Francisco came in, a solemn, quiet, little, refined-looking man, thick and neat in his clothes. Someone whispered after he left that he was in love with a society girl, but he felt the difference in their social classes, and he would never smudge her name by asking her to marry him. And somebody else added that the girl herself had openly

Figure 89 A

Luzare Laid To Rest

declared her love for Francisco.

Night and dark blueness outside heightened the sadness. The wind in the patio cried with unusual strength. Suddenly the quietus was rent by a piercing scream from upstairs. Dashing up ahead, Margarita found little Isabel still crouched over Charlene. Snatching her off the baby's body, Margarita spanked her hard and sent her sprawling onto the floor. Charlene's cherubic face was bloody with scratches. But by the time Anabella arrived, Margarita had already sponged the baby's face clean. Anabella rasped, "Why did you spank my child? She doesn't realize what she is doing."

Margarita hissed, "That's what you always say. She could kill my baby, and you wouldn't care."

Rafael, trying to effect peace, declared, "I'm glad you did it, Margarita. This child never minds anybody." And with that, he and his family retired to the back of the house.

Margarita had promised her mother after the "ca-ca" fracas that she would not lay her hand on Isabel again. That had been the day when she came upstairs and found that Isabel had accomplished a bowel movement on her blue rug. When she scolded her, the little girl turned her pouting mouth up insolently and with her foot scuffed the stuff deeper into the rug. Margarita grabbed the child and spanked her until her undersides were welted red. When the little girl finally escaped, she ran screaming to her mother. After Libia heard the story from Anabella, she reprimanded Margarita sternly and forbade her from correcting Anabella's child again. And Margarita kept her promise until this moment.

The next day at twelve, the three brothers lifted the coffin of their father onto their shoulders, carried it across the street, and down the two blocks to the little church their mother had founded. There, after the requiem was heard, the coffin was put into a carriage pulled by three white, net-draped horses and was drawn away to the cemetery. The horses walked slowly, in a trained pace, their fringed tassels shaking with every step. Seven coaches of flowers followed the carriage. And Otilio Ulate Blanco, President of the Republic, attended the services to do Luzare personal homage. Thus it was on December 3, 1949, that Luzare Constant, at the age of seventy-seven, was laid to rest. Though not in Esmeralda's dirt. He had long ago bought a lot for himself and his new family.

And Barr, who had been told by Margarita of the death, attended. For the rapprochement, he wore a bright tie and blue suit amongst the mourners in black. He shook each brother's hand, mellowed by sorrow, thanked them for coming, and said that he felt a family should all be together in times of grief.

At home, Libia grieved a loss known only fully to herself. Luzare was a contradiction made flesh. When she expected sympathy and understanding, he burst forth in a temper. When she dreaded harshness, he had oftentimes shown an uncommon generosity and something akin to tenderness. When she craved bounty, he was churlish. But in the last two weeks of his life, she had known a Luzare, refined by the furnace of his afflictions, a lovable companion. They enjoyed a friendship that was sweetened and blended by the mutual interests of a lifetime spent together. Only she knew such an irreplaceable loss. She bowed her head and said a requiescat.

Figure 89 B

Luzare's Funeral Procession

Figure 89 C

The Final Resting Place

CHAPTER THIRTY-FOUR

Entombment Of Her Soul
1949-1950

T HE NEXT FEW DAYS, THE house was filled with sympathetic visitors. Libia sat in the parlor and received them all graciously. Telegrams and postcards edged in black stacked up on the hall table. Luzare had been just a man who walked with a sense of integrity, and he had not been forgotten in death. The newspapers carried his picture and the biography of his phenomenal rise to prominence.

Each night for nine days, an altar, fashioned by Libia, with a big table draped in black against a background of a white curtain, flickered with tapers. A crucifix flanked the wall where Luzare died. Mourners sought out the room and lingered lachrymosely. Curiosity seekers filled and cluttered the place. People who had never had reason to gain entrance into the house before now roamed idly throughout the rooms. A gossipy neighbor whom Libia had always ignored paid her respects and then inquired in a simpering voice, "Well, Libia, now that your husband is gone, you will be well fixed. Lots of us can't feel so sad about your circumstances."

Libia stiffened and drew her handkerchief away from her nose. She lashed out, "Money! I am not thinking of money. I have not even heard the will. I am thinking of what I have lost. I am sorry, but you will have to go. I don't feel well, excuse me." And she retired to her bedroom, leaving the long-tongued woman to find her own way out.

Margarita found herself looking forward to Stefano, an octogenarian who walked as straight as a cane itself and who, many years ago, had served as a chauffeur for Luzare and as a handyman for Esmeralda. Margarita listened spellbound, chilled as Stefano, with wall-eyed seriousness, told story after story of unhappy, restless spirits who walked the earth, seeking their living enemies or searching for ways to regain their own souls. The convivial old braggart remained all his life a bachelor. But even at his age, he never missed seeing a comely figure. Upon his arrival every evening, he would always go into the kitchen, where the servant stood perpetually washing cups. He would give her a good stinging whack across her posterior with his long, bony fingers and laugh into her startled, angry face. Sipping his coffee, he would then contemplate her high-pointed breasts, tell her of their beauty, and vow he would give up his bachelorhood for her. Finishing his coffee, he would put down his cup, go back up the hall, seat himself, and in a very few minutes an interested audience of mourners would be clustered about him.

He was partial to stories of Llorona, the crying horse woman, and always included at least one hair-raising story about her. The first night he was reminded of a story that don Luzare had told him long ago. A happening that don Luzare himself experienced, and who could say that it was not true? Thus Stefano began his tale.

> "Once, don Luzare said he attended a house party. This was when he was just a young man. There were a bunch of boys and girls together at a private home. During the night, don Luzare said he felt an urge of nature, and he went to the outhouse. But when he was about to open

the door, out came a woman. Don Luzare had never seen this woman before. He looked at her. She was beautiful, and he kept wondering who she was. Her hair was long and blond, and the nightdress she had on was thin about her body. Still, he didn't speak to her. When he came back to bed, he asked the other boys in the room who the blond girl was. They all said, "*It's impossible! There is no blond girl in the party.*" One of the boys took a flare, and they started moving about the rooms. About that time they heard horses, like a herd of horses, except the noise seemed to be coming from under the house. One of the boys took the light and crawled under the house. In a minute he called everybody else to come and see. There they were, clear enough to be seen by everybody: hoof marks under the house. The next day the party broke up. All the girls were too scared to stay any longer. Llorona always comes whenever she suspects impure love. You can count on her."

Everybody in the room shuddered. Another night Stefano had a more chilling story of Llorona. This time he vouched for the veracity of it because he had seen proof of it himself.

"One time," he said, "Hernon, the cleaning boy who used to be in the house where I worked, went down to Heredia, his home. He left late one night, after twelve, and was waiting on the street for a bus with his suitcase in his hand. But he decided he would hitchhike a ride if he could. Just about that time along came an old car, but it was odd in a way. It had a chauffeur in it. Hernon asked if he could catch a ride. The man nodded, and Hernon climbed into the back seat. And there she was, sitting there with her long blond hair, so beautiful, in her loose gown, a regular vision, more like an angel. Hernon told me he didn't speak to her. He just looked at her. Finally he touched her arms; he patted her hands, and she returned the pats. He moved closer; he wanted to kiss her. He did kiss her, and she returned the kiss. But he became too passionate, too eager. The beautiful woman turned her face for a moment. When she faced him again, it was a hideous face, the face of a mule, long with big teeth. It gaped its mouth wide at him and made a screaming sound, a horrible noise. Hernon was so scared he jumped out of the moving car and broke his hand. The driver looked back at that moment, and he jumped too. Hernon came back to work with his hand all bound up and said it would never happen to him again. He said he would never try to catch another ride."

Stefano leaned back, and on this night ventured another tale. He apologized for not ever having seen the Llorona himself but said he had seen Cadejo. And with that his audience shivered. Then Stefano went on,

"Now this black dog is like Llorona. It always appears in the middle of the night. Black, black it is, and about the size of a horse. One night after twelve, I was walking down the street. Nobody but myself was afoot. When suddenly it crossed the street and came right in front of me, its head bent low, a strange-looking thing, and even as I had my eyes right on it, it disappeared, right in front of my very eyes. The moon was full and bright, but it went poof, away into nowhere." And he sounded a warning note with "And if you ever see such an animal, better you don't try to touch it because it is really the devil."

Stefano was always the last to leave, and Margarita dreaded climbing the stairs after the house was darkened. Once in bed, she always slept with the light shining in her eyes. She hoped after the nine days of mourning were over, her mother, softened, would relent and consent to Barr's returning to the house. Libia, however, was adamant. She did not even bother to reply but with her hand waved the thought farther away. Margarita pondered her mother's justice. Barr wasn't any more at fault in the fight than Rafael, and his punishment shouldn't last forever.

On Christmas Eve night, while Anabella was preparing the table for the big late meal, Margarita, as slight-fingered as a gypsy, held her paper bag low and scooped her spoils from the table, all the while keeping her eye on Anabella's svelte figure and its graceful flow of movements back and forth to the kitchen.

With her bag stuck under her jacket, she went to see Barr. The streets were already a flow of riotous merrymakers. As soon as she reached Barr's hotel room, she pulled him out into the gaiety. She was stultified by black and was tired of low, gloomy voices. There was an ennui about death. She had had enough tears. She wanted to laugh! Tying a red shawl over her black-clad shoulders and donning a tall stovepipe hat she had lifted from a drunk passerby, she and Barr jostled through the giant mob onto the park, where thousands were throwing confetti, blowing paper horns and whistles, popping balloons, and drinking cheap whiskey from long bottles.

At eleven, hilariously happy, Margarita and Barr worked their way through the drunken mobs to the hotel room. Margarita spread a newspaper on the dirty, littered floor, and there they sat down mirthfully for a feast. With laughter they ate their Christmas Eve meal. An apple for each, some grapes, a fat, thick tamale that had been succulently prepared by Grandmother Catalina's hand, and some chocolate. After their meal, Margarita crawled into bed beside her husband. Unlike her wedding night, there was now no reluctance. She would never keep him waiting again. Hers was the same impatience as his, and it consumed her until she could be consumed no more.

Her bare shoulders felt the coolness and chill of the early morning. She was suddenly wide awake. Standing tremblingly cold and bare-limbed before the open window, she listened to the grave voice of the cathedral bell speaking vibrantly, *I sleep not. Neither do I slumber. For the God of the City watches for the morning!* Strongly he clanged, *Arise, come. I will give you beauty for ashes, white for the scarlet of your soul!* A great gust seemed to search out the innermost parts of her being. Her very spirit was overwhelmed. She felt small, trapped, and as frightened as the moment when, at seven, she crawled through an air window and went under the house. She

Figure 90 A

The Entombment Of Her Soul

heard footsteps overhead, but when she called out, nobody heard. The dust closed soft and powdery over her hands as she crawled. And a black, hairy tarantula with a big, round body rose from its dirt nidus, stretched out its legs, stopped and stared at her for a long moment, then walked away on its many long, crablike legs.

And now, in the entombment of her soul, voices and faces called to her. There was a young boy's face, Edwin. And Jaime with his absurd bravado smile. Next Maurice shook his powerful mane like a gentle lion, and Barton leaned in and took a peek while his hair glinted in the sun. Then there came a baby's face, dimpled and fresh. "Who had cared for Charlene last night?" she suddenly wondered. Behind all the faces, her mother's sweet voice seemed to be begging her to remain and go to Mass. She wanted to scream and free herself from her damnation, but it was like a nightmare in which she could utter no sound.

Slowly, slowly, she looked about her. The shabby room was a loathsome sight in the morning's clean light. Old newspapers, cigarette butts, and liquor bottles cluttered the floor. A Ferris wheel made of toothpicks balanced precariously on the dresser, made by Barr's hand, but it was too weak to touch. Barr's dirty clothes were flung carelessly about. Trash, unsightly trash, all of it.

Barr lay on the bed, an arm over his face. Her trash. He was hers, and she was his. There was no way to dislodge his being from hers. In some odd way, by submitting to his passion, he had become her passion. He had ravished her, and now he was her ravishment.

PURE, the church bell clanged, *Pure*. "*What was 'pure'*?" she thought. Had she ever felt spotless and good? She remembered there had been a time when she, a little girl dressed in white, held a lily in one hand and waited to go to the rail for her first communion. There had been a wondrous singing noise in her head. She felt light, lifted up, as if she had only to hold up her feet and she would float upwards and out of the church, then up into heaven. But now she could not remember the sound of the singing noise. That was gone, like all her young years of childhood and innocence. It was all gone.

She roused herself with a shudder, reached for her undergarments, and wondered if it would not be a good idea for Barr to approach

Ricardo about sending her and Barr back to the United States. Now was the time to ask, while Ricardo was still sad.

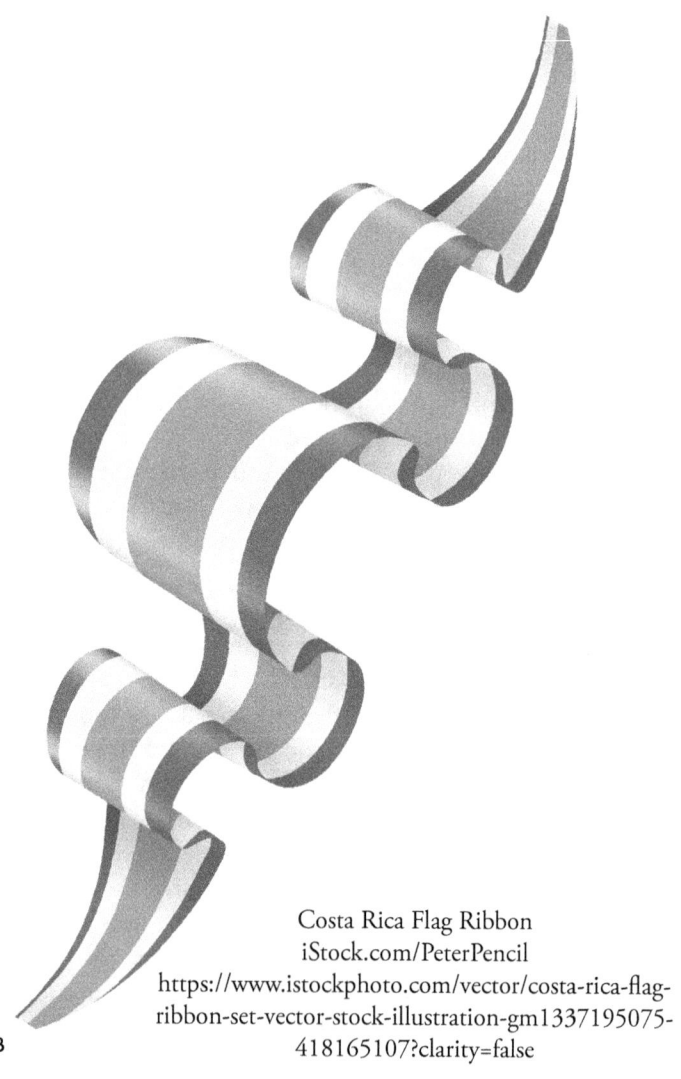

Costa Rica Flag Ribbon
iStock.com/PeterPencil
https://www.istockphoto.com/vector/costa-rica-flag-ribbon-set-vector-stock-illustration-gm1337195075-418165107?clarity=false

Figure 90 B

CHAPTER 34

Glossary

Abase - Belittle or degrades
Abashed - Ashamed, embarrassed.
Abattoir - Slaughterhouse
Abejones - Beetles.
Abetted - To help or encourage someone to do something wrong.
Abhorred - Regard with disgust and hatred.
Abhorrence - A feeling of repulsion or hatred for a person or thing.
Abito - Nun's habit dress.
Ablution - Washing or a cleaning of oneself, for personal hygiene or a ritual washing.
Ablutions - The act of washing oneself.
Abodes - Homes.
Abolished - Formally put an end to.
Accosted - Approach and address a person boldly or aggressively.
Acknowledge - To accept or recognize.
Acquiesced - Consented.
Addled - Confused.
Admonition - Warning.
Affable - Friendly, good-natured or easy to talk to.
Affected - Behaving, acting or speaking in a fake or assumed way to impress others.
Affluent - Wealthy.
Aghast - Horrified, shocked, stunned.
Agonizingly - Causing great physical or mental pain.
Allied - To join in an alliance.
Amble- Walk slowly and relaxed.
Amiably - In a friendly and pleasant manner.
Ammoniated - Treated or infused with ammonia.
Aquiline - Like an eagle.
Archer - British inventor of the acid used to etch glass photograph negatives.
Ardor - Enthusiasm or passion.
Arrogant - Having an exaggerated sense of one's own importance or ability.
Ascertain - Make sure of.
Ascot - Broad silk necktie.
Askance - Sideways, tilted.
Asp - Snake-like.
Assiduousness - With great care and attention.
Assuage - To ease, pacify, quiet, to put an end to by satisfying.
Asunder - Apart; divided.
Attired – Dressed in a fashionable and slightly formal way.
August - Majestic or dignified.
Auspicious - Favorable, showing future success.
Austere - Severe, stern or strict in manner, attitude or appearance.
Austerity - Sternness or severity of manner.
Averted - Turned away.
Bacchic tear - Drunken merrymaking time.
Bacinilla - Chamber pot.
Balustrades - Railing supported by decorative posts.
Banish - Drive away.
Barrage - Massive outpouring.
Barrister - Lawyer with ability to advocate in higher courts.
Basking - To expose oneself to pleasant warmth.
Beckoned - Signal someone to come or follow.
Bedecked – Decorated.
Bedizen - Dressed up or decorated gaudily.
Bedlam - A scene of uproar and confusion.
Bedridden - Cofined to bed.
Benignly - Kindly, gently.
Benison - Blessing.
Bereft - Deprived of or lacking.
Beseeching - Earnest, urgent pleading.

Besought - Beg for urgently or anxiously.

Bestirred - Roused. Became motivated.

Betrothed - Engaged.

Bewilderedly - Deeply or utterly confused.

Bewitching - Enchanting or delightful.

Bickering - Arguing over unimportant, petty matters.

Bidden - Told, instructed.

Billowing - Filled with air and swelling outward.

Bland - Lacking strong features or characteristics.

Blighted - Spoiled or damaged.

Blundered - Move unsteadily or confusedly.

Blurting - To utter abruptly and without thinking.

Bobble - An error.

Bodice - A garment that covers the torso from the neck to the waist.

Boggy - Too wet and muddy to be easily walked on.

Bootees - A usually ankle-length boot, slipper, or sock.

Borne - Carried or transported by the thing specified.

Bouffant - Puffed out.

Brandishing - To shake or wave menacingly.

Brazenly - In a bold and shameless way.

Brigades de Choque - Shock Brigades.

Brilliantes - Glittering ornaments.

Broach - Raise (a sensitive or difficult subject) for discussion.

Brocade - A rich fabric woven with a raised pattern, typically with gold or silver thread.

Brusquely - Rudely.

Burr - Trilling or fluttering of the letter "r."

Buttresses - Walls, sources of defense.

Ca-ca - Spanish word that means poop, garbage or crap, depending on the context.

Caballeros - Gentlemen.

Cached - Hidden or stored somewhere.

Cadejo - A supernatural spirit that appears as a dog-shaped creature with blue eyes when it is calm and red eyes when it is attacking.

Campesinos - Peasants.

Capacious - Having a lot of space inside; roomy.

Capricious - Given to sudden and unaccountable changes of mood or behavior. Unpredictable.

Caraja - Damn.

Carajitas - Little girls. Vulgar.

Carajo - Dick, prick. Vulgar.

Carmine - A vivid crimson (red) color.

Carnicería - Butcher shop.

Carousers - People partying, drinking to excess, speaking and laughing loudly.

Cartago - Cartago is the head city of Cartago canton of the Cartago Province in Costa Rica.

Cassimere - A woollen suiting cloth of plain or twill weave.

Cast - To make a mental or visual search.

Caterwauled - Make a shrill howling or wailing noise like that of a cat.

Cavalier - Showing a lack of proper concern.

Chicanery - Using trickery to achieve a political purpose.

Churlish - Rude, mean.

Cleft - A split or opening.

Clique - A small, exclusive group of people not allowing others to join.

Cloistered - Kept away from the outside world; sheltered.

Cloyed - To supply with an unwanted or distasteful excess.

Coaxing - Gently and persistently persuasive.

Cocked - Tilt or turn up or to one side.

Coherence - Understanding what happened. Putting the pieces together logically.

Coiffure - Deprived of or lacking.

Colic - When a healthy baby cries or fusses frequently for no clear reason.

Comerciantes - Traders.

Compelled but repulsed - Forced to do something distasteful.

Compromised - Settled a dispute by mutual concession.

Conchitas - Peasant girls.

Concho - Peasant, Slang.

Concise - Giving a lot of information clearly and in a few words.

Concoction - Mixture of various ingredients.

Concottic - To make something, usually food, by adding several different parts together, often in a way that is original or not planned.

Confounded - Confused.

Conniving - Sneaky, scheming or conspiring.

Conscientious - Wishing to do what is right.

Consoled - Comforted someone in grief or sorrow.

Consternation - Feelings of anxiety or dismay.

Constrained - Forced restriction.

Contemptuously - In a scornful way that shows disdain.

Contrite - Feeling or expressing remorse or sorrow.

Contrition - Feeling remorseful and penitent.

Contrive - Invent something cleverly or deceptively.

Convivial - Friendly, lively and enjoyable.

Coquettish - Flirtatious manner.

Corda - Latin for "Lift up your hearts" or literally, "Upwards hearts." It is the opening dialogue to the Preface of the Eucharistic Prayer or Anaphora in Christian liturgies.

Countenance - Dishonest or unprincipled facial expression.

Courtier - Person who attends a royal court as a companion or adviser.

Cozen - To deceive, win over, or induce to do something by coaxing and wheedling or shrewd trickery.

Credulity - Willingness to believe that something is real or true.

Cremitas - Cremitas de leche is a custard-like dish.

Crevice - Narrow opening.

Cronies - Close friends or companions.

Crowing - Boasting.

Cuerda - Rope or line.

Cuerdas - Live music festival highlighting in Latin genres such as bolero, cumbia, salsa, merengue, etc., and folklore.

Culler - One who picks out from others, separates.

Culprits - Person who is responsible for a crime or other misdeed.

Curvaceous - Attractively curved shape

Cynical - Distrustful of human sincerity or integrity.

Daintily - In a way that shows fine or delicate manners.

Dastardly - Wicked and cruel.

Debilitated - Very weakened.

Décolletage - A woman's shoulders and chest exposed by the low top edge of a dress.

Decorum - Failure to observe behavior in keeping with good taste and propriety.

Deftly - Skillful and quick in movement.

Degenerate - Immoral or corrupt.

Dejectedly - Unhappy, disappointed, without hope.

Dejection - Sad, in low spirits.

Delirious - Confused and disoriented.

Demurely - Appealing.

Demurred - Raise doubts or objections or show reluctance.

Denouncement - To condemn openly as being wrong or reprehensible.

Deplorably - Very bad and should be disapproved of.

Deprecatingly - Showing you think something is of little value or importance.

Derision - Scornful ridicule or mockery.

Derisive - Expressing ridicule or contempt.

Desolate - Deserted, lonely or gloomy.

Despoiled - Steal or violently remove.

Despondency - Being extremely low in spirits.

Desultory - Lacking a plan, purpose or enthusiasm.

Diadentro - Indentured servant.

Diario de Costa Rica - A newspaper.

Didactic - Intended to teach, particularly in having moral instruction.

Dike - Fix or spruce up in order to look better.

Dilapidated - In a state of disrepair.

Dilated - To become wider, larger or more open.

Dilatory - Slow to act.

Din - A loud, unpleasant and prolonged noise.

Dingy - Gloomy and drab.

Dirgeful - Mournful.

Dirges - Songs and hymns for the dead.

Discerned - Recognize, perceive.

Disconcerting - Causing worry.

Discord - Disagreement between people.

Disdainfully - With disapproval or contempt.

Disembarked – Left. Got off.

Disingenuous - Not sincere.

Dismounted – Got off

Dispelled - Made to disappear.

Dispersing - Moving away.

Disquieted - A feeling of anxiety or worry. Uneasy or troubled.

Distorted - Pulled or twisted out of shape.

Distraught - Deeply upset and agitated.

Dives - A rich man who ignored the poor Lazarus and ended up in hell.

Divine - Foretell.

Docile - Ready to accept control or instruction. Submissive.

Doffed - Tip the head in salutation.

Doggedly - Stubbornly persevering.

Doily - Small ornamental mat made of knotted yarn.

Dolefully - Filled with or expressing grief.

Dour - Stern, harsh.

Drab - Lacking brightness or interest, very dull.

Dray horse - A horse pulling a vehicle used to haul goods; a strong cart or wagon without sides.

Drudgery - Hard menial or dull work.

Duped - Fooled or deceived.

Effigy - Model of a person.

Effusive - With feelings of gratitude, pleasure and enthusiasm.

Effusively - Unrestrained or excessive in emotional expression.

Ejercicios Espirituales - Spiritual Exercises.

Elongated - Long and slender.

Emaciated - Abnormally thin or weak.

Embarazada - Pregnant.

Emboldened - Given courage, confidence or nerve to do something or behave in a certain way.

Empathetic - Showing an ability to understand and share the feelings of another.

Emphasizing - To stress the importance of something.

Enceinte - Pregnant state.

Enervated - Drained of energy.

Ennui - A feeling of weariness and dissatisfaction.

Enraptured - Giving intense pleasure or joy to.

Ensconced - Settled in a comfortable, safe or secret place.

Ensigns - Symbols.

Enthralled - Completely interested.

Entourage - A group of people attending or surrounding someone.

Entreating - Pleading.

Enumerating - Mention several items one by one.

Erizo - Hedgehog.

Eschew - Deliberately avoid using.

Escutcheon - Shield or emblem around a keyhole or door handle bearing a coat of arms.

Espied - Catch sight of.

Estrangement - No longer being on friendly terms or part of a social group.

Estrous - In heat.

Evasive - Not clear or direct.

Exasperated - Intensely irritated and frustrated.

Exhilarated - Very happy, animated or excited.

Extricate - Free from a constraint, remove.

Exuberance - Full of energy and excitement.

Facile - Doing something easily or with ease, but insincere.

Fantasia - A partially improvised, free flowing piece of music.

Fantoccini - Puppets animated by moving wires or mechanical.

Fastidious - Very attentive to and concerned about accuracy and detail.

Fatuous - Foolish, silly or pointless.

Fawn - Light yellowish-brown color.

Feckless - Lacking initiative or strength of character; irresponsible.

Fending - Resisting with no help.

Fetid - Smelling extremely unpleasant.

Filigreed - Decorated ornamental work.

Finca - Estate, Land, Property.

Fisticuffs - Fighting with the fists.

Flabbergasted - Overcome with astonishment.

Flaxen-haired - Pale yellow hair.

Fleetingly - For a very short time.

Flitted - Move swiftly and lightly.

Florid - Flushed red.

Flounced - Moved in an exaggerated way.

Flourish - A bold, extravagant gesture or action, to attract the attention of others.

Flourishing - Developing rapidly and successfully.

Flumped - Sat down heavily.

Flustered - Agitated or confused.

Fluttered - Fly unsteadily or hover by flapping the wings quickly and lightly.

Fondled - Stroke or caress lovingly.

Foreboding - Feeling that something bad will happen.

Fortified - Made stronger.

Fracas - A noisy disturbance or quarrel.

Frantically - In a distraught way owing to fear, anxiety or other emotion.

Frenzied - Wildly excited, uncontrolled.

Frenzy - Uncontrolled excitement or wild behavior.

Fuchsia - Vivid purplish-red color.

Fumbled - Use the hands clumsily while doing or handling something.

Furrowed - Covered in long, narrow trenches.

Galled - To irritate or aggravate.

Garrish - Unpleasantly bright and showy.

Gaunt - Excessively thin and bony.

Giddy - Dizzy, silly, happy.

Girted - To brace, prepare oneself for action.

Glower - To look or stare with sullen annoyance or anger.

Glowered - Having an angry or sullen look on one's face.

Glowering - To look or stare with sullen annoyance or anger.

Gluttonous - Eating and drinking more than needed.

Gnawed - To cause constant distress.

Grabble - Feel or search with the hands, grope about.

Grappling - Fighting in order to win.

Grisly - Causing horror or disgust.

Grotesquely - In a repulsively ugly or distorted manner.

Guaro - Guaro, or Cacique, the official brand, is the national liquor of Costa Rica. It is made from sugar cane and is similar to a white rum.

Guileless - Innocent.
Haberdashery - Men's clothing and accessories.
Habituated - Accustomed or used to something.
Habitué - Person who may be regularly found in or at a certain place or kind of place.
Haggard - Exhausted or distraught.
Hallow cheeks - Old looking dark skin.
Harangued - Give a long, passionate speech.
Harked - Listened.
Harlot - Prostitute.
Harpy - A grasping, unpleasant woman.
Haughtily - Unfriendly, scornfully and with a manner of superiority.
Hauteur - Arrogance or haughtiness.
Heaved - Said with effort or force.
Heedful - Aware of and attentive to.
Hemstitching - Sewing to make decorative drawn thread work.
Hilarity - Great cheerfulness.
Hodgepodge - A confused mixture.
Hoisted - Raised or lifted.
Horrendous - Horrifying.
Humanístico - Humanism. (emphasizes the individual and social potential)
Hysteria - Exaggerated or uncontrollable emotion or excitement.
Hysterically - With wildly uncontrolled emotion.
Idyllic - Peaceful.
Illicit - Forbidden by law, rules or custom.
Illicitly - Improper or in an immoral condition.
Illustrious - Well known, respected and admired for past achievements.
Imbecilic - Foolish or stupid.
Immaculate - Perfectly clean, neat or tidy.
Imparted - Made known.
Impeccable - Of the highest standards, free from fault or blame.
Impecunious - Having little or no money.
Impelling - Urging (someone) to do something.
Imperceptible - Unable to be noticed.
Impious - Lack of respect.
Impish - Inclined to do slightly naughty things for fun; mischievous.
Implore - Beg someone desperately to do something.
Improvised - Figure it out as you go type of person.
Inaccessible - Unable to be reached or entered.
Inattentive - Not paying attention to something.
Incessant - Continuing without pause or interruption.
Incongruous - Not in harmony or keeping with the surroundings.
Inconscient - Mindless with no planning.
Incumbency - Obligatory rest.
Indefatigable - Persisting tirelessly.
Indignation - Anger or annoyance.
Indolence - Laziness.
Inevitable - Certain to happen; unavoidable.
Inexorable - Impossible to stop or prevent.
Inexplicable - Unable to be explained or accounted for.
Ingenious - Clever.
Ingeniously - Original, inventive, intelligent.
Innate - Inborn; natural.
Innuendos - Remarks that suggests something but does not refer to it directly.
Inscrutability - Difficult to understand.
Insensate - Lacking physical sensation.
Insidiously - In a gradual, subtle way, but with harmful effects.
Insidiousness - Subtle but continually causing harm.
Insinuation - Indirect or sly hint.
Insistent - Demanding something; not allowing refusal.
Insolently - Rudely disrespectful.
Instigation - Causing an event or situa-

tion.
Intimidated - Frightened.
Intolerably - Unable to endure.
Intrepidly - In a fearless, daring or bold manner.
Intricate - Very complicated or detailed.
Inundations - Flooding.
Irazú - The highest volcano in Costa Rica.
Ire - Anger.
Irked - Irritated or annoyed.
Irksome - Annoying.
Jardinières - Ornamental stand for plants or flowers; a usually ceramic flowerpot holder.
Jauntily - In a way that shows that you are happy and confident.
Jeer - Make rude and mocking remarks.
Jig - Lively dance.
Joséfinas - Dancers and entertainers in bright and cheerful colors and even more garish petticoats, suits and shirts. This is the Costa Rican typical costume being formed today and taking a place in the culture of the country.
Juniper - Deep earthy greens with blue undertones.
Kaleidoscope - Complex pattern of changing colors or shapes.
Kef - A dreamy state brought on by a sudden fever.
Kewpie - A doll having rosy cheeks and a curl of hair on its head.
Kiosco - Band stand.
Knurly - Rough, twisted, gnarly.
La Negrita - Costa Rica's patron saint.
La Sabana - A giant green area with trails winding through, it is one of the top summer venues for big events in Costa Rica.
Lachrymosely - Given to tears or weeping.
Laconically - Short and to the point, possibly seeming rude.
Laggards - Someone who falls behind.
Lamentations - Passionate expression of grief or sorrow.

Lamenting - Mourn aloud.
Lanky - Straight, thin and usually greasy.
Lascivious - Showing an offensive sexual desire.
Lathery - Foamy.
Lavandera - Washer woman.
Lavandería - Laundry lady.
Lavatory - Washbasin.
Lavishly - In a very rich, elaborate or luxurious manner.
Lianas - Plants with long, flexible, climbing stems that are rooted in the ground, and usually have long dangling branches.
Libertine - Acting without moral principles especially in sexual matters.
Lilting - Characterized by a pleasant, gentle rising and falling.
Linguistic - Having studied language.
Loath - Unwilling.
Loathsome - Disgusting, repulsive.
Loitering - Act of standing or waiting around idly.
Loki - A mischievous and sometimes evil god.
Loll - Sit, lie or stand in a lazy, relaxed way.
Lolling - Hanging loosely out of the mouth.
Loping - Running with long, bounding strides.
Lucid - Easy to understand.
Ludicrously - Amusing, foolish.
Lull - A temporary interval of quiet.
Lulled - Soothed, calmed.
Lulling - Soothing.
Luxuriantly - Elegantly.
Mace - A weapon or symbol of authority.
Maddening - Extremely annoying; infuriating.
Maelstrom - A powerful whirlpool.
Magnanimity - Generosity.
Malapert - Boldly disrespectful to a person of higher standing.
Malicious - Intending or intended to do harm.

These Are Not Señoritas

Mandarin - Chinese.

Manna - Miraculously supplied as food.

Marimba - Musical instrument consisting of wooden bars that are struck by mallets. Below each bar is a resonator pipe that amplifies its sound.

Marred - Damage, ruin or disfigure.

Matrimony - Marriage.

Mauve - Pale purple.

Meager - Lacking in quantity or quality.

Meekness - Ready to accept control or instruction. Submissive.

Melancholia - Deep sadness or gloom.

Mellifluous - Sweet smelling.

Menacing - Threatening.

Mesmerize - Hypnotize.

Meticulously - Showing great attention to detail; very thoroughly.

Metternich - Austrian statesman who formed alliance against Napoleon I.

Mew - To be caged. Here cage.

Mewing - High-pitched cries.

Micah 6:8 - "And that doth the Lord require of thee, but to do justly, and to love mercy, and to walk humbly."

Mirador windows - Designed to give an extensive view.

Mire - Wet or muddy ground.

Mired - Stuck or entangled.

Mirthfully - Full of gladness and merriment.

Miscreant - One who is sorry for behaving badly.

Mock - Not authentic or real, fake.

Mollifying - Calming someone down.

Moorland - An area of acidic ground with low growing grasses, vegetation.

Mortification - Great embarrassment and shame.

Mosaico - Tiled floor.

Mulled - Think about or consider.

Multitudinous – Many people, packed crowd.

Mundane - Lacking interest or excitement.

Mused - Absorbed in thought.

Mussed - Untidy or messy.

Mutinous - Rebellious.

Mystified - Utterly bewildered or perplexed or confused.

Natant - Floating.

Nebulous - Vague.

Nettled - Irritate or annoy.

Niminy-piminy - Formal, correct in behavior that is not sincere. Prissy, prim, finicky, dainty.

Noire - A person or thing that you dislike very much or that annoys you.

Noisome - Extremely offensive.

Nostalgia - A sentimental longing or affection for the past.

Novios – Boyfriends

Noxious - Harmful, poisonous or very unpleasant.

Nymphs - Mythological nature spirits imagined as a beautiful maidens inhabiting rivers andwoods.

Oblige - Help, do a favor for.

Oblivious - Not aware of or not concerned about what is happening around one.

Obsequious - Obedient or attentive to an excessive or servile degree.

Obstreperous - Noisy and difficult to control.

Obstreperously - Stubbornly resistant to control.

Offhandedly - Without much thought or interest.

Ogled - Stare in a excessive or sexually desiring manner.

Olla - A pot.

Ominous - Giving the impression something bad or unpleasant is going to happen.

Ominously - Warned of coming evil or disaster.

Opulence - Great wealth or luxuriousness.

Oraciones de la mañana - Morning prayers.

Oraciones de la noche - Night prayers.

Ostracized - Excluded from a society or group.

Otilio Ulate - Otilio Ulate Blanco (August 25, 1891 – October 10, 1973) served as President of Costa Rica from 1949 to 1953.

Overwrought - In a state of nervous excitement or anxiety.

Painstakingly - With great care and thoroughness.

Pall – To become unhappy, hopeless.

Pan Dulce - Sweet bread.

Parturient - About to give birth; in labor.

Parvenu - One of obscure origin who has gained wealth, influence. Derogatory.

Patent leather - Leather with a glossy varnished surface.

Patois - The dialect of the common people of a region.

Patrician - Aristocratic.

Peaked - Having a sickly appearance.

Peccadillo - A small, relatively unimportant offense.

Peccavi - An acknowledgment of sin.

Peered - Look carefully or with difficulty.

Pedagogued - Taught.

Penance - Voluntary self-punishment as an outward expression for having done wrong.

Pensively - Engaged in deep and serious thought.

Peon - A worker, a laborer or a person who does hard or dull work.

Perfidious - Deceitful and tending to betray.

Perpetually - In a way that never ends or changes.

Persistent - Continuing firmly in a course of action.

Pertinacious - Holding firmly to an opinion or a course of action.

Perturbation - Anxiety; mental uneasiness.

Perugino - Italian Renaissance painter.

Pestiferous - Carrying infection and disease.

Petulance - Quality of being childishly sulky or bad-tempered.

Phenomena - A fact or event in nature or society that is not fully understood.

Piddled - Spend time aimlessly.

Piety - Religious or reverant.

Pinioned - Hold the arms or legs.

Pious - Devoutly religious.

Piquant - Interesting and exciting, especially because of being mysterious.

Piqued - A feeling of irritation or resentment resulting from a slight to one's pride.

Plaintive - Sounding sad and mournful.

Platanos - Bananas.

Platanos maduros - Side dish prepared from sweet plantains.

Plato - Bowl, Container.

Plies - Leather straps of the whip.

Poás - An active volcano in Central Costa Rica.

Pomposity - Arrogant, self-important.

Ponder - Think about carefully, consider.

Ponderous - Having great weight.

Portal - Large and imposing doorway decoration.

Poster - A decorative item hung above or around a bed.

Potsherd - Speckled appearance. i.e. Liver or age spots.

Pragmatic - Practical, Sensible.

Prattle - To talk or chatter idly or meaninglessly.

Predatory - Seeking to exploit or oppress others.

Prescribed - Advised.

Pretentious - Attempting to impress by affecting greater importance than is actually possessed.

Priggish - Self-righteously moralistic and superior.

Procuring - To get or obtain something by special effort.

Prodding - Poking, pushing.

Prognostication - Action of foretelling or prophesying future events.

Prone - Having a tendency or inclination.

Protracted - Lasting for a long time.

Protuberance - Bulging or jutting out.

Proud - The swollen flesh that surrounds a healing wound.

Provender - Food meant to sustain people.

Providential - Occurring at a favorable time.

Provoked - Stimulate or give rise to a reaction or emotion.

Proximity - Nearness in space.

Prudential - Involving or showing care and forethought.

Puerile - Childishly silly and trivial.

Pulperías - Grocery stores.

Puntarenas - A city on the Pacific coast of Costa Rica.

Puntarenas - Known as the "Pearl of the Pacific," Puntarenas is the largest province of Costa Rica.

Purveyed - Provide or supply.

Puta - Prostitute.

Putrefying - Festering or rotting.

Quagmire- Difficult.

Quaint - Attractively unusual or old-fashioned.

Quandary - A state of not being able to decide what to do about a situation in which you are involved.

Quaver - Tremble.

Quavering - Trembling.

Querulousness - Grumbling.

Quixotic - Unrealistic and impractical.

Rabble - Numerous, noisy shouting mob.

Rakishly - In a careless, charming way.

Ramrod - A rod for ramming down the charge of a muzzleloading firearm.

Ransack - Look through thoroughly and in a reckless manner.

Ranting - A long, angry and impassioned speech.

Rapaciousness - Showing a strong wish to take things for yourself.

Rapier - A thin, light, long, sharp-pointed sword.

Rapturous - Expressing great pleasure, enthusiasm, excitement or great joy.

Rapturously - In a way that shows extreme pleasure and happiness.

Raved - Talked wildly or irrationally.

Ravenous - Very hungry.

Ravenously - Extremely hungry way.

Ravished - Filled with intense delight and desire.

Rebuke - Sharp disapproval.

Reeled - Lose one's balance.

Reiterated - Say again, repeat.

Relentlessly - In an unceasingly intense or harsh way.

Relish - Enjoy greatly.

Reminiscing - Recalling past experiences or events with pleasure or nostalgia.

Repartee - Quick, witty replies.

Repast - Meal.

Replete - Gorged, full.

Repress - To hold back, prevent or subdue something by force.

Reprisal - An act of retaliation.

Repulsed, Compelled but - Forced to do something distasteful.

Requiescat - A wish or prayer for the repose of a dead person.

Requite - Pay, reimburse.

Rescinded - Revoke, cancel or repeal.

Resonant - Deep, clear and continuing to sound.

Resorted - Adopt an undesirable course of action to resolve a difficult situation.

Resounding - Loud and clear.

Resplendent - Attractive and impressive through being richly colorful.

Retaliated - Make an attack or assault in return for a similar attack.

Reticence - Unwillingness to do or talk about something.

Retort - A sharp, angry reply to a remark

someone has made.

Retorted - To remark in a sharp, angry or wittily direct manner.

Retorting - A quick, witty response.

Retribution - Punishment inflicted on someone as vengeance.

Ribaldly - Coarsely or obscenely humorous.

Rifled - Searched or plundered through in order to steal.

Roily - Turbulent.

Rollickingly - Carefree and high-spirited.

Roma Ida - On August 2, 1944, nearly 3,000 Roma and Sinti women, men and children were murdered in the gas chambers of Auschwitz-Birkenau.

Rooted - To search or dig about for something in a casual way.

Routed - Defeated and caused to retreat in disorder.

Ruefully - In a way that expresses sorrow or regret.

Rummaged - Search unsystematically and untidily through a mass or receptacle

Ruse - Action intended to deceive someone.

Sal Uvina - Digestive aid with sheep salt.

Sallow - Yellowish and looking unhealthy.

Sanctimoniously - As if one is morally better.

Santamaría - National hero of Costa Rica.

Sarcastically - Mockingly, meaning the opposite of what was said.

Sashayed - Walking confidently while moving your hips from side to side in a way that attracts attention.

Sated - Satisfied.

Satyr - A class of lustful, drunken woodland gods with horse or goat ears.

Sauntered - Walk in a slow, relaxed manner, without hurry or effort.

Scanty - Small, limited, meagre.

Scathingly - Harshly critical, harmful or painful.

Scowled - Frown in an angry or bad-tempered way.

Secreted - Hidden, concealed.

Sedate - Dignified.

Segregation - Action or state of setting someone or something apart from others.

Self-abnegating - Self-denying.

Semblance - Outward appearance of something when the reality is different.

Sensuously - Involving gratification of the senses, especially in a sexual way.

Sequestered - Isolated and hidden away.

Sequined - Covered in or decorated withsmall, shiny disks.

Serenely - In a calm, peaceful and untroubled manner.

Severe - Plain.

Sheepishly - Embarrassed due to shame.

Shucked - Pulled off, got rid of.

Shushed - Quiet.

Sidled - Move gradually up to someone.

Sidled - Walk trying not to be noticed.

Siloam - The Pool of Siloam was a source of water and life for Jerusalem, especially during times of crisis. It was also the place where Jesus healed a blind man and revealed his glory.

Simpered - Smile in an affectedly coy, silly or ingratiating manner.

Slough - A dropping off.

Smoldering - Burning slowly.

Snappishly - To break upon suddenly with sharp, angry word.

Solicitous - Showing interest or concern.

Somnambulist - A sleep disorder that involves partial arousal and performing activities while asleep.

Somnolent - Sleepy; drowsy.

Sordid - Involving actions and motives that arouse moral distaste and contempt.

Sordidness - Morally degraded.

Soughing - Moaning or sighing sound.

Spartan - Simple and severe with no comfort.

Spatulated - Flat and spread out.

Spluttered - Make a series of short explosive spitting or choking sounds.

Spray - Floral arrangement commonly used as a commemorative offering.

Squelched - Put an end to it.

Stammer - Speak with sudden involuntary pauses and repeat the initial letters of words.

Stealthily - So as not to be seen or heard.

Stifled - Restrained or stoped.

Stifling - Very hot and causing difficulties in breathing.

Stigmata - Mark of disgrace.

Stinted - Held back, limited.

Stultified - To have a dulling or inhibiting effect on.

Sublimely - Awe-inspiringly grand, excellent or impressive.

Subservient - Prepared to obey others unquestioningly.

Subtle - Not obvious or noticeable.

Succumbed - Submited or yielded.

Sulked - To be silent and bad-tempered out of annoyance or disappointment.

Sullenly - Gloomy.

Sultry - Attractive in a way that suggests a passionate nature.

Sumptuous - Splendid, expensive-looking, magnificent.

Sundry - Various.

Suppressing - Forcibly put an end to.

Surreptitious - Kept secret, especially because it would not be approved of.

Suspiros - Crispy and light meringue cookies.

Svelte - Slender or graceful in figure.

Swank - Stylish, elegant.

T.B. - Tuberculosis.

TACA - TACA Airlines, originally named Central American Air Transports, was founded in 1931 in Honduras.

Tacacos - It's a tasty little green fruit, eaten like a vegetable . It is only grown and enjoyed in Costa Rica.

Taciturnity - Silent, reserved.

Taffeta - A fine lustrous silk or similar

synthetic fabric with a crisp texture.

Tallow - Animal fat used to make candles.

Tannhäuser - An 1845 3-act opera by Richard Wagner (1813-1883).

Tatterdemalion - Tattered or dilapidated.

Taunt - A scornful remark.

Taunted - Provoke or challenge (someone) with insulting remarks.

Taunting - Arousing mild sexual excitement or interest.

Taunting - Intentionally annoying and upsetting.

Tedious - Too long, slow or dull.

Tempestuously - With strong emotions.

Tenure – Time holding of an office.

Terse - Abrupt.

Ticos - Costa Ricans are recognized as Ticos and it is what they proudly call themselves.

Timbre - Quality and tone of a musical sound or voice.

Timidity - Lack of courage or confidence.

Toalla - Shawl,Towel, Wrap.

Tonsorial - Relating to barbering or hairdressing.

Tousled - Untidy, messed up.

Trabajadores del café - Coffee workers.

Tranquility - A calmness characterized by tiredness or inactivity.

Travail - The labor of childbirth.

Traversing - Pass through or cross over.

Travesty - Distorted representation of something.

Trilled - Quick wavering sounds like a bird.

Trod - Walked.

Trousseau - The clothes, household linen and other belongings collected by a bride for her marriage.

Turrialba - An active volcano in central Costa Rica.

Umbra - The darkest part of a shadow.

Uncomprehendingly - Not understanding.

Uncouth - Lacking good manners.

Unction - Action of anointing someone with oil or ointment as a religious rite

Unctuous - Excessively or ingratiatingly flattering.

Unpretentiously - Modestly.

Unremitting - Non-stopping effort.

Unrequited - Not returned or rewarded.

Upheaval - A violent or sudden change or disruption to something.

Ushering - Escorting.

Vehemence - Strong feeling or passion.

Veranera - Thorny, shrubby vine or tree is native to Brazil and Peru, and is cultivated as an ornamental plant in tropical regions of the world.

Verdulería - Green or vegetable grocery.

Veritable - Very or extremely, often used to emphasize something positive or impressive.

Vexed - Annoyed, frustrated or worried.

Vigorously - In a way that involves physical strength, effort or energy.

Viperous - Malicious. Like a snake.

Vivaciously - Lively and spirited.

Vivacity - Attractively lively and animated.

Voluptuous - Shapely and sexually attractive.

Voraciously - A craving for something else.

Wafted - Pass easily or gently through or as if through the air.

Wan - Faint, weak.

Wanly - Weakly.

Waywardness - Stubborn, independent, finding their own way and not easily controlled.

Whiled - Pass time in a leisurely manner.

Whimsical - Playfully old-fashioned or fanciful in an appealing and amusing way.

Whimsically - In a fanciful manner.

Whimsy - To satisfy an unusual, unexpected or fanciful idea to stop anger.

Wiles - Ways to trick someone to do something.

Winnower - One who separates or gets rid of the bad or undesirable.

Winsome - Attractive or appealing in appearance or character.

Wistfully - A feeling of vague or regretful longing.

Wizened - Shriveled or wrinkled.

Wolfed - Eat food quickly and voraciously or ravenously.

Writhing - Twisting and squirming.

Wroth - Angry, enraged.

Yen - A longing or yearning.

Yoke - Joining together.

Yoke – Waist.